THE
BURNING
LIBRARY

ALSO BY GILLY MACMILLAN

The Manor House
The Long Weekend
To Tell You the Truth
The Nanny
I Know You Know
Odd Child Out
The Perfect Girl
What She Knew

THE
BURNING
LIBRARY

A NOVEL

GILLY
MACMILLAN

WILLIAM MORROW
An Imprint of HarperCollinsPublishers

Without limiting the exclusive rights of any author, contributor or the publisher of this publication, any unauthorized use of this publication to train generative artificial intelligence (AI) technologies is expressly prohibited. HarperCollins also exercise their rights under Article 4(3) of the Digital Single Market Directive 2019/790 and expressly reserve this publication from the text and data mining exception.

This is a work of fiction. Names, characters, places, and incidents are products of the author's imagination or are used fictitiously and are not to be construed as real. Any resemblance to actual events, locales, organizations, or persons, living or dead, is entirely coincidental.

THE BURNING LIBRARY. Copyright © 2025 by Gilly Macmillan. All rights reserved. Printed in the United States of America. No part of this book may be used or reproduced in any manner whatsoever without written permission except in the case of brief quotations embodied in critical articles and reviews. For information, address HarperCollins Publishers, 195 Broadway, New York, NY 10007. In Europe, HarperCollins Publishers, Macken House, 39/40 Mayor Street Upper, Dublin 1, D01 C9W8, Ireland.

HarperCollins books may be purchased for educational, business, or sales promotional use. For information, please email the Special Markets Department at SPsales@harpercollins.com.

hc.com

FIRST EDITION

Designed by Nancy Singer

Library of Congress Cataloging-in-Publication Data

Names: Macmillan, Gilly, author.
Title: The burning library : a novel / Gilly Macmillan.
Description: First edition. | New York, NY : William Morrow, 2025.
Identifiers: LCCN 2025000600 | ISBN 9780063422919 (hardcover) | ISBN 9780063422933 (paperback) | ISBN 9780063422940 (ebook)
Subjects: LCGFT: Thrillers (Fiction) | Novels.
Classification: LCC PR6113.A269 B87 2025 | DDC 823/.92—dc23/
eng/20250107
LC record available at https://lccn.loc.gov/2025000600

ISBN 978-0-06-342291-9

25 26 27 28 29 LBC 5 4 3 2 1

For Rose, Max, and Louis

THE
BURNING
LIBRARY

PROLOGUE

LOCH MOIDART, WESTERN ISLES, SCOTLAND

The storm passed and a double rainbow appeared over the loch. Eleanor Bruton noticed that the kayak and the tent had gone, and she felt uneasy.

She'd been watching them for two days and two nights: the red tandem kayak pulled up onto the beach in front of the ruins of the ancient castle, the two women and the small dome of blue nylon they slept under.

The women looked young, strong, and competent. They were dressed in shorts and fleece jackets, wore their hair tied back in ponytails, and laid their wet suits neatly over the kayak to dry. They passed the time hiking and exploring the castle.

Until the storm the weather had mostly been fine, and on mornings, and in the early evenings, while they cooked on their small camp stove, the women sometimes stood at the edge of the water and stared directly across the loch toward Eleanor's home. Each time, Eleanor lowered her binoculars and stepped back from the window, her heart thumping.

Their behavior wasn't that unusual. Most of the campers who made it to the remote beach below the castle stared over the water at the stone cottage, and presumably speculated about who lived there, just above the shoreline, nestled among oak trees and heathers and mossy undergrowth, but there was something about those two that had made the back of Eleanor's neck prickle.

No trace of them remained now, except for depressions in the sand where the kayak and tent had been, and the wind would erase those soon.

Dusk was falling but hadn't yet erased the last vestiges of light. She panned the shoreline with her binoculars one last time, then the expanse of the loch, which was glassy in places, choppy in others. The loch was tidal, one end of it open to the sea. Strong currents flowed beneath its surface.

She saw no sign of a red kayak, or of the women, just a sea eagle, talons dripping as it snatched a fish from the water. She tracked it through the binoculars until it disappeared, then lowered them and questioned whether there was a good reason for her anxiety. It would be best not to ruin an evening's work by overreacting. She'd made that mistake before, too often, and lost valuable time.

She asked herself firmly whether her anxiety was just a product of her imagination, which had been increasingly unruly lately, or whether she'd truly seen something troubling. It was hard to say, if she was honest, but she decided enough time had been spent speculating and she should pull herself together. There was work to do.

She put the binoculars away, turned back to her kitchen table. Carefully laid out in front of her was an ancient piece of embroidery, torn along one edge.

Chaos surrounded it: printed papers and handwritten notes, piles of illustrated reference books, volumes of poetry, of symbolism, of heraldry, and several foreign-language dictionaries.

The notes wouldn't be there long. Each night, she burned her work. The fireplace was already stacked with some of today's pages. It had become a ritual she enjoyed, watching her handwriting disappear in the flames. No matter what frustrations or breakthroughs she'd experienced that day, she was mesmerized and calmed by the nightly fire, by how the edges of the pages curled as they burned, by the way they held their shape momentarily once they'd turned to ash but before they crumbled.

It was necessary to burn them. She must leave no trace of her workings. What useful things she'd discovered and recorded so far were for her eyes and the eyes of her sisters only, and she'd encoded and hidden them carefully.

She touched the brooch pinned on her blouse: a wheel, with spurs, made from gold and enameled, a reminder of the cause she'd sacrificed everything for.

Somewhere, in one of these books or in her encyclopedic memory, were the answers to deciphering the puzzle the embroidery fragment posed. She could feel in her bones that she was just a hair's breadth away from finding what she needed. It would be quietly revolutionary.

She switched on a magnifying lamp and peered at the embroidery through it. The individual threads came into sharp focus. She wasn't given to fantasy, but she felt a strong connection across the centuries to the person who had made this. She was surely a woman. Female solidarity was a beautiful thing, Eleanor believed; its roots didn't just grow sideways, binding us to the women who lived alongside us, but also deep, connecting us to the past. Women needed to support one another. It was a terrible shame that not everyone agreed on how.

Eleanor was so absorbed in the fragment and all that it meant to her that she didn't hear them coming.

The cottage door gave in on the first kick. Before she could get to her feet, one of the women struck the back of Eleanor's head with a rock. Eleanor fell to the floor, blood oozed from the wound, and her consciousness began to slip away.

The last words she heard were whispered close to her ear:

"You shouldn't take what isn't yours."

To: Elly Gibbs
From: Adam White
Subject: Anya Brown press release next steps
Date: February 15, 2024

Elly,

Final text (attached) just approved by Anya and her supervisor, Alice Trevelyan (Professor of Manuscript Studies). This is a great story for us with wide appeal. We'd like to give it a big push and it would be good to discuss graphics as well as marketing strategy and potential tie-ins with you.

I'm thinking for starters we submit to all media to coincide with a burst on our socials. Are you free for a zoom or a call to discuss?

Best,
Adam
Adam White
Press Office, Oxford University

PRESS RELEASE

OXFORD PALEOGRAPHER DECODES FORGOTTEN LANGUAGE

Oxford University's Dr. Anya Brown, 26, has solved an ancient mystery while studying for her PhD, finding the key to deciphering a cryptic manuscript, known as Folio 9, which has perplexed some of the world's finest minds.

Dr. Brown's supervisor, Professor Alice Trevelyan of Hartland College, said, "Anya's achievement is nothing short of exceptional. This is a very exciting development, and she is an exceptional young talent."

Folio 9 was discovered two years ago in the Hartland College Library and made available online. Since then, many distinguished cryptographers, linguists, and paleologists have all attempted to decipher it. None have succeeded. Until now.

For more information, please contact Adam White at the University Press Office.

CHAPTER ONE

Anya

The press release made me anxious. Feels crazy to admit that now, after everything, but it's true. I was happiest avoiding attention. Years of solitary study in libraries and archives had fired up my brain but also created the perfect environment for my introvert tendencies to blossom and thrive.

Then there was that thing I felt shame over.

When I told Sid, he said I was suffering from impostor syndrome and that I should be proud of what I'd achieved. End of story. I loved how concise and sweet he was. I loved his composure. I loved everything about him.

Mum had more to say. On a video call from the hospital where she'd been admitted after a tough bout of chemo, she looked gaunt but didn't hold back. "If your father hadn't rejected you, you wouldn't feel this way. It's his fault you can't enjoy your success. Don't give him the win. This is an incredible achievement." Eyes shining, she wept tears that were plump with pride and revenge fantasies against the man who'd abandoned us both after she got pregnant with me.

Mum's carer, Viv, gently took the phone from her and told me

Mum had made sure there wasn't a soul in the hospital who didn't know what I'd done. We're both so proud of you, she said.

Professor Trevelyan was enthusiastic and pragmatic. On brand. "The press release is terrific. You deserve it, and you should be delighted. I know plenty of academics who would kill for this kind of attention."

It meant a lot to have her approval because she was my supervisor, and even after three years working with her, she made me nervous. There was a hawklike quality about her, laser vision and sharp talons elegantly packaged in silk and cashmere. I had a work crush on her. Everyone with a pulse did.

I knew how lucky I was to be surrounded by so much support. Even though I still had doubts, I tried to appear pleased by the articles and interviews that followed. Mostly, it wasn't too hard because they focused on Folio 9 and didn't get personal, with one exception: "As her translation of Folio 9 makes headlines, Anya Brown is living the girl nerd dream. Are Doc Martens the new blue stockings?" So much was wrong with that. It was Dr. Anya Brown, for starters. Some things even an introvert like me wants to stand up for.

"Of course, it's written by a male journalist," Mum said.

A while later, she sent me one of the riddles she loved to make up:

> *I'm concealed 'til I pop*
> *I'm mellow but I crush*
> *I seethe but I dazzle*
> *I'm chill but I blush*
> *What am I?*
> Who *am I!?*

It took me a few minutes to decode, as usual. I had the memory for images, but Mum had a love of wordplay and a very quick mind; her riddles were personalized and clever. The "What am I?" was a glass of pink fizz, our name for pink prosecco, the celebration drink of choice in our home. Mum kept a bottle hidden in the back of the fridge and brought it out with ceremony if the occasion warranted it. We never had the money for real champagne, but prosecco hit the spot. The "Who am I?" took me a few more minutes—because who immediately recognizes himself or herself through the eyes of another person, even a loved one?—but I realized that it was me, and I felt the love. Be yourself, she was telling me, and be proud.

Professor Trevelyan had little patience with having to repeat herself, but I couldn't let things lie. I went back to her and said, "This feels wrong because I couldn't have done it if I didn't have an eidetic memory." Having a memory like mine felt like cheating, because I remembered everything I'd ever seen, in intricate detail. I felt as if I'd been given a gift that gave me an unfair advantage, instead of earning my stripes.

She arched an eyebrow and retorted, "By chance or luck or whatsoever cause . . ."

It took me a moment to realize that she was quoting Chaucer and that I shouldn't downplay my success. She added, "You didn't achieve this just because of your exceptional memory, Anya. It's been extremely helpful, no one's going to deny that, but it was your hard work and talent as a scholar that got you over the line. If you hadn't studied so hard you wouldn't have been able to make the connections that you needed to translate Folio 9. Possessing a memory as good as yours in no way diminishes your achievement. Don't dwell on it, Anya. Focus on what's next. You're about to be in demand."

She was right. Job offers rolled in, dazzling me. Mostly they came from departments I'd longed to work in, at some of the best universities and institutions in the world. There were two outliers, and both were unexpected.

The first arrived via Trevelyan herself. She invited me to a meeting in her rooms. When I got there, a man was already seated in half shadow by the leaded window, which had a view of the college's garden and the stained-glass window of its ancient chapel. It was a damp, cold day. The buds on the magnolia tree were swollen. A crow pecked at the lawn and unearthed a struggling worm.

Trevelyan introduced the man to me, offering shortbread and jasmine tea that she poured into her best set of cups. Steam trailed from the spout of the teapot, dampening her cuffs. I noticed she was wearing a silk blouse that I'd only seen before at formal dinners.

The man was tall and pale, with a long, narrow nose and rimless glasses. His suit was beautifully tailored, his long legs elegantly crossed. He wore brogues that were hand tooled. I'd learned to notice this kind of detail since coming to Oxford: things that signaled wealth and power.

He asked me if I'd ever considered working for the Ministry of Defense, and it took me a moment to understand that he was from MI5 and he was inviting me to become a spy. While I thought about my answer, the bells in the chapel chimed solemnly, and I realized that Trevelyan must genuinely have faith in my abilities, or she wouldn't have let this meeting happen.

I told the man no, thank you, because I couldn't imagine living a life where I wasn't allowed to tell people what I did. My mother and Sid were everything to me. How could I have the normal existence I longed for if I had to look over my shoulder 24-7 or sleep with one eye open?

Which, of course, turned out to be ironic.

The other unexpected offer came from Scotland.

To: Anya Brown
From: Diana Cornish
Subject: Interview The Institute of Manuscript
    Studies, St. Andrews
Date: March 20, 2024

Dear Dr. Brown,

I hope you don't mind me contacting you unsolicited. I wouldn't do so if I didn't think I had something to say that might be of interest to you.

I've read your work on Folio 9 and to say that I'm impressed would be an understatement. Congratulations on an outstanding achievement. Our institute in St. Andrews has a very special opening for a new staff member, and we feel strongly that you'd be an excellent fit. We're not your run-of-the-mill university department; we pride ourselves on being better than that.

I appreciate that you've probably had a lot of interest (and probably some sterling offers) already, but if you could spare some time to have a chat with me, I'd much appreciate it, and I know you won't regret it.

I hope to hear from you.

With warmest wishes,
Professor Diana Cornish
The Institute of Manuscript Studies
St. Andrews

The email from St. Andrews arrived just at the right time to intrigue me.

I'd had a great interview with Yale University, where they'd hinted heavily that I would be receiving an offer from them, which was the dream. Yale's Beinecke Library was home to an incredible collection of ancient texts, including the Voynich manuscript, the most famous untranslatable text in the world, and probably the most mysterious. But there was a catch. I knew, deep in my heart of hearts, that even if they made me an offer, I couldn't accept it, because how could I put an ocean between me and Mum? Her health was on a downward trajectory that none of us could ignore, no matter how much she wanted us to. Of course, she was desperate for me to go to wherever was most prestigious and gave me the best opportunities. *Follow your dreams, Anya. Don't compromise your life for other people. Don't let this bloody cancer affect your decision. And never make decisions because of a man!* I listened to her, but I couldn't ignore reality. I knew that if I went to Yale, every time I got onto a plane, I'd worry I'd never see her again.

And there was the small matter of being in love with Sid.

I'd considered staying at Oxford, but I'd been there seven years already, and Professor Trevelyan and I agreed that a change was a good idea. Cambridge had made an approach but was out of the question; I would never set foot in that city. There were other excellent universities in the UK, but with Yale casting a long shadow I was struggling to feel passionate enough about any of them. The St. Andrews email, though, was intriguing.

I forwarded it to Professor Trevelyan for a sanity check. I hadn't heard of the Institute of Manuscript Studies before, which seemed like it should be a red flag.

She replied immediately: "I don't think you have anything to lose by meeting Professor Cornish, and you might have a lot to gain. The Institute of Manuscript Studies is small but elite. This could be very good for you and suit your personal circumstances. Even if you're not interested in what the professor is offering, she's a great contact to have."

I put a lot of store in what Trevelyan said. She'd been incredibly supportive through my PhD and even more so lately, when I was becoming reluctant to burden Mum with my problems. She'd stepped up. I wrote back to Professor Cornish and told her I'd be happy to meet her in London.

Trevelyan told me a little more about the Institute. It was small and had only been founded five years earlier. Not many people knew much about it, but among those who did, it was very well respected; it was also exceptionally well funded.

I did a little research myself. The Institute's website was bare bones, but I studied the staff's headshots and short bios. I hadn't met any of them before, or seen them speak at conferences, though I was aware of an excellent publication by one of them: Karen Lynch. I also couldn't find them mentioned on sites where students review their professors, which I found curious, but Trevelyan shrugged it off. "Students tend to leave reviews when they have something to complain about. Maybe theirs don't."

Maybe, I thought, happy to let Trevelyan call that one for me, a decision that seems painfully naïve to me now.

PROFESSOR CORNISH ARRANGED TO MEET ME THE FOLLOWING WEEK AT the offices of *The Wimpole Magazine*, on the corner of a cobbled, pedestrianized street in Bloomsbury lined with Georgian houses. At street level their elegant, bowed shop fronts were beautifully kept, and the old streetlamps gave the scene the half-real quality of a film set.

The magazine occupied a whole house, on the corner, five stories tall. A brass plaque beside the door announced it discreetly. I was curious to see inside, because the magazine was over a century old and highly esteemed in niche academic circles. The joke went that it had more footnotes than subscribers.

I rang the buzzer at 11 a.m. precisely. It was genteel and shabby inside, two small, cluttered offices downstairs, a staircase in the narrow hallway between them. I climbed to the second floor, as directed. Professor Cornish stepped onto the landing as I reached the top, as if she'd been listening for me.

"Dr. Brown?"

"Yes. Anya Brown."

Her smile was warm, and her handshake firm. She was poised, a slender brunette, with smooth, olive skin and lively eyes. I guessed she was in her late thirties. Her hair hung long and loose in soft, glossy curls, and she was darkly chic, wearing all black except for a colorful silk scarf tied at her neck.

"Diana Cornish," she said. "Call me Diana."

She showed me into a corner room with windows on two walls, looking south and west. Leather-bound collections of the magazine going back a hundred years filled rows of bookshelves. We sat in high-backed armchairs on either side of an elegant fireplace, its marble surround carved with a riotous frieze of Bacchanalian figures. It was out of place among the stiff furnishings.

She fixed me with a bright gaze. "I expect it's very likely that on paper St. Andrews may not be your first choice for the next step of your career, but I'm hoping I can convince you to change your mind." Her half smile hinted that she knew something I didn't. "We recruit very rarely, because we can afford to wait years for the right candidate, Dr. Brown, and we think that's you."

Mortifyingly, I blushed and muttered, "Please, call me Anya."

"Our institute is unusual because we're the recipient of a substantial endowment, which gives us valuable independence and the opportunity to be extremely selective when we recruit staff and students. We make outstanding offers, but only to the people we really want. Our offers include very generous remuneration and exceptional accommodation. You won't find that anywhere else."

She more than had my attention now. I was as flat broke as any PhD student, and the other universities were offering amazing jobs but at the usual low salaries.

"Your PhD is remarkable. The sort of breakthrough that happens once in a generation. It makes you a perfect fit for us. As well as a generous package, we want to offer you the opportunity to develop at St. Andrews. We'll keep your teaching duties very light so you can focus on your personal research projects. Whatever you need, including travel, we'll fully support you. The endowment ensures that you won't find yourself in competition for any resources and there'll be no pressure to publish frequently. We prioritize quality over quantity."

"May I ask who endows you?"

"They prefer to remain anonymous." She smiled warmly. "Any questions?"

"What's the accommodation like?"

"It's a very pretty cottage, with two bedrooms, the perfect size for one person, or for a couple. Do you have a partner?"

"My boyfriend is finishing his PhD in computer science at Oxford."

"We can explore opportunities for him at the university here, if it's something you'd both like."

"I'll talk to him about it," I said. "That could be amazing."

"Let me know." She smiled. "The cottage faces the sea. When you lie in bed you can hear the waves. St. Andrews is a magical place, Anya." She had a look in her eye as if she was talking about something she really loved. It was powerful. "There's one more thing I should mention: our benefactor has made it known that if we recruit you, and *only* you, they'll make available for study an outstanding collection of manuscripts. They've been in private hands for centuries and will be yours to devote your research time to *if and only if* you accept our offer."

"Would I have heard of this collection?"

She shook her head. "I doubt it. How about you come and see for yourself?"

The bait she'd cast was irresistible.

"I'd love to."

Diana

Professor Diana Cornish watched through the window as Anya Brown walked away from the offices of *The Wimpole Magazine* in the direction of Bloomsbury Square. She had her phone out; she was barely paying attention to where she was going.

The interview had gone well, Diana felt. You couldn't mistake the spark in Anya's eye, especially when she'd heard about the collection of manuscripts. Diana was hopeful that she'd done enough to lure Anya to St. Andrews.

In truth, so much work had gone into making this interview happen that failure wasn't an option.

She picked up her phone. Using an encrypted chat, she sent a message to Professor Alice Trevelyan at Oxford.

It went well, I think. Let me know when you hear from her.

I just did. She's very excited. Well done!

Diana exhaled lightly, with relief. She was confident in her abilities, but you could never be certain.

She looked up as the magazine's editor in chief slipped into the room and joined Diana at the window. They watched as Anya Brown reached the end of the street and waited to cross the road.

"How did it go?"

"Alice and I are hopeful."

"Alice has heard from her already?"

Diana nodded. "Yes, and it was very positive."

"That's a good sign."

The editor in chief was named Charlotte Craven. Her silver hair was cut into a bob and blown dry in soft waves. She wore a fitted soft-pink cashmere sweater, discreet yet expensive jewelry, and beautifully cut trousers. Nobody knew quite how old she was, but her contacts included very influential names from as far back as the seventies.

Charlotte had access to powerful people and back rooms all over the city. She knew everybody who was anybody in the world of art and antiquities. When she socialized, she dined in the most private of homes. If she went to an exhibition, it was usually outside of visiting hours, by invitation. In public she was seen only at the most exclusive viewing parties.

In secret, she was also a senior member of a society of women called the Fellowship of the Larks. Since the Larks considered it safer not to have an official meeting place, when appropriate Charlotte occasionally allowed their business to take place at the magazine. Anya Brown's interview was one of those times.

"So, she'll come to St. Andrews?" Charlotte asked.

"I think so."

"Any concerns?"

"We need to reassure her that she can take leave in the event her mother's health deteriorates."

"Of course."

"And I dangled an opportunity for her boyfriend, as discussed. Anya's pretty reserved, but I got the feeling he's very important to her, and Alice agrees."

"We can use that, but can we deliver on the promise of a job for him?"

"Absolutely," Diana said. "The head of the computer science department at St. Andrews made some unfortunate choices when he was at a conference recently. We have video he won't want his family to see, so I'm sure he can come up with something."

"Could the boyfriend be a danger to us? Given his specialty?"

"Anyone could be a danger to us, and we'll be keeping a very close eye on them both to make sure things don't turn out that way. If you look at it another way, there's a best-case scenario where we could make use of his skills, depending on how things turn out, of course."

"True. I like your optimism. Let's hope it's not misplaced. We should get Anya up to St. Andrews as soon as possible to seal the deal."

Diana nodded.

Charlotte took her seat behind the desk. "I have news."

"What news?"

Charlotte smiled. "Eleanor Bruton is dead."

Diana felt a rush of emotions: relief and elation that the Kats had been so stupid as to let Eleanor be found so easily, and regret that she'd been denied the chance to tell Eleanor what a talentless, dreary little dishwasher she was before she died.

"Now, that is good news," she said.

"I thought you'd be pleased."

"When?"

"Last week."

"Where did they find her?"

"A privately owned island in the Western Isles."

"Did she have the embroidery?"

"Yes. Do you want to see it?"

"Of course."

Charlotte removed a slender box from her desk drawer and handed it to Diana. Nestled inside was a fragile fragment of embroidery, the upper edge ripped away along a diagonal. What remained was decorated with three complete roundels, one in the center and the others lower left and lower right, each containing a profile of a different woman. A partial roundel, upper right, contained just a woman's neck; her head had been torn away. The roundels were surrounded by densely sewn and very detailed foliage. Beneath each one was a letter—an initial relating to the women depicted?—woven into the foliage, almost obscured by it. She could also see a shield shape. Heraldic? That could be a clue. She squinted at it, but it was impossible to make out what was inside or around it, though she thought maybe she could see a pair of wings. Part of what might be the bottom of a second shield was visible just below the torn edge, though most of that had frayed away.

Diana let out a low whistle. They'd been looking for this for so long.

The embroidery's frailty didn't surprise her, but it alarmed her. It was a reminder of how vulnerable the objects they sought were. If this fragment was too degraded, the Larks might have lost the means to find the prize they'd been seeking for so long: an extremely valuable book, known as *The Book of Wonder*.

"It's not in great condition," she said.

"I know," Charlotte replied. "But it could be worse."

Diana heard the hope in Charlotte's voice, and the determination. The embroidery was, they believed, one of the objects that was the key to finding the book. With the help of Anya Brown, they hoped to have the other soon. If it had survived its own journey through the centuries.

"Do we know if Eleanor Bruton got anywhere interpreting this?" Diana asked.

"We don't think so. Our girls turned the place inside out. They found books, but nothing else of use. There were also a lot of signs that Eleanor wasn't looking after herself. The place was a mess. Rotting food, unwashed bedding on the sofa downstairs."

Diana snorted. "I thought she was supposed to be a model housewife."

"The girls said it was so bad that they wondered if she'd been losing her mind a little. They also found a lot of ashes in the stove, which might indicate she was burning her notes."

"Perhaps she was afraid we'd find her. I hope so. I hope she was terrified."

"Indeed. But it does mean we have no idea what she may have discovered about the embroidery and who she told."

"Hopefully she spent so many years playing trad wife that her brain atrophied."

"We both know that's wishful thinking."

"True. Hopefully we can bring more expertise to it than she had. If she died a week ago, her lot must know by now. Any repercussions yet?"

Charlotte shook her head. "No. But it's only a matter of time. The Kats will act, we just don't know when, or how."

"It'll be slow, because they'll need to cook supper or iron underwear for their husbands or their daddies first. How do they not understand that giving up your independence so willingly humiliates all women? They are such sanctimonious bitches, and it will be my greatest pleasure in life to make sure their organization collapses."

"Mine, too," Charlotte said. "But don't forget they got to the embroidery before we did. We can't underestimate them."

Diana said, "Trust me, I don't. But I will wipe that smugness off their faces if it's the last thing I do."

Clio

In the heart of London's West End, a stone's throw from the north bank of the River Thames, a group of detectives were gathered in the basement of Gordon's Wine Bar. It was a disparate crew. The cragged and weary old guard, a lot of life between the eyes, some of them deep in the wine, were crowding the cheese boards like gannets. A younger crowd was there, too, leaner, fitter, ambition running hard through their veins. Some of them didn't know Detective Sargeant Lillian Shapiro too well, but they knew to turn up to her retirement do and press hands. They aspired to climb the ranks.

For the four remaining members of Scotland Yard's Art and Antiques Squad it was more personal; they would miss her deeply, and the person who would miss her the most was Detective Constable Clio Spicer. She stood quietly at the edge of the group, sipping fizzy water. Lillian had mentored her since she joined the squad two years ago. Now Clio would no longer enjoy her protection, and it left her feeling as if she'd lost a layer of skin.

The wine bar's basement resembled a subterranean encampment, carved out through centuries of use, a warren of small rooms and cellars, some vaulted and so low a grown man could hardly stand. If the corners were cobwebbed, it was too velvety dark to see them. Flickering candlelight brought the place partly to life, exaggerating facial expressions and revealing the uneven cellar walls and the framed yellowed newspaper cuttings and old playbills hanging near the bar. Chairs were liver-brown wood, tables upturned barrels. In the door's draft a white-haired man in a three-piece suit and an expensive greatcoat was asleep in his chair, cradling his walking stick like a bishop's crozier.

If the ghosts of London's past roamed the city seeking familiar spaces, then they surely met down here sometimes, Clio thought. And if they did, they surely traded information in whispers, the way people always have done and always would do, the sort of whispers that detectives made it their business to hear, which was precisely why she loved her job.

She stood with her back against the wall and sipped her drink, sober and watchful as a judge while her colleagues got drunker. When she started in the squad, Lillian had advised her either to drink like a man and make sure she could keep up or to stay sober at events like these. Clio chose the latter.

She could feel that the evening was at its tipping point. Most of her colleagues had drunk enough alcohol that tongues were loosening and inhibitions were evanescing, sizzling to nothing in the candle flames or falling to be trampled underfoot on the sticky floor. Soon, the hands of one or two of the men would wander—they all knew who—and there weren't many female targets. It was time for Clio to leave.

She pushed through the crowd to find Lillian and say goodbye but Lillian was nowhere to be seen. Clio headed to the ladies' bathroom and found her there, washing her hands. Their eyes met in the mirror. Clio opened her mouth to say goodbye, but something serious in Lillian's expression made her hesitate.

"You off?" Lillian asked. Her eyes were the same steel blue as the River Thames.

Clio nodded.

"I'll come with you."

"But it's your party."

"They don't need me anymore. It's been a feat of endurance to stay here this long, and there's something I need to talk to you about."

Outside, Villiers Street was crowded with pedestrians, but the air was fresher, and the temperature bit just hard enough to be invigorating. The slice of night sky visible between the buildings was artificially brightened, the city's lights turning it from black to gray. Shop windows and streetlamps made the wet paving stones glow golden and threw long shadows between the strides of commuters and nightlife seekers who passed each other without a glance.

"Walk with me," Lillian said. It sounded more like an order than a request, even though she no longer had authority over Clio, hadn't since five that evening. Clio owed her far too much to care.

At the bottom of the street, beside the railway arches, the entrance to Embankment Station glowed. Above and behind it, the white struts of Hungerford Bridge were lit blue and pink. Clio and Lillian cut through the station and climbed the steps onto the bridge. Trains rumbled back and forth across it in a blur of lit windows and squealing brakes. On the opposite bank, the London Eye was turning slowly, lit cerise. The river ran fast and dark below the bridge, offering the city a choppy reflection of itself. As they walked toward the middle of the bridge, a sharp wind tugged at their hair, at the ends of Clio's scarf, at the belt and lapels of Lillian's coat. It felt good to be out there after the stuffy bar. Clio didn't think she would ever tire of London.

Lillian stopped halfway across, and she and Clio stood close, but not touching, facing east, toward the City. A lump sat in Clio's throat and she felt a little hollow. Missing Lillian was going to be hard.

"For a while now, I've been agonizing over whether to tell you something," Lillian said. "There's a mystery I've been investigating—unofficially—for years."

Clio glanced at her in surprise, because Lillian did everything by the book, in fact she insisted on it, but Lillian didn't meet her gaze; she stared out at the river as if there was something out there, on the wind, in the water, or veiled by the bright lights. She said, "If I'm honest, it's become an obsession. If I'm *really* honest, it's been an obsession for decades, and I thought I'd got to a place where I could let it go, but something happened very recently, and I've realized that I can't."

Clio wasn't sure how to respond, so she did what Lillian herself had trained her to do: kept her mouth shut and waited for the other person to fill the silence until she understood more. Her heart beat a little faster than usual.

"Do you remember the famous British Museum theft of 1968?" Lillian asked.

It was impossible for Clio to remember every one of the seven hundred thousand entries in the national database of stolen or lost works of art and antiquities, but Lillian knew she had an exceptional memory for the unusual cases, and it didn't take Clio long to recall it.

"Was it an ambush? A van loaded with treasures that had been bequeathed to the British Museum was held up on Russell Square when it was on its way to deliver them to the museum."

"Do you remember what they stole?"

Clio frowned. "A collection of gemstones? And wasn't there something else, something obscure? A piece of fabric, maybe?"

"Yes. It was a very old fragment of embroidery that had been in possession of one family for over a century. Before it was shipped to the museum it was briefly examined by one of the curators, who thought it was likely to be part of an old bookbinding, probably the front cover. From the Middle Ages onward you can find examples of manuscripts and books that have fabric glued onto the outside of their covers. They're pretty rare, because textiles are so vulnerable to damage, so we see very few of them. The curator's notes are brief, because he was chiefly a gemstone specialist, but he described it as intricate and beautiful, depicting portraits of five women with foliate decoration, some geometric patterning, and heraldry motifs that he didn't identify. He guesstimated the date as sometime during the fifteenth century."

Clio remembered more details about the case. "Wasn't the embroidery damaged during the ambush?"

"A piece of it was ripped away. The van driver had been hit on the head, but he regained consciousness as the thief was taking the embroidery out of its storage box, and he lunged for it. He got hold of it, but of course it was fragile, and it ripped into two pieces. The thief ran off with the bigger bit and disappeared without a trace. The piece that the driver was left holding is just under a third of the original and is on display today in the Medieval Europe gallery at the British Museum. It's known as the Everly Binding, because the bequest came from the Everly family, but, disappointingly, it's not much to look at. To quote Lord Everly's daughter, 'That bastard thief took the interesting part.'"

Clio stared down the river, toward the glittering lights of the City of London, where many of their investigations started or finished. The work of the Art and Antiques Squad was mostly focused on fraud. They tracked money and artworks around the world, encountering extraordinary wealth belonging to powerful, secretive, and dangerous people, uncovering, if they were lucky and dogged enough, layers of deceit. The stakes were always high.

The embroidery seemed like small fry by comparison.

"Why are you interested in this?" Clio asked.

"Because I just heard that a woman called Eleanor Bruton died."

CHAPTER TWO

Anya

After the interview, I called Mum from Paddington Station as I waited for my train. I hadn't been able to speak to her yet that day and I was worried about her. She was in hospital and had been having a rough time of it. People thronged the concourse as the phone rang. The departures board rippled with changing information.

Finally, Viv answered. After Mum's first round of chemo, she and I had realized she couldn't cope alone. I offered to suspend my studies and come home to take care of her myself, but Mum wouldn't hear of it. She said she'd find the money from somewhere to pay for help. *I won't let this fucking cancer compromise your future as well as mine.* My mother had a potty mouth but a warm heart and buckets of courage. She hired Viv, who cost a fortune but was worth every penny.

Viv looked harassed. "Your mum's not doing great today," she said, and my heart sank. I heard Mum say, "Don't tell her that," as she took the phone.

"I'm fine," she said. Was she having trouble holding the phone, or purposely angling it so I couldn't see her properly? Sometimes she did that when she was looking rough and she didn't want me to see.

The screen showed a slice of the ceiling of her ward, then the curtain around her bed. It wobbled again, and her forehead came into view. "How are *you*?" she asked.

"I can't see you, Mum. Can you move the phone?"

The image onscreen wobbled again. Finally, I saw her face. She looked terrible, and I felt the usual grip of panic and the urge to go to her immediately, even though she'd hate it if I did.

"I had a really great interview today," I told her.

"Who with this time?"

"St. Andrews."

Her eyes narrowed. "What about America?"

"I'm just looking at all my options before I make a final decision. St. Andrews contacted me."

She started to speak. I only caught a few words—"Yale" and "you must" and "don't"—before she got caught up in a coughing fit and dropped the phone.

"Are you okay?" I shouted.

Viv's face appeared on the screen. "Sorry," she said. "She's okay but it's been a rough evening. She's been drifting in and out and hallucinating from the morphine. Earlier she thought she could see a mouse in the corner of the room. There was nothing there, but she was convinced."

This was the trade-off that we had to manage on Mum's bad days: pain versus coherence.

"Maybe it would be best to call back tomorrow," Viv suggested.

I hung up. Before Mum was diagnosed, I didn't know that illness could feel like such an impossibly sad and heavy weight. The everyday evils of treatment, the torment of hope, and the crush of disappointment were horrendous. Then there was the huge, unthinkable fear of losing her completely.

The symbols for death were some of the first I'd learned when I started my studies at uni. In Western art and literature, it's the grim reaper, scythe, skull, cloak, and hourglass. Other cultures associate death with the jackal, the crow, the death's-head hawk moth, the vulture, and more. We all know this. They're some of the most recognizable symbols in the world.

I was adding to them as Mum's illness progressed, as we met more sick people and their families, other repeat customers on the oncology ward. I knew that death could also look like a letter from the hospital, the somber expression on a doctor's face. Bad blood results. A sinister shadow on a scan. An invitation to talk in a private room.

Those things could also scythe you down with brutal efficiency.

What I didn't yet know was that the grim reaper can look exactly like someone you know.

WHEN I GOT BACK TO OXFORD, SID WAS SITTING IN MY BED, WORKING ON his laptop. He looked studious and sweet. There was no one I'd rather have come back to.

We lived in adjacent Oxford colleges but since we met a year ago, we'd been inseparable. He was my first serious relationship, the first man I'd fallen hard for. We barely fought, and we laughed a lot. It had been fun, and perfect, and easy so far, but now, with the future looming, we had hard decisions to make. What to prioritize? Our relationship or our work? We were both ambitious.

When I'd first mentioned Yale, Sid said, "If you go, you won't come back."

I'd wanted to protest that it wasn't true, but he was probably right. I'd thought of a solution, though: "You could apply for jobs on the East Coast of the US, too. Why not?"

He shook his head. "For starters, getting a visa won't be easy. I'd have to get an employer to sponsor me, which would limit my options. If I want to work on Lucis it'll be much easier to do here, because I can pick up work whenever I need it if I get short of funds."

My friend Ella once asked me, "Do you even have a computer science boyfriend if he doesn't have a tech start-up dream?" Lucis was Sid's dream. He believed it had huge potential. He was a security researcher, specializing in defenses against malware. If you met Sid, you wouldn't immediately have him down as a fighter, but that's what he was: a warrior on the front line of the arms race to develop tech that could outwit cybercriminals.

I sat on the bed beside him and rested my head on his shoulder. He closed his laptop. "How was it?" He sounded guarded, as if he was braced for me to say it went badly, especially because I hadn't messaged him from the train. I wanted to see his reaction in person.

"It was great. They've invited me to visit them in St. Andrews, and I'm going to go."

He moved so he could see my face. He thought I was kidding. "Really?"

"They want you to come with me. Plus, they're making me a crazy good offer."

"How crazy?"

"Fifty grand."

His eyes popped.

"There's more. I'll have research freedom and barely any teaching. She also mentioned a private collection of manuscripts that's never been studied before. They're going to let me work on it. They're also offering me a rent-free cottage with a sea view and two bedrooms."

"Bloody hell, Anya!" he said. Then, cautiously, "What about Yale?"

I didn't answer the question directly, because in my heart of hearts, I did still want to go to Yale, but I could also see a way that St. Andrews could work better for me and for Sid. I couldn't forget Mum in all this, either. She was desperate for me to go to Yale, but I couldn't be that far away from her while she was so sick.

"This is obviously hypothetical until they actually make me an offer, but would you consider moving to Scotland with me? Professor Cornish mentioned that they could look into finding you work opportunities at the university, but even if that doesn't happen you could concentrate on developing Lucis and we could both live off my salary."

"Now *that* is an interesting idea," he said. I watched him think about it, watched the smile spread across his face.

"Come with me to visit? If it turns out it's all a fever dream, at least we get a free weekend away by the sea."

"Yes. Obviously, yes!" he said.

Here's something I wonder, now that I have the bittersweet benefit of hindsight: If the Institute's recruitment process hadn't worked just the way they planned it, would they have got to me some other way?

I think they would have.

Clio

On the morning after Lillian's retirement party, Clio arrived early at the British Museum and flashed her badge to bypass the lines. Visitors were already crowding the ground-floor galleries, streaming toward the Rosetta stone and the Egyptian mummies. Upstairs, the Medieval Europe gallery was relatively empty.

Clio barely glanced at the famous rotunda or at the exhibits. Her expertise was in modern art: Impressionists, Post-Impressionists, Surrealists. She'd always found medieval art and artifacts somewhat creepy, and nothing she saw as she walked through the gallery changed her opinion. A lot of the artifacts and paintings on display were simultaneously familiar and strange, unsettling versions of modern things, as if humankind hadn't so much progressed over the past few hundred years as gone a little sideways. But perhaps she shouldn't be too cynical. It could be a useful trait at work but a downer outside of it.

She stopped beneath a sign: "The Everly Bequest: Medieval Treasures." It marked the entrance to a very small room, big enough for only five or six people to enter at once.

Lillian was already seated on the narrow bench set against the right-hand wall of the gallery, facing the display cabinet, which ran the length of the wall opposite. An information panel told the story of the van ambush in Russell Square and the recovery of most of the stolen artifacts. It was entertaining and included copies of old newspaper articles and photographs. The embroidery, by far the least valuable piece, only got a small mention.

The back and sides of the display cabinet were painted velvety black; the shelves were glass. It was lit from the top, the lights angled to make the treasures glow, especially the gold.

Lillian indicated that Clio take a seat beside her, and when she did, she saw that she was sitting in front of the embroidery. It was at eye level. She leaned forward to study it. It had been ripped diagonally, across the bottom. Through glass it was impossible to look as closely as she wanted, but she was surprised to see that it was quite gorgeous. The linen was fragile, the frayed edges especially so, and the threads were extremely fine. What she hadn't been able to see online was how prettily the metallic ones glinted when light struck them.

She saw better, too, how lovely the intact portrait on the upper left corner was, and the foliage around it, that seemed to have a letter *I* within it at the bottom of the roundel that framed the portrait, or perhaps it was a Roman numeral, and she felt it a shame that the other portrait, on the upper right, had been ripped through, leaving only part of another woman's head visible. There was another detail, too, part of a geometric shape containing a sort of pattern. It was positioned between the two roundels but ripped so badly it was impossible to tell anything from it.

"What do you think?" Lillian asked.

"It's much more impressive than in the photographs I saw online. It has life in it. What a shame it got ruined."

"I agree." Lillian folded her hands on her lap. Was it Clio's imagination, or were they shaking? She looked away, uncomfortable witnessing vulnerability in someone she looked up to so much.

"I need to tell you a story," Lillian said. "And everything I'm about to say is true."

Clio thought that was a strange thing to say. Lillian's hands were clasped so tightly now that the knuckles were white. She exhaled, nerves on her breath, before she spoke.

"There are two very different, very powerful groups of women that exist today, in almost total secrecy. They are hiding in plain sight, embedded in our society. Both are fighting for the same goal, which is to improve the right of women to live free from violence and discrimination, but they can't agree on how to achieve it. Their methods and ideologies don't align."

"How so? And whatever happened to women supporting women?"

"Indeed," Lillian said. "Their differences lie in how they gain and exercise power. The Larks believe women should obtain influence by shattering the glass ceiling. By contrast, the Katherinites, or Kats, as they call themselves, think it's better to maintain traditional roles as wives and mothers, and to exercise power by manipulating, or persuading, the men in their lives to act in their interests. It's a more softly, softly approach than the Larks'."

"The traditional way of doing things versus feminism," Clio said.

"Sort of. Broadly, yes. Though it's a little more nuanced, I think."

"Why those names?"

"Kats is after St. Katherine of Alexandria. They call themselves the Order of St. Katherine. They even have a creed. I think it's probably quite a long document. I've only discovered a couple of lines from it, but they're illuminating." She handed her phone to Clio. On the Notes app were a few lines of text:

> We will whisper in the ears of powerful men. We will be their wives and their mothers, their confidantes and advisers. We believe that in the image of the saint, we owe our fidelity to our fellow women.

"Wow," Clio said. "So they use men to get the power they want?"

"Exactly," Lillian said.

Clio's eyes fell on the embroidery. She had no idea how it might fit into all this. "What's the other group called again?" she asked.

"They call themselves Larks."

"Because?"

"Again, guessing, but I think because larks sing in the morning—"

"A new dawn for women?" Clio interrupted, and Lillian nodded.

"Could be. That would be my best guess, too. The Kats are well hidden, often embedded in powerful families, but the Larks can be easier to identify, because they often hold influential jobs. I believe they're well established in academic circles, and they likely have strong professional connections in all sorts of places. I suspect their network is extensive."

"How are these groups structured? How big are they?" Clio asked.

"I don't know how big they are. I would love to. They likely both have top-down, pyramid power structures, like the Freemasons. Both groups scout and recruit aggressively at grassroots level. The Kats are entrenched in the Women's Institute, in church groups and volunteer organizations that are predominantly run by women. We've heard of both groups recruiting through book groups and PTAs. The Larks are also involved with professional organizations and guilds. Sometimes, an affiliation with one group or the other runs through the women in a family, especially the Kats. I believe both also operate small cells of women who do their dirty work for them."

"Dirty work? Like?"

"When they clash, it can turn lethal. As Eleanor Bruton found out."

Clio remembered the name from their talk on the bridge. She was starting to feel intrigued. "So who's in charge?"

"That's something else I'd love to know. I'm pretty sure I've identified some of the women who operate at high levels within both groups, but I haven't got to the top."

"And you think one of these groups murdered Eleanor Bruton?"

"I do. I believe she was working for the Kats and was a victim of the Larks."

They fell silent. Clio tried to process what she'd heard. The room—its dark shadows and glittering contents, the reflective glass—was starting to feel oppressive. Her eyes lit on the embroidery once again. The small sign beside it estimated that it dated from the fifteenth century.

"How long have these groups been operating?" she asked.

"For hundreds of years, I believe. There are long periods of time when they go quiet, but others when they seem more active. If you look back carefully you can sometimes see the hand of one or the other of them in significant historic events, though it's almost always impossible to prove it."

Clio had seen Lillian excited before, and determined, but she'd never got an obsessive vibe off her the way she did now. It rang some alarm bells. As if she sensed it, Lillian said, "Look, I don't need you to get too involved in this, or even to believe it. All I'm asking is that you get some information from the Scottish police about Eleanor Bruton's death for me. I can't do it myself, not now that I'm retired. It might attract too much attention. The timing is terrible."

Clio would rather not, because of the alarm bells and the way Lillian looked: pale, edgy, stressed. She wondered if Lillian was trying to distract herself from her retirement. On the other hand, she was very aware of how much Lillian had done for her, and what harm could it do, really? "Sure. I can ask. Tell me about the case."

Lillian paused while a security guard walked past the gallery entrance, then lowered her voice almost to a whisper.

"Eleanor Bruton died three weeks ago, on an island in Scotland. The location of her death was odd in itself, because apparently, she'd been a committed wife and mother and a pillar of the community in her village in the south of England for most of her adult life."

"Was she a Kat?" Clio asked.

"Maybe. Though her husband, who died a few years ago, was undistinguished. But she could have been a sleeper asset, someone they waited to use until they needed her. This is why I want to know more about her. Eight months before her death, she left her family home very abruptly and went to live alone on this remote island. Her son and daughter-in-law were living with her, and the move shocked them because it was very out of character. They'd recently had a baby, her first grandchild, who she loved. But more important than any of that, and the reason I wanted to meet you here, is that shortly before she left for Scotland, a much-loved but incomplete piece of embroidery disappeared from the home of a woman Eleanor had befriended and cared for in the last weeks of her life. It was about the size and shape of the missing piece from the Everly embroidery."

The security guard appeared again, pacing in the other direction, giving them a long glance as she passed.

"We should leave," Lillian whispered. "They have eyes and ears everywhere." She stood abruptly and left the gallery. The museum was busier now. Clio followed her downstairs and outside.

They emerged beneath the shelter of the stately columns holding up the museum's grand portico. Clio noted Lillian scanning the crowds outside. It was raining hard and umbrellas and hoods were up everywhere, making it hard to see people's faces.

In the gloomy daylight, Lillian looked more troubled than Clio had ever seen her. "Don't underestimate these women. I lost a colleague to them; she was also a dear friend. And don't mention this to anyone on the team. You must be very careful."

Clio had to stand close to hear Lillian over the rain. She found herself staring at her mentor, trying to figure out whether she really knew her at all. The Lillian she'd been used to was measured and calm; she rarely showed fear, never got dramatic. This felt far from normal.

The rain intensified, coming down so hard that the black cabs on Great Russell Street slowed to a crawl, and even so, their tires sent up arcs of water and their brake lights strobed brightly; red light refracted into fragments in the spray, and was reflected in the pooled water on the road.

"I'll be in touch," Lillian said.

Clio's phone rang. "Wait," she said. She needed to see who was calling because she was supposed to be in the office, but she wanted to ask one more thing. Lillian didn't hear or didn't care. She hurried down the steps as Clio took the call. As she spoke to a colleague, Clio watched Lillian run through the rain across the area in front of the museum and out through the wrought-iron gates. A few seconds later she heard the squeal of brakes, a thud, a scream, raised voices. The world seemed to stop. Clio instinctively held her breath, unable to move until her body forced out a lungful of air, then she ran after Lillian.

A black cab was parked at an angle across the street. Bystanders were gathering. Lillian lay in the middle of the road, unmoving, eyes wide open, staring at the sky. Blood seeped from a wound at the back of her head. A channel of rushing rainwater swept it away. Time slowed for Clio.

She knelt beside her friend. A drop of rain landed on Lillian's eyeball and rolled away, sliding down her temple, just like a tear, but Lillian didn't blink or flinch. Clio choked back a sob as she tried her best to staunch the head wound, but even before she heard sirens, she knew there was no saving her. Lillian was dead, and Clio couldn't help wondering if it was something to do with what she'd just been told.

Anya

Two weeks after my interview with Professor Diana Cornish, Sid and I took a predawn flight to Edinburgh and white-knuckled the drive north to St. Andrews under sheets of rain that slicked the roads and drenched the countryside, glazing it inky green.

Mum was better, back at home, though frail and still upset about my talking to St. Andrews. She'd thought Yale was a done deal and that it was best for me. I tried to reassure her that her illness had nothing to do with my decision to interview more widely, but she switched tack, accusing me of wanting to stay in the UK because of Sid.

Never, ever make a life decision based on a man, Anya. Promise me you won't! If there's one thing I've learned from what your father did to us . . .

I was tired of hearing that. It made me sad and angry that my father had treated her so badly, but I resented her assumption that I was destined to repeat her mistakes, and that Sid might not be a good man. For now, I decided not to tell her about the trip to Scotland. I didn't want her more agitated than she already was.

As we reached St. Andrews, the rain stopped. We parked and entered the town through the old medieval gate. It was a small, stolid place, predominantly low buildings built from gray sandstone, hewn into rough rectangular blocks, some tinged with variants of the color of rust, and every sill, corner, and carving weather worn and time softened so there wasn't a sharp edge to be seen, yet there was also the sense that this place could never be cowed by its wild location.

In place of Oxford's multiple, ethereal spires, St. Andrews had just four, and they were stark in silhouette against an unforgiving sky that had hardened from slate to granite as we'd traveled north. If any of Oxford's marshy air had lingered in our lungs, the north wind scoured it out in moments, with harsh gusts of fresh, salty air that we could taste.

Like the simplest line drawing of an arrowhead, three main roads led from one end of town to the other, converging on the headland, funneling visitors toward the remains of an extensive medieval holy complex, as they had done for centuries.

We took a meandering dogleg path, weaving through alleyways that connected those roads, some no wider than a person. These spaces between the streets, at the backs of houses, shops, and pubs, all of them accessible only on foot, felt like the true heart of the place. They were full of life, developed haphazardly over time. Behind thick walls and through open gates and doorways we caught glimpses of gardens, greenhouses, buildings that extended back in unexpected ways, courtyards with communal washing lines, staircases crawling up the rear of buildings, balconies, picture windows, secretive and private exits and entrances. It felt as if the way people lived back there might not have changed much for centuries.

But all roads led to the headland in the end, and it was spectacular. The sea was wild and loud, the wind stiff. Waves rushed from horizon to shore and broke violently over rocky outcrops and the harbor wall. We stood on the cliff top beneath the old walls of the cathedral complex and its ruins. The remaining structures were skeletal, but the spires and towers still stood proud and tall. Shipping must have used them to navigate for centuries. A sign informed us that St. Andrews had once been the "Jerusalem of the North," and I could believe it. The grandeur of the place hadn't been chastened by ruination.

"Imagine the storms they must get up here," Sid said. "It's like we're standing at the edge of the world."

He wasn't wrong. By comparison Oxford suddenly felt far too precious a place, far too self-absorbed. The idea of St. Andrews's potential and its possibilities began to grow in me. It was a smaller town, but you could be a bigger person here, with a wider mind, I thought.

We drank coffee and ate pancakes and bacon at a café just yards from cathedral ruins. A sign in the window boasted that Prince

William used to meet up there with his girlfriend, Kate. We emerged in time to make the short walk to South Court, where the Institute of Manuscript Studies was based.

The entrance was via a short, low tunnel that cut through a building fronting South Street. Sid wished me luck and left me there. To settle my nerves, I focused on the sound of my footsteps, which scraped and echoed as I walked through the tunnel.

It opened out onto a small, enclosed courtyard, no bigger than half a tennis court. Part paved and part cobbled, it was surrounded by white-rendered buildings whose windows overlooked the small space blankly. A gnarled tree grew in one corner of the yard on a patch of earth, its canopy wide and low enough to make a man stoop; a smattering of yellowed leaves had fallen below it.

I climbed a set of stone steps. The Institute was marked by a discreet plaque, and I pushed the buzzer beside it. Diana Cornish opened the door almost immediately.

"You made it!" she said. "Welcome! Come in!"

The interior was gorgeous. Medieval-scale rooms with uneven, lime-washed walls, floors made from wide planks of oak or flagstone, an ancient fireplace that had pride of place. Everything was beautifully restored and simply decorated to showcase the building's age, simplicity, and quirkiness.

Cornish indicated the foot of a narrow staircase that disappeared behind a wall. "We each have an office upstairs," she said. "They have lovely views, which I'll show you later, but first come and meet everyone. We're so excited you're here."

She led me toward the back of the building, which opened out into a surprise: a large, tall-ceilinged extension, with two walls and the ceiling made from glass. It was stunning. A large oval table that could seat at least ten occupied one end of the room, where it was widest; the other end tapered to a cozy nook where a woodstove was lit, a small sofa and two chairs gathered around it, upholstered in jewel-like colors. Three women were sitting around the fire. They rose to their feet, and I recognized them from their headshots on the website.

Giulia Orlando wore an elegant shift dress and boots. She couldn't have been more than thirty. Beneath high cheekbones, her smile was fluid and generous. I knew from her bio that she'd studied in Rome before completing a PhD in Paris. She spoke Spanish, Dutch, French, and Italian as well as reading Latin and Old English. She was a reader in paleography, her specialty manuscripts from the fourteenth century. Our research interests were closely aligned. She took my hand between hers and shook it warmly.

"So good to meet you," she said. I heard a trace of an Italian accent.

The handshake from Karen Lynch was more reserved. She was in her forties, a slender, fit-looking woman with a steady, blue-eyed gaze. Her hair was a furious shade of red, closely cropped. She wore dark jeans and a loose-knit sweater over a striped top.

"A pleasure to meet you." Her accent was softly Scottish.

"I loved your paper on female mystics," I said. It was one of the few publications by members of this institute I'd been able to track down, a work of exhaustive research and meticulous conclusions but extremely readable.

She studied me for a second, then thanked me. I got the feeling that whatever Diana Cornish might have told them about me, Karen Lynch would be making up her own mind.

Sarabeth Schilders had pure white hair, pinned into a fraying bun. The frames of her glasses were thick and stylish. She pulled me in for an unexpected hug, enfolding me briefly in the colorful, drapey jacket she wore, then releasing me only partly, to clutch me by my upper arms.

"Welcome to St. Andrews, Dr. Brown. Your PhD is one of the most remarkable pieces of work I've ever read. It's a privilege to have you here."

I felt embarrassed, that niggle of shame about my natural advantage making itself felt. "Thank you. Please, call me Anya."

"Why don't we let Anya sit down before we pepper her with questions," Diana said.

I sat. They were all smiling at me, apart from Karen, but I got the feeling she didn't smile much.

"Tell us about this exceptional memory of yours," Sarabeth said. "I envy it." I wasn't surprised she knew. I'd mentioned it in some of my interviews, to mitigate the guilt.

"I have an eidetic memory. I can remember everything I see, in detail."

"Isn't it unusual for an eidetic memory to last into adulthood?"

"Very."

"You're a lucky woman, then," Giulia said.

"It's definitely part luck, but also part nurture. My mother believed that if she actively encouraged me to use my memory, it might last into adulthood, and thanks to her, it has."

"That was very clever of her," Sarabeth said. "How did she do it?"

"She taught me a bunch of techniques for cultivating memory, mnemonics and such, but she also exposed me to a wealth of visual stimuli when I was a child and encouraged me to talk about what I saw. Even when I was very little, I remember looking at images and illustrations in books with her. She'd ask me simple questions, like what the best and worst bits of each picture were and why I thought so. It got me into the habit of taking my time to look at things carefully, and it's helped me to retain my recall."

"Can you remember everything?" Giulia asked. "Sounds, too?"

I shook my head. "Just what I see."

"These images your mother showed you, what were they of?" Diana asked.

"Paintings, drawings, sculpture, architecture, textiles. She took me to museums when we could afford it, or we got books out of the library. She worked as a book restorer, so we'd also look at illustrations in the books she was working on and designs on their bindings."

"She trained you well," Diana said.

"She did and I don't take it for granted."

"So, your mother essentially loaded up your brain with visual references and you applied this library of images to Folio 9 and were able to make connections that others couldn't because they were focused on decoding the language without the visual context," Karen said.

"Exactly. Folio 9 had been looked at by a linguist and a few paleographers, and they couldn't crack it, but Professor Trevelyan and I wondered if the images in it could give us the key to its contents."

"And so it came to pass," Karen said.

I flinched at the tone in her voice, because it sounded as if it held an edge of sarcasm, but when I looked at her there was no trace of it in her expression. She was smiling kindly, and I relaxed.

"Well, thank goodness you and Professor Trevelyan got your heads together on it," Diana said.

"Have you applied this to any other manuscripts?" Giulia asked. "I wonder how many might benefit."

"Not yet," I said. "But I've wondered, too."

We talked for an hour or more, unpicking my work on Folio 9. They were generous with their praise, asked intelligent questions, and I relaxed as the interview passed. By the end, I felt like I'd found my people.

The rest of the day passed in a whirlwind. They treated Sid and me to lunch. Giulia and her husband, Paul, showed us where we might live. It was an old fisherman's cottage, two stories and in the middle of a terrace. It was being gutted for a total renovation. We put on hard hats and trod carefully on the exposed joists and over the dirt floor, where archaeologists had dug an exploration pit before okaying the build. From its narrow garden and back windows, it had a partial view of the cathedral ruins. From the front, even over the metal hoardings erected around it, sunshine poured through the salt-crusted windows, and the view of the ocean was spectacular.

Giulia showed me the plans for the finished building while Paul and Sid stood outside, arms folded, chatting. It seemed like they were getting along nicely, and I liked Giulia, too.

"The cottage will look mostly the same from the front," she said. "But the roof will be raised and the attic made into an extra room."

I thought it was going to be perfect.

CHAPTER THREE

Anya

That evening, I waited alone outside the hotel for Diana to pick me up. It was dark already. Sid had gone out to meet Paul and Giulia at the pub. They'd promised him some good whiskey.

I was riddled with nerves, partly in case the manuscripts were disappointing—the Bodleian Library was a hard act to live up to, as was the promise of the Beinecke—but also in case the benefactor didn't like me. Neither Diana Cornish nor her colleagues had given anything away about this mysterious person, and I didn't know what to imagine, but I had a feeling they might be the one to make a final decision on whether or not I received a formal offer from the Institute.

At seven on the dot, a smart town car with tinted windows pulled up outside the hotel. I watched as a female driver got out and opened a back door. She said, "Ms. Brown?"

"For me?" I asked. She nodded. Feeling self-conscious, I slid into the back to find Diana there already.

She greeted me with a mischievous smile, as if we were complicit in an adventure. I was running on adrenaline. She pulled some paperwork from her bag. "I'm sorry to be boring, but would you mind signing this? It's an NDA."

I skimmed it. It forbade me from discussing anything about this evening, including who I met, and where, what was said, and anything I saw. I signed and handed it back to her. It made me hopeful about the quality of what I was going to see. In my prior experience of manuscript collectors, secrecy levels had a direct relationship to the value of the collection.

A few turns out of town the streetlights gave way to pitch darkness, and I lost my sense of direction. The headlamps illuminated fragments of the countryside as we drove: a stone bridge, dense forest on either side of the road, its understory wadded with thickets of bracken and bramble. After about half an hour, a well-kept wall, maybe eight or nine feet high. We drove alongside it for long enough to suggest that we were adjacent to a large private estate and pulled up in front of a grand pair of gates.

The glassy eye of a camera swiveled and trained itself on the driver. Seconds later, the gates swung open smoothly. They were topped with razor wire. The car rolled down a long driveway, and a building loomed into view. It wasn't so much a house as a small castle, its exterior spotlit dramatically. It looked very old and was hemmed in closely by pitch dark forest.

We mounted the steps beneath a sky clotted with stars, as the town car cruised around the side of the building to park out of sight. Diana pulled a thick cord, and a bell chimed inside. We were let in by a housekeeper who asked us to follow her.

I didn't expect to recognize the person who rose from one of the red couches as we entered a large sitting room wrapped in wooden paneling.

She was casually dressed, wore glasses with tortoiseshell frames, and had long, straight hair, honey tinted, framing a beautiful, heart-shaped face. She was startlingly familiar, but I couldn't place her. She saw my confusion and looked amused.

"Hello, I'm Tracy," she said, and I realized with a shock that I was in the presence of a woman who'd mysteriously disappeared from public life at the peak of her fame just a couple of years before.

Tracy Lock was a British actress who'd had Hollywood in thrall before making herself invisible without explanation. There had been some rumored sightings here and there, but nothing confirmed. The media occasionally erupted with speculation over whether she'd suffered a terrible accident, or had a drug problem, or bad plastic surgery, yet here she was, looking perfectly sober and extremely beautiful, her face unaltered so far as I could tell.

"I've been so looking forward to meeting you," she said, as if this were the most normal thing in the world. "Are you ready to see the manuscripts?"

I glanced at Diana, as if I needed her permission. She was smiling.

"Yes, please." I must have sounded as eager as a child, because they both laughed.

"Follow me," Tracy said.

I wished Sid were there. I would tell him all about it later, I thought, before remembering that the NDA forbade it.

We followed Tracy as she led us away from the reception area of the castle and down a stone-floored corridor also paneled from floor to ceiling. Guns and ornate, historic swords were hung along its length. A suit of armor was mounted at the far end.

"Excuse the *Game of Thrones* décor," Tracy said.

At the end of the corridor, we seemed to be entering a more private wing of the castle where the rooms were smaller and felt more lived in. She stopped outside a heavy metal door. It was modern; it looked like the entrance to a vault.

"Would you mind leaving your phone and bag out here?" she asked.

"Of course," I said. I put my phone on a small table and my bag on the floor beneath it.

"Ready?" she asked.

I nodded. My heart was thudding. I followed her into a small, circular space, more like a chamber than a room. I figured there must be a tower at the back of the castle, and we were on its ground floor. To one side, a spiral staircase led up. There was a single window, glazed with glass stained in shades of amber that reminded me of apothecary jars.

A plain wooden desk was positioned beneath the window. On its surface, a lamp and two wooden book stands. Each one held a manuscript, which was closed, just the edges of the pages visible, the promise of what they might contain tantalizing.

"Tell us what you see," Tracy said.

I approached them with my heart in my mouth and was drawn to the one on the left, the plainer of the two. An important manuscript will often declare itself with an ornate cover, perhaps embossed leatherwork, or fine embroidery on sumptuous velvet—some are studded with jewels—but not this one. It didn't mean there was nothing remarkable inside, though.

Before touching it, I examined it visually first, as I'd been trained to do. I spoke aloud as I did. "Manuscript is approximately twenty-five by fifteen centimeters. Plain binding, probably in either goat or calfskin. Unadorned. In excellent condition. Can I open it?"

"Of course," Tracy said. She took a step closer. I felt her proximity viscerally. Diana stayed back. I got a strong sense that they'd performed this bit of theater before and they knew their parts well, and it made me wonder who might have done this before me.

"What's the provenance?" I asked. It's the first question you want an answer to in the art and antiquities world. Where and when an object or work of art was made or discovered, and who has owned it over the years, can help you to tell the difference between a fake and something authentic, though I was pretty sure I knew what I was dealing with here. You get a feeling in your gut when something is real.

Tracy waved a finger, chiding me. "Tell us what you think first."

I turned some pages. The parchment crinkled between my fingers. "It's pharmacological and has exceptionally fine and detailed illustrations. Based on the handwriting, I'd date it to the sixteenth century. The style of the illustrations supports this because—"

Tracy leaned across me and shut the book with a snap. I flinched.

"Very good," she said.

I was taken aback. It was like the weather had suddenly changed. Were there pages she didn't want me to see or remember? Or was she just being proprietorial? I glanced at Diana. She smiled damply, as if Tracy's behavior was to be expected and must be tolerated. Perhaps that little display of knowledge was all she'd needed from me.

I knew from experience that collectors will go to extremes to pursue certain objects and are extremely protective of their treasures, sometimes to the point of obsession. I'd heard stories of other academics glimpsing exceptional manuscripts that they never saw again because of a collector's whim.

Tracy Lock was an extraordinary person. If she could vanish when there was global interest in her, then she could make these manuscripts disappear from my life in a heartbeat. Don't let her rattle you, I told myself. This is a test.

I said, "Thank you for showing me. It's exquisite." And it was probably worth a couple of million. She looked at me until I felt uncomfortable.

"What about the other one?" she asked.

More nervous than ever, I stuttered a little on my visual description of the second manuscript. It was bound in red leather, with metal clasps, and my hands trembled as I opened it.

"It's an alchemical text," I said as I leafed through the first few pages. I saw images of apparatuses and emblems, of magical and mystical processes. "Not a copy of any books from the known canon. It seems to be unique." I wanted to ask where it was from, but she'd said no questions about provenance, and I wasn't about to upset her again.

This time, Tracy closed the book carefully. She had a small smile on her lips, and I hoped it meant that I'd pleased her. Diana seemed to pick up on some invisible cue, and as quickly as it had begun, our meeting was over. When we stepped out of the castle the silence was broken only by an owl hooting and the moon had risen above the trees.

Diana and I didn't talk in the car. Drivers have ears, I thought, conscious of the NDA. Through the car window I could see the moon, hovering behind clouds shaped like torn strips of paper.

At the hotel, Diana got out of the car when I did, and we stood under the rich red awning outside the entrance. Inside, a party of well-heeled men was joking around in the lobby.

The doorman opened the door, but she gestured for him to shut it again, so we were alone.

"How big is the collection?" I asked.

"Nearly two hundred volumes. The books you saw are representative of the quality of the rest."

"Why are they suddenly available for study? And why me?"

"We think you have the talent to do the collection justice. We like your modesty and the breadth of your learning. We like the way you think. I hope you're convinced by what you've seen today."

"Do you think Tracy is convinced by me?" Sid would have told me not to ask. Trevelyan and my mother would have said the same. Clearly, Diana Cornish was still trying to persuade me to join the Institute. But my anxiety was always there like a tiny stone in my shoe, irritating me and demanding my attention.

"You have nothing to worry about. Enjoy the rest of your evening, and safe travels in the morning. All we ask is that if you want to accept our offer, you let us know by end of day tomorrow."

I messaged Sid asking where he was, and he came down to meet me in the cozy hotel bar. We had a nightcap beside the crackling fire. He told me about his evening. He'd had a nice time, was a little buzzed. "Paul's nice. Reserved, but a good bloke. I could see myself going for a pint with him, and he's offered to take me bouldering if we move here."

I loved that Sid was already imagining himself here, because I was, too. I told him what I could about my evening, which wasn't a lot, because of the NDA, but he got the gist.

"Will you accept the offer?" he asked.

"Only if you want this, too."

"I could make it work." He smiled and held up his glass, and I chinked mine against it.

"Are you sure?"

He nodded. "That's a tight deadline she's given you to respond. They must be keen. Will you tell her tonight?"

"I think we should sleep on it," I said, because he'd had a few to drink and I didn't want either of us to rush into a decision, but in my gut, I already knew what my answer would be.

Clio

Clio attended Lillian's cremation on a bleak day in Essex. It seemed Lillian had almost no family; her job had been her life. Clio thought of the friend who Lillian said she'd lost and felt her absence. She wept silently in the second row of the nondenominational chapel during the service and fought to hold back tears the next day back at work, when she couldn't concentrate because her mind's eye kept replaying the moments after Lillian's death in excruciatingly vivid detail. The rain, the blood, the absence of life in Lillian's open eyes. Her boss offered her a week of compassionate leave, and she took it, but once she got home, she had no idea what to do with herself.

The intensity of her grief was surprising and oppressive. She felt as if the walls of her flat were closing in around her. The first night of her leave she lay in bed, so physically tense her muscles ached and emotionally fretful, unable to sleep. She spent hours watching shadows move across the ceiling as cars drove by, their headlamps sweeping the room.

By morning, she decided the only way to get through this was to do the thing that Lillian had asked her to. From her work account, she sent an email full of questions to the Scottish police and got a quick reply.

To: Clio Spicer
From: Rory Thomson
Re: Eleanor Bruton
Date: April 8, 2024

Hi Clio,

Happy to help. Eleanor Bruton's death was an open-and-shut case for us.

I'm attaching the official on-scene report, autopsy report, and a transcript of an interview with Simon Bruton, the deceased's son.

If you don't fancy plowing through them, main points are as follows:

Mrs. Bruton's body was found by a local fisherman who was collecting his lobster pots. Her swimsuit had snagged on some rocks in Lythe Bay, an inlet on the coast of the mainland. She was face down in the water and in a bad way. We don't know how long the body had been there, but the weather had been poor for at least four days, with big swells and high tides.

There was trauma to her head consistent with falling onto the rocks or being washed up hard against them and abrasions on her face, hands, and feet that were consistent with the body having traveled in the water postmortem. The fisherman pulled her body onto his boat and took her to shore. The body was bloated, and the autopsy report noted that her skin had marked wrinkling and had sloughed in places, suggesting prolonged immersion. The report also confirms that there was water and debris in her lungs, so we know she was alive when she went into the sea.

After a search of the east side of the island we discovered a towel, and a dry robe had been left tucked into some rocks in a small cove closer to the cottage. A thermos of tea was with it.

A search of Mrs. Bruton's cottage found it to be immaculate. There was a pan of soup on the hob and some dough had been left to rise on the kitchen sideboard. We found sprigs of heather in a jug on the table. There was no note.

Ian Robertson, who had been bringing her groceries to the island, said that he'd once seen Mrs. Bruton swimming and once spotted her wearing the dry robe, too. She'd been on the island for eight months.

We spoke to Mrs. Bruton's son, Simon. He asserted that she wasn't the type to consider taking her own life, although he also mentioned that he and his wife thought it was out of character that she'd moved to Scotland. Between us, I'd have traveled some distance to avoid him if I were her. I got the feeling that most of his objection to her moving had been the loss of free childcare, so we took that with a pinch of salt.

The coroner ruled it an accident, and I think she was right. The likelihood is that Mrs. Bruton slipped off the rocks when entering the water. She wasn't the first to drown there and she won't be the last. Loch Moidart is connected to the sea and is tidal. The currents are strong, and the water is very cold.

Please be in touch if there's anything else you need from us.

Rory
DC Rory Thomson
Major Investigation Team, Glasgow

Clio read the email carefully, then the attachments. They included the address of the cottage. She looked it up online and found that it was available for rent. Impulsively, she booked it for a few nights, threw some stuff in a bag, and began the journey up north. It would be a distraction, she thought. A way to tamp down her feelings about Lillian, channel them into action so she didn't dwell on her grief. Lillian wouldn't want that.

She broke the drive overnight in a motel where the décor matched her sense of desolation but felt better the next morning when she reached the Scottish Highlands, whose beauty left her a little awestruck. When she stopped for provisions in Fort William, she felt like she could breathe easier, as if the sights and sounds of this quest were replacing some of her muddled grief, or at least distracting from it.

After another hour of driving, she found herself standing on the shore of Loch Moidart beside the ruins of an ancient castle, watching a man load her things onto his boat. The island had no shop, no public transport, no access via land. She would be there for four nights.

Choppy waves roughed the loch's surface. The water looked dark and deep, even though the sky was bright with autumn sun. The loch and its surroundings were wilder and more intimidating than they'd looked in the online pictures, and she thought, What am I doing here? But it was too late to turn back now.

The man's hand swallowed hers as he helped her onto the boat. It was small and low to the water. As he readied them to leave the dock, the lenses of his sunglasses reflected the sky, the water, the castle, the prehistoric-looking copse on a tiny islet out in the loch. Clio could also see a reflection of herself perched in the prow of the boat, dwarfed by everything.

"What brings you here?" he asked once they were free of snaking sandbars and in open water, headed directly for a pier on spindly wooden posts that reached out from the island. She could see the cottage she'd booked. It was built from gray island stone and was flat fronted, with four windows, symmetrically arranged two on each side of the front door, one atop the other. It looked like a child's drawing of a cottage.

"Bird-watching," she said. A pair of brand-new binoculars, purchased in Fort William, hung around her neck.

He slowed the boat as they approached the pier, and the water behind it churned and frothed. He killed the engine, tied the boat to a post, and helped her out. The pier was scarcely wide enough for two people to walk along it together, so she followed him. The water looked gelatinous and dark through the wooden slats. It slapped the stilts and the rocky shoreline.

On land they followed a path. Where the shore ended, woodland began, and they were quickly surrounded by trees as far as she could see; some had trunks as thick as a man's torso. Silver lichen clung to the branches. The leafy canopy of goldening green twitched and rustled above, and the ground was so thickly carpeted with acid-green moss that it was hard to know what was beneath it: stone or loam or fallen timber. Rich green scents thickened the air. Clio's lungs felt more capacious with each breath. It was an otherworldly place.

They passed a small shed tucked to one side of the path, and the man—Ian Robertson, his name was, the same man who had looked after Eleanor Bruton when she lived here—yanked the door open and took a glance inside before shutting it again.

"What's that for?" Clio asked.

"It's where we leave groceries for long-term tenants, the ones who don't like to be disturbed."

"I guess if you want solitude, this is the place to come."

"Yeah. Tenants leave trash there for us to pick up. It's a good system, except when something tries to nest in there."

"I guess you get a lot of people wanting solitude?"

He shrugged. "Some do. We had a woman staying until earlier this year for eight months."

That would be Eleanor, Clio knew. He said no more about her. Not a good idea to tell a new tenant that the previous one had died here, she supposed.

"Eight months of solitude is a lot," she said, hoping to draw him out, but he shrugged and said, "Suits some people."

The cottage stood in a glade just above the shore. They approached the back of it down a slope. He dropped her bag in a small boot room inside the back door. "Make yourself at home. There's a house book with all the instructions you should need. I'll be here Friday same time to pick you up unless I hear from you in the meantime. If the weather looks bad, I'll be in touch. If you can't get a phone signal here, you need to walk further around the island."

Clio checked her phone. One bar, which disappeared as she looked.

"Any questions?" he asked. She could tell he wanted to go. It was going to be dark soon. She was thinking there was probably something she should ask, but nothing came to mind. When the back door shut behind him, she heard total silence and felt the weight of stillness in the air.

She explored the space. The ground floor was one large room, kitchen and living space combined, two sofas around a stove, a large pine dining table that could seat six. The furnishings were colorful and warm. Logs and kindling were stacked by the fireplace. Two big windows borrowed watery light from outside that illuminated the interior softly. She got a fire lit after a few attempts, made a cup of tea, and spent a long time staring out the window.

"You know what, boss," she said aloud, addressing Lillian. The sound of her voice was awkward in the quiet. What was she doing talking to a dead person? She carried on anyway. "I don't know what happened to Eleanor Bruton, but if I was going to murder someone, this would be a perfect place to do it."

A murder here would be without witnesses. The water provided an easy way to dispose of a body. The problem was access.

Pockmarks appeared on the surface of the loch. Rain. In a heartbeat, Clio was transported back to London, to the moment of Lillian's death, to the questions nobody could answer. Like, why was there a CCTV glitch in one of the most camera-heavy areas of London for a couple of hours on that morning? Was it by chance or design that the number plate of the hit-and-run vehicle had been partially obscured? For Clio, these were already two coincidences too many.

Then there was the bad luck of the sudden downpour and the crowded streets and the fact that the accident had happened in the blink of an eye, meaning most witnesses had been preoccupied with wrangling umbrellas, or blinkered by hoods, or running for shelter. All the police had been able to glean from interviews was that the car that struck Lillian was likely a black sedan.

This had all needled at Clio. So had Lillian's warning that she should be very careful.

When she gave her own statement to colleagues about that morning, she told them that she and Lillian had met for coffee and a wander through the museum. She described it as a personal goodbye after the big party, and nobody seemed to doubt it. They knew the two women were close.

Clio felt uncomfortable hiding information from them. It felt like a risk to lie, but also a risk to tell them the truth, because part of her believed that Lillian's death, just like Eleanor Bruton's, might not have been an accident.

Diana

When Diana arrived to update her colleagues on how things had gone with Anya and Tracy, she found Sarabeth Schilders, Karen Lynch, and Giulia Orlando waiting for her. They'd drawn the blinds in the back room of the Institute of Manuscript Studies, and the space was dimly lit.

"It went well," she said before they asked. It would be the first thing they wanted to know. This had been so long in the planning. Everything was coming together. Finally. "Anya was blown away by the manuscripts. As we agreed, I asked her to let us know by end of day tomorrow if she wants the position."

"Why not give her a little more time?" Giulia asked. "What if having such a tight deadline puts her off?"

"I'm only following orders," Diana said. "As you know."

"Do you think she'll go for it?" Sarabeth asked.

"I think so. She was like a kid in a candy shop around the manuscripts."

"Go figure," Giulia said.

"Do you think she believes that Tracy is the benefactor?" Karen asked.

"I don't think we have anything to worry about there," Diana said.

"I mean, why would she doubt it?" Sarabeth snapped.

Karen shrugged. "She's a clever girl."

"We've been very careful," Diana reassured her. "I won't keep you much longer. I just wanted to check in in person before Anya and Sid leave town. Giulia, anything to add?"

"Paul and I took Sid out for a drink. He seems like a nice guy. He loved the cottage. He and Paul got on very well, too. Paul offered to take him bouldering if they move here, and Sid seemed keen."

"Good. Any red flags?"

Giulia shook her head. "No. He had a lot of questions about the Wi-Fi that we had no clue how to answer."

"Let's make sure we get answers for him and reassure them that everything can be made just the way they want it. Sarabeth?"

The older woman frowned as she polished the lenses of her glasses with the sleeve of her jacket. "I think we're on the cusp of winning this and doing some very serious damage to the Kats, so let's not fuck it up. My main concern isn't whether Anya Brown will agree to work with us, because I think she will. It's how we stop the Kats getting to her like they got to the others."

"We'll take good care of Anya Brown."

"They got to the others."

Diana bit her lip. Sarabeth was wrong, but she couldn't know the truth. And her concern was valid. The Kats were deadly when they wanted or needed to be.

She said, "Of course we won't let anything happen to Anya.

She's our best and last hope to transform this organization in our lifetimes."

Clio

Clio's sleep was wrecked again once she started thinking about Lillian. She lay in bed but kept the curtains open, because out here on the island who was going to look in? The only artificial lights she could see were pinpricks, shining from properties on the other side of the loch. There were no headlamps to rake the ceiling here.

Even though she felt blanketed by the deepest darkness she'd ever experienced, it couldn't muffle her recall of the morning Lillian died. Memories surfaced as abruptly as flipped tarot cards, riddling her with grief and uncertainty.

Tired of lying in bed, she got up early and watched dawn break over the loch, the sky oozing sherbet pinks and oranges onto the glassy water and misting the ruined castle with watery light. She held her breath as a red stag stalked the edge of the forest right outside the window. A cup of black tea warmed her hands. She blinked in the rising steam and the stag was gone. She watched a heron fly past, wings beating silently just a few feet above the water, and then, for the first time since Lillian died, she broke down the way she needed to and cried uncontrollably.

When her fit of weeping had subsided, she felt steely inside and determined.

She got dressed and went out. The forest receded around her in dark and darker shades of green, but the sun had risen high enough that here and there the edges of things seemed tinged with gold. Wet leaves stuck to her boots as she walked the path that led around the perimeter of the island. Now and then, something living crashed or flapped in the undergrowth, startling her, but she never saw what it was. She was guided by a hand-drawn map of the island she'd found in the house book, and her goal was to reach Seal Cove, where Eleanor's body had been discovered.

She knew she was close when she heard waves scraping a pebbly shore, the inhalations and exhalations of the loch. A ridge of large stones and a patch of coarse sand lay between her and the water. The stones were slippery, and everything on the shore was dressed in seaweed, colored briny red and yellow. There were strong smells of both freshness and decay.

The loch was mostly calm, though she could see muscular ripples offshore that hinted at currents easily strong enough to claim Eleanor Bruton's body. At the shore's edge a flat shelf of rock was visible just beneath the water's surface. If I wanted to swim, Clio thought, that's where I'd get in. She could see that if she slipped over in that spot, it would be easy to sustain a significant head injury, and with no one around to help, she'd be in trouble.

It relaxed her a little, because it made the story about Eleanor's death seem entirely believable, even if she would still like to know why Eleanor had come here. There were many less remote places to hide out, places with fewer practical challenges for someone living alone, places you didn't need a boat to access, places with a shop. But maybe that was the point; maybe Eleanor wanted to make herself as difficult to reach as possible. Maybe she wanted to deter visitors. Maybe she came here with the embroidery for some reason, but died by accident. Though that didn't explain why it wasn't found among her things. Maybe her only reason for coming was to escape her family. Not all women wanted to be free childcare providers. Perhaps she hadn't been as excited about her grandchild as her family believed.

Clio hiked farther around the island until her legs ached and her stomach growled. When she got back to the cottage, she ate hungrily then fell asleep on the sofa and woke late in the afternoon, disorientated, groggy, and a little chilly. But it felt good to have slept. She'd been running on too few hours of rest since Lillian died.

She went upstairs and ran a bath in the claw-footed tub, which had chipped enamel and cranky taps. The water was hot, but the pressure was poor, and the tub was deep. It would take a while to fill.

It was getting dark and she noticed a man in a boat on the loch, so she went to pull the drapes before she undressed. They were made from heavy, worn green velvet and moved easily enough along the wooden rail they hung on, until the bottom of one snagged against the leg of a chair.

Clio reached down to unsnag it, but it was caught firm at the hem. She grabbed a handful of the fabric and yanked, but it didn't come loose. She knelt to inspect it more closely. There was something sewn into the hem; it crinkled as her hand closed around it. She worked the drape loose, turned the hem up, and saw a line of stitching, neat and new.

She fetched a kitchen knife to cut the threads and pulled out an ordinary white envelope. It was unmarked but sealed, a gap at one end just wide enough for her to slip her little finger into. She tore it open and found a sheet of paper inside.

She unfolded it. At the top of the page there was a simple line drawing of a sun, with wavy rays. Beneath it, a handwritten poem. She read it and said, "Holy shit."

> *If you read this, I may be dead,*
> *But I leave you with this little thread.*
> *Your first refuge and your first inn,*
> *Is a city to house deserving women.*
> *He who on the ladder has the sacred bird displayed,*
> *Was where two men hang but St. Eustace did fade.*
> *Where horse and man cross Styx with Big Dog,*
> *A visit here could lift the fog.*
> *But if you share this castle view,*
> *You may soon be dead, too.*

CHAPTER FOUR

Anya

Summer passed quickly. I couldn't wait to make the move to St. Andrews. In August, I packed up my life in Oxford and said a temporary goodbye to Sid, who was staying to finish up his PhD. I wanted to have some time with Mum before I went up to Scotland.

Viv took some time off, so it was just Mum and me for a whole fortnight. We pottered: baking, doing some gentle work in her cottage garden, a little walking, playing card games and chess. As she got stronger, we started to feel hopeful that she would be able to endure a new round of chemo in September, which was what her doctors recommended.

My decision to accept the job in St. Andrews caused friction. No matter how often I told Mum that it wasn't a compromise, I couldn't convince her. In the end, we avoided the topic because both of us got upset if it came up. But in September, when Viv was back and Sid and I were packed up and ready to go, Mum wished us luck and gave us both a big, tight hug. She and Viv waved us off from the cottage gate.

Viv is here, so I will be fine. Go live your life.

We were at the tail end of the summer's heat wave, and the

countryside looked baked as we drove north, everything waiting for rain. Air shimmered over the asphalt on the motorway and Sid's old car had no air-conditioning, so we drove with the windows wide open, buffeted by the hot draft, the music cranked up.

"Do you realize this is the first road trip we've made together?" Sid asked. He was shouting to make himself heard.

"I don't know why we didn't do it before."

"We were working too hard."

"True. But I think it was worth it, don't you, Dr. Hill?" Sid had successfully defended his PhD with no corrections.

"I do, Dr. Brown."

We smiled at each other. "Do you think that'll ever get old?" I asked.

"I hope not," he said. "It doesn't even feel real yet."

St. Andrews looked completely different from our first visit, like a summer resort. The North Sea was a glassy sheet, and the beach could have been Mediterranean. Golfers speckled the old and new courses and packed the terraces outside the hotels. We heard American accents everywhere.

The renovated cottage was gorgeous. Wooden floors, fresh white paint, cute kitchen and bathroom, brand-new windows throughout framing the stunning views. When we opened them, a salty breeze made the muslin curtains dance. We took the second-floor room at the front for our bedroom, and Sid moved his work stuff into the attic, where he had views to both sides of the building.

My new colleagues had left a welcome basket and stocked the fridge. In the evening we made a picnic and took it to West Sands Beach, where we found a nice spot in front of the dunes. The tips of the golden grasses twitched. Sand stretched a mile in either direction. In the distance, across the water, we could see our cottage.

We sat shoulder to shoulder and toasted our future with warm beer, chatting as the light faded gently, smudging outlines, softly shrouding the town and the ocean.

Mum had had some words of advice for me before we left.

Living together for the first time is bumpy. Make sure you communicate.

We had that covered, I thought. I'd met a gentle, intelligent man. We loved each other and talked to each other, so we'd figure it out. I couldn't remember ever feeling so hopeful.

"You happy?" Sid asked.

"Yeah," I said. "Very."

"Me, too."

We stayed until the temperature dropped and we could barely see in front of us, then we gathered our stuff and walked home in the darkness. Stars blanketed the sky, brighter than we were used to, and Sid pointed out the constellations he knew.

I could have written a paper about astrology as it appeared in manuscripts, how it was used in alchemy, witchcraft, medicine, or whatever else you wanted to know about, but I realized I'd never studied the stars themselves as intently as I did that night.

They created a sense of wonder in me; I thought they were beautiful, an ancient world in themselves, a silent witness both to history and to our future. I felt more viscerally tethered than ever to the ancient texts I studied.

When I tried to explain what I was thinking to Sid, he said, "But stars are so much older than humanity. We're irrelevant to them. Did you know that any element heavier than helium needs to be forged in a star?"

"I didn't," I said. The science felt irrelevant to me just then, because I was too lost in my thoughts about history and symbols, about the stories men and women tell themselves as they try to predict their destinies.

It amazes me now that even though I was immersed in the world of ancient signs and symbols, I saw no omens in my own life.

Instead, I believed Sid and I had enough agency to shape who and what we became, and that idea kept me smiling as we walked hand in hand back to the cottage beneath the canopy of indifferent stars.

Diana

Diana Cornish sat in her office overlooking South Street, which was just waking up to a sharp wind and smatterings of icy rain. Autumn had arrived overnight, the way it did here. The children who lived in the town house opposite had just left for school. A few early-bird university staff were on their way to their departments. On a morning like this, it was tempting to envy such ordinary academic lives.

At the far end of South Street, only a few hundred yards to the east, the sun was rising behind the cathedral ruins, visible when there was a break in the clouds. It was a sight Diana usually enjoyed: the sun's rays aligned with the east-west axis of the cathedral, pouring through the orifices where its great windows had once been, telling the town it was time to wake, to work. But not this morning. She'd been up all night, managing a devastating crisis as best she could remotely, grabbing just a few hours' sleep on the sofa.

She heard a soft knock on her door. "Come in," she said.

Sarabeth entered, her coat still on. "What's happened?"

It was a terrible thing to have to pass on bad news, even when it was expected. "The Kats have struck back. Revenge for Eleanor Bruton's death."

Sarabeth paled. "What have they done?"

"They burned down Kamila Newman's lab last night. All her work is lost."

"Dear God. Is she okay?"

"She has some nasty burns to her hands. She's in hospital but stable. They're saying she's lucky; it could easily have been so much worse." Watching Sarabeth's reaction to the news made Diana feel the ice-cold shock of hearing it herself all over again.

"Is everything gone?"

"All of it. Millions of pounds of investment and over a decade of work."

"Christ," Sarabeth said.

"It was only a matter of time before they acted. We knew that."

"And yet it doesn't make it any easier."

"I know."

Sarabeth stared out the window. She blinked back tears. When she turned back to Diana, her expression was steely. "What are we going to do about it?"

"I've had a thought. Jamie Whitelaw is a third-year student here. I'm not sure if you've come across him?"

"I know we've been keeping tabs on him. His mother is Amelia Whitelaw?"

"Exactly. Her sister is treasurer of the Order of St. Katherine."

"What are you suggesting?"

"Jamie's a star player on the university rugby team. He has the potential to be an international. I was thinking, wouldn't it be a shame if he suffered a career-ending injury?"

Sarabeth smiled.

"The rugby club has a social tomorrow night, at the student union. I expect Jamie will drink a lot, as usual. He might have an accident on the way home."

"That will hurt them."

"It's the best we can do at short notice. We need to strike back fast. Charlotte agrees."

"As do I. Who started the fire at the lab, do we know?"

"Not yet. Charlotte thinks it could have been one of the women who worked in the canteen."

"Nobody checked her out?"

"An oversight we're going to have to live with." Diana hated to make mistakes. They weighed on her. She wondered if she looked as tired as she felt. Her adrenaline was dipping, and there was still so much to do.

"Can you please tell our girls about our plans for Jamie? I would do it myself, but Charlotte wants me in London. She promises me it's good news. She wants me to bring Anya, too, to introduce her to the benefactor. She says it's time."

"It's way too soon for her to meet him. We need to get her settled here first."

"I agree. I said the same, but Charlotte wants what she wants. She's spooked. She has been since we disposed of Eleanor Bruton."

"It's not like her to be so squeamish," Sarabeth said. "She'd also do well to remember that the Order of St. Katherine isn't averse to taking lethal action. We're more certain than ever that they killed that detective, by the way, Lillian Shapiro."

Sarabeth was always braver talking about Charlotte than to her face, Diana thought, but it was pointless to say so. "I thought they must have," she said. "Shapiro must have been digging and got too close, so they've done us a favor, too."

"We always knew that there would be a human cost to finding *The Book of Wonder*," Sarabeth said.

"We did," Diana agreed, though she thought Sarabeth sounded haughty, which bothered her. For Diana this wasn't a comfortable thing to think about, let alone talk about. It was time to end the conversation.

"Are you clear on what needs doing about Jamie Whitelaw?"

"Crystal clear."

"Thank you." Diana stood and smoothed the front of her skirt. "Okay. We must be ready for Anya's arrival."

"She's a born teacher's pet, so I imagine that will be any minute now."

Diana allowed herself to laugh. "Indeed. The timing of everything is terrible, so it's all the more important that her first day is a good one, especially as I need to tell her that she and I are traveling to London tonight."

Sarabeth reached out, took Diana's hand, and squeezed it briefly before letting go. "Anya Brown may be valuable property, but she's also just a pawn, *our* pawn, and we've planned our moves."

Yes, Diana thought. We have. But she never stopped worrying whether they'd thought enough moves ahead to avoid being checkmated by the Kats, because whoever found *The Book of Wonder* first would use it to become immensely more powerful, and to crush their opposition.

Clio

Every so often, over the summer, Clio had taken out the poem and read it again.

After discovering it, she'd left the island earlier than planned, finding enough cell reception to call for a boat to her get back to the mainland the next day. Family emergency, she'd lied. She'd stashed the poem and its envelope in a freezer bag, the closest thing to an evidence bag she could find, and brought them with her.

Once she was off the island, away from its isolation and the strangeness of its otherworldly atmosphere, she found she wasn't sure what to do about the poem. At first, she felt determined to show it to her boss or to the Scottish police and insist that Eleanor's death be reinvestigated, but her rational mind reasserted itself when she thought about how her colleagues might react. She was going to sound like a fool if she claimed it was evidence of anything on its own. And she couldn't forget Lillian's warning not to let anyone know what she was doing.

She also couldn't prove who had written the poem or hidden it—the fact that it was carefully printed in block capitals would make handwriting analysis very difficult, even if she did manage to get a sample of Eleanor Bruton's writing. And then there was the fact that she hadn't the first clue how to interpret the poem. For all she knew it could be part of a prank, perhaps a game played by a family staying at the cottage. Maybe an elaborate treasure hunt or an attempt to terrify a sibling.

She put off a decision all summer and threw herself back into work. Operation Platinum, a demanding investigation into a forged painting and an associated money-laundering ring, was helpfully all-consuming. She did a lot of overtime, some undercover work. She performed well, got some praise, got noticed. It helped to keep her grief at bay.

In September, two things happened.

First, there was a lull at work, and she started to think about Lillian and about the poem again. She did a bit of quiet digging and found an address for Eleanor Bruton's family home.

Second, she was sent to Bristol to assist the Avon and Somerset Police on an inquiry. When she was looking at transport options for the journey, she realized that if she drove, it would be easy to take a quick detour to the Bruton house. It was too tempting to resist.

THE SLEEPY VILLAGE WHERE ELEANOR BRUTON HAD LIVED LOOKED PIC-ture perfect. Thatched cottages surrounded a duck pond overhung by a weeping willow, its fronds trailing in the water. To one side was the village green, with a pretty cricket pavilion and a well-worn pitch.

She followed the GPS down a narrow lane and parked at the end beside an ancient village church. The old graveyard encircling the church had beautiful views of the chalk hills around it.

The Old Vicarage was directly across the road from the church, a large house built from the same red brick as the cottages, probably Georgian, Clio thought. There was a sense of comfortable neglect. Roses rambled over the porch, just about still in flower, long, whippy stems tangled and in need of pruning.

Clio rang the bell. It chimed deep inside the house, and a dog barked. When the door opened a heavyset Labrador barreled out and greeted her as if they were old friends.

"Barney! Shush! Down!" The woman grabbed the dog by its collar and pulled it back into the house. She was in her early thirties, Clio guessed. They were of a similar age. The woman was slim and fit looking, with flushed cheeks and long, uncombed blond hair. She wore skinny jeans, Uggs, and a Breton top.

Clio flashed her badge. "I'm sorry I didn't call ahead, but I was wondering if you have a few minutes to talk about Eleanor Bruton?" She spoke softly, conscious of the family's loss, but the woman answered brusquely: "Oh, God. We thought all that was done with."

"It's just a couple of extra questions, nothing to be alarmed about."

"Well, look, yes, of course, come in, I suppose. The baby's just waking up, so do you mind waiting while I get Simon?"

In the sitting room at the front of the house a carriage clock ticked somberly on the mantel shelf. The décor was old-fashioned: hunting prints and dowdy landscapes in elaborate frames, some sepia-toned photographs of family members (she assumed), stiff in Victorian finery.

Clio examined the bookshelves. She found *Debrett's Peerage* and multiple biographies of male politicians and explorers. There was a collection of books relating to the Roman Empire. Clio was cautious about stereotyping—if there was one thing her job had taught her, it was that you shouldn't—but the interests on display seemed very masculine.

Simon Bruton was a big man with doleful eyes, fleshy cheeks, and a prematurely thinning crown of fine, pale hair. He wore the country uniform of the well-to-do: checked shirt, corduroy trousers, and a vest.

"DC Clio Spicer," she said. "From the Scotland Yard Art and Antiques Squad." She showed him her badge and omitted to tell him that this wasn't, strictly, official business.

"How can I help you?"

Clio offered her condolences for his loss, and he thanked her gruffly, showing a little more emotion than his wife. She asked, "Are you aware of whether your mother came into possession of a piece of embroidery before her death?"

"She did, and I wish I'd thrown the bloody thing in the bin when I had the chance. Mummy was obsessed with it. Why do you ask? Was it valuable?"

"I'm working on a case it might be relevant to, but I'm afraid I'm not allowed to share details. As to value, I'm not sure."

"I wanted to get it valued, but Mummy ran off to Scotland and took it with her before I had a chance to. When they sent her things back after she died, it wasn't there."

"Are you sure she took it?"

"I saw her pack it myself."

Clio felt goose bumps as he carried on talking. "Honestly, the whole thing was so bizarre. She took off without any warning after our baby was born. The last time she saw him he was five months old, and he's eighteen months now. Can you believe it? One minute she was saying she was *so* looking forward to being a grandmother, the next, she does a disappearing act."

"Can you describe the embroidery?"

"Not very big, maybe two-thirds the size of an A4 piece of paper, torn across the top. Tatty. Old."

"Any idea where she got it from?"

"No. There was a horrible accusation from the family who live at the manor house that she stole it from them. I didn't for an instant believe it, because Mummy never broke the law. It's unthinkable, and they had a nerve to even suggest it after she cared for one of their relatives."

Clearly, he still felt very angry about this. Clio asked, "Where *do* you think she got it from?"

"She'd been collecting scraps of fabric for years, from second-hand shops, jumble sales, and the like, because she did a lot of sewing. She was into all that Women's Institute sort of stuff. Crafts and the like. Flower arranging for the church. Her collection's still here. You're welcome to look at it if you'd like."

She followed him through the house to a room at the back, which was small but cheerfully furnished and decorated. A large window overlooked a well-stocked garden that was settling into its autumn droop. A botanical print of a palm frond hung prominently on the wall beside it.

"This is where Mummy spent her time whenever me and Daddy didn't need her," Simon said. Clio glanced at him to see if he detected anything wrong with still calling his mother "Mummy" at his age or with the casual sexism he was displaying. Apparently not.

She was drawn to a circular table nestled in the window, piled with books.

"That's Mummy's booky-wooky table," Simon said. "That's what we called it."

"Right," Clio said. What a way to infantilize Eleanor Bruton's interests.

Simon opened the lid of a wooden chest. "Here's the box of rags." Again, a casually derogatory description. Maybe Eleanor Bruton had a better sense of humor about such things than I do, Clio thought. She hoped so.

Fabric swatches were folded neatly inside the chest, silks, linens, and cottons in all colors, some embroidered or trimmed with lace. Clio carefully removed some of them. Simon stood over her for a few moments, then his phone rang. "I'll leave you to it," he said, and stepped out to take the call.

Clio rummaged through everything in the chest, but there was nothing of interest. None of the fabric seemed particularly old or special. She examined some of the books on the table. They were highbrow, and niche, histories of bookbinding and embroidery. Again, she felt goose bumps, and she had just started to flick through one of them when Simon's voice startled her.

"She was always reading," he said, watching her from the

doorway. "She belonged to a book club. They would meet here sometimes."

"What kind of book club?"

"Fiction reading. Women's books."

Clio held up the book she was holding. "Did she ever talk about these books?"

He shook his head. "I think those are her old university books. She went to Cambridge. That's where she met Daddy."

Clio knew he was wrong. The book she was holding had a library sticker and bar code inside the front cover. Eleanor had borrowed it from a library in Salisbury. Presumably, she was supposed to have returned it by now.

Simon's phone rang again. He glanced at it. "Busy morning," he said.

She took the hint. "I should leave you in peace," she said. "Thanks so much for your time."

Clio sat in her car for a few moments after leaving the Brutons' house. If Eleanor Bruton had been educating herself about embroidery and bookbinding, then she must have at least suspected that her piece of fabric had something to do with the fragment in the British Museum. It was too much of a coincidence otherwise.

Lillian had believed they were related, too.

Goose bumps. For the third time.

Anya

Sid was sleeping peacefully beside me when I woke up early to the sound of the ocean. I drank my coffee in a cozy spot on the window seat. It was my first day at work, and I was a bag of nervous energy.

I was counting on this place to take the doubts that had plagued me and disperse them over that cold North Sea, leaving them adrift, unable to find their way back to me. I was excited about the manuscripts, about where they might lead me.

The walk to the Institute took no more than five minutes, just the right amount of time to get soaked and cold. I was early and the place felt empty, office doors shut.

The secretary, a gentle, soft-spoken older woman with a Scottish accent, let me in and showed me up to my office.

It was a good room with a view of the courtyard and a large desk where I could spread out books and papers. There was also a comfortable office chair, a generous wall of shelving, and a sofa and easy chair where I imagined myself running tutorials. I unpacked the few books I'd carried in with me and heard voices drifting up from the courtyard, so I peeked out the window.

Students, passing through, were exchanging a few words with Giulia Orlando, who was standing on the steps. It was time to go downstairs and say hello, find out what plans my colleagues had for me today. I took a deep breath, hoping it would gift me some courage, and heard Professor Trevelyan's words: *You have a gift, but you're an exceptional scholar, too.*

Downstairs, in the beautiful back room, Diana Cornish was with Sarabeth Schilders and Karen Lynch. A pot of coffee and some pastries were laid out and the fire was already lit. We exchanged pleasantries and news about our summers until Giulia joined us.

"So good to see you, Anya," she said.

"We feel very lucky," Diana said. "Okay, to business. We meet together once a week, generally on Friday mornings, depending on everyone's schedule."

She handed me a sheet of paper. "These are the teaching hours we currently have scheduled for you."

There was almost nothing on it. Just one lecture on Folio 9 and two seminars weekly. I looked at her in surprise.

"It's not a lot, because we want to give you as much time as possible with the manuscripts," she said. "And on that note, I hope you won't mind accompanying me to London tonight."

"Tonight?"

"Our benefactor would like to meet you in person." Diana caught my expression. "Ah. You assumed Tracy was the benefactor, which is understandable, but no, she's not. He's looking forward to meeting you, though."

I tried not to show it, but I felt blindsided. The benefactor's identity mattered, because signing up to work on their collection meant signing up to some kind of relationship with them and whatever that entailed, good, bad, or ugly. It wasn't a relationship I was comfortable in committing to without meeting them first, or at least knowing who they were, but it seemed that was exactly what had happened. I wondered why they hadn't been clearer with me about this and kicked myself for making the assumption about Tracy.

"Who is he?" I asked.

Diana didn't answer the question. Instead, she told me they'd booked me a flight and a hotel, that the secretary would have details for me later. "I'm busy all day today," she said. "But I'll meet you tomorrow morning, in London, and I can't wait! In the meantime, Sarabeth and Giulia will make sure you feel at home."

"Who *is* the benefactor?" I repeated the question. She was on her feet already, exuding an air of busyness and importance.

"Don't sound so worried!" she said. "I'll introduce you in person tomorrow." I felt gently chided, as if I'd been silly to ask, and I was too embarrassed to ask again in front of everyone.

I spent the morning settling in. I organized my office and met the students who would be in my seminar groups. The secretary ran me through a bunch of admin and their security systems. She gave me a pass, a card with my new email address and a temporary password on it, and my itinerary for London.

Sarabeth suggested I go home at lunchtime to pack. Back at the cottage I found Sid in his office, setting up his tech.

"I think they should have asked if I wanted to go before booking everything," I shouted up to him, as I threw things into a bag I'd only just unpacked.

"It's only twenty-four hours. It might be fun." He was coming down the stairs. "Where are you staying?"

I checked. "Mayfair."

"And you're complaining?" he asked.

I googled the hotel. It was fancy. "I guess I'm spoiled already," I said.

When it was time to go, he hugged me tight. "See you tomorrow." I felt silly for making a fuss. This was my new life. This was work now.

As I arrived at the airport, I got a message from Mum hoping I'd had a good first day. Once I was through a long security line I called her back.

Viv answered. "She's gone to bed, I'm afraid. Do you want me to wake her?"

"No," I said, feeling a little twinge of guilt. "How has she been?"

"Average, I'd say. We managed a walk to the post office, which was good, and she got a letter with the date of the next scan. It's in November."

"That's good about the scan," I said, though I felt deeply anxious about what it might show.

"How was your day? She was dying to know."

"It was great," I said. "Tell her I'm sorry I missed her."

I felt bad. Until I'd started the new job, we'd spoken every day since she was diagnosed.

CHAPTER FIVE

Diana

Diana Cornish boarded the Caledonian Express train bound for London's Euston Station at Leuchars, just west of St. Andrews, at 23:28 in the evening. As it pulled away from the station she made her way down the swaying corridor in search of her cabin. Inside were two narrow bunks. She lay down, fully dressed, on the bottom one and fell asleep at around midnight.

Outside, the Scottish countryside rushed past in the darkness. Diana slept as the train slipped over the border into England. Her alarm woke her just before it pulled into Preston at 04:35. Minutes later, Charlotte Craven, the editor in chief of *The Wimpole Magazine* and high-ranking member of the Fellowship of the Larks, boarded the train.

They met in the dining car. It was as dim and empty as an Edward Hopper bar, Diana thought. No one to overhear them, and preferable to their tiny cabins, which were too cramped to talk in comfortably.

They sat in a booth. Charlotte set some knitting on the table in front of her. Diana did the same with a pen and puzzle book. Charlotte had never knitted anything in her life—she preferred to buy cashmere in Edinburgh—and Diana was more accustomed to working on complex logistical problems than simple word searches, but they left these carefully selected symbols in view, knowing their power to render two women unremarkable.

"Anya Brown?" Charlotte asked.

"She arrived at the hotel in London. She wasn't happy about leaving St. Andrews so soon. We should have given her more time to settle in at the Institute before bringing her to him; it feels hasty."

Charlotte waited as another passenger walked through the dining car. Once they were alone again, she said, "I need you to trust me. This isn't just a knee-jerk reaction to the arson attack. I have good news, too. Last night I had dinner with a businesswoman, one of us."

"Have I heard of her?"

"Undoubtedly."

"A collector?"

"She enjoys acquiring seventeenth-century books and drawings relating to a very specific theme, and I've been able to help her with that."

Diana raised an eyebrow. No point in asking more, because Charlotte wouldn't tell. One of the most effective ways Charlotte extended her networks was through her work advising private collectors. The more niche their interests, the more they needed her, and her reputation for discretion.

"She says she knows of a site that's perfect, but we have to act fast," Charlotte said.

"Where is it?"

"Beside the river in Greenwich, within half an hour of central London by public transport. It couldn't be better. I've spoken briefly to one of our friends in the City for advice on negotiating a long-term lease—in this case she recommends we ask for a term of one hundred years—and she stressed the importance of proving our credibility. The fact that we're proposing to build a foundation doesn't help, because it means we won't be generating cash on site. Obviously, lettors prefer tenants who are running a provably profitable business because they want to be certain that they can cover the lease. So, that's a challenge for us, and they'll see us as a risk in that respect. We'll need to show them a massive chunk of cash to offset our lack of balance sheets and credit facilities."

Diana felt her heart rate quicken. This was a welcome bit of good news, and it explained the rush on getting Anya down here. They would have to accelerate their plans.

Charlotte said, "There's also the fact that we're a loose coalition of women, not a corporation or a structured organization, and not a man in sight. That could work against us."

"Of course," Diana said. "Our old friend misogyny."

The carriage listed to one side as the train took a bend, then straightened again. Outside, the sky was brightening, a slight silver stain spreading like mercury on the horizon.

"But if Anya Brown does what we need her to, it shouldn't be an issue. We'll have enough money that no one will say no to us," Charlotte said.

The Book of Wonder was worth millions. If Anya played her part and the Larks found it, they could make enough from its sale to fund their foundation. But they had to hurry. The Order of St. Katherine valued the book equally, but for a different reason. They considered it to be the foundational text for their cause. If they got their hands on it first, they would lock it in a vault somewhere instead of using it to make useful change for women, but even behind the door of a safe it would bring them power. An object like that created reverence and obedience through its mystique and uniqueness. It would give the Kats something to gather around, something to entice new believers with. It would be their Bible.

The main lights in the dining carriage came on suddenly. Staff were arriving to prepare for breakfast service. They couldn't talk openly here any longer.

"I'll do everything I can to ensure she delivers," Diana assured Charlotte.

Charlotte nodded. "We may not get another opportunity like this again, not in our lifetimes. This is a pivotal moment for the Fellowship. It's taken more than a hundred years of work to get us here."

As if Diana didn't know that. Charlotte could be patronizing sometimes, but Diana was used to it. She looked out the window and allowed herself a quiet moment of satisfaction. She'd learned so much since they'd founded the Institute. Starting small, somewhere out of the way, had given them space to enjoy some successes and make some mistakes and learn from both. The plan to scale up to a foundation was a huge step, but she was hoping for a significant role in the new organization. She felt she'd proved herself.

They ordered breakfast as the train entered London's outskirts.

Charlotte was looking at her phone. Diana stared out the window. The suburbs were, truly, a graveyard of female ambition, she thought. Here were women tending to homes, taking jobs that could fit around childcare or around their husbands. Compromising. It pained her to think of it.

Lights shone from the windows of the houses. Women were waking up, facing their reflections, their husbands, packing their children's lunches. Some might be waking feeling loved and fulfilled, but so many would already be engaging in self-criticism, in domestic scuffles. They might be experiencing violence. She'd seen it firsthand. The drudgery and subjugation of domestic married life had worn her own mother down and, Diana was certain of it, contributed to her ill health and early death.

They rolled onward through a commercial district of offices, bars, and shops. The streetlamps were still on, with their false promise of security. Diana thought of all the women discovered dead or hurt by men in places just like this. Women weren't safe anywhere. This simple but horrendous truth was at the core of everything the Larks did. Diana could think of no better cause to dedicate her life to.

The train pushed deeper into the metropolis, and her tired eyes drank in everything she saw. The City of London looked dazzling, such confident geometry in the architecture, lines straight as a bullet's path, curves that were elegant yet robust. How bold did the steel and concrete look? It was virile design. She even saw a muscular touch of poetry in the way two skyscrapers framed the falling moon while their mirrored flanks reflected the burgeoning sunrise. Stunning. Powerful.

Diana wondered if this was how the world appeared to Anya Brown: if everything she saw was inextricably linked to something else, everything suggesting a dozen connections, good and bad. It could be overwhelming, she supposed. It invited the question: Was every talent a gift? But that was Anya's problem, not hers. The world kept turning. Days broke, one after the next, and sometimes the pace of their progress could feel horribly slow, but not right now. They were Larks. They welcomed new dawns. And maybe, finally, the sun was breaking on a world in which they would be making a difference.

She looked at Charlotte. "I'm going to freshen up."

She was brushing her teeth when she heard a knock on her door. She let Charlotte in.

Charlotte handed her a thick envelope, the contents soft enough that the paper crinkled beneath Diana's fingers.

"The embroidery," Charlotte said. "I think you should have it. Keep it safe until you are back in St. Andrews. When the time's right to show it to Anya, don't hesitate. But remember, we need to know she's completely on board with the new benefactor before you let her see it. Otherwise, she'll be a liability."

Diana's heart beat a little faster. This was more proof that things were accelerating. It was an unexpected responsibility, but she was up to it.

When Charlotte had gone, Diana slipped the embroidery into a zipped compartment of her handbag. She hesitated, wondering if she could keep it closer to her somehow, because if it were mislaid, it would be a disaster, but she had no suitable pockets.

The bag would be fine for now. She wouldn't let it out of her sight. When she picked it up, it felt as if she were carrying a bomb.

Sid

Sid sat at his desk in the attic of the cottage. He had a view of the big sky and the ocean, and its wildness was bringing him joy. Oxford had felt so dull by comparison, so stultifying. He felt like he could achieve here, like he had the time and space and energy to focus on Lucis and really make something of it.

It was a welcome surge of optimism, because he hadn't slept well. Without Anya home to distract him, he'd got spooked late yesterday evening. On a walk before bed, he'd discovered that there was a dearth of street lighting at this end of town. The ruins behind the cottage weren't lit at all. There were shadows on shadows everywhere, and the ocean's roar had sounded unnervingly close. The wind had howled all night, too.

He checked his email, pleased to see confirmation for a meeting scheduled for the next day with a professor at the computer science department. He was looking forward to it, hoping for a part-time position to earn him some money so he could contribute something to the household. It would be nice to meet some like-minded people, too. He was hopeful that he and Giulia Orlando's partner, Paul, might hang out together, but he would need more friends of his own up here. He had no intention of being dependent on Anya for everything.

He drained the last of his coffee, and felt the caffeine doing its good work. Ready to start, he reached for his headphones but heard the doorbell chime. He considered ignoring it, but they'd ordered a bunch of stuff for the cottage, and it was raining, and the cottage's small porch didn't provide much shelter.

A woman stood outside staring up at the roof. She had the look of a busybody, and Sid's heart sank, because he was itching to be at his desk, getting on, but there was no avoiding her now.

"Hi," he said. "Can I help?"

"You are?" A brusque question, but she sounded friendly enough.

"I'm Sid Hill. I just moved in here with my girlfriend."

She shook his hand firmly. "I'm Maggie from next door. Nice to meet you. We have a leak in our front bedroom, and I think it's a problem from your side."

Sid stepped out and joined her in looking up at the roofline, where the cottages were adjoining. Everything looked fine to him. "There's nothing leaking on our side, but we've only been here a couple of days. I could ask my landlord."

"Would you mind? Diana Cornish never answers my messages. I'm getting stonewalled by her secretary. Just like last spring when I called to ask about a girl who lived here. My tenants and I were anxious because she left very abruptly."

"Oh, dear," Sid said blandly, to discourage her from chatting, but Maggie was on a roll, barely drawing breath before she carried on talking.

"She disappeared in the middle of the night and left quite a lot of her stuff here. My tenants said it didn't seem like her to do something like that. Their impression was that she was a courteous person and they considered themselves friends of hers, though of course they questioned this afterward, when she didn't respond to any of their messages. Anyway, I phoned Diana about it and the secretary wouldn't put me through, so I called in at the Institute and she was extremely abrupt with me. She said Diana had told her to tell me that it was nothing to worry about, the girl changed her mind and left her job at the university."

Sid blinked at her. This was a lot of information. "I mean, it happens," he said. He was thinking of the time he messaged a guy on his course who he'd been partnered with to do a presentation, and the guy had messaged back that he'd left Oxford and returned home. Nobody had noticed. "University populations are always in flux, especially when there are a lot of international students."

She looked at him sharply. "It was very *fishy*," she said. "Though she was foreign."

"Okay," he said. "Well, I should get back to work."

"Of course. It was nice to meet you. I'm Maggie."

"Maggie," Sid repeated. Had she forgotten she'd told him already? Perhaps she was losing her marbles. She looked quite old, which made him worry that she was lonely. "Nice to meet you, too."

He opened the cottage door. She stayed where she was, looking up at the roof even though the rain had begun to fall harder. As he went inside, he suddenly felt as if her gaze was burning into his back, but when he turned to shut the door behind him, she was walking away.

He was going to have to watch out for her and make sure she didn't get in the habit of interrupting him during work hours. The last thing he wanted was a needy neighbor.

Diana

Diana Cornish and Charlotte Craven disembarked separately when the train arrived at Euston. Charlotte got into a waiting town car, and Diana slipped into the crowd of commuters thronging the entrance to the tube station. If they ran into each other later, in public, they would greet one other as if they were merely professional acquaintances, nothing more.

Diana took the Victoria Line to Victoria Station, then changed to the District Line and got off at West Brompton. She wasn't feeling the lack of sleep yet. Her adrenaline was pumping, her mind buzzing. Charlotte had inspired her. She should have trusted that everything was being done for the right reasons. Now that she was reassured, she was one hundred percent committed to making sure things went well between Anya and the benefactor.

But there was something she needed to do before she met with Anya later.

Deep inside, in a secret place, she was carrying a hunger for a man she should have left a long time ago, once he'd outlived his usefulness to the Larks. But she couldn't give him up. It was a weakness, she knew it, and a violation of one of the Larks' unbreakable rules, but her life was already full of risk, and she felt she could handle this one. She undertook so much selfless work for the cause, and she wanted just this one thing for herself.

She had seduced Henry Macdonald two years earlier. To be more precise, she'd seduced married Judge Henry Macdonald, father of two, and she'd done it to help to get a law enacted, a law designed to protect women, a law that Judge Macdonald had a lot of sway over.

He wasn't the first powerful man Diana had become intimate with in order to influence him, and she wasn't the first of the Larks to do it. There was a long tradition of exerting control this way in the Fellowship, and in the Order of St. Katherine, too. But unlike the Kats, the Larks never married them.

Judge Macdonald opened the door of his flat and kissed Diana with so much feeling that her self-control evaporated.

I'm in love with him, she thought. That was the terrible truth of it, the thing she could barely admit to herself. He was her Achilles' heel, and she knew it, but she fell into his arms anyway.

Diana left Henry's flat alone, one hour later, slipping out of his building at Chelsea Harbor and taking a cab to her hotel. She felt the same way she usually did after seeing him: physical satiety and guilt.

At the hotel she went to her room and lay on the bed. She had some time to rest before leaving to meet Anya. She checked the news on her phone, scrolling until she saw a headline that caught her attention.

"She Deserves a Name, and She Deserves Justice."

POLICE APPEAL FOR HELP IDENTIFYING BODY OF WOMAN

Police are appealing for help in identifying a young woman whose body was recovered from the bank of the Thames at Shingles Riverbank in Putney two weeks ago, when police were called to reports of a person discovered by a dog walker.

No personal property was found. Fingerprint tests were conducted but were negative. The recovered body was sent to the coroner's office and details were uploaded onto the UK Missing Persons database.

The death is being treated as suspicious. The body is very badly decomposed.

Detective Inspector Jason Dench said, "We're working hard on identifying the body and pursuing several lines of investigation regarding the tragic circumstances in which this young woman may have ended up dying. We're now asking for help from the public to identify her."

A spokeswoman for the WeAreAlive Trust, a charity dedicated to eradicating modern slavery, said, "Given this young woman's Asian descent and the difficulty in identifying her, we believe it's likely that this young woman was a victim of people trafficking. We urge anyone with information to support the police in identifying her so that she doesn't become an anonymous crime statistic. She may have suffered extreme abuse and exploitation, but she also has a family somewhere. She deserves a name, and she deserves justice."

There was a photograph of where the body was found. Diana had a sickening feeling as she looked at it. It had been her job to make sure the body disappeared forever, and she'd failed.

Clio

Clio drove through the village and made a turn down an unmarked lane bordered by rolling fields. She couldn't have known that Sherston Hall was down there; there was no sign, just two worn stone columns on either side of the lane's entrance, but that's what the GPS told her, so she kept going. The sun lurked behind a row of trees atop a ridge in the landscape and threw striae of smoldering golden light between their trunks.

When Sherston Hall came into view she caught her breath. It was impossibly large and fine. It surely had to be Grade I listed, with its gorgeous neoclassical façade hugged by two beautifully proportioned, symmetrical wings, fronted by a huge terrace with an ornate balustrade. Access to the terrace was up a wide stone staircase.

She parked out front, in a sea of pea gravel. There was doubtless another out-of-sight parking area somewhere, where vehicles wouldn't spoil the view of or from the house, but she quite enjoyed the comedy of her small, city-dinged Renault against such a grand backdrop. As she began the climb up the wide stone steps to the entrance a man appeared through a small door that was set within the house's grand double doors.

He was tidily dressed in jeans, a button-down shirt, and a lightweight sport coat. Nice brogues, polished and worn. An affable smile.

"Can I help you?" he asked in a smooth tone of voice that struck just the right note of friendliness and authority to let her know that she was being handled. He was staff, then. She hadn't been sure. She flashed her badge and told him why she was there.

"I'll see if Lady Arden is available," he said, poker-faced. He had Clio wait in the gracious entrance hall, where decorative plasterwork swirled playfully across walls painted a delicate pale gray. The balustrade on the elegant staircase curled with rococo twirls, the floor was marble, and between the flourishes of ornamental plaster huge paintings hung, life-size portraits of bewigged aristocratic women posed against bucolic backgrounds, wearing tight bodices and plumped-up skirts like puffs of silken cloud.

He returned quickly, his soles clip-clipping on the marble flooring, and Clio followed him down a corridor wide and long enough to play cricket in. It was the sort of home where the owners were aristocratic enough that they probably did.

He showed her into a large and gracious drawing room where Lady Arden sat on a wide sofa facing the door. It was upholstered in primrose yellow, and she occupied the middle seat, an aged charcoal whippet curled up beside her, unbothered by Clio's arrival. A fire crackled in the hearth. There were more oil paintings in here, and a collection of drawings. Side tables offered homes to an ornate chinoiserie vase, bottles of alcohol, and a gathering of silver-framed photographs. It had echoes of the Brutons' home but was much grander.

Lady Arden was an older woman, in her late sixties, Clio guessed, beautifully preserved, with exceptional bone structure and glacial-blue eyes. She was slender bordering on skinny and wore jeans and a black sweater, her collar a white lace crown that stood up around the base of her neck, like an homage to Tudor royalty, who, to be fair, she could well be related to. A thick strand of pearls hung over her sweater. The matching earrings were large enough to stretch her earlobes. She smelled of something expensive and exuded confidence from every pore.

"Do have a seat," she said. "It's lovely to meet you." The sentiment in her words didn't carry over to her tone of voice or her expression, where a trace of a smile appeared only fleetingly before her face settled back into looking stony. There were some women, Clio thought, who had the ability to make you wither in their presence. Lady Arden was surely one of them, but Lillian had been, too, and, in her mentor's honor, Clio was determined that she would not wilt.

"No, thank you. I'm trying to trace a piece of embroidery that Eleanor Bruton had in her possession, and I heard it might have been here?"

"Who?" Lady Arden said.

"Eleanor Bruton. From the Old Vicarage in the village. I was told she was a frequent visitor here when a relative of yours was ill."

"Oh, yes. She did visit rather tirelessly. A very boring woman, but my sister-in-law had a high tolerance for life's strugglers."

Her snobbery, Clio thought, was so uncompromising, it was borderline magnificent.

"The embroidery belonged to my sister-in-law. She was living with us here while she was ill. Bloody brutal cancer. It ravaged her. Took her very quickly. After she died, the embroidery disappeared. I don't know where it went, and I don't really care. It had some sentimental value to her, I believe, but it was very tatty and ragged. I didn't see what the fuss was about."

With such an embarrassment of extraordinary objects and artworks around her, Clio supposed this made sense.

"Why was Eleanor Bruton suspected?"

"Visitors who aren't close friends often have sticky fingers."

"Was Eleanor close to your sister-in-law?"

Lady Arden shrugged. "Not particularly. She was a church busybody. One of those types who *gather* around the bedsides of the sick and dying to nurture because they haven't got anything better to do. I shan't allow it when it's my time. It's pure voyeurism, if you ask me." She shuddered performatively.

"Who noticed the embroidery was missing?"

"That would be my niece. Mostly absent while her mother was dying, quick to arrive when it was time to collect her things, and apparently adept at pushing through probate at record speed. She made a lot of noise about the embroidery because apparently, my sister-in-law had promised to give it to her. She made a tremendous fuss about having had an emotional attachment to it, though you'd have thought we might have seen her more if that were true. Why do you want to know?"

Clio wondered how honest to be. "They have eyes and ears everywhere," Lillian had said. They were often embedded in powerful families.

"I'm not sure," she lied. "My superiors don't tell me everything. I'm just here to ask the questions and I'm very grateful for your time." She stood. Lady Arden watched her appraisingly, as if skeptical, and Clio felt a ripple of alarm. The man who'd shown her in appeared in the doorway. Had he been listening? Lady Arden nodded at him.

"I'll see you out," he said.

Out front, Clio asked, "What's your role in the household?"

"I'm Lady Arden's butler."

"People still have those?"

"Very much so."

When she reached the bottom of the steps he said, "Someone else came asking about the embroidery."

He had her attention. "Who?" she asked.

"An academic from St. Andrews University. A woman. She said she was working on historical bookbindings."

"Did she speak to Lady Arden?"

"Just to me. Lady Arden wasn't here at the time."

"When was this?"

"It was last autumn, almost a year ago. She was quite persistent, to the point where I thought she might become a nuisance, but we never saw her again."

"What was her name?"

"I can't remember off the top of my head, but I took a note of it somewhere. It was a foreign name."

Clio handed him a card. "Could you get in touch if you find it? Let me know?"

"Of course. Is there something special about the embroidery?"

She didn't have to lie. "I really don't know."

But she was beginning to believe there might be.

Olivia

Olivia Macdonald, wife of Judge Henry Macdonald, glanced out the window as she put on her necklace, a gold chain with a pendant in the shape of a spiked wheel.

Outside, she could see the gardener working on the rambling rose at the entrance to the walled garden, pruning its thorny, lashing branches into submission. Henry would want to tour the walled garden when he came home this weekend. It was his pride and joy, and now it would be looking lovely for him, which was good, but Olivia struggled to feel as happy about that as she might usually.

She was having what she called one of her bittersweet days.

Her husband had been with his mistress, Diana Cornish. Bitter thought.

But Diana was unaware that Henry's wife was a member of the Order of St. Katherine who knew all about the affair. Sweet thought.

Outwitting Diana Cornish was satisfying. As for the affair being a source of pain? As every member of the Order of St. Katherine must, Olivia understood, accepted, and made the best of the realities of her marriage. She well knew that the garden was only Henry's second-favorite place to be. The first was in Diana's arms. Men will be men. You did not try to change them; you worked with what you had.

Downstairs, she made tea and toast, which she spread thickly with her homemade marmalade, then sat down at the kitchen table and opened her laptop.

The screen saver was a photograph of their twin boys from a few years ago, when they were still sweet. Now, on the cusp of turning fifteen, they reminded her more of giant slugs, dull, oily creatures who were apparently semi-blind when it came to finding any of their possessions and permanently in great need of food, sleep, and charging cables.

There was work to do, with them, but Olivia wasn't fazed. This was just a phase. She had a plan to turn them into fine young men, and she had the time to do it, since no member of the Order had a job outside the family once her marriage was established. It wasn't allowed. That didn't bother her, either. Ultimately, it was wives and mothers who held all the power in a family, even if the men thought they did.

Multiple folders floated on the home screen of her MacBook, with labels like "Family," "Volunteering," "Housekeeping," and "Holidays." The app bar glowed with bland software icons, nothing that might attract the attention of her sons (who anyway tended to regard her and her interests as if both were transparent), or even Henry, who was a great deal sharper and more attentive than his offspring but nevertheless content to imagine that Olivia *wished* to spend most if not all her days in service to him and their family.

She clicked through a few menus to reach the app she kept hidden: encrypted audio software. She opened it, slotted earbuds in, and made a call.

"Hi!" Conchita answered immediately.

"Hi, sweetie," Olivia said. "Well done."

"Thank you."

There were nanny cams hidden throughout Henry and Olivia's London flat, including the bedroom. Henry had no idea. Olivia visited the property so rarely that he considered it his private space, for all intents and purposes.

Olivia hadn't watched any of the recordings of her husband making love to Diana Cornish since the first time. Once had been enough. His tenderness had been the most difficult thing to witness.

The rest was just biology. Urges. But she'd watched the feed from the hallway camera this morning, and seen Conchita let herself into the flat while Henry and Diana were in the bedroom.

"It was pretty easy," Conchita said.

Olivia knew this already. The footage had shown Conchita, wearing a cleaning tabard over a hoodie, cheap black leggings, and sneakers, slip inside and make it the work of seconds to pick up Diana's coat from the chair in the hallway, to remove Diana's phone from its pocket, and to install an app that would allow them to monitor all Diana's phone activity. Conchita knew Diana's passcode because it had been recorded by the cameras before. They had to do this often, because Diana changed her phone frequently, which meant that the information they got from it was only patchy, but it was better than nothing.

"Is it working?" Olivia asked.

"Yes. I'll send you the report later."

"Thank you. Can we make it twice daily, please."

"Is something wrong?" Twice daily was more than normal.

"We weren't expecting Diana to be in London, and Anya Brown has traveled down, too, which seems very soon after her arrival in St. Andrews. It doesn't feel right."

"Are they reacting to the attack on the lab?"

"It's possible."

"Doing something with the embroidery?"

She was deeply worried that the Fellowship of the Larks had hired Anya to work for them at the Institute, which everyone knew was a front for their hunt for *The Book of Wonder*.

Her worry went far deeper than just bitterness that the Fellowship of the Larks had outplayed them over the embroidery. Her fear was that they were closer to finding *The Book of Wonder* than she knew.

The thought that it could be sold tore a piece from her. It would be devastating to the Order of St. Katherine. *The Book of Wonder* was an indescribably important text. For the Order it had the status of a lost relic. It was the first link in a centuries-old chain of women working quietly and with dignity to help one another, for the good of society. It represented their ideological soul.

She couldn't share her thoughts with Conchita. The Order had a strict hierarchy, and you didn't share information down the ranks.

"I don't know," she said.

There was silence on the other end of the line, then Conchita asked, "Do you want me to do something more?"

"No. We'll watch and wait for now. Thank you. You know how important you are to us, don't you, Conchita?"

Conchita was an asset; she had a promising future with the Order.

"I don't dress up as a cleaner for just anybody. Of course I know."

She would also have to curb that tone if she was going to make a good marriage.

Diana

Diana sat at the desk in her hotel room in London. She was trying, and failing, to thread a needle. When she flubbed it for the fourth time, she swore in frustration.

Reading the article about the body had thrown her. The arson attack had thrown her. The lack of sleep was catching up with her. This was a difficult day, and it had barely started, though thank God for Henry. The hour she'd spent with him had passed far too quickly, but it had been perfect, and it would sustain her.

She tried with the needle one more time, and this time the thread slipped through its eye. She sighed with relief and laid it down on the desk, then unbuttoned her blouse and removed it, reached behind her to unclip her bra, and took that off, too. It had full cups, and she ran her fingers around one of them and examined it under the desk light. It had a thin, soft layer of padding. She took her nail scissors and, holding the bra even closer to the lamp, made some small snips until she'd opened up a few centimeters where the cup met the underwire.

She removed the embroidery from her bag. Wincing because she was afraid it would cause damage, she folded it a few times so that it was smaller than her bra cup. Luckily it wasn't too bulky. She eased it into the cup, between the padding and the fabric that sat next to her skin, so that it wouldn't show when she wore it. When she slipped the bra back on she could barely feel it was there. She looked in the mirror, turning this way and that. No one looking at her would ever guess it was in there.

She removed the bra again, picked up the threaded needle and, using tiny stitches in a technique her mother had taught her, she sewed up the gap she'd made as delicately and invisibly as possible. When she finished, she was pleased with what she'd done.

A lot had gone wrong in the last twenty-four hours. Two disasters already, and while Diana wasn't superstitious, she couldn't help thinking that bad luck is reputed to come in threes.

Sewing the embroidery into her underwear made her feel better. She was damned if she was going to take any more risks by having it anywhere other than right next to her skin.

She got dressed again. It was time to meet Anya Brown.

God help me, she thought as she left the hotel and stepped out into the city. I need this to go well.

Anya

I'd never woken up in Mayfair before, never drawn back the curtains to catch the sun rising on such valuable real estate, never looked down on so many sleek, expensive vehicles waiting to ferry sleek, expensive people to wherever they went every day. It was a very polished scene, topiary in heavy pots and chessboard-tiled walkways, impeccably groomed dogs and elegant wrought-iron railings.

I sent Sid a photo of the hotel's sumptuous breakfast buffet. He sent one back of his mug of tea and bowl of cornflakes with a sad-face emoji.

While I was eating, Mum messaged me with another riddle, which made me smile, because it meant she wasn't feeling too bad. It was a tough one.

> *Precious gown and wooden throne*
> *Has ancient archetype outgrown.*
> *By larvae of wasp and flock of sheep,*
> *Where golden vine o'er poison creeps,*
> *Six hands four feet make ten,*
> *Among horned lady and horseless men.*

I got the third line first. Wasp larvae caused oak galls to form on the trunks of oak trees. These growths were used to make the ink used in many medieval manuscripts. The vellum for a large manuscript often required the slaughter of one or more flocks of sheep or goats. A manuscript gave context to the first line: precious gown and wooden throne. The most expensive color to make was blue, implying this concerned a woman in a blue gown, seated on a wooden throne. I thought immediately of the Virgin Mary, but the second line brought that into question. Mary was a classic archetypal woman, not an evolved one.

The bottom three lines were a test of my memory. Because Mum was contrary, horseless men made me think of the four horsemen of the Apocalypse, and I guessed that it meant there were four men in the image and one woman. "Horned" could relate to a hat or headpiece. I thought of those strange medieval hats that women wore. My memory whirred until I smiled. I had it.

The riddle was describing a manuscript illustration of Christine de Pizan, the first professional female author, fourteenth-century defender of women's rights, and therefore smasher of archetypes. In the picture, she was seated on a wooden throne, teaching four men who looked displeased to be at the intellectual mercy of a woman. Only four feet were visible in the image—well, three and a half, if I was to be precise—and the hands of only three of the people had been painted, including Christine's, which were, as I remembered, elegantly posed over the manuscript. She'd been an intellectual powerhouse, and here she was, both in a manuscript and teaching from one.

Never content putting just one meaning into her riddles when there could be two, this was Mum's way of saying F**k the patriarchy and show them what you're made of!

I sent a reply: Love you too x

Diana had asked me to meet her in Green Park and it was gorgeous that morning. Falling copper leaves twisted gently as they fell through the still autumn air, and slivers of mist lingered here and there. Diana sat on a bench, talking on her phone. She hung up as soon as she saw me and rose to kiss me on both cheeks, as if we were society friends, and I had another of those moments where my life didn't seem like it belonged to me.

We walked toward Buckingham Palace, skirting the tourists gathering outside the gates. Diana kept the conversation light. Was I okay walking? she asked. She loved Green Park; it was one of her favorite places in London, and on a day like this . . .

She hardly drew breath. I barely knew her, but this seemed unlike her. I sensed that she was anxious, and her nerves were contagious. I began to feel wary.

We turned onto Grosvenor Place and then almost immediately off it into a residential enclave in deepest Belgravia. Diana led me to a row of mews cottages. "Here we are," she said. The sweet little road was cobbled; window boxes burst with trailing ivy and flowering heathers. The mews cottages were an eclectic mix of styles. Some had basements dug out. They must be worth millions. At the end of the row, a dead end, she stopped.

"Ready?" she asked.

"Sure," I said. My heart was beating, though.

"Diana, how lovely to see you." The woman who answered the door looked to be in her forties, with long blond hair, a husky voice, skin that had seen some treatments. She wore wide-legged sweatpants, and a baggy sweatshirt and sheepskin slippers. She was somehow familiar to me, but I couldn't place her.

She turned to me after they embraced. "This is very special, Anya." We're not being formal then, I thought. I was crap at knowing how to talk to rich people, so this whole exchange was a source of anxiety for me. I usually solved it by being overly ingratiating, then castigating myself later for it because that kind of behavior was against my beliefs, the opposite of what Mum had taught me. *Nobody is above or beneath you.*

She held out both hands. I hesitated, then let her take mine. I hadn't expected the meeting to happen in a private home, and it threw me.

"I'm Cece. Thank you so much for coming today. We're thrilled to meet you," she said, and I said, "It's nice to meet you," but my voice sounded tight and my smile felt fake.

Diana had been here before, because she knew to remove her shoes. I took mine off, too, and we followed Cece along a narrow hallway carpeted thickly in cream. The walls were painted white and hung with modern artwork. I saw a Basquiat drawing. "He's upstairs," Cece said.

Diana knocked on a door at the top of the stairs. It was slightly ajar.

"Come in." A man's voice.

We entered. The room faced the street. Slats on the shutters were tilted, ensuring privacy, filtering the light. Stunning artworks caught my eye: a large de Kooning *Woman* in oil, a Jackson Pollock sketch, works by Miró and Chagall. A Giacometti sculpture stood on a table in the corner of the room, barely there.

A ripple of anticipation ran up my spine. This man wasn't just a collector of old texts, or of London's finest real estate, but of modern art, too, of fluid, brave painting that was expressive and imaginative, a little wild, violent, even, in the case of the de Kooning.

It was exciting to think what that might mean for his manuscript collection.

He was approaching me. I clocked his silver hair, the glint of the heavy timepiece on his wrist. He took three rangy strides across the room toward me, quicker than I was expecting.

"Hello," I started to say but the breath was punched out of me as he wrapped his arms around me. The amber smell of his cologne was pungent. I heard Diana say, "Oh!" and his words, slightly muffled but audible: "Anya, my God, I've waited so long for this. Thank you so much. *Thank you*."

He loosened his grip on me a little. I put my hand to my cheek. It was wet. Was he crying? Then I really saw him.

"Oh my God," I said.

I'd seen him online, but never in person. For years, I'd googled him obsessively—his wife, his children, their privileged lives—until I'd forced myself to stop because it was unhealthy and it wasn't going to change anything and I never wanted Mum to find out what I was doing. This man and his wife hadn't wanted anything to do with me, until now. I was the baby he had decided wasn't good enough for him before I was even born.

And Cece. She was, of course, Cecilia Beaufort. The woman he'd married after abandoning me and Mum. I hadn't recognized her. I should have.

"Dad," I said. The word left my mouth involuntarily. Just saying it felt like a betrayal of Mum.

CHAPTER SIX

Sid

Sid arrived promptly at the Jack Cole building for computer science. It was a flat-roofed two-story building on a modern campus, a short walk outside the ancient town walls, an exposed site, separated but hardly sheltered from the ocean by the Old Course.

The sky felt bigger out here, and there was plentiful space around the buildings. A large parking lot was almost full, the leaves on the trees around it just turning from green to gold. It had the feeling of an out-of-town science park, and Sid liked it.

Professor Cameron Johns assessed him from behind an uncluttered desk. He looked like he had zero body fat, and his skin was weathered and tanned. Sid held his gaze calmly and reckoned him to be in his forties, a runner. The office was compact and faced the ocean. Its window glass was clouded from the salty air.

"This request from Professor Cornish to give you some work is unusual," Johns said. "Generally, I prefer to hire my own staff."

Sid was thrown by the acid in his tone. Diana Cornish had assured him he would be welcomed here, and he and Johns had exchanged emails over the summer that had seemed fine. Though, come to think of it, maybe they'd been rather terse. A cold feeling lodged itself in Sid's chest. Had he got this wrong? Was he being foisted on this department? That would be humiliating.

"I gather from Professor Cornish that your partner is considered invaluable to her institute," Johns said.

"She's a new hire there, yes."

"So that's why you're here, too? Happy wife, happy life?"

Sid couldn't believe how quickly this was going south. It was mortifying. He said, "I think there might have been a misunderstanding. If there's nothing for me here, I won't waste any more of your time."

Johns picked up a ballpoint pen and clicked the button on the end against his desk. The sound grated on Sid's nerves. He felt ready to walk out. "How's your wife finding life at the Institute?" Johns asked.

"We're not married."

"It's brave of you to relocate for a partner at this early stage of your career. Not many men would do that."

"I'm working on a project of my own. Look, this has been a mistake." He stood, but Johns waved at him to sit back down.

"Okay," he said. "I'm giving you a hard time. I'm sorry. You're talented and your work is impressive. We both know it. I just don't like being told how to run my own department. But here we are. I already have a department fully staffed with people who went through the normal recruitment process to get here, so I can't offer you teaching just now because it would be at the expense of one of them, but I have an opening for an assistant on a project of mine that's in the cybersecurity arena. You'd be supervising a few postgrads for a couple of days a week. How does that sound?"

Sid was tempted to refuse because his pride was hurt, he didn't love the way Johns was speaking about Anya or to him, and it seemed like he'd walked right into some messy politics, *but* Johns was offering him a bone and it was probably wise to take it for now. St. Andrews didn't have too many employment options for him.

"Sure," he said. "Sounds interesting. Thank you."

"Okay. I'll be in touch with a start date. It'll probably be in a couple of weeks, after we settle the new students. In the meantime, we'll fix you up with access to the lab and some desk space."

At reception Sid scribbled his initials in the sign-out column of the visitor book and asked about getting his pass. The receptionist gave him a temporary one to use for now. As he was leaving, she called out, "Hold on. There's an envelope here for you, too."

She passed it to him. His name was neatly handwritten on the front in block capitals. He frowned at it. Who knew he was going to be here?

"Do you know who left this?" he asked.

"I don't. Sorry. I found it with the post when I got in this morning. I almost threw it away, but Cameron mentioned you were coming in."

The phone rang and she answered it. Sid opened the envelope as he crossed the parking lot. It contained a single sheet of paper with just seven words printed on it:

"You need to know about Minxu Peng."

Anya

"Dad" was the most loaded word of my childhood.

If you'd looked at Wikipedia the day Diana Cornish and my father ambushed me in his mews house, it would have told you that for many years Magnus Beaufort was mostly known for his work as a consultant nephrologist at Addenbrooke's Hospital in Cambridge, and for the limited philanthropy he engaged in using the significant fortune he inherited from his eminent physician father, who had, in turn, inherited a great deal of money from Magnus's grandfather. If there was one thing Beaufort men were good at, it was turning money into more money.

You would have learned that Magnus had enhanced this fortune when he'd helped to develop a drug that was later approved and sold at a scandalously high price. What might have interested you, too, was the paragraph about what he wanted to do with the money. My father, who had rejected his own flesh and blood, was paradoxically very interested in immortalizing his legacy in bricks and mortar instead. In the eponymous Magnus Beaufort Library, to be specific.

Designed by a leading architect, a man who had worked on world-class buildings across the globe, the library was intended to be an exceptionally avant-garde and inspiring space, but also one of the most technologically advanced libraries and teaching spaces in the world.

Critics weighed in as soon as the plans were made public. They said the design was terrible and impossible to realize in the materials suggested, that the materials themselves were flawed and ugly, that the site was wrong, that the construction was going to run catastrophically over budget. They asked whether the millions and millions it would cost couldn't be better spent elsewhere. They wrote that the Magnus Beaufort Library was a vanity project.

Mum said the same: *Of course, Narcissus named it after himself.*

My father went into whitewash mode, writing robust op-eds in defense of his library and throwing money at reading and literacy programs for children and in prisons. He released patents for his drug so that third-world countries could make it, but nobody forgot how many had died in such places while his company raked in millions in the West. Even as he broke a sweat ostentatiously doing good, even as they broke ground on the library, the controversy waged on. Magnus Beaufort had a PR problem, and it couldn't have delighted my mother more.

The prospect of watching his library get built in a dominant position was one of the reasons I would never study or teach at Cambridge University. The other was the danger of running into one of my half siblings. There were three of them. I saw them on social media but had no idea whether they knew I existed or not.

Now, here I was, in my father's arms, in his mews house, under the watchful eye of Diana Cornish. Magnus Beaufort and I had never touched before. A deeply buried part of me wanted him to hold me longer, but I was trembling because he felt so forbidden and because I was so angry with him.

Over his shoulder, I stared at the de Kooning painting, at the woman's body exploded in streaks of fleshy paint. It was what he'd done to Mum. He'd blown her life up, and mine. I wrenched myself out of his grip.

"You look just like my mother," Dad said. His eyes were glassy. With tears? I felt unbearably raw, and my anger flared. How could he be having a *moment* where he was *feeling his feelings* because I reminded him of my grandmother, who I'd never met? It was too much.

I ran down the stairs so fast, I almost slipped, and ignored their shouts behind me. I didn't stop to put my shoes on, just grabbed them and burst onto the street in my socks. I stood, shocked, blinking in the daylight, feeling as if the little street was pivoting around me. When I heard them behind me I took off.

I didn't know where I was going. I just ran and walked and ran again until I felt like the mews house was lost behind me and I became aware of a stabbing pain in the side of my foot. I sank down with my back to someone's wall in a quiet corner and tears rolled down my cheeks. I gripped my foot where it hurt, and when I took my hand away there was blood on it.

"She's here!" My father knelt beside me. He put his hand on my shoulder. I felt as if it was scorching me. I slapped it away.

"Fuck off!"

He stood up, backed away. He looked distraught. Cece was there. He said, "I don't know if I should hug her." It made me even more angry. If he was my father, he should *know* the right thing to do. Not that I did. I wanted never to see him again, but then I'd wanted him all my life and here he was. So. Very. Close.

Diana knelt beside me. "Are you hurt?"

"I'm fine." She had a lot to answer for. I was so angry with her, and I could see in her eyes that she knew it.

My father said, "I think that foot needs attention."

"It's fine." I stood up. Diana offered me her hand, but I ignored it. I tried to walk, but it hurt badly, and blood smeared the pavement. My sock was soaked red. I sat down again.

My father approached. I wrapped my arms around my knees defensively, but he didn't touch me this time.

"Let us help you with that foot and my driver will take you anywhere you want afterward. I promise. I also think Diana has some explaining to do. To both of us."

I looked at her. She nodded. My foot was throbbing like crazy. The sight of blood made me queasy. Something in me gave up fighting, and I let him help me up.

It was my first proper look at him. We had the same eyes. I knew there were similarities between us from when I'd obsessively searched the internet for pictures of him, but seeing it in the flesh was totally different. It was like a body shock, a too-real and therefore surreal replay of all the fantasies I'd ever had about meeting him.

I hated him for what he'd done to us. The way Mum told it, he'd refused to have anything to do with her after she got pregnant with me. It happened when they were young, but not too young. His family had money. He'd told her he loved her. But when push came to shove, he told her that she wasn't "the right kind of girl" for his family, that he would be having nothing more to do with her, or with me.

Your father has a cold, cold heart. And the same eyes as me.

He offered me his arm, but I leaned on Diana and limped back to the house on her arm.

I was silent, but my anger was swelling. She'd ambushed me. Had she ambushed him, too? He'd made it sound that way, but Magnus Beaufort was a very good liar.

"THE BIGGEST PROJECT"

Feature, *Telegraph Magazine*

February 3, 2024

Libraries are in Magnus Beaufort's family. He welcomed me to his home in Cambridge to talk about his latest project and why it's personal.

There's a room at the end of a corridor in Beaufort's spacious home on a leafy street in Cambridge that he—entrepreneur, physician, collector, and philanthropist—cleans himself.

"I won't let anyone in here except family."

Inside, we admire the interior, but not all of it. The room and its contents burned 25 years ago, and although he's had it made safe, Beaufort hasn't been able to bring himself to restore it fully.

Beaufort is coy about why, at first. Over lunch in the Orangery that has a charming view of their garden, with a planting design originally provided by Gertrude Jekyll for Beaufort's grandmother, and exquisitely maintained by this generation of Beauforts, we're joined by his charming wife, Cece (CEO of makeup and fashion brand cEcE).

"Magnus doesn't like to talk about it," she says. "It's painful."

She's referring to the fire that consumed the private library built by Beaufort's grandfather and destroyed his collection of rare and special manuscripts.

Beaufort has a distant look in his eyes. "It's still painful," he says. "I mean, thank God there was no loss of life, but what you need to understand is that the collection was so special to our family that quite apart from the monetary and historical value of what we'd lost, it felt as if we'd lost part of ourselves, too."

I do understand. His patrician features are softened by grief as he recalls the years his father and grandfather spent building the collection, with its emphasis on rare medical texts. Although, as Beaufort is keen to point out, they collected many other exceptional manuscripts, too.

The loss of his family's collection is the reason he wants to build the Magnus Beaufort Library and why he's determined not to let the project fail, even in the face of fierce opposition.

"Book collecting is heroic," he says. "I believe that. Over the centuries, men have risked their lives to collect manuscripts because they knew that without preserving the knowledge we've accumulated over millennia, we're doomed to live in very dark times."

The Beauforts are keen to talk about their enthusiasm for the initiatives they're funding to boost literacy. "We love doing all this grassroots work, it's what gets us up in the morning, but we think it's also important to gift this new institution to the nation. We feel it's the only way to make up for the loss of the books that burned on our family's watch."

It's hard to tear myself away from the Beauforts' beautiful home, but tear away we must. After a short drive we don hard hats and inspect the site where the new library is beginning to rise from the ground. As Beaufort describes his vision, I understand that it will be magnificent.

"Once the doors of this building are open, the new manuscripts I've been acquiring will become the cornerstone of a brand-new collection."

It takes a man with vision, determination, and very deep pockets to conceive and deliver a project like this. To steer it past criticism and gift it to the nation, it takes a titan with a tear in his eye.

Detractors should make no mistake: the Magnus Beaufort Library is a phoenix rising from the ashes, and it will also be a jewel in the crown of this nation.

Sid

Sid read the note again: "You need to know about Minxu Peng."

Surely, it couldn't be for him. He'd never heard that name before. He considered going back to ask the receptionist if she knew more than she'd said, but that seemed unlikely. The note could hardly have been left for him by mistake because it was so obviously deliberate: the fact that it had arrived at the department on the day he was due to be there, the careful printing of his name on the envelope.

Back at the cottage, he took the note upstairs and set it down by his desk. He sent Professor Johns an email thanking him for the chat and the offer of work and saying he was looking forward to starting. He thought about asking if Johns knew who Minxu Peng was but decided against it for now. Better to keep things simple with that man. The situation was already tricky enough.

He did an online search for Minxu Peng. A few pages of results appeared, and he scrolled idly down them, but they seemed irrelevant. He spotted one link that looked promising, but when he clicked on it, it led to an error notification. He clicked back to the results page and took another look at the link. It contained just enough information to suggest that Minxu Peng might be associated with the Center for Computing and Business at the Hunan Normal University in China. He found the university's website and a page for the Center for Computing and Business. There were no staff photographs, but it had a list of staff members. Minxu Peng wasn't included on it, but another of the names he'd seen on the obsolete link was. That person was now the director of the center.

"Right place," he said aloud. "Wrong time."

He felt as if he'd been set a puzzle, like the riddles Anya and her mum exchanged. Occam's razor: most straightforward approach first, he thought. He ran a simple cache search, putting the address of the dead web page he found earlier into the search bar and searching for saved versions of it, but drew a blank. Next, he opened a piece of software built to search billions of archived web pages for content and entered a few terms. This time, he got lucky.

Alongside seven others, Minxu Peng was listed as a member of the Center for Computing and Business in 2018. Her specialty was cybersecurity, the same as Sid's.

It felt like he was getting somewhere. He screenshotted the page and saved it. Now he was intrigued.

Anya

Magnus bound up my foot, neatly and carefully, while I stared at his surgeon's hands and imagined them holding a blade and cutting into other people's skin to avoid thinking about how intimate the moment was.

I didn't want to let him play dad *or* doctor. He didn't deserve it. Where was he when I fell off my bike or grazed my knees as a kid? Where was he when my appendix burst, or when I got strep throat? Where was he when Mum got her diagnosis?

He looked up at me and said, "I'm sorry this has been such a horrible shock for you. I was under the impression that you knew we were going to meet."

We both looked at Diana. She sat with her back to the window, and her face was in shadow. Her hands were clasped in her lap. But her posture was straight and strong.

She said, "I should have been honest with you both, and I'm sorry I wasn't. For what it's worth, I had my reasons. Your father has an exceptional collection of manuscripts, which will be the foundation of his new library and which he's willing to make available for study to the very best and very brightest. He asked us to find the right person for the job."

I heard Mum's voice: *Excellence is the only thing he values. People are commodities to him. They're disposable.*

Diana went on: "We found you, Anya. Your eidetic memory,

your linguistic knowledge, the breadth of your learning and experience. It's exceptional. Was I less than honest about the situation to bring you together? Yes, because I didn't think you'd agree to meet otherwise. Am I sorry? I don't know yet."

I was very angry with her, but part of me admired her honesty.

Magnus said, "I don't know if it helps to hear this, but I felt the same as you when Diana first proposed this. But the more I thought about it, the more it seemed right. At the very least, my hope was, *is*, that we can have a fruitful working relationship that helps your career and helps us get to know one another."

"You've never been interested in helping me."

"Is that what your mother told you? Did she tell you how often I tried? And how often she knocked me back?"

I bit my lip.

"I hurt her," he said. "I own it. The way I treated you both was unforgivable, but I was very young and very stupid. I can't change the past, but I can try to improve things for us now."

Don't believe a word that man says.

I couldn't hear it. "I want to leave," I said.

He messaged his driver. I didn't want to use his car, but my foot was throbbing, and I knew I couldn't walk far on it. When it arrived, Diana got in with me.

"No," I said.

"Give me one more chance," she said. "You don't know everything, and I owe you the full picture."

I didn't know what to say or whether to trust her. I still felt ambushed, angry, used. She saw my indecision and leaned forward to talk to the driver.

"Could you please take us to Cecil Court."

WE GOT OUT OF THE CAR NEAR THE NATIONAL PORTRAIT GALLERY. WE WERE in the heart of London's theater district, busy with billboards and traffic, on the roads and on foot. I followed Diana down a short, pedestrianized street leading toward Covent Garden. It was lined with small, independent bookshops, specializing in first and rare editions. A book lover's paradise.

She entered one of the smallest, and I followed. Barely more than a shop front, where a handful of books were displayed on a pyramid-shaped stand, it felt cramped inside. A woman with mussed gray hair and tortoiseshell reading glasses on a chain sat behind a small desk in the corner. She took one look at Diana, then at me, and said, "Downstairs is free."

The steps to the basement were narrow and precipitous. Diana flicked a switch, and a strip light came on overhead, bright and with a persistent hum. The space was home to piles of cardboard boxes. Some had been opened and were packed with books. Two stacks of folding chairs leaned against a wall, as if meetings regularly took place down here. The only natural light came from a frosted window set high up, through which we could see the blurred silhouettes of a security grille and the feet of passersby. In the back corner was a tiny cloakroom beside a small kitchenette. The walls were painted white and plastered with posters advertising bygone literary events.

Diana took two chairs and unfolded them with a deft shake. She placed them in the middle of the room, one facing the other. "Coffee?" she asked. "Cup of tea?"

I shook my head.

She sat in one of the chairs, and after a moment's hesitation I took the other. She said, "I'll get straight to the point, because I appreciate that this morning came as a shock. For what it's worth, I didn't want to introduce you to Magnus that way, but here we are."

I started to speak, but she held up a finger. "Let me finish, if you don't mind. Then I'm happy to hear whatever you want to say. I know you must be feeling used."

I nodded.

"What do you know about your father's manuscript collection?"

"It burned," I said. It was a story I'd heard many times from my mother.

There was no one in your father's house that night. They were all staying in London. I saw the neighbors interviewed on the news. They had smelled the smoke first and called the firefighters, but by the time the fire trucks arrived, the flames had taken hold and it was too late to save the library. The neighbors spoke vividly about how horrible the smell of burning vellum was and how the ashes of the burnt manuscripts floated through the smoky dawn like fireflies. Your dad and your granddad, who was still alive then, rushed back from London and in the papers the next day there was a photograph of them looking stricken in front of the charred remains of the library.

"It did," Diana said. "What else do you know about it?"

"He has people scouring auctions and collections around the world looking for manuscripts important enough to replace the ones he lost." Just like Ashurbanipal, just like the other men throughout history who'd made it their life's work to create libraries.

"What do you know about the contents of the collection?"

While my parents were dating, my mother had only been allowed to see the collection once, a source of bitterness to her.

Of all the people who could be trusted with the books, a restorer has to be high on the list, but of course I wasn't good enough for them.

I only knew what she'd told me about it and what I'd read about the collection online. "Not a lot," I said.

"It was world class. The medical books dated back to the ancient Greeks and possibly earlier. Your grandfather had also managed to bring together some of the lost volumes from the library of John Dee. Books on alchemy and sorcery. He had some exquisite texts in Arabic. Early treatises on mathematics. Books on Jewish mysticism. The collection was eclectic and esoteric. What your great-grandfather, grandfather, and father all had in common was that every book they acquired was the very best. So the loss was unimaginable."

I heard your grandfather collapsed when he saw the burnt out library, and your father refused to talk about it for a long time.

"I know," I said.

"Of course."

She leaned forward, a new intensity in her eyes. It reminded me of the first day we met. She said, "How would you feel if I told you that the collection survived the fire?"

"I would tell you that you're wrong."

"I'm not. The core of the collection survived. Some of the best books had been moved to another location before the fire. Afterward, it was decided to keep them there and to tell no one, because it was such a lucky escape. Your father and grandfather were terrified that whoever burned down the library would come after the books again."

"No. That can't be." The total destruction of the collection was part of the lore of the Beaufort family.

"It can and it is. Your father's family are very good at keeping secrets."

That was true. My father kept me a secret. I wasn't mentioned in any of his official biographies.

"What you showed me at Tracy's, was that—"

I remembered every detail of those manuscripts. Their quality and rarity had been exceptional.

"They were part of his original collection, yes."

"How many books survived?"

"About two hundred. Ten percent of the collection, but the finest ten percent. If you agree to work on your father's collection, you'll have access to them all. They've never been properly looked at, certainly not published on."

This I knew to be true. My grandfather had famously kept the collection closely guarded, which had appalled Mum.

Your father's library contained extraordinary books. Books that were believed to have been lost to humanity. The Beaufort men had no problem believing themselves to be worthy keepers of the manuscripts, and they also believed nobody else was worthy of seeing them. The manuscripts were for their eyes and the eyes of their heirs only. That was the scale of their self-importance.

Diana took a piece of paper from her bag and passed it to me. "This is a comprehensive list of the surviving manuscripts."

I took it from her and read it. I was amazed.

"They're your birthright," Diana said. "Now, tell me I did the wrong thing getting you and him together. Tell me I was wrong, and you'll never see this list again, let alone any more of the manuscripts."

CHAPTER SEVEN

Sid

Sid fetched himself a coffee, then dove deeper into the mystery of Minxu Peng and found more interesting results online.

He discovered that she'd published some papers that had some crossover with his concept for Lucis. Unfortunately, they were in Mandarin, so he couldn't read them, but it deepened his feeling that she was someone of interest specifically to him.

He remembered a Chinese colleague at Oxford complaining about how hard it was to get Westerners to write his name consistently, and Sid wondered if Minxu Peng had the same problem. He tried searching again, using variations of her name, and stumbled on a headshot attached to the name Peng Minzhu. Her eyes danced with intelligence beneath a thick fringe of hair. If the photo was recent, she couldn't be much older than him and Anya now.

The caption read: "New Appointment to the FX Trading Team." He read the article. She'd got a job at a foreign exchange trading desk within a major investment bank, where she was working as a security analyst in the in-house red team. It made sense, given her background. She'd likely be testing the exchange's security controls.

His doorbell rang. He jogged downstairs to answer it, but froze when he saw it was his neighbor again. She was peering through the front window, trying to see in. He cursed and wondered if he could make himself invisible if he stood very still, but it was too late. She waved at him.

He opened the door, thinking that he must order a doorbell camera.

"Sorry to bother you again," she said.

"It's fine," Sid lied.

She handed him a package. "This came while you were out this morning."

"Thanks," he said. "Appreciate it." It was a book he'd ordered. He felt guilty for thinking that she was interrupting him for no reason.

As he was about to shut the door, something from their previous conversation snagged, a possible but not probable coincidence. Worth asking about, though.

"The woman who lived in our cottage, the one you said disappeared? Did you say she was from abroad?"

"Yes, from China."

"What was her name?"

"Minnie. Min for short. Why do you ask?"

"Can I show you a photograph?"

He ran upstairs and grabbed his laptop, brought it down, and showed her the headshot of Minxu Peng that he'd found.

"Yes," she said. "That's her."

Anya

I was furious as I paced the basement of the bookshop in Cecil Court. Diana seemed so smug, sitting there in front of me, telling me things that I didn't know about my father, trying to get me to do what she and he wanted. Clearly, neither of them understood me at all.

"I won't work with him," I told Diana. "Not for any manuscript. I won't betray my mum like that. Period. I quit."

"You can't," she said.

"No, I can. I quit."

"Really, you can't."

"I just did."

I walked out, slamming the door behind me. I was so angry that the pain in my foot almost felt good. I walked in a random direction, hardly noticing or caring where I was going, just wanting to get away. The streets were swarming with tourists. I ducked into a side alley that ran behind a row of shops.

Partway down it I heard a car crawling behind me. I sped up to reach a recessed doorway where I could get out of its way and heard the car speed up, too. I glanced behind me, nervous. It was gaining ground and speed. The wing mirror clipped a garbage bin and knocked it over.

My gaze met the driver's, but the car didn't slow. My body understood what my mind was slow to process: it wasn't going to stop. I turned and ran, slipping into the doorway just in time to feel a buffet of air as the car shot past, inches away. My heart had never thumped so hard.

I peered out. The car was still in the alley, parked about fifty yards up. The reverse lights came on and it began to move back, gathering speed again. It felt wet, sticky, and warm inside my shoe. My foot was actively bleeding again. I couldn't possibly outrun the car. I tried to open the door I was hiding beside, but couldn't. I slammed myself hard against it and fell through.

I found myself in a storeroom. Boxes of pasta, flour, canned tomatoes, and huge cans of olive oil lined the shelves, alongside wine and biscuits. A huge refrigerator hummed in one corner. I looked for a way out. Chunky plastic strips hung over an open doorway. I pushed through them and found myself in a fancy delicatessen.

"Hey!" a man called out. He and I were behind a counter where prosciutto and salami hung and fresh pasta was stacked onto wooden trays. He was operating an industrial-scale meat slicer. I slipped around the counter to the door, and he shouted again. "Hey! What are you doing?"

I was too afraid to stop. I emerged onto a small street lined with genteel shops. It was free of crowds and I felt very visible, a moving target. Every step I took left bloody marks on the pavement. I scraped my foot against the curb, trying to wipe the sole of my shoe clean, and limped on.

There was a tube station down the street, at an intersection, and I headed toward it. About fifty yards away, I saw a black sedan car turn in, identical to the one that had menaced me.

A van pulled between us, blocking the view. I wasn't sure if the driver had seen me or not. I crossed the street as quickly as I could and crashed into a shop whose window display of bolts of fabric and ribbons was as brash and colorful as fireworks.

A woman stood behind a cutting table covered in deep red silk, pattern pieces pinned to it. A tape measure hung around her neck; half-moon glasses sat halfway down her nose. She held an oversized pair of scissors. "Can I help you?"

"There's a man."

It was all I needed to say; she understood.

"In the back," she said. "The changing area in the corner."

I did as I was told, finding myself in a room full of haberdashery supplies. In the corner a tiny changing area was enclosed by a curtain. I pulled it around me, trying to make sure it didn't gape. I sat on the chair that just fit into the space, hugged my arms around my chest, and tried not to shake.

Minutes ticked by. I heard nothing from the front of the shop apart from the scratch and snip of fabric being cut, and I began to doubt myself.

Had I run from the car for no reason? Imagined it was pursuing me? Who had sent it? Diana? How?

She'd told me I couldn't quit, and the way she'd said it was calm, resigned almost; she had no doubt about it. Was this what she meant? That they'd find me and bring me back?

What the hell was this Institute if you couldn't leave it?

I jumped at the sound of jangling bells. Someone had come into the shop.

"Can I help you?" the shopkeeper asked. I held my breath.

A woman's voice answered, "I'm looking for my friend. She's in a bit of a state. Has she come in, or have you seen her go past?" She proceeded to give a full description of me. How tall I was, my hair color, exactly what I was wearing. My mouth dried out. I tried not to make any noise. I was hardly breathing. "We're really worried about her," the woman said. "She hasn't been taking her meds. She may be showing signs of paranoia."

My chest started to heave, a panic attack coming on. I clapped my hand over my mouth, smelled fear on my breath. I shut my eyes.

"I'm afraid I haven't seen her," the shopkeeper said. "I'm so sorry. That sounds very worrying. Would you like to leave your number in case she comes in? I can give you a call if she does."

"Thank you, that would be great," the woman said. She sounded so calm, so rational. I might have believed her if I were the shopkeeper.

"What's her name?"

"Anya Brown."

"Good luck finding her."

It felt like an impossibly long time before the shop door opened and shut again. I heard it being locked. I didn't dare move until the shopkeeper pulled back the curtain.

"Did I do the right thing?"

"Yes. Thank you."

"I knew she was a wrong 'un," the shopkeeper said.

"How?"

"She didn't mention your name. And when she did, she told me your full name. Women don't do that. The names of our female friends roll off our tongues easily."

"I can't thank you enough."

"Should I call the police for you?"

What would I say? That someone tried to run me over? Had they? My gut said yes, I'd certainly thought so at the time, but could I prove it? I didn't have the car's number plate, and I didn't know if the alleyway had CCTV. I imagined myself telling an officer that I'd *thought* I was in danger but had no proof. It didn't go well. I shook my head. "I'd rather go home."

"Okay, but you're hurt." She was looking at my bloody shoe. "Let's deal with that first." I winced as she removed the dressing and redid it, unwrapping my father's work, wadding clean cotton over it, binding it with a strip of linen. I eased my sneaker back on.

"Are you sure you don't want to stay here a bit longer?" she asked.

I shook my head. I wanted to be somewhere they couldn't find me. I wanted to call Sid. I felt too vulnerable here.

"You can leave through the back. There's a footpath. The tube station is just two hundred yards away."

"I can't thank you enough."

"Be safe."

The footpath behind the shop was narrow, bordered by tall brick walls. At the end, I watched the street for a while before stepping out. There were no black sedan cars in sight, just taxis, a bus, regular cars.

The tube station wasn't far, as she'd said, but I'd have to cross the street to reach it. I had to work up the courage to go for it. I took a deep breath, stepped out, and walked up along the street as fast as I could. I was hoping to dart across, but traffic was too dense and fast moving. I would have to use the crossing. I jabbed at the pedestrian button and waited impatiently for the vehicles to stop.

Before the light turned green, a man in dark glasses linked his arm through mine and pulled me against him.

"Hello, Anya," he said. "Stay calm. Let's go this way."

I tried to yank my arm away, but he was too strong. He kept a smile on his face. To someone watching, we probably looked like a playful couple.

He put his mouth to my ear, as if we were lovers. I froze. He said, "Don't fight me. We wouldn't want you to get hurt."

Diana

Diana stood in the ladies' restroom off the lobby of a glistening tower less than half a mile from the building called the Gherkin in the City of London. The room was fancy, tricked out in marble, lit like a dressing room, folded hand towels beside the basins. The stalls were empty; she was alone, apart from the multiple reflections of herself in all the mirrors.

She washed her hands slowly. She had five minutes before she was due upstairs, enough time to compose herself. Charlotte mustn't see any worry in her face, no hint at all that Anya was AWOL and the body of an Asian woman had been found in the Thames.

As to that, Diana had a contact in the police who might be able to tell her more, but she was loath to get in touch yet. Better to wait a little. She'd had scares like this before that had turned out to be nothing. She looked at her reflection, searching for signs of stress on her face. Sometimes she wished it showed more. People assumed she was infinitely capable, but everybody had a breaking point.

I could do it all, she thought, if other people didn't make changes, like compressing the timeline for Anya Brown to deliver. This morning was proof that that wasn't working, that they'd moved too fast bringing Anya Brown here, and Diana had been right to call it. The question was, would anyone listen to her now, even after she'd been proved right?

It was so important that they got this right. They were gambling with the highest of stakes. Lives had been lost and deep down, this troubled Diana, even though she understood the deaths had been necessary. You couldn't play with fire unless you accepted you might be burned, and that went for both the Kats and the Larks.

However, the ultimate gamble was whether the objects they were seeking would lead them to *The Book of Wonder*. If they didn't, all this effort would have been spent and lives would have been lost for nothing, and that, she knew, would keep her up at night for the rest of her life.

But she mustn't let doubt get in her way. She was as confident as she could be that they were on the right track. They'd based their decision on information passed from woman to woman in whispers over centuries. Some dismissed them as nonsense, but Diana was convinced they had truth in them.

The whispers suggested that clues to the location of *The Book of Wonder* were encoded somewhere or somehow in Magnus Beaufort's collection and within the embroidery, too. Diana just had to bring the relevant objects together and have the means to interpret them.

"I insist that we keep the embroidery from Anya until we're sure she's loyal to us. We don't want her seeing it, then putting two and two together once she has access to his collection. She could go rogue," Charlotte had said.

Diana believed there was sense in that approach—Anya was a very bright girl—but she wondered if Charlotte might revise it now that timing was a more urgent issue. The Fellowship of the Larks weren't the only ones looking for *The Book of Wonder*. The Order of St. Katherine were, too. It was a race. But Diana believed the Larks had the upper hand now. The Kats didn't have Anya, and, more important, they didn't know that the Beaufort collection had survived. Yet. Diana didn't underestimate their ability to find out.

She really needed to talk to Charlotte about the necessity of not rushing this.

She closed her eyes, placed the palms of her hands on her belly, and inhaled slowly and deeply, then exhaled. When she opened her eyes again, she saw reflections of herself everywhere—the room was a hall of mirrors—but she looked calm and composed, her shoulders back, her head high, and she took some strength from that. She would go to this meeting and press palms with Charlotte's City contact. Then she would locate Anya and talk to her again. Hopefully, she'd have had a chance to cool down by then. She hadn't fled out of town; the tracker on her phone told Diana that Anya was still in Central London.

She was a bright girl. She would come to see that there was only one sensible choice she could make. Certainly, it was worth giving her time and space to allow her to think the decision had been hers to make. And if she didn't make the right choice, well, Diana didn't love threatening people, but if it came to it, she would.

She wasn't worried about Magnus. He'd be fine if he got what he wanted in the end. His self-absorption was truly a gift, on occasion.

The express elevator took her up to the forty-fourth floor in seconds. It was on the outside of the building and its glass walls offered majestic views of London's most iconic sights. The day was clear, and in the far distance, Diana saw planes circling Heathrow Airport. The River Thames cut its serpentine path through the City like a mythological beast. Perspective was always useful. You had to think big and be bold to achieve anything meaningful. Women wouldn't have better lives unless they were brave.

The elevator stopped and its doors slid open. Diana stepped out, looking perfectly composed. She approached a curved reception desk.

"I'm here to see Bridget Farley," she told the polished receptionist.

The meeting room was finer than Diana had imagined. Carpet thick enough to threaten the stability of her heels, a view just as good as the one from the elevator. They were directly above the Tower of London. Charlotte Craven was already in the room. Bridget Farley was, too. She sat at the head of a large conference table, polished to a gleam.

Bridget wore a dark pantsuit and cream blouse, heavily accessorized by chunky gold jewelry. She had glossy red curls, emeralds in her ears, and a vintage Rolex on her wrist. Diana had a lot of admiration for Bridget. She'd smashed through the glass ceiling, making her a powerful ally for the Larks, but she was tricky to handle. Bridget wasn't known to be a good team player. Bridget believed that Bridget was always right.

Diana shook hands with her. Bridget's grip was assertive, as usual. They sat.

"I have good news and bad," Bridget said. "The good news is that we are fully supportive of your venture and can help you arrange funding. The bad news is that we can raise only half of what you'll need, and we've been unable to secure any other backers. It's disappointing. To secure the site, you'll need to find an extra twenty million pounds. I hate to admit it, but I've run out of rope to get that for you, and believe me, I've tried every contact I know."

Charlotte and Diana exchanged a glance. Charlotte nodded.

"We have a source for the money," Diana said. "Our only obstacle is an unpredictable timeline in terms of liquidity."

"Investors hate two things: lack of liquidity and unpredictability. Can you give me an estimate?"

"We should have access to the full amount in three months," Charlotte said. Diana smiled to cover up the rush of doubt she felt. It was an audacious claim. They hadn't agreed that Charlotte could promise this. She likely wouldn't have if she'd known that right now, Anya Brown was probably trying to figure out a future where she didn't have anything to do with her father or his collection.

Bridget smiled. "Three months is doable. These things take time, anyway. So long as you can guarantee it."

"I guarantee it," Charlotte said, boldly.

Diana kept her mouth shut, but she felt as if this might be the straw that broke her back. Even if she got Anya back on board in the next twenty-four hours, three months could prove impossible. But it was an unbreakable rule of the Fellowship of the Larks that you never contradicted your sisters in public. If you did, there would be consequences.

Sid

Sid's neighbor peered at the photograph he'd found online of Minxu Peng.

"Yes," she said. "That's her. Can I ask why you have this?"

He told her about the anonymous note he'd received and the searches he'd done. She said, "I think we'd better have a little chat. Would you like a cup of tea?"

Her cottage wasn't as nice as his and Anya's place. It shared the views but the interior had the bleak feel of a student rental, with cheap fittings and drafty windows that rattled in the wind.

"Take a seat, dear." As Maggie made tea, Sid sat at the table, which was covered with a neatly organized array of folders, a laptop, an iPad, and a notebook. It looked very businesslike, not what he was expecting.

She set down mugs of tea and sat.

"I need to tell you something," she said. "And it might sound crazy, but bear with me, because I promise it's true."

"Okay," he said quietly. He was starting to feel uneasy.

"Min—Minxu—has come to harm, I'm sure of it."

"For real?"

"It's very real. We think Min got hurt because she knew too much."

"Too much about what?"

"About what the Institute is doing. Ask yourself why someone like Min, who trained in your specialty, was given a job at the Institute."

"I don't know." He hadn't had a chance to think about it properly, but it was odd. "I'm sorry, but who are you exactly?" he asked.

"I'm an investigator. I've been looking into Min's disappearance on behalf of her family. Her parents desperately want to find their daughter."

Sid stared. She looked nothing like how he imagined a private investigator would. "I guess you're going to tell me next that your name isn't Maggie." He laughed, but she didn't crack a smile.

"My name is Mel Drummond." She handed him a card. It had a company name on it: Drummond Private Investigations.

"No way." This couldn't be real. Unless it could.

Two things occurred to him. First, that anyone could get a card printed up and claim they were a PI. Second, that if she *was* telling the truth, all of this wasn't just deeply strange, it was extremely unnerving. The smile fell from his face. "I don't understand. What's going on?"

"Okay," she said. "Buckle up. I started looking into Min's disappearance when she'd been missing for a few weeks. This was last March. Her parents hired me because they live in China, they don't speak good English, and they don't have the money to stay here for as long as it would take to look for her themselves. Between us, we've tried very hard to make police here take Min's disappearance seriously, but as there was no sign of foul play, it's been impossible to persuade them to investigate. From their point of view, Min was an adult, she wasn't new to this country, and she was free to do what she wanted. They noted her as a missing person but refused to do more."

"What makes you think differently?"

"Things her family told me. Her parents and brother say that her behavior since she arrived in St. Andrews at the start of the last academic year had become secretive and anxious. They described it as paranoia. When she first arrived here, she was in daily contact with them, which was normal for her, but by the time she disappeared they were barely hearing from her. It was out of character. We told the police this, but it didn't have much weight, because the story the Institute was telling about Min was different. Diana Cornish and her colleagues insisted she'd been fine, a pleasure to have as a colleague. Nothing to see here, basically. According to them, Min had been talking for a while about quitting and traveling around the UK, so when she left, they weren't surprised. They had no explanation as to why she disappeared in the middle of the night.

Their only response was to suggest that Min's neighbors had been mistaken. It didn't help that they were students, so of course they partied sometimes, though not that night. The Institute also told police that Min had complained about her parents and found them very overbearing. They painted a picture of her family as extremely pushy, hinting that they were people she might want to disappear from. Basically, they stereotyped her parents appallingly, and the police seemed happy to believe it."

Sid felt the burn of anger. He hated bigotry. "What's your impression of her parents?"

"Lovely people. Caring and supportive. Not pushy at all. I might be wrong, of course, but I'm a decent judge of people, and that's what my gut tells me. Min's brother says the same, so there's that, too."

Sid thought about it. "So how are you justifying hanging around here to Diana? Why ask me to tell her you were here? Because there's no roof leak, is there?"

She shook her head. "No. I've just moved in here. I'm not the landlady; I'm renting the cottage. I took over the lease this summer, when the students left, to put pressure on Diana Cornish. I asked you to mention me to her for the same reason. The Institute needs to know that Min hasn't been forgotten."

"What will that achieve?" Sid asked.

"It might help to keep you and Anya safe."

"Safe from what?" he asked. His unease was growing into fear.

"I believe the Institute had something to do with Min's disappearance, and I believe Anya is in danger, too."

"That's a hell of an accusation."

"I know, and I can't prove it yet."

"Why aren't you afraid of them?"

"I'm very afraid, but I take precautions."

He tried to process what he was hearing. "Did you leave the note for me at the computer science department?" he asked.

"No, and I don't know who did, but I'd love to find out. Can I show you something?" She opened her laptop and angled it so he could see the screen.

"This is a screenshot of a D&D chat. Do you see the user called ScotchEgg? That's Paul Fields, the husband of Anya's new colleague, Giulia Orlando. Have you met her?"

"I've met them both," Sid said. "You're watching him online?"

"It's my job."

"Are you watching me, too?"

"I tried. You cover your tracks too well."

Sid smiled.

"Look what Paul's saying." Mel pointed to the screen.

SCOTCHEGG: Does anyone know how to find out if police located someone who went missing?

"He deleted the question later. This is a screenshot," Mel said.

"Did anyone reply?"

"They did, but they didn't take him seriously."

"Do you think he means Minxu?"

"I don't know for sure, but quite possibly."

"Have you talked to him?"

"No, because I don't know what his motives are for posting this."

"Is he doing it because of or in spite of Giulia, you mean?" Sid said.

"Exactly that."

"Do you think it was Paul who left the note for me?" Sid asked, then, thinking aloud, "But how would he have known I was going to the computer science department?"

"Did you tell anyone?"

He shook his head. "But Anya could have mentioned it to Giulia."

"Or he made an educated guess. Does he know much about you?"

Sid thought back to their night out, the chat over some whiskey shots. "The basics, so yeah, he might have guessed, but why not talk to me? Or slip a note through the cottage door?"

"I don't know. Not a lot about this makes sense, but what I know for sure is that the Institute has lied about Min, and lying about a young woman's disappearance is a very serious thing to do, so you've got to wonder why."

"Do you have theories?"

"They must be hiding something; I just don't know what. Have you tried searching online for any of the women who work there? You won't find much. That's a red flag to me."

Sid remembered Anya saying the same when the Institute first approached her, but he hadn't given it much thought at the time, busy as he was with his PhD. After they'd been dazzled by the offer, it wasn't something either of them had considered. We should have, he thought. *I* should have.

"Somebody's done a very good job of keeping information about them out of the public domain," she said.

"Min could easily have done it if she has a background like mine. She's almost invisible online, too. Could the Institute be secretive because of something they're working on?"

"They claim to work on manuscripts. If that's true, what's there to hide?"

"I don't know."

"I have a theory that Min could have been investing money for the Institute, possibly even laundering or day-trading. She told her brother she was using her experience in the trading world. He'd pressed her on it, because he couldn't understand why someone like her ended up working here."

"But Anya is just a historian. She really is here to study manuscripts. Why would she be in danger?"

"She might not be, but if I were Anya, at the very least I'd want to know who my employers really are, because the Institute is not what it seems."

CHAPTER EIGHT

Anya

The man held my arm tightly as he marched me around the corner to where the car was waiting on a quiet street. There was nothing I could do. He was built like an ox. And when I saw Magnus in the car, I realized he was my father's driver.

I tried to thump Magnus. I wasn't a violent person, but I was scared enough that the impulse to lash out overtook me. He caught my arms easily, and it made me feel weak.

"You tried to run me over," I said, and my voice shook with the accusation.

"No. That was a mistake. Another car, a different driver. I'm very sorry. There were a few of us looking for you. Diana said you'd run off and were very distressed. Do you understand? We were looking for you for your own good. Frightening you was a mistake."

"You nearly killed me."

"No. Not me. And he didn't. He just frightened you."

His grip on my wrists was strong and tightening.

"You're hurting me."

He dropped them. "I'm sorry."

I lunged for the door handle and yanked it, but the door was locked. I yanked again and again until Magnus said, "That won't work," and I slumped into the corner where the seat met the door.

A woman sat in the front passenger seat. She had an earpiece in. "Did you come into the shop looking for me?" I asked her. "Lying about me?" I added, but she didn't answer. Nobody did. The indicator light ticked and the driver pulled the car out smoothly into the moving traffic.

"How did you find me?" I asked. I poked her shoulder. "I'm talking to you!"

"Bloody footprints," Magnus said. "You left a trail of them. We knew you were in the shop. It was a matter of waiting for you to come out. I was worried about you."

He made it sound so normal, to wait for someone and snatch them off the street. I could imagine him telling the police the same thing and imagine them believing he was a concerned parent. A good man.

Your father is not the saint people think he is.

Magnus said, "Can I take you somewhere so we can talk? We could get lunch. My club is near here."

I looked at the backs of the man and woman in the front of the car. How much of what they were hearing did they know already? Were they paid enough to see nothing and hear nothing, whatever went on around them?

"We can talk here. You have five minutes, then you let me out."

He said, "Diana betrayed us both this morning. Please believe me when I say I genuinely believed that you wanted to reconcile with me, and the idea of it had brought me so much joy. Since the day you were born, your absence has been a gaping hole in my life. A chasm."

I bit my lip. I could hardly bear to look at him. Why hadn't he approached me since I'd been an adult, then? Mum hadn't been able to gatekeep me for years.

He's a liar.

But the child in me had always wanted to hear words like these, to know that I'd meant *something* to him, to believe that in his heart of hearts he'd wanted me then and wanted me now.

"I treated your mother very badly and hurt her deeply. I'm not surprised Rose turned away from me the way she did. I don't blame her."

"You don't get to talk about blame," I shot back. "You lost that right when you told her we weren't good enough for you."

"I know." He put his hands up. "Sorry! I'm so very sorry that I did that. I feel terrible about it, and I can't imagine how much it must have hurt you. All I can say is that I did it because I was immature enough to believe my family knew best. They put enormous pressure on me, which was monstrous of them, but I was very young at the time. Your mother and I, we were both just babies, really. I'm not trying to excuse myself for what I did, because it was heinous, but it might help you understand the situation. If you care to."

I did care to understand, but I wouldn't give him the satisfaction of knowing he was getting through to me. Not yet. He hadn't convinced me that his intentions were good. But his words were getting through my emotional armor. I'd spent my life trying to rewrite the stories about him that Mum had told, always hoping for a plausible reason for what he did, one that wasn't to do with me. Always dreaming of a happier ending. What child abandoned or mistreated by a parent doesn't wish the same?

"I see myself in you, Anya," he said. "I think you're incredibly smart, so let me say this plainly. If we can put our emotions aside for a moment, consider this: I need someone gifted, whom I can trust absolutely, to work on my manuscripts. Working on my manuscripts could help your career immeasurably. If you can't forgive me, then I'll make sure I keep out of your way entirely. But if you're even a little bit interested in seeing if we can build a relationship, we can do that however you want. I don't put myself in other people's hands very often, but I'll make an exception for you, Anya. You are terribly important to me."

"How do you know you can trust me?" I asked. I wanted to turn the tables back on him a little.

He tries to disempower everyone around him.

"You're my flesh and blood. I know you."

Boom. I had to hand it to him. He knew all the right things to say. I just had to decide whether I believed him. But it was very tempting to.

"This is your birthright," he added.

"What about your other children?" He had three. They were still school age. I'd stalked them on social media. "Do they know about me?"

"They do, and they'd like to meet you."

It changed the game, knowing that I might gain half siblings, that it wouldn't just be him. Because he was damaged goods, a page full of corrections, inkblots. Imperfect. But getting to know my half siblings might give me a chance to turn a pristine new page.

"If I study the manuscripts, the ones that everyone believes were burned, can I publish my work?"

"Good question. The idea is to reveal that the manuscripts survived the fire at the same time as publishing your work on them. We intend to make a big noise about both. Everybody will be talking about it."

He's never selfless. He always has an agenda.

The penny dropped. "This is about your library, isn't it? You'll do this to coincide with the opening of the library."

"That is the plan," he conceded.

It was clever. He would be able to open the library with a core of exceptional manuscripts and scholarship already attached to them that would enhance the family name. It would be a terrific PR stunt. I would have bet he was also considering whether he could get a good emotional story out of it, too: Magnus Beaufort, contrite and reconciled with his estranged daughter and her mother.

"You want me to enhance your vanity project. Your library."

Libraries had burnished the reputations of so many men throughout history, and guaranteed them a place in it: Bodley, Beinecke, Ashurbanipal, and all the others who'd dreamed that dream. There was a reason that American presidents founded libraries after leaving office, even if they weren't readers.

"My library is a gift to the nation. I believe I have a moral obligation to use my privilege for good, when and where I can."

He sounded like a press release. I thought I knew better. "You're afraid of dying."

"I will die, like everyone else."

"But your name will forever be attached to the library. That's as close to immortal as a man can get."

"Is it so terrible that a project appeals to a man's vanity if that is far outweighed by its contribution to society?"

Was it terrible? Probably not. Wasn't life a series of compromises? I felt very tired. The throbbing in my foot was insistent.

"Anya, I badly want you to be part of this because I want this to be our family's legacy, not just mine. Please consider it."

I looked out the window. I had no idea where we were. The streets outside looked smart.

I thought of Mum, just getting by from one medical appointment to the next, from one health crisis to the next, living in desperate fear of her treatment options running out, or of being unable to access the right drugs, reliant on Viv, who was great, but a huge cost herself.

I said, "I'll do this on one condition."

"Anything."

"My mother has lymphoma. Stage IV. She's one of the unlucky ones with a poor prognosis. I want you to help her. I want you to get her the best treatment in the world. There's a trial. In the US. A new drug that's showing incredible results for her type of the disease, but we have no hope of getting it here. I want you to get her put on the trial."

"I would love to." He didn't sound surprised. He already knew she was ill. That cut me to the bone. "Will she let me help?"

I'd rather die than beg him for charity. Literally.

"No. That's your challenge. Figure out how to help without her knowing."

"I think I can do that," he said.

"If you can, we have a deal."

Diana

Diana watched London crawl by as she sat in the back of the town car. She wasn't unhappy to be in traffic; it was a chance to close her eyes for a few minutes, to catch her breath. This was starting to feel like the longest day of her life.

Charlotte rode ahead, in the same car as Bridget Farley and Bridget's assistant. They were traveling in convoy from Bridget's office to the site in South London that the Institute was hoping to lease.

The visit had been Bridget's idea, one that had occurred to her during their meeting. "There's a wonderful young architect I'd like you to meet. She's up and coming. I think she's a promising talent and a project like this could make her career. Let me see if she can meet us at the site."

Of course, Bridget's engagement with the project was a good sign, and of course, Diana couldn't refuse, even though she was itching to check on Anya.

Diana considered whether to message her but decided against it. She would give her time and space for a little longer. She hadn't had a chance to discuss Anya with Charlotte yet. Charlotte would doubtless argue that they should scoop Anya up immediately and put pressure on her, possibly threaten her, but Diana thought she knew Anya better. She was confident that she could handle this herself. If this time pressure could be removed, she'd have the whole thing in hand already.

She yawned, staving off exhaustion. Sometimes, the Larks' mission felt like a house of cards that she had sole responsibility for.

She reminded herself again that the Kats had clearly come to the same conclusion about the path to finding *The Book of Wonder*. If they hadn't, they wouldn't have gone to so much trouble to find the embroidery, and Eleanor Bruton wouldn't have holed up on a remote Scottish island with it. The Larks just needed to stay at least one step ahead of them, to reach the prize first.

Her phone vibrated. A notification from Magnus. She read his message—Anya's on board. She was hugely relieved but also unsettled that he had got to Anya before she did. She had too many plates spinning, she knew, but she supposed Shakespeare was right when he wrote that all's well that ends well, and this was good news, if Magnus was right. He tended to be a bull in a china shop when it came to negotiations, but with Anya he could pull emotional levers like no one else, and he was undoubtedly manipulative enough to do so.

So, Anya was a problem solved for now at least, which was excellent. It reminded her that it was important to hold her nerve and not assume that she needed to be the one to put out every fire. Sometimes, she caught a break. Sometimes, just when she thought the center wasn't going to hold, things went her way.

The car stopped. "This is it," the driver said.

They were in a wasteland, in north Greenwich, a site on the edge of the River Thames almost opposite London City Airport. Diana had seen photographs, but she hadn't appreciated what an amazing location this was until now. It would be the perfect place for the Fellowship to construct its flagship building for the Lark Foundation. An appropriate setting for them to bring their mission out into the open, with the means and structure to make meaningful improvements to women's lives.

Charlotte and Bridget were already out of their car and had walked ahead. Bridget's assistant stayed in the car, working on a laptop. She glanced at Diana but didn't smile. Charlotte and Bridget stood at the edge of the site, with their backs to the water. Charlotte was pointing to something. Their shoulders were almost touching, and Diana wondered how deep the connection between them went. Charlotte was so good at fostering these relationships. Behind them, the river coursed toward the Thames Barrier.

As Diana approached, Charlotte and Bridget moved on, but she was content to stay behind and let them talk. Bridget was Charlotte's contact, and she would want to lead this. There was a reason she had chosen to travel with Bridget, not with Diana, and it was wise to be sensitive to her wishes.

Diana followed at a distance as they walked the perimeter of the site. Seagulls squabbled over something on the pebbly shore. It would be dark soon.

A black cab pulled up beside the two sleek town cars. Diana watched as a woman got out. She carried a large messenger bag. Diana waved to her, and she waved back. It must be the architect.

She looked to see where Bridget and Charlotte had got to. They were quite far ahead now and had reached a corner of the site that bordered a set of unused railway arches, old structures built from red brick, probably Victorian.

Diana waited for the architect to join her. It would be nice to get a moment alone with her to hear about her vision for their building. As she approached, Diana saw she was surprisingly tall. Her blond hair was cut into a shaggy bob. She wore black boots, tailored black trousers, and a coat whose silhouette seemed sculpted. Her glasses had thick black frames. Diana smiled. This was exactly the uniform she'd expect a young architect to wear, but so long as this woman could design a building worthy of the Foundation, it didn't matter if her clothing was a cliché.

They shook hands and introduced themselves.

The architect's name was Naomi Lee and her palms were clammy, suggesting nerves lay beneath her poise. She must want this very badly, Diana thought, which was a good thing, and not surprising. A project on this scale was a huge opportunity for her and she could be a very good fit for the Larks' ethos. Launching the career of a young female architect was just the sort of work the Larks were dedicated to.

They set off to join Charlotte and Bridget, who were standing outside the railway arches. The space beneath each arch was closed off with a pair of large wooden doors. They'd been neglected. Chipped paint and rotten planks, their edges nibbled by decay. Diana wondered if the architect would want to preserve some of these features or raze it all.

"What else have you worked on?" she asked the architect.

"Until recently I've been working with a practice in the UAE. Some very exciting things happening out there."

"There's a lot of money washing around, I suppose."

"Yes, and a hunger for buildings that innovate."

She would probably raze the arches, then. But Diana didn't have a problem with that. Sometimes you needed to destroy to create.

Ahead, Bridget wrenched open one of the big doors. Charlotte followed her inside.

"Now I'm trying to start my own practice in London," the architect said. "I've done a couple of private homes, but I want to work on bigger projects. Something like this would be the dream."

I'll bet it would, Diana thought. The architect would have to earn her place on this, but Diana liked her confidence already. It was women like her who would inherit the benefits of what Diana was working for and build on that. Amazing how a short conversation and a bit of good news from Magnus could kindle hope and inject energy into a crappy day.

They arrived at the arches. Diana gestured for the architect to enter the space first. The door swung shut behind them.

Charlotte and Bridget were standing beneath a lightbulb that hung from the tall arched ceiling. The bulb cast a desultory glow, illuminating the exposed brick on the underside of the arch. Water dripped from it. In a corner two pigeons huddled on a ledge near a hole in the wall that opened to daylight. The acoustics were strange, distorting and amplifying their cooing and scratching, magnifying the sound of dripping water.

Introductions over, the architect said, "So, there's a viewpoint on the top of the arches that we can access from here. You can see the whole site from there. It might be a good place to explain some of my preliminary concepts."

"Great," Bridget said.

"Great," the architect echoed back. Everyone was smiling. "It's a bit of a dodgy climb, so watch your step. Maybe best to use phone lights. I promise it's worth it!"

Bridget led and Charlotte followed.

The architect said, "We probably shouldn't have more than two people on the stairs at once. I don't know how much weight they'll bear."

Diana waited as Charlotte and Bridget climbed. The stairs were made from metal that was rusted in places. It wasn't clear how firmly they were attached to the wall. Light from Charlotte's and Bridget's phones bounced off the surfaces, then they disappeared through the door at the top of the stairs. Their voices suddenly sounded quite far away.

"After you," the architect said.

Diana stepped toward the staircase and directed the light from her phone onto the first few treads.

She didn't immediately sense danger when she felt the barrel of a gun nestle in the pocket at the base of her skull. The sensation was cold and strangely simple. She hadn't processed what it was or what it meant before the architect pulled the trigger a millisecond later.

The sound of the shot was a dull thud, the silencer doing its work.

Diana's body fell backward. The architect stepped neatly out of its way, and it landed hard on the damp floor. A halo of blood emerged from the wound in Diana's head as the architect watched. It was viscous and berry red.

Bridget made her way carefully back down the stairs and knelt to inspect the body to make sure Diana was dead. She took care to avoid the blood.

Charlotte stood at the top, watching, shock on her face, the color draining from it, before she descended.

"For God's sake, Bridget," she said. "Did it have to be so quick?"

"She was a liability. We agreed she had to go."

"We only just agreed it!"

"You know the policy. We eradicate problems as soon as we identify them. Do you have a problem with that?"

"She did good work, and she was a friend." There was a snag in Charlotte's voice.

"A friend carrying on an affair with Judge Henry Macdonald after we got what we wanted from him. A friend whose affair with him compromised us because she was too blind to see that his wife was one of them. A friend who made a fucking mess of disposing of the Chinese girl's body, because it just washed up. And, yes, the DNA is a match. I don't enjoy firefighting. Larks do their jobs properly or they go."

"I know *why* we've done this," Charlotte snapped. "It doesn't mean I'm happy about how and when. We could have afforded her a little more dignity than this. And how do I explain it? It's going to bring a world of unwanted attention to the Institute when we could really do without it."

Bridget stepped around the body and walked toward the sliver of natural light slicing through the doorway. At the door she turned back and said, "Get Anya Brown in front of that embroidery and those books."

Charlotte was still staring at the body. "Well, here's the thing," she said. "I gave the embroidery to Diana." She picked up Diana's bag and rifled through it. Then her pockets. "It's not here," she said.

"Then check her bloody hotel room."

The "architect" stood silently by. She said nothing; she was paid to have no memory of what she saw or heard and no comment, but she felt happy. One clean, professional shot was always the goal. It was important to end a life efficiently, when it was deserved. And thank God she didn't have to pretend to know about architecture anymore.

"Can I move her now?" she asked.

"Yes," Bridget snapped. "You know what to do."

Charlotte looked at her. "What do you mean?"

Sid

Sid left his neighbor's cottage after about an hour, feeling blindsided. While he was with her, he'd found her convincing, but now that he was back home, alone, he wasn't so sure. He had zero appetite for believing that his new life was going to implode, and on that basis alone the temptation not to believe her was strong.

He paced the cottage. Several times he started to call Anya, but didn't go through with it. If his neighbor was wrong, he didn't need to bother Anya; he could tell her all about it when she got home. It might even entertain her. But if his neighbor was right, best not to tell Anya when she was with Diana Cornish. She would feel afraid, and might not be able to hide how she felt. That could be dangerous. He decided he would hold out until she got home and talk to her in person.

He sent her a quick text: How are you doing? Good day?

She didn't reply right away. Sid decided he would try to find out more. He didn't have a number for Paul, but he knew where he lived, because Paul and Giulia had taken him on a walking tour past their house the first time he visited. Sid vaguely remembered that Paul ran the admin side of his business from their place. Hopefully, he would be home and Giulia would not.

Sid walked around the headland, following the walls of the cathedral complex. The sea glinted silver where the sun broke through. Waves broke over the harbor walls.

Paul and Giulia lived in a modern place just behind East Sands Beach, overlooking the Kinness Burn, a wide, shallow stream. A heron stood in the water, still as stone, and gulls shrieked overhead, but the sound fought to be heard over the clanging of cables against the masts of the boats docked at the mouth of the burn.

The house was part painted white and part clad in weathered wood. It had large picture windows and a balcony at the back, overlooking the street. In the yard a small silver birch offered some privacy but not much.

Sid pressed the buzzer and waited. He was about to give up when Paul answered. He looked disheveled, as if he'd just pulled on his clothes, and he'd lost weight, too. Shockingly, he was a shadow of the man Sid had met before.

"Good to see you," Paul said.

"I'm sorry to drop in on you, but I was wondering if you were free for a chat?"

Paul glanced over Sid's shoulder, then smiled tightly. "No worries. Come in."

"Are you sure this is okay?"

"Yeah, yeah. Do you want a coffee? I could use one."

Sid took a seat on a stool at the kitchen island. Paul opened the blinds, and the drab outside light drifted into the open-plan space. The décor was simple, but expensive. Designer lamps and abstract paintings brought color to the sleek, minimalist furnishings.

Paul prepared coffee. As he set the French press and two mugs out on the island, Sid noticed his hands were shaking.

Paul said, "I've been meaning to get in touch, mate. Just been a bit busy. How's it going? The cottage working out for you?"

"Yeah, great. We like it." Sid paused. "Can I ask you about a woman who lived there before me and Anya?"

"Not sure I know much about that," Paul said.

"She worked for the Institute. Her name was Minxu, or Min."

"Oh, yeah, maybe Giulia mentioned her. What's this about, mate?"

"Do you know what kind of work Minxu did?"

Paul shrugged. "I dunno. Historical stuff, I guess, like the others. Giulia didn't talk about her much. I don't think she was there long." His words couldn't have sounded blander, but there was a muscle twitching in his jaw. Sid watched him carefully.

"Did she leave abruptly?" Paul would surely know this, as it was his job to manage the cottage.

"Yeah, I think she did. I'd forgotten, but now you say it." Paul plunged the French press, poured the coffee. There was that tremor again.

"Milk or sugar?" he asked.

"Black's fine."

"Yeah," Paul said as he slid Sid's mug toward him. "It's coming back to me a bit. I think Min might have had some family troubles. They wanted her home."

"Right," Sid said. "Makes sense."

Paul took a sip of coffee and put his cup down. He seemed to have to force himself to raise his eyes to meet Sid's, and when he did, he shook his head. Sid felt his stomach lurch, because there was no mistaking what he saw in Paul's expression. It was pure fear.

Clio

Clio waited at Harringay Green Lanes tube station, her usual coffee order in hand. Large latte, fully caffeinated. The train arrived in a screech of brakes and a rush of hot, stinky air. Clio stepped on board, grateful that it wasn't too full. She'd always been an early bird because she felt it gave her an advantage. What was that old saying about women in the workplace? They had to work twice as hard for half as much.

She was getting used to the office without Lillian. They all were; it had been hard for everybody. Usually, Clio tried not to think about it, but since she'd been to Wiltshire and spoken to Lady Arden she couldn't get Lillian out of her mind. She wondered if she should give that butler a call, find out if he had a name for the woman who'd been to the house to ask about the embroidery before she did.

At the office, she squeezed past her colleagues' desks to reach her own. Since Lillian retired, and, ominously, hadn't been replaced,

Scotland Yard's Art and Antiques Squad office space consisted of just four desks and four officers, in a cramped corner of a large open-plan workspace. They were responsible for policing the second-largest art market in the world. As her boss was fond of reminding them, Italy employed two hundred carabinieri to do the same job.

Clio loved her work, though. It was a man's world but not overtly misogynist. Nothing she couldn't handle, anyway. The humor tended toward childish, not harmful. If it crossed a line, Clio gave as good as she got, just the way Lillian taught her.

"Catch-up?" A rhetorical question from the boss, Detective Inspector Tim Keenan. A career burdened by groaning caseloads, two divorces, and a chronic case of mortal ennui had etched deep lines on his face.

"Yep. Coming," she said.

They gathered in a meeting room. Clio listened carefully to updates on a major fraud case. It was complicated, the money trail long and complex, leading from London via Paris to some shell companies registered in the Bahamas.

"So, there's that," Tim said, "and we've had an email from a CID colleague asking for help. I'll read it to you. 'Dog walker found a body in the early hours this morning in a park in Tower Hamlets. The body has been laid out in a weird way on a chalk drawing.' She's sent a photo, but I haven't looked at it yet. They're asking for help to interpret it."

He swiveled his laptop so everyone could see the screen. The photograph was horrendous.

They were looking at a dead female, with an exit wound in her forehead. She was dressed in an old-fashioned costume: a dark red dress, low cut, with white details on the cuffs and the décolletage, and a tasseled scarf wrapped loosely around her head, like a turban. Her body lay on its side, posed in a sort of crouch, knees bent, bare feet slightly separated, toes pointed.

Her arms were arranged so that one hand was bent toward her

bosom, and in it was a long, feathery palm frond. The other hand was resting on a chalk drawing of a spiked wheel. Chalk had also been used to draw a crown on her head, topped by a line that could suggest a halo, and elsewhere it had been heavily applied to create a rectangle around her body, framing it from the waist up. Suddenly, the symbolism made sense to Clio. "This is supposed to represent an actual painting, Artemisia Gentileschi's portrait of St. Katherine of Alexandria. It's in the National Gallery. May I?"

Tim pushed the laptop toward her. Clio made a new tab and brought up an image of the painting beside the photograph the detective had sent so she could show them the similarities. The painting was one of her favorites, which made this feel strangely personal. She studied both images closely.

Where else had she seen a palm frond lately? The answer came to her suddenly: it was in a botanical print on the wall of Eleanor Bruton's study. Which made her think of something else: the sun that Eleanor Bruton had drawn at the top of her poem. What if it wasn't a sun, but a wheel just like this one? Spiked, or flaming. Eleanor was no artist, but it didn't matter which she'd intended—both were symbols of Saint Katherine.

Which begged the question: Was this murder linked to the group that Lillian had described?

"Have they identified the woman?" Clio asked.

"Yes, she had ID on her. She's a professor, called Diana Cornish. She works for the Institute of Manuscript Studies in St. Andrews."

Clio stiffened. "What did you say?" It was a couple of weeks since she'd spoken to the butler at Lady Arden's home, and he'd told her that it was someone from St. Andrews who'd asked about the embroidery. She *needed* to follow that up now.

As Tim repeated what he'd said, she felt as if every nerve in her body was twitching. Lillian might not have wanted her to tell anyone that she was looking into Eleanor, but she couldn't keep everything to herself now. If she compromised a murder investigation by withholding what she knew, she could lose her job. That couldn't happen.

Besides, she trusted Tim. She said, "Boss, can we talk in private? I need to show you something, and I need to tell you what I did on leave."

Anya

I scanned the timetable board at King's Cross Station, looking for the train to Cambridge. Platform 8. In fifteen minutes.

I couldn't believe I was going there for the first time in my life. But I'd do anything for Mum, even the one thing I swore I wouldn't.

The train whisked me north of London into a rural landscape that flattened out as we traveled. The sky stretched wider. The horizon lengthened.

Magnus wanted me to come and look at more of his manuscripts before I went back up north. He said he kept ten of his favorites in Cambridge because he couldn't bear to be parted from them. The rest were in Scotland, at Tracy's castle, where he felt they were safest. "We can go today," he said. "My driver will take us."

Sid had messaged to ask how I was doing. He'd freak out if I told him what had happened and where I was going, and I couldn't talk now because the train was crowded and I didn't want to be overheard. For all I knew, Magnus could have someone watching me. If he could have me snatched off the pavement in Central London, who knew what else he was capable of?

I wrote: You wouldn't believe how my day is going. I'll call later.

I messaged Diana to let her know what I was doing but didn't get a reply.

I thought about Mum. Telling her anything about today was totally out of the question; she must never know. But it would be hard because she and I had never kept secrets from each other.

As the train pulled in, my eyes were glued to the sign saying "Cambridge" as it slid past the window, proof my world had been knocked off kilter. I walked from the station into the center. When I got there, I felt strangely at home, which was disconcerting. I knew this world of colleges and their courtyards, of clipped lawns, streets full of students and dons, and porters in their waistcoats and hats at the college gates. Even the air was marshy and close, just like Oxford's.

I had an hour to kill before meeting my father. I went to see the site where his library would be built, drawn there like a moth to a flame.

Tall hoardings surrounded the lot. It was adjacent to Magnus's former college. A crane was at work, hoisting up a beam. The building had risen two stories from the ground already. The hoardings were covered in signs advertising the builders and architects, with an artist's rendering of what the library would eventually look like and an electronic countdown clock to the date it should be finished.

I'd seen pictures online already, but in person it was so much more impressive. Its sheer size and the audacity of raising such a modern building in the heart of the medieval city were breathtaking. It was remarkable that one man could do this and give it his name. It was ambition on a phenomenal scale.

My phone buzzed. Mum. My heart skipped a beat, and I debated whether to answer, because the scale of my emotional betrayal of her felt overwhelming, and I didn't know if or how I could keep that out of my voice or my face, but I didn't want her to worry. And I needed to know how she was.

All this will be worth it, I told myself, if it means she gets what she needs. I took a deep breath and accepted the video call.

"Hi, love," she said. "How are you?" Her face popped up on my screen. She looked much better than I was expecting. I sat on a low wall in front of a tree so she couldn't tell where I was.

"I'm good," I said. "Down in London for a couple of days for work. What about you? You look great."

In the background, on her end, I heard a strange noise.

"Is that Viv?" I asked.

"Viv is whooping! I've had some amazing news."

He couldn't have made this happen so soon, could he? "What news?"

"Somebody called from the oncology unit to say that a clinical trial in America is recruiting new patients for a trial with that drug, the one they said wasn't available here because it was too expensive. Anyway, I'm eligible! I'm in! All expenses paid. Apparently, I'm perfect for it."

I choked up. "That's brilliant, Mum!"

"I know! I can't believe it."

Had it really been that easy for my father to buy Mum the chance of more life, of a cure even? It was breathtaking. I tried to think what I would ask, if this truly was news to me.

"Who's running the trial?"

"Oh, I can't remember. I wasn't listening properly once they gave me the news. They're going to email me, so I'll forward it to you. I think they said it was a private clinic."

"It's spectacular news, Mum. I'm so happy for you."

Viv poked her head into the frame, a smile wrapped around her face. She waved and gave a thumbs-up before disappearing again.

I chatted to Mum a little longer. She was so upbeat, I forgot where I was for a few blissful minutes. I kissed my fingers and put them to the screen as we said goodbye. She was still connected when bells began to ring. The clock on the college tower was chiming, and it was very distinctive.

I jabbed at the button to end the call. She'd lived in Cambridge with my dad. I was afraid she'd recognize the sound. For a few moments I stared at the phone screen, afraid she'd call back and ask where I was, but she didn't and I relaxed fractionally.

While we'd been speaking, the sun had moved, and the shadow of the library was reaching across the pavement, almost touching the tips of my shoes. I checked the time. My father would be waiting for me.

CHAPTER NINE

Sid

Sid watched Paul closely. The fear in his eyes intensified as he changed the subject brusquely.

"What are you up to this morning, mate?" he asked. "Do you fancy a short hike? I could show you Maiden Rock. It's not a challenging route, your grandma could do it, but it's a cool rock formation."

"Sure," Sid said. "That'd be nice." He wasn't dressed for it, and the weather looked unreliable, but somehow, he didn't think the hike was the point. He felt a growing sense of dread. If he hadn't had the conversation with Mel next door, the self-styled private investigator, he would have thought Paul was behaving weirdly. If Paul was presenting more normally he could have written her off as a nut. For them both to be like this, Sid had to believe something bad was really happening.

They left the house and crossed a wooden pedestrian bridge onto East Sands Beach under a mackerel sky. The tide was half in and half out. Waves rushed and pounded the shore, throwing up a light mist. The sun was a dim halo behind the clouds. Where the waves dragged the beach they left a mirrored sheen on the sand, blending light, water, sea, sky, and sun. Paul and Sid walked where the sand was dry and powdery, scattered with pebbles and shells. There were just a few other souls out, most with dogs. Sid couldn't enjoy it. His body felt tight with anxiety.

Paul, head down, remained silent until they passed the university's Institute of Oceanography. At the far end of the beach they took an empty footpath leading over the cliffs. Away from people, Paul relaxed fractionally.

"You got the note," he said.

"I did. Why not just talk to me? Or leave it at the cottage?"

"Because they're watching your place and they're listening to everything we say. Did you look Minxu up?"

"'They'?"

"The Institute."

"Why would they do that?" Sid's heart began to pound the back of his ribs.

"Control," Paul said, as if it were obvious. "Did you look up Minxu?"

"I looked, but I didn't find much." Sid wasn't ready to share what Mel had told him yet. First, he wanted to know what Paul would say.

"I thought you might be able to find more than me because you're a computer person. I want to know if she's okay."

"Why wouldn't she be?"

Paul shook his head. A dog walker was approaching from the other direction, almost close enough to overhear them. They passed him in silence. To the right of the path was a holiday park, multiple tidy units, mostly empty, facing the sea. Just beyond, the path narrowed, and it was no longer surfaced. The mottled clouds were gathering into darker, heavier masses.

Atop the cliff, they reached an empty bench, angled for the view back toward St. Andrews. Sid hoped they might sit there and talk, but Paul said, "It's this way." Sid followed him reluctantly down a rutted track. Gorse scratched his arms, and he had to keep his distance from Paul to avoid the thorny shoots that whipped back as Paul pushed past them. A squall whipped over the open water and drenched them when it hit land.

"Should we turn back?" Sid shouted into the wind. The path was steep now, and fast becoming more liquid than solid. His feet were wet. His sneakers had poor grip.

"We can shelter at the rock." Paul forged on, and Sid followed unhappily.

Maiden Rock was a solitary sandstone outcrop on a deserted rocky beach, tall and looming, eroded into an otherworldly silhouette. It reminded Sid of the weather-beaten cathedral ruins. They leaned against it, poorly sheltered, until the rain ceased.

Paul pulled his hood back. Sid did the same, and his stomach curled when he realized that Paul had been crying. Paul stared grimly at the ocean as he talked.

"I'm so fucking scared. All the time, I'm scared. I wake up with my heart pounding. My dreams are nightmares. I feel like I should know what to do, but I don't. It never stops, and I'm so fucking sick of it."

Sid put a hand on Paul's shoulder. The man was shaking. *"Why are you so scared?"*

"Because people disappear from the Institute. Min wasn't the first."

"Who else?" Sid's fear level went up a notch.

"She was called Zofia. She disappeared four months before Min. They hired her from Poland. She was an expert in Renaissance textiles. Giulia and I got friendly with her." He wiped his eyes roughly with the back of his hand, but the tears kept coming and the shaking didn't stop.

"What happened to Zofia?"

"She went hiking one day last November and didn't come back. They found her car parked at the train station local to the hike. It was locked, with no personal effects left inside it. There was no

CCTV, it was too remote. The Institute said Zofia went back to Poland. Basically, the same story they told about Min. But the thing is, I *know* she didn't go back to Poland."

"How?"

"I'm not proud of this, but we'd been getting closer emotionally during her first year at the Institute. And I know, I'm a heel. But Giulia spends all hours at the Institute, and it's all small talk when she gets home. It had been dead between us for a while. I was fucking lonely."

"I'm sorry," Sid said.

"I was with Zofia the day she disappeared. Nobody knows that except you, but we went hiking together. We had a beautiful day. We walked and talked and decided we wanted to be together. I was going to tell Giulia about me and Zofia that night, but Zofia never came back. She'd suggested we drive to the hiking spot separately, and I wish we hadn't, God, how I wish I could go back to that day and be braver. I was just so scared of Giulia finding out before I had the chance to tell her. I *know* Zofia didn't have her passport with her because I went to the cottage to look for her when she didn't come home that night, and it was there. All her things were. The police took everything away a few days later but I saw it with my own eyes that first night. Something happened to her, I know it did. I *felt* it. She was my soulmate."

"God, mate, I'm sorry. This is awful. Did you talk to the police?"

"I was thinking about it, but I've got to be honest, I bottled out of it. I didn't want anyone to know about our relationship." Paul paused, then said, "Maybe that was bad. But I'm scared. I can't stop being scared. Giulia is one of them."

Sid felt so far in over his head it was terrifying. "Does Zofia have family?" he asked, thinking of what his neighbor had said about Min's parents, how desperate they were to find their daughter.

"She was estranged from them. I thought about trying to find them, but I didn't know how to start."

"So what do you think happened to her?"

"Something bad." Paul seemed to notice just then that his hands were shaking. He shoved them into his pockets. He wasn't on the edge, Sid thought, but already over it.

Paul said, "Don't mention this to Anya, will you? You can't tell anyone. We must be careful, so, so careful."

"I won't," Sid lied.

"The thing is, I don't know what to do about any of it." Paul looked ashen, broken.

Sid felt jolted. How was he supposed to know? He said, "I'm not sure, either. But we're going to keep talking to each other, okay?"

"It's been heavy, carrying this. It's been this massive weight on my shoulders."

Had Giulia noticed a change in him? Sid wondered. He needed a timeline. One woman disappearing was extremely worrying; for two to disappear from the same workplace was surely something no one could ignore, even the most incompetent police force. How high up did this go? He was beginning to wonder, though he didn't want to fall down a conspiracy rabbit hole. He wondered if his neighbor knew about Zofia and assumed she didn't. He needed to tell her.

Far out to sea, more sheets of rain had materialized and were sweeping across the ocean toward them. They needed to get out of there soon or the path would be impossible to climb, but this moment felt fragile. If he didn't handle it right, Sid wasn't sure if Paul would confide in him again.

"Are you and Giulia okay now?" he asked. He thought about when he'd first met them. He'd only spent a couple of hours with them, and they'd seemed happy, but of course he hadn't really paid much attention. He'd been dazzled by what was on offer for him and Anya.

"After Zofia happened, I still wanted to leave Giulia. I kept thinking maybe Zofia would get in touch and I could go join her, but I never heard from her again. I had a breakdown, lost my job as a climbing instructor. Giulia looked after me, and the Institute offered me work and I took it. I doubted myself, mate. I hit rock bottom. And then it started to seem like it hadn't happened the way I thought it had, and I started to believe maybe I got it wrong, that Zofia never loved me, and I convinced myself to believe that until Min went just four months later."

"I'm sorry," Sid said. Could there be an innocent explanation for any of this? He was worried there couldn't.

Paul wiped his eyes with his sleeve, roughly, and seemed to regain awareness of their surroundings. "There's more rain coming. And the tide's rising. We should head up."

The sky was a mess of fluid cloud, the sheets of rain closer than ever, the ocean restless and oily. Sid slipped and cursed as they climbed.

He was glad to see the bench when they reached the top, but two women stood by it, blocking the way, their heads bent over a laminated map. They were young and fit, wearing walking boots and leggings that revealed the muscled contours of their legs. Both wore baseball caps and had their hair tied in ponytails. Walking poles hung from their wrists. Serious hikers, Sid thought.

They were close to the women now, but neither looked up or moved out of the way as they approached.

"Ladies," Paul said. "Morning."

Unsmiling, they stepped out of the way. One of them nodded curtly. Sid met her eyes and instantly recoiled at the flinty coldness in them. As he and Paul walked on, Sid looked back over his shoulder, as drawn to that gaze as he'd been repelled by it, because it felt as if it was personal somehow. The women stood shoulder to shoulder, staring back. Blatantly. If they'd been men, it would have been threatening.

Sid told himself not to let Paul's paranoia infect him. They were just hikers.

It was vital he keep his own head together if he was going to work out what was happening and what to do.

Anya

My father's house in Cambridge was a mansion distinguished enough to have its own Wikipedia page. His family had owned it for three generations. It occupied a spacious and very private end lot on a beautiful wide street just a ten-minute walk from the library site.

The street was lined with mature beech trees, grown so large their roots had forced up paving stones; their trunks were thick and gnarled. The leaves were starting to turn, from acid green into copper. Beechnuts fell around me, plinking onto the roofs of the high-end vehicles parked along the verges and crunching beneath my shoes.

I walked through a set of open gates onto a wide, paved driveway. A perfectly shiny Ferrari was parked in front of a large garage. The home looked to be Victorian, and Gothic in style, though it was hard to see much evidence of its age in the fabric of the building. Every inch had been restored and maintained. Window frames gleamed with white paint; the stonework was pristine, the yew globes in the front garden immaculately clipped. There wasn't a stray leaf on the ground. Beneath it all, I wondered if the old bones of the house could breathe.

Your father's a control freak.

Evidence of Magnus's obsession with legacy was here, too, in the family motto chipped into stone above the door, the cuts, appropriately enough, surgically clean. The motto: *Ingenio et industria*. By wit and industry. So squeaky clean.

He opened the door himself and let me in. I rubbernecked shamelessly. My greedy eyes didn't want to miss a thing. I'd had to imagine his family home for so many years; seeing it for myself felt unreal. It was a riot of rich Victorian architecture: a finely etched glass porch door, original, beautifully tiled floors, molded ceilings, brass hardware on the doors, William Morris wallpaper, glass lanterns, intricately carved banisters, unfeasibly large bouquets of fresh flowers spraying from urns on polished side tables. There were family portraits, too. My father and, presumably, my grandfather and great-grandfather beside him.

"I made some calls," he said. "For your mother."

"I heard from her. It seems like you got her on the trial. Thank you."

Dust motes spiraled in a shaft of sunshine that crept through a doorway from a room I couldn't see into. This place was impressive, but lugubrious. It was hard to imagine Mum here; she must have found it stifling.

I was kicking myself for not approaching Magnus for help earlier. I'd been so passive where he was concerned, so eager not to upset Mum. Why did I buy into her invective so wholly that I didn't even think to ask one of the most medically well-connected men in the country to help us? Why didn't I make my own mind up about that as she got sicker? Perhaps I needed to grow up. In answer, I heard her.

Don't deal with the devil.

I tried to ignore her, but she was persistent.

If you give your father an inch, he'll take a thousand miles.

"This way," he said, and I followed him.

I was alert for any sign of my half siblings, even though they were surely at school. It was hard to believe I was in the family home, the place I might have grown up in if things had been different.

It was also hard to believe it *was* a family home. It was more like a museum.

At the end of one wing of the house, in a room with tall, arched windows, designed to make the most of its garden views, he invited me to sit down.

I took a seat opposite the windows. I felt buzzed but edgy, too. I'd been running on adrenaline for too many hours. I'd taken painkillers for my foot, but they were wearing off.

There were four professional archival boxes on the table in front of me and two empty book stands. I inched forward to look at the boxes but didn't touch. They were plain and unlabeled, cream colored, not a fingerprint on them. Magnus hit a button on the wall and semi-sheer blinds rose from the base of each window to the top. The light in the room dimmed to a pearly gray and the air felt soupy.

"Which would you like to open first?" he asked, and I flinched, because the question had echoes of my childhood birthday parties. At every single one, I'd fantasized that he would turn up to surprise me.

"You choose," I said.

He opened the one closest to him and extracted a white bag, which he handed to me. I loosened its drawstring and removed a book. Written in Latin and exquisitely illustrated, it was a medical encyclopedia.

"Fifteenth century?" I asked.

My father nodded.

"German," I said.

"Yes." He looked lit up, as if he'd been waiting for this, for me to prove my expertise, and it delighted him. I didn't want that to mean something to me, but it did.

I turned the pages. Here was a Tree of Life, a Zodiac man, a Tower of Wisdom. There were astrological diagrams, recipes for remedies, and instructions for bloodletting. The illustrations were of exceptional quality, the colors so fresh on the page it was as if they'd just been mixed, as if the scribe's brush were sitting to the side, still wet with paint.

He had more to show me: an extremely rare and very early Bible with fascinating riddles, manicules, and annotations in the margins, a Celtic codex not dissimilar to the mind-blowing *Book of Kells*, Ireland's national treasure. A gorgeous little book of hours. Treasures, all of them. He watched me intently as I examined them.

"Do you have a favorite?" I asked. A collector's favorite piece can reveal a lot about them. I was eager to know everything I could about him but didn't want to give him the satisfaction of asking directly.

He smiled, as if he knew my game. "I love them all," he said. "You could make a lifetime's work of studying this collection. If I hadn't chosen medicine, that would be my dream. Next best thing is that you do it."

"Why recruit me to St. Andrews, not Cambridge?"

"The manuscripts live up there. As I said, it's where they're most secure. Did you enjoy meeting Tracy? Isn't she exquisite?" He caught my expression and backtracked. "I mean, you can see why the camera loved her, can't you?"

I nodded slightly, but he'd sounded a bit creepy to me, and I wondered about their relationship.

"Let me ask you a question: Why so self-deprecating in your interviews about Folio 9? You should be proud of your talent. If you were—" He stopped, catching himself.

I stared. His words got right under my skin. My interviews were, of course, available for anyone to find, but it unnerved and annoyed me to think of him reading them and judging me. "If I were what?" I asked. "One of your children?"

He shook his head, but we both knew that's what he was about to say, and it cut like a knife.

"I think you gave up your right to offer me advice when you decided to abandon me before I was born," I said. "You don't get to parent me. It's not part of our deal."

His lips twisted, and I was glad to see that I could get to him. "Understood," he said.

I closed the books. "Thanks for showing me these." We put them back in their boxes and he pressed the button that made the blinds open. We both blinked in the light. I still wasn't used to seeing my eyes in his face. "I need to ask you something," I said.

"Anything."

"If I decide I don't want to work with you at any point, will you stop helping Mum?"

He winced. "How little you think of me."

"Will you?"

"I promise I'll do everything I can to help your mother, for as long as she'll let me."

He makes promises as easily as he breaks them.

I didn't trust him, but his word was all I had to go on. I thought of Mum on the phone earlier, how happy and hopeful she'd sounded for the first time in what felt like forever.

He said, "Anya, before you leave, can I hug you?"

"No," I said.

"Fair enough. A handshake?" He held his hand out. Now there was a glint of mischief in his eyes. "Don't leave me hanging."

He can be charming when he wants to be.

I hesitated before reaching across some of the most valuable manuscripts in the world and shaking my father's hand. His grip was too firm. It hurt a little. He was smiling, but I was remembering how hard he'd held me in the car earlier, hard enough to bruise his own flesh and blood.

He'll crush anything and anyone that gets in his way.

Clio

Clio told her boss what she'd discovered: the delicate threads linking Eleanor Bruton and an embroidery fragment to the Institute of Manuscript Studies at St. Andrews. DI Tim Keenan had his best poker face on as she did. She admired how he never made snap judgments, preferring to consider things carefully before making up his mind. As Lillian said: He swivels the jar and looks at a specimen from all angles before classifying it.

When Clio had finished her story and shown Tim a photo of Eleanor's poem, he said, "If these were different times, I'd greenlight this, because I can smell trouble here the same as you can, but I need everyone on Operation Platinum."

Clio nodded. She knew. She watched him carefully, still mindful of Lillian's warning, but he wasn't reacting any differently from usual. He said, "But why don't you liaise with the officer who made the inquiry. Let them know we think she's been deliberately posed as St. Katherine and tell them everything you've just told me."

"Will do."

She composed the email, laying everything out carefully, and paused before hitting send. She added a cheeky request to see the crime-scene report, justifying it by suggesting her department might have more useful expertise to add. The reply came promptly.

To: Clio Spicer
From: Izzy Adefope
Re: Operation Saint
Date: September 18, 2024

Hi Clio,

Thanks so much for your team's prompt input. Much appreciated. As you can see, it arrived in time to inspire the name of our operation.

Below is a list of personal items found at the scene. ID was straightforward. A bag left beside her body contained her wallet and driver's license. Whoever did this made no attempt to disguise her identity.

Lack of blood or any other evidence around the body leads us to assume that she was killed elsewhere and moved to the location where she was found. Cause of death is a single bullet wound to the back of the neck. Bullet exited through the forehead. Either the shooter got lucky, or they knew what they were doing. We're leaning toward it being a professional hit.

For obvious reasons we have a strong working theory that the death was intended as a message. Your info strengthens that hypothesis. The location of the body dovetails with the St. Katherine theme. The park where she was found is on Butcher Lane in Limehouse, next door to an organization called the Royal Foundation of St. Catherine. (FYI: Spellings of Saint Katherine of Alexandria's name are interchangeable. Whether it's with a *k* or a *c*, it's the same saint so the location where this body has been left is unlikely to be a coincidence given your theory on the costume and the pose.)

We have no idea yet who this symbolic message might be for or from, and we're holding off publicizing any details for as long as we can, to give us space to make inquiries before the internet gets hold of it and speculation goes through the roof.

What we've established so far is that Professor Cornish worked for the Institute of Manuscript Studies in St. Andrews, Scotland. We haven't located any next of kin yet. If we can't identify anyone soon, we'll contact the Institute to inform her colleagues and see if they can assist with that.

If you or your team have more thoughts, I'd love to hear them. None of us has expertise in the art or rare book world. We're all Philistines, basically. Thanks for your assistance to date.

Izzy
DC Izzy Adefope
Murder Squad

LIST OF PERSONAL ITEMS FOUND AT THE SCENE

Bra

Knickers

Dress (possibly from a costume)

Headscarf (possibly from a costume)

Handbag

Bag contents:

iPhone

Sewing kit

Wallet including bank cards, Oyster card, and library card

Tampons

Makeup

Clio took a moment to process what she'd read.

With Eleanor Bruton dead, too, possibly murdered because she had the embroidery in her possession, she was starting to think that the fragment of embroidery might be lethal. Unfortunately, there was no sign of it among the list of things recovered with Diana's body. It would have been helpful if it were. She might have got some answers from it.

She replied to Izzy, telling her about Eleanor Bruton and the embroidery, as well as the connection between them and Diana Cornish's place of work, and she attached a link to the British Museum fragment for context. She omitted explaining how she'd found out about Eleanor. She didn't want to mention Lillian just yet. She asked if they'd discovered where Diana had been staying in London or been able to retrace any of her movements yet.

The reply was brief: "Thanks! No. I'll let you know when we do."

She looked up a number for Lady Arden's home in Wiltshire. The butler was on leave for the day; she left a message, asking if he could call her back and let her know if he'd found the name of the person who had visited asking after the embroidery.

Clio thought about Eleanor Bruton. She remembered the overdue library book she'd seen in her office and picked up the phone to call Salisbury Library. They confirmed that there were ten books overdue on Eleanor Bruton's account, all special orders. Eleanor was supposed to have returned them over a year ago. They read Clio a list of titles. They included books on medieval symbolism, the fabric trade in medieval Italy (Clio remembered that book), early clothing, and medieval bookbinding techniques.

She thought of Eleanor Bruton's poem sewn into the curtains in Scotland and looked again at the list of items recovered from Diana's bag.

"Sewing kit" stood out. Her eyes kept returning to it. It wasn't something you'd expect to have in your bag unless you'd had a recent use for it, an occasion to sew.

Coincidence? Probably. But stranger things had happened.

She sent a reply to Izzy Adefope: "Any chance I can inspect the evidence?"

CHAPTER TEN

Sid

Sid said goodbye to Paul and watched as he walked away. The man looked broken.

He was unsure where to go. If he believed everything he'd heard, he had to consider the possibility that the cottage was under surveillance and his and Anya's devices were, too.

He checked his phone. Anya had sent a slightly cryptic message: You wouldn't believe how my day is going. I'll call later. He wrote back: Same! He was dreading telling her what he'd learned. It felt more important than ever to do it in person.

The possibility of surveillance at the cottage was a problem he didn't know how to solve, but he knew how to operate online without leaving a trace. He had a USB with the Tails operating system loaded on it.

He went back to the cottage, changed out of his wet clothes, and decided he didn't feel like being there at all. Even if he could evade any online monitoring, the idea that he might be being watched was too creepy. He grabbed his laptop and the USB. They'd work just as well anywhere else. In Oxford he could have gone to a cybercafé, but he knew there were none in St. Andrews, so he walked back to the computer science department, deep in his head.

The lab was opposite the Jack Cole building, housed in a low, bunker-like structure on a square plan, constructed from brown brick punctuated with tall, tinted windows, through which it was just possible to glimpse rows of desks and computers.

He used his new pass to get inside and settled down in a discreet corner.

Once he'd inserted the USB into his laptop, and booted into Tails, his fingers hovered over the keyboard. It was important to be smart and methodical about this. He decided on the question he wanted to answer first: What was the Institute hiding? He started by reminding himself what they *were* letting people see online.

From their website he noted the full names of the staff members and their specialties. He ran searches for every name, and it was just as Anya and his neighbor had said: there wasn't much to find.

Two scholarly articles by Karen Lynch came up, and a photograph of Diana Cornish at a society event seven years prior. He tried searching archived pages, just as he'd done for Min, but got nothing. If these women had been scrubbed from the internet, someone had done a better job for them than they had for Min.

He mustn't forget Zofia. He needed to get her surname from Paul, and he should probably do that in person. For now, he made do with searching for "Zofia missing Scotland," but nothing came up.

Time to change tack. He returned to the Institute's website, screenshotted headshots of the staff, then ran a reverse image search on the picture of Sarabeth Schilders.

She appeared on a website linked to Amsterdam University, promoting a conference for academics involved in finance. It had taken place in 2003. Sarabeth was listed as a professor of economics. The Institute's website said her specialty was Renaissance women. So she'd had two decades to make a career change, from finance to medieval history. It was a hell of a coincidence that she and Min had both made such radical career moves and both ended up with the same specialty and working at the same place.

He did the same search for Giulia Orlando. Her photograph appeared embedded in an article about young cryptocurrency dealers. Giulia was in the background of a picture that had been, according to its caption, shot at a party on a private Caribbean island. She was standing behind a famous model and looked almost unrecognizable. Her hair was ironed straight and worn long and loose. She wore the skimpiest of dresses. Her face was flushed and painted with flowers, which framed her eyes and had tendrils that curled across her temples, circling small, sparkling jeweled dots. She couldn't have looked more different from the Giulia he'd met, who dressed conservatively and had given no hint that she was hosting this party animal.

He read the article, noting that it was written in 2018. The "hedonism"-themed party was an exclusive event for cryptocurrency workers and influencers. The article dropped the names of some high-profile celebrity attendees and described a sumptuous menu involving enormous amounts of fresh seafood and cocktails that had been specially created to match. Sid could only imagine the industrial levels of drug-taking going on off camera. This was a universe far removed from the Institute and from the Giulia he'd met.

He wondered why these images hadn't been scrubbed. Had someone left them online on purpose? If not, it was a hell of an oversight.

His image search for Karen Lynch returned a lot of results, but they were more what he'd expect. Karen cropped up as long as a decade ago at medieval history conferences and in previous academic roles, teaching in the history department at King's College London, and as a PhD student at Harvard. There was nothing unusual in her history, so far as he could tell.

He moved on to Diana Cornish. That search immediately threw up the photograph he'd already seen, of Diana at a society party, and he found another picture of a much younger Diana, one of a group of four in a graduation photograph. He zoomed in. The caption told him that the group were graduating from Oxford

University. Diana was recognizable, and one of the other women looked familiar, too. He scanned the names listed: "Alice Trevelyan (First Class Honors: Medieval Languages)." Alice Trevelyan and Diana had studied together. It surprised him. So far as he remembered from what Anya had said, Professor Trevelyan had claimed only to know Diana professionally.

He messaged Anya: Did you know Trevelyan and Cornish were at Oxford together as undergrads?

He'd never liked Trevelyan much. She was a strange woman, a little cold. In retrospect, he wondered if she and Anya had become worryingly close. Sid knew a lot of graduates who formed tight relationships with their supervisors, but no one whose supervisor paid quite so much attention to them as Professor Alice Trevelyan had to Anya. Had it been kindness, or something else? It was Trevelyan, after all, who'd strongly encouraged her to consider St. Andrews.

At every turn Sid was hoping to find something that proved his fears were unfounded, but things got more complicated, and more concerning, as he looked deeper into them. He just wanted everything to be fine, but it was crystal clear that nothing was, absolutely nothing at all.

Anya

I took another crowded train back to London. Time was tight. My flight was that evening, and I needed to get to the airport. Diana still hadn't replied to my message, and I wondered how things would be between us now. I could never trust her again, that was for sure, but she would be getting what she wanted from me, so hopefully we could work together smoothly enough. Still, her silence worried me. I thought about sending her another message but decided to hold off. Let her come to me.

Sid had messaged again, asking if I knew that Trevelyan and Diana had studied together. I hadn't known, but after today, it didn't surprise me, though it increased my sense of feeling watched and controlled. I wrote back: Makes sense. How do you know?

I got across London on the tube and arrived back at Paddington Station, eyes glazed with tiredness, my foot screaming to have the weight taken off it. I sat on a bench and was dully watching pigeons pecking at crumbs as I waited to board the train to the airport when Viv called.

"Anya, love, your mum's just been readmitted to hospital. She's got another infection, and they're worried it's sepsis."

"I'm coming," I said.

I swapped platforms and just scored a standing-room spot on a crowded commuter train heading out west. My phone lit up with terrifying updates from Viv during the journey.

> Her blood pressure plummeted she almost fainted.
>
> She's having IV ibuprofen and antibiotics, and her temp is down but it still isn't as low as they'd like.
>
> I've told her you're coming but I don't know if she's taken it in. She's calling for you.

Tell her I'll be there as fast as I can, I wrote back.

BRISTOL ROYAL INFIRMARY WAS A MISHMASH OF BUILDINGS, OLD AND NEW, in the city center. The layout and signage were confusing no matter how often you'd been there. I arrived twenty minutes before the end of visiting hours on the acute emergency ward, jabbing at the elevator buttons, running down corridors to make it on time.

The ward, for four people, was full, curtains pulled around two of the beds, but not Mum's. Viv sat beside the head of the bed. There was a bloody mess around the canula on the back of Mum's hand, and she was pretty out of it, but she squeezed my hand when I kissed her, and I wiped away the tears slipping down her hot cheek. As I stroked her hair I whispered that she was going to be fine, that she needed to hang in there, that she could do this, that it was a piece of cake.

It seemed like I'd only been there for moments when the nurse said, "We'll take good care of her tonight. Visiting hours start again at ten tomorrow," and I realized she was telling us to go.

In the multistory parking lot just up the street, Viv momentarily forgot where she'd parked the car. The composure she'd had on the ward slipped and she looked exhausted. "She was fine," she said. "We were still celebrating the news about the clinical trial; she was on such a high. Then she threw up and her temperature spiked. I called her treatment team, and they said to bring her in. By the time we got here she could barely walk."

I knew what she needed to hear: "You did the right thing. Thank you for being there for her. I don't know what we'd do without you."

We took the elevator up to a floor of the parking lot that had mostly emptied out. Mum's car sat all alone in its spot, parked badly. The tires squealed as we inched down the spiral ramps, and Viv hit the brakes too soon and too hard all the way home.

She and Mum had left the cottage in such a hurry, there were no lights on when we arrived and it was pitch dark.

We went straight to bed. It felt like the longest day of my life. I unwrapped my foot in the bathroom and sat on the edge of the bath to re-dress the wound. It was angry and sore. I stood on one foot to brush my teeth. The bathroom mirror had a chip in the corner that had been there my whole life. In the reflection I could see lines drawn on the edge of the door where Mum had marked my height as I grew up. I remembered how it felt to stand there as she balanced a pencil on my head to make those marks.

When I looked at my face it was a shock to see Magnus staring back at me. His eyes, anyway. I wondered how Mum had felt seeing him in me every single day as I grew. How she felt about that now. It made me visualize the rest of him, and I hated it. It felt wrong to imagine his face here, in my childhood home, our sanctum, though it niggled at me that he'd suggested Mum had kept him away. I turned my back on the mirror until I was ready to rinse and left the room without looking again.

I messaged Sid, wondering if he was still awake.

Can you call?

The idea of telling him everything that had happened was daunting. A changed *me* might mean a changed *us*. But I shouldn't catastrophize. I got into my childhood bed. My body sank gratefully into its familiar hollows, but nothing felt the same. It was like the day Mum was diagnosed. You know you've already changed forever, but you don't know how yet, or whether you'll sink or swim.

It was impossible to sleep. Everything that had happened fought for space in my head. I wondered if Magnus could help Mum through this new crisis. Maybe get her in a private room, summon specialists. I considered calling him. Before I'd left Cambridge he'd given me his number, promising he'd respond, day or night, if I contacted him.

"I barely sleep," he'd said. "It's a curse and a privilege. Sometimes at night I visit my manuscripts. I look at them in candlelight and feel like a time traveler."

Such theater.

I called Mum and she didn't pick up so I tried the main number for her ward. Cell service at the cottage was poor, which was frustrating, but eventually I spoke to a nurse who reassured me that Mum was stable and settled for the night.

I wondered whether to tell Viv. She'd want to know, but she needed rest as much as I did. I opened the door and saw that the light was still on in her bedroom. I could hear faint voices, as if she was listening to something. I crossed the landing. It sounded like a podcast. I heard: "Manifest your perfect partnership."

I rapped on her door softly. "Viv, sorry to interrupt, but I just spoke to the nurse and Mum's stable."

The voice went immediately silent. She'd muted it. "Thanks," she said.

"I thought you'd want to know."

I stood there for a moment, but she didn't say anything else. I imagined her waiting for me to leave. She felt so much like part of the family that sometimes, I forgot we paid her to look after Mum, that I should respect her boundaries. Perhaps I shouldn't have disturbed her. "Good night, then," I said.

"Good night."

I crept back to bed. Sid called.

"Hey," he said. "Are you at the airport?" His voice was muted, and I heard background noise, as if he was out somewhere. I checked the time. It was almost eleven.

"No, I'm at the cottage. I had to miss my flight. Mum's in the hospital again."

"Oh, God. What's happening?"

I told him. Reception was lousy again, so we kept losing each other. I didn't want to try to explain about Magnus over a bad line.

"Where are you?" I asked.

"I'm at the computer science department."

"Oh," I said. "That's nice."

"Listen, I'll come and join you," he said.

"You don't need to. It's okay."

"I'll book the morning flight to Bristol."

"Sid, it's okay, really. I'm okay. Why don't we speak in the morning? She could have turned a corner by then. I'll call you from the hospital. It'll be better reception."

"I'm coming."

It wasn't worth arguing about and I was secretly pleased. After we hung up, I took some more painkillers for my foot, and as soon as they kicked in sleep snatched me and dragged me into Boschian nightmares where my mother was screaming and all the shadows had eyes, and when I startled awake in the small hours I didn't know if they were a reaction to what I'd been through that day or a premonition of worse.

Sid

As soon as he got off the phone with Anya, Sid booked a flight to Bristol for first thing the next morning.

The lab was emptying out. It was too early in the academic year for students to be pulling all-nighters. Sid planned to stay there until he found some answers.

He bought himself a refrigerator-stunned sandwich and an energy drink from a vending machine. When he sat back down, he realized he hadn't done any digging on Paul yet, so he typed "Paul Fields," hit the search button, and found a Facebook page.

One year ago, Paul had been working for a local climbing company and was listed as a guide. Before that, he'd been based in Anglesey for a few years. And before that, in Northern Italy. Sid wondered if it was where he'd met Giulia. He found only one post from the past year: a bleak shot of the ocean, from the beach in front of Paul and Giulia's house, captioned: "Gray days." It was a literal description of the scene but a sharp contrast in tone from the upbeat posts of previous years, where Paul showed off his travels and his climbing achievements. Sid searched the other social media platforms, but Paul was absent.

He thought of the broken man he'd just met with. The drop-off in activity on Facebook matched up with the timeline Paul had given for his decline in mental health. It made him more plausible. Sid rubbed his eyes. What happened to people when they came here? Was it going to happen to him and Anya?

He expanded his search to the deep web, which didn't tell him anything new. Then, to the dark web. As before, he ran spiderweb searches for a range of terms: Diana Cornish, Anya Brown, Sarabeth Schilders, Giulia Orlando, Karen Lynch, Institute of Manuscript Studies St. Andrews, Paul Fields, Folio 9, Alice Trevelyan, and Minxu Peng.

The only one that threw up interesting results was Folio 9. A few usernames were associated with the term across a range of forums. The search did its work of finding out where they congregated. It was in a private, invitation-only forum called "Suspicious Minds."

Sid frowned. He would have to get into it by impersonating one of the chat members. Not impossible. He had a text file of hundreds of thousands of common passwords. He ran an automated spam attack on the forum that tried every password in combination with each of the usernames, and he was in.

The chat participants presented as nerdy medieval academics who were spooked and obsessed with ensuring their privacy. Sid allowed himself a small smile at that—clearly, none of them had IT expertise or they'd have been way more careful—but it soon faded when he found a mention of Folio 9 and of Alice Trevelyan in the same sentence, followed by the killer line:

> I have definitive proof that Folio 9 was forged.

He stared at it. If true, this could be devastating for Anya. *If.* The skin on the back of his neck crawled. He wanted to know more, but that was all it said.

He spent hours searching, typing in combinations of his search terms, but nothing else came up. It was almost midnight when he walked home to grab his passport and a few hours' sleep before getting a taxi to the airport.

Outside, the deep darkness beyond the campus lights spooked him. He took the main road into town, then walked up North Street.

He knew he was close to the cottage when he passed beneath the tower of St. Salvator's Chapel. A rowdy group of students walked toward him, on the other side of the road, drinking beer and sharing boxes of fish and chips.

At first, he was grateful to have company on the quiet streets, then he did a double take, his brain telling him urgently that one of the women he'd seen on the footpath with Paul was part of the group. He stared, unsure now, unable to identify her from behind, but also certain he was right. He could have been. The group had just passed a narrow alleyway that she could have disappeared into. She could even be standing in the shadows and watching from there, right now.

He hesitated, wondering if he should check, then shuddered involuntarily, as if someone had walked over his grave. He was too spooked to chase anyone down a dark alleyway, and he had a flight to catch in a few hours' time. He hurried to the top of North Street and cut toward the Scores. He knew he wouldn't sleep, but he couldn't wait to be out of town and with Anya.

Anya

I woke at six the next morning, sitting bolt upright, my skin slick with sweat and my jaw aching with tension.

Magnus and his London home had appeared in my nightmare: his face looming, then dissolving and reforming as the de Kooning oil of the obliterated woman I'd seen on the wall of his London house, the thick paint twitching, then writhing, becoming a backdrop to my mother's painful death. Horrific.

I found a message from Sid on my phone.

> On my way to the airport landing in Bristol around 10. I'll come straight to the hospital.

I couldn't wait to see him.

I was still expecting a reply from Diana and was surprised she hadn't responded yet. I checked that the message I'd sent her last night had gone through: I had to miss my flight back to Scotland. Mum is very unwell, so I'm home, and will be needed here for a few more days. I'll be back as soon as possible.

It said the message had been delivered. Maybe she wasn't awake yet, or maybe she was punishing me. I had no mental bandwidth free to think about it.

Viv was already in the kitchen when I went down, ready to go. I drove us in Mum's car. We barely talked on the journey. We never had much to say to each other when it was just the two of us, but the silence was comfortable enough.

Mum had improved a little, the antibiotics doing their work. The nurse was propping her up when we arrived. She told me Mum had had some episodes of rigor overnight.

"It's the worst, darling," Mum said. "You feel so cold, but they take the blankets off you."

"That's because you'd overheat dangerously otherwise," the nurse said. She was taking Mum's blood pressure. I watched the cuff squeeze Mum's too-thin arm. She'd been through so much already. Too much.

"We've brought you some pajamas and some other bits," I said. "Viv packed a bag for you."

"That's lovely. I'll change later. I'm a little tired now." Her voice tapered off.

"She's going to need a lot of rest," the nurse said. She hooked up a new transfusion of antibiotics and ibuprofen. Mum shut her eyes. The nurse left the cubicle and pulled the curtain shut, and I let Mum doze while I unpacked the things we'd brought for her and set them up as nicely as I could in the cramped cubicle. A phone charger, Kindle, ChapStick, some snacks, spare underwear and nightwear, a cardigan. If they kept her in longer, we'd bring more stuff. It was a routine we knew well by now.

I sat beside Mum. Me on one side, Viv on the other. It was chatty on the ward; visitors gathered around the other beds, but we were mostly quiet. I drew Mum's curtain so we were shielded from the room but could enjoy the daylight from the window beside her bed. I found some comfort in watching the peaceful rise and fall of her chest. Her body seemed less stressed than it had last night. It gave me a little hope.

I don't know how long I'd been there when Sid peeked through the curtains gently and said, "Knock, knock." Mum's eyes fluttered open. He'd bought a bar of her favorite chocolate. "For when you feel well enough," he said.

"Thank you, dear Sid. What are you even doing here?" she chided him, but she squeezed his hand affectionately. He found another chair and put it beside mine. Viv offered to fetch us drinks from the café. Sid tried talking to Mum, but she fell asleep again, this time with her mouth open. It made her look older than her years.

We sat for a while before he whispered, "She doesn't look great."

I didn't want to hear it. I never wanted to hear it from anyone else when she wasn't doing so well, even though I always knew. "She's a lot better than last night."

"Is she out of danger?"

"They say she's going in the right direction. Apparently the first twenty-four hours is crucial."

"I need to talk to you about something," he said. "Privately."

I glanced at Mum. She was asleep. It might be hard to chat later, with Viv around. She had a way of hovering. "What is it?"

He pulled his chair closer to mine and lowered his voice. He talked urgently and told me what he'd discovered about the Institute. It left me reeling. I had so many questions. He answered what he could.

I said, "I need to tell you something, too."

I checked again that Mum was asleep before whispering: "I met my dad. It's him who owns the manuscripts they want me to study. He's the bloody benefactor. I went to his house in Cambridge."

"Cambridge!" he echoed, a little too loud. He knew I'd sworn never to go there.

I shushed him, but Mum stirred. Her eyes opened, and they lit on me.

She smiled weakly. "Did I tell you about the clinical trial?" she asked.

"You did. It's amazing news." My stomach lurched. Why was she confused? She hadn't been earlier. Her head fell back on the pillow, and she turned her face to the window. Raindrops were slipping down the glass. Her skin was dull and pale, apart from the bright fever spots on her cheeks and neck, and the damp light washed her grayer.

I met Sid's eye. *We'll talk more later*, I mouthed. I hadn't yet told him about the pact I'd made with Magnus. It felt as if everything we'd wished for had been exploded, but Mum was the priority right now. Nothing else mattered.

It seemed to cost her a lot of effort just to move her head. She turned it slowly to look at me, and said, "Oh, yes, I remember now. You were in Cambridge when we phoned you."

My stomach clenched. "No," I said. "I went to London. You just overheard Sid say Cambridge. He was talking about something else."

I tried to hold her gaze casually.

I always know when you're lying, Anya.

She said, "No, my love. You were in Cambridge. I heard St. Leo's clock chiming in the background when we were speaking. I know that sound."

"No," I said. It came across as meek and unconvincing.

We eyeballed each other. I couldn't let her know I'd been there. I wouldn't. I thought she was about to speak when her eyelids drooped and her head lolled. The oximeter alarm went off.

"Get the nurse! Quick!"

Sid swept the curtain aside. Viv was standing right behind it. She looked startled.

"I just arrived!" she said, as if we'd asked.

Sid dashed past her to fetch someone. I ignored her.

"Mum!" I shook her shoulder gently but couldn't rouse her. "Mum!" I held her face between my hands. Her neck was limp, and her head was heavy.

A medical team ran in. I moved aside. Viv stared from the end of the bed. I heard her say, "I'm in the way." She stepped aside as everyone converged on Mum.

The medics worked on her, putting an oxygen mask on, running checks, monitoring her oxygen levels until they were back in the normal range, and after some heart-stopping moments Mum was there again.

"She fainted," the doctor said. "We'll give her something to bring her blood pressure up."

We were always lurching from one crisis to the next. Where Mum's lymphoma was concerned the ground beneath our feet was never stable. I found it exhausting trying to keep my balance and stay strong for her.

Her eyes were open again, but she lapsed back into confusion. She was mumbling. Sid slipped his arm around me, holding me as if he knew I was afraid that I might fall. I felt his heart thumping as hard and as fast as mine was.

We kept vigil beside the bed. Mum was very drowsy. The nurse checked her blood pressure every few minutes until she was sure it had stabilized. "She's doing well now," she said. "We'll check again in half an hour." She left Sid and me alone with Mum.

"How long do you think Viv was behind the curtain?" I asked.

"I don't know," Sid said. "Maybe a while? The way she reacted, it was like she'd been eavesdropping."

"I think she was just startled when you drew back the curtain. The situation was scary. Don't you think?"

"I'm not so sure."

Viv

Viv barely looked where she was going when she left the ward. She was seeking a quiet spot to make a phone call. A recess where some empty wheelchairs were parked would do. She tucked herself in beside them and pulled out her phone.

Finally, she had information. Anya Brown had met with her father to work on part of his manuscript collection that was up in Scotland, and she didn't want her mother to know. Sid was suspicious of Anya's colleagues. These were golden nuggets of information, both highly valuable to the Kats, she was sure of it.

Information is precious. Their motto. *Her* motto, too, since she'd joined the Order.

Her heart was racing. She put her hand to her chest and felt it pound. This was exhilarating, because it had been a long time coming. Not that she'd minded caring for Rose Brown. Being of service was a special sort of calling, and Rose had been an uncomplaining patient and surprisingly good company in spite of her views on men and marriage. But a breakthrough like this was what Viv had been waiting for.

She made the call. When her mentor answered she heard herself gabbling as she relayed everything she'd learned and held her breath as she waited for the reaction.

"This is excellent work," Judith said.

Viv had never met Judith, but she liked to imagine that she had a beautiful home, a detached house with a large garden, thoughtfully decorated. A real home for her and her family. Judith hadn't told her many details about her private life because the Order had strict rules about privacy. All Viv knew was that she was married.

As Judith talked, Viv basked in the praise, and her fingertips found her favorite charm on her bracelet: St. Katherine's wheel. They traced its small circumference, bumping over the nubs along its outer edge. What comfort it gave her. What strength.

"Keep doing what you're doing," Judith said. "Stay close to them, keep your ears open, and report everything, especially information regarding the manuscripts. Pay extra attention to that, please. I'm going to let everyone know about your superb work. You'll be very well rewarded for this."

Her words made Viv feel warm and wanted. She was invisible to so many people, but never to the Order.

When the call ended she made her way back to the ward. Her expression soured as she went. Anya Brown really got on Viv's nerves.

If Anya were a proper, dutiful daughter, who took responsibility, then she'd stay home and care for her mother instead of chasing a career. Even worse, was Anya's attitude to her boyfriend. She didn't know how lucky she was to have a good man like him, and it was a disgrace the way she put her career before her relationship. It was Viv's opinion that Anya should have modified her ambitions to support his. But it was all take, take, take with Anya. She'd made that lovely man trail after her in a way that must be humiliating for him. And what's more, Rose was paying a small fortune for Viv's services while Anya was away doing whatever she wanted. Did Anya never think that her mother might prefer to get the cottage roof fixed? Or to take a holiday when she was well enough?

If Viv had ever had the chance to get a man like Sid, she'd have done everything to support him. He was handsome and clever and kind. Life with a man like him was all Viv had ever wanted. For decades she'd dreamed of it. Babies. A family. A passport into the world of married couples. But most of all, a man who she could support and, when necessary, gently guide.

The bones of men are the scaffold on which we hang our power.

Such a powerful phrase from the Order. It thrilled her.

The Order had promised her they would do what they could to help her find a suitable match if she worked hard for them. She'd simply had bad luck so far, they assured her, but they planned to change that. Many men became newly available for marriage in their fifties, dumped by selfish, impulsive women who saw married life as drudgery. Some of those men, sadly, would be snapped up by much younger women. Everyone knew that, and it was unfortunate for the older widows and spinsters, but it was a part of man's nature that they simply had to accept. They would do their best to find Viv a husband as soon as she'd finished this assignment successfully.

She'd reached the door of the ward, and she pressed the buzzer. The plan was to apologize for rushing away so abruptly. She would explain that it all just got too much for her, that she should have listened to Anya's advice to rest more. She'd got emotional, she would say, but she was fine now.

They'd swallow that explanation easily because they thought she was just another middle-aged woman fulfilled by a life of service. That was fine by Viv. It was the reason the Order was so effective. She muttered another of their maxims as she waited:

"Service is our camouflage. Invisibility is our strength. We build power in the shadows."

She loved that.

A nurse answered the intercom. "I'm here to see Rose Brown," Viv said, facing the camera. The door buzzed open, and she entered the ward.

She was ready to do whatever was necessary. When her mentor had explained what her final instructions might include, Viv hadn't balked. As Judith knew, it wouldn't be the first time Viv had helped someone over to the other side.

CHAPTER ELEVEN

Clio

Clio met DC Izzy Adefope at the evidence-storage facility. Diana Cornish's clothing and belongings had been bagged up and were laid out on a table.

Clio liked Izzy immediately. They were of a similar age, and Izzy was doing the job Clio would have gone for if she hadn't landed her role in the Art and Antiques Squad. The Murder Squad wasn't for the fainthearted, and Izzy had an implacability about her that Clio admired and recognized as a necessary requisite for any woman who wanted to succeed in criminal investigations.

Gloves on, she looked through Diana's belongings. The dress was badly made, unlined, and made from cheap fabric, the sort of minimum-quality stuff you'd invest in for a fancy-dress party or for Halloween. The headscarf was also cheap: an unhemmed strip of muslin that could easily be purchased by the meter.

"This does look like a costume," Clio said.

"We're looking online to see if we can find it, but we're also considering whether it was specially made to match the clothes in the portrait of St. Katherine you sent us."

The professor's underwear was of a completely different quality: black lace and silk. Sexy. Expensive.

"How do you afford this stuff on a professor's salary?" Clio asked.

Izzy shrugged. "She had no husband, no kids. Her salary was her own."

"Even so. Are these real?" Clio held up a bag containing two pearl earrings.

"We think so. And the necklace."

"That's a big diamond."

"She definitely had money to spend on herself."

"Unless someone bought these things for her."

"We've found no sign that she was in a relationship. Her parents are deceased so maybe she inherited money. We spoke to her colleagues this morning, and according to them she was wedded to her work. They seem to be the closest thing she had to a family. We're working on getting into her phone still."

Clio picked up the sewing kit that had drawn her here. It was the cheapest of things, the kind of kit hotels give out for free, a needle threader and needle attached to a soft piece of cardboard. A few loops of yarn in black, blue, and white. The needle was threaded with a short length of black cotton.

"She used this," Clio said.

"Somebody did."

Clio couldn't shake a gut feeling that there were connections to be made between Eleanor Bruton's sewing of her letter into the curtain, and the embroidery, and this, but she kept the idea to herself for now because she wanted to impress Izzy. It was good for women in the police force to make connections with one another; she wasn't going to start saying anything Izzy might think was outlandish or stupid.

Diana's handbag was black, also expensive. It was by Chanel. Clio inspected it, looking for places where it might have needed a small repair, but it was in good shape, and it would have been hard to sew, if not impossible, with such a flimsy needle. Besides, nobody repaired handbags in an emergency. You repaired sweaters or shirts. You sewed on buttons that had fallen off. Because there were no bloodstains on the dress, it was likely that whatever Diana had been wearing when she was killed had been removed and replaced with this costume. Perhaps the repair had been to some item of clothing they were yet to find or might never find.

Unless.

Izzy's phone rang. "Excuse me, I need to take this," she said.

Clio reached for the evidence bag containing Diana's black underwear. The panties were skimpy, with no visible repairs. The bra was lightly padded, the cups covered in lace.

Izzy's conversation got heated, quickly. "Sorry," she mouthed to Clio, and stepped out of the room.

Clio removed the bra from the evidence bag. It looked normal, but when she ran her fingers along the seams and around the underwire, they caught on something beneath one of the cups, and the cup itself felt different from the other one. It was slightly more padded.

Clio peered at it closely. At the base of the cup, there was a very small, very neat row of hand-stitching. She had nothing to unpick it with and couldn't remove her gloves without contaminating the evidence. She tugged at it gently, and the flimsy thread snapped, allowing her to ease her fingertips inside, and remove a very fragile piece of embroidery.

She caught her breath.

Anya

I told Sid everything and he did the same.

It was overwhelming. So many things didn't make sense to us, but we could barely process them while Mum's body was fighting so hard and while Viv was fussing around us. For the first time, I found her overbearing.

"Do you think Viv only feels good when she's caring for people?" I whispered that night. We were in the small sitting room in the cottage. I'd told Viv she could go home, but she said she preferred to stay, that she wouldn't be able to relax while Mum was so sick. She was in the kitchen, preparing us a meal we hadn't asked for, didn't want, and knew would taste like ashes in our mouths.

"I don't know," Sid said. "I think it's odd."

"What do you mean?" I asked.

"Everything feels disturbing."

"Not Viv, though," I whispered. "She's annoying but surely not disturbing."

He couldn't reply because Viv appeared in the doorway, startling us both.

"Dinner won't be long," she said. She was wearing Mum's apron. I tried to look at her with fresh eyes, but all I saw was a woman who'd been invaluable to us. I glanced back at Sid. He was watching her very carefully, which unsettled me, but I thought, What harm could she possibly do?

THE NEXT MORNING IT WAS GOOD NEWS AT THE HOSPITAL. MUM WAS VISI-bly improved, sitting up in bed. We had a long hug. "We got you back," I said.

"I feel human again."

I hadn't been there more than half an hour when I got a message from Magnus.

> Good news that your mother is better. Flights are
> booked for you and Sid to return to Edinburgh later
> today. Work starts at the castle tomorrow. Rose will be
> in good hands.

I showed it to Sid, who swore. "How does he know?"

"I don't want to go back."

"I don't, either, but I don't see that we have a choice."

The airport was crowded when we arrived in the early evening. We got food and found seats overlooking the runways. Fatigue hit like a sledgehammer. I laid my head on Sid's shoulder and let the rising planes mesmerize me.

"I've been thinking about the cottage," Sid said. "When they renovated it, it would have been the easiest thing in the world to install surveillance, hidden cameras, or microphones at the very least."

He was convinced they were monitoring our phone activity, too. I saved our seats while he went to buy cheap burner phones for us both. I didn't know if it was an overreaction or not. It was growing darker outside; the window glass reflected the airport interior brightly enough that I could watch Sid walking away. A woman caught my eye. She was sitting a few rows behind me, to the side, a laptop open on her knee. She was watching Sid, too. It was more than a glance. She swiveled her neck to see where he was going. I wondered if she thought he was hot. He was a low-key guy; he didn't get a lot of open attention from women, so I wasn't used to it. I felt a little jealousy rise, but when she turned her head back, I looked away so she didn't catch me staring, and when I checked back, she'd gone.

I told Sid when he returned.

"What did she look like?" he asked.

I tried to remember. "Long hair in a pony, tucked beneath a baseball cap. A lot of makeup. Scarf up around her neck. Sweatshirt. She looked like a fitness influencer."

He said she could be one of the women who he'd seen in St. Andrews. I tried to spot her again, but she'd disappeared. At the gate and in Edinburgh, he scanned the people around us, asking me, "Is that her?" but we didn't see her again.

It felt as if we'd let go of reality, as if paranoia was our new normal.

When we got to the cottage, I was about to put my key in the lock when Sid put his hand on my arm. "Remember: act naturally."

I nodded, but once we were inside, it was so hard. If there's one thing creepier than feeling watched, it's when you don't know where you're being watched from. My skin crawled. I wanted to leave. Somehow, though, we got through the time until bed, and it was a relief to be in the dark holding hands beneath the covers.

Sleep came slowly, and once again, it was tangled with nightmares.

Sarabeth

Sarabeth Schilders threw a treat for her puppy, a Scottish terrier named Hypatia, and watched approvingly as the little dog ate it. Hypatia's tail wagged madly, and this made Sarabeth feel happy. It was late in the evening, and they were the only occupants of her dusty, book-filled house on Hope Street in St. Andrews.

"Good girl," she said. "Who's a good girl? Are you ready for walkies?"

Every night they took a turn around the block so Hypatia could do her business. Sarabeth took down Hypatia's leash and harness from a peg in the hall, and began the difficult job of attaching both to the dog's wriggly body. The job was only half finished when her phone rang. She ignored it. But it rang again, and again, until she picked up. Her heart skipped a beat when she saw who the caller was.

"Sarabeth Schilders," she said.

"It's Charlotte Craven."

Diana's boss. The puppy started yapping. With the side of her foot Sarabeth slid the dog across the tiled floor into the utility room and shut the door on her. The yapping became inaudible as she went to her study and sat down at her desk. Charlotte only called Diana, usually. There was a hierarchy in the Fellowship, and this was a break of protocol. It was a bad sign.

She cried when Charlotte told her that Diana had died, and

how. Sarabeth wasn't close to many people, but Diana had been an exception. She'd also been an extraordinarily effective member of the Fellowship.

"This is a terrible blow," she said, once she'd found her voice. Then, "And so brazen. Those fucking women."

"I know," Charlotte said. "There will be retribution. In the meantime, I need you to handle things up there for me. I'll call Giulia and Karen and tell them about Diana, but I need you to tell Anya. The details about how her body was found are being suppressed for now, while police investigate, so we'll let Anya believe it was a mugging that went wrong."

Sarabeth pushed her glasses up her nose. "I'll do it in the morning."

"Thank you. And for stepping up."

"I'll do her proud."

Sarabeth sat for a long time in the dark after ending the call. She forgot about the dog. Tears ran down her cheeks and she tasted them on her lips.

If she was in charge up here, if she was to take on the mantle of Diana's power, then she would clean house. And if the Order of St. Katherine was willing to be this brutal, then Sarabeth would be, too. A clean house meant a strong, efficient house.

She mulled over this until her tears had dried, then she remembered Hypatia and the outing she needed. They walked the dark streets until the dog whimpered to go home. Sarabeth picked her up and kissed her. By the time she let them both back into the house, she knew exactly where her housecleaning would start.

Anya Brown was an asset that needed protecting at all costs. Sarabeth was convinced that the combination of her visual memory and her academic brilliance was uniquely suited to the work they needed her to do. She was honored to take on the role of looking after her. She'd backed Diana one hundred percent when Diana had suggested hiring Anya, even when Magnus had pushed back. He hadn't wanted to complicate his situation. He made Sarabeth sick to her stomach.

If the problem wasn't the Order of St. Katherine, it was always men.

To protect Anya and the ambitions of the Fellowship, she could remove that particular obstacle. Their best operatives were already following Sid. As soon as he got back to St. Andrews, she would tell them to find a way to deal with him permanently.

Clio

The door of the evidence room swung open, startling Clio. DC Izzy Adefope came in, frowning.

"We have to leave," she said. "We shouldn't be here."

"What? Why?"

"That was my boss calling. He told me not to do anything more on this case. Like, stop. Now." She made a cutting motion across her neck. "I'm being transferred onto something else. My whole team is."

"Transferred onto what?"

"He didn't say."

"Who's taking over this case?"

"He is."

"Did he say why?"

Izzy shook her head. "I should go."

Clio hesitated; she couldn't leave the embroidery. She said, "I can finish up here if you need to leave." She moved slightly to her left, to obscure the embroidery from Izzy's view, but Izzy caught it.

"What's that?" she asked.

Clio decided to be bold; it was what Lillian would have done. "You never saw it."

Izzy chewed her lip as she looked at the embroidery. Her expression was stony. Clio's heart sank. *Crap.* It was just her luck to be in the room with a Goody Two-shoes. She decided to double down on Lillian's brand of tough, anyway. "All I want is a photograph. It'll still be here when your boss comes looking."

"I hate him!" Izzy blurted out. "All he wants is to get in my pants. Since he found out he's not going to be able to, he's decided it's fun to demean me in front of the team whenever he gets the chance."

Clio swallowed. "I'm sorry," she said. "What's his name?"

"Tony Axford."

It was always good to know.

"Do what you want," Izzy said. "Just make sure you leave it as we found it."

"Thank you. If I can ever do you a favor in return."

"I'll keep in touch. Good to meet you, Clio."

"Be safe," Clio said.

She laid out the embroidery and photographed it carefully, including close-ups, then refolded it and tucked it back into the bra. She had no means to sew it back up, but she tucked the lining back into the underwire as best she could using her fingernail, though with gloves on, it wasn't easy. She returned it to the evidence bag.

On the street, she wondered if she should call in. Her boss, Tim, might have heard by now that she was off the case.

Her phone rang with an unknown number.

"Clio Spicer," she said.

"Oh hello, Detective, this is Mark Ward, Lady Arden's butler from Sherston Hall. I have that name for you. The woman who came to us asking about the embroidery was called Zofia Danek." Even over the phone he was smooth. She wondered what it cost to employ a man like him.

"And you said she worked for the University of St. Andrews?"

"That's what she told me."

Clio thanked him.

She could call in or she could eke out a few more minutes to work on this. She slipped into a café across the street, where she found a quiet booth in the back. She ordered food and a coffee, and hit the phone to make some discreet inquiries as to the whereabouts of Zofia Danek.

CHAPTER TWELVE

Anya

Over breakfast, Sid told me he was going to spend the day at the computer science department. He sounded stilted, and so did I when I replied to say I hoped he had a nice day. It was impossible to remember what I would normally say, or how I normally behaved.

Sarabeth called me early. "I have some very difficult news to tell you. There's no easy way to say this, but Diana died yesterday. She was mugged in London, and it seems to have gone wrong. She was found in a park in East London with a head injury and died in hospital without regaining consciousness. If it's any consolation, the doctor said it would have been quick. I'm so sorry, Anya. Please take the day off if you want."

She sounded terribly upset. I told her how sorry I was, too. The shock was intense. I wasn't sure how I got the words out. It was hardly credible that Diana had died, especially as I'd been with her only a few days earlier. I felt as if this was something I could hardly process on top of everything else. My mind was stretched to breaking.

The car arrived to pick me up. Nobody had canceled it, and even though my brain was sludge, I decided to work. It felt better to be on autopilot doing what Magnus wanted me to do, doing what I *knew*, than staying at the cottage, feeling watched or heard, feeling as if another cluster bomb had gone off in my head and not knowing how to reassemble the pieces. Sid stepped outside with me when I was leaving and told me to call him if I needed him, to come home if everything got too much.

I thought about Diana on the journey to the castle. How much I'd liked her at first, how charismatic she was, how the last time I'd made this trip was with her. It seemed impossible that she was gone. I watched the back of the driver's head, too, and wondered who they really worked for. I was becoming as paranoid as Sid.

Rain fell in shards and the wipers were working overtime. As we drove up the long drive the castle looked gloomy and spectral ahead, here one moment, obliterated by the wipers the next. They scraped the windscreen, and the sound cut right through me.

Tracy's housekeeper greeted me at the door and showed me in. The castle was busier than before, the atmosphere more alive. Florists were positioning an exuberant display on a table in the middle of the entrance hall, and there were staff working in the formal dining room, laying the table for what looked as if it would be a sumptuous dinner. Polished cutlery and elaborate candelabra gleamed. The room's tall ceiling was intricately painted with medieval designs. Vast tapestries hung from the walls and chandeliers fashioned from deer antlers were suspended on long chains secured to the dark beams crisscrossing the ceiling. I could hear chatter and the sounds of work coming from the kitchen and the aromas drifting out smelled delicious.

The housekeeper led me away from the bustle and into the more private wing of the castle, where the tower was. She asked me to leave my bag and devices on a table outside the door like I had before. I did it but kept my burner phone on me, hidden in a pocket. Tracy was waiting in the room at the base of the tower, where I'd seen the manuscripts on my first visit.

She must have to hide when they had people in the castle, I

thought, and I wondered who the dinner was for. Perhaps there was a select group of people, like my father, who knew where she lived and could be trusted to keep it a secret.

I had no time to dwell, though. Focusing on the collection was what mattered and the sooner I started, the sooner I could deliver on my side of the deal I'd made with Magnus and guarantee the best treatment for Mum.

Tracy looked stressed and I wondered how close she'd been to Diana and whether grief was the reason, but I didn't know whether to mention it to her. I wasn't sure if she knew yet.

"Ready to get started?" she asked, and I told her I couldn't wait. "Let's go," she said. I followed her up the spiral stairs; the room above was empty, a circular stone void, harboring echoes, its windows glazed arrow slits, with narrow views over the forest below and the hills beyond.

Tracy opened a wooden door that, curiously, led from the tower back into the main body of the castle, as if the tower had been constructed as an elaborate entranceway. The door was so thick and dark and worn that it had to be ancient. Tracy hit the lights and we entered a small, square chamber paneled from floor to ceiling. The paneling was inlaid with intricate patterns and pictures, trompe l'oeils, made with such skill that images seemed to leap out from the wall in 3D. I turned a full circle to take it all in. It was incredible. There were musical instruments, books, a dagger, a pipe, and more, all attributes of an educated gentleman from medieval Italy, all arranged in trompe l'oeil cabinets or displayed on trompe l'oeil shelves. I'd seen it before.

"Is this a copy of the study in the Ducal Palace in Gubbio, Italy?" I asked.

"Yes. The laird who built this place made a trip to Italy and fell so much in love with what he saw that he had his own version made here."

This place was full of surprises. Using a key fob, Tracy unlocked yet another door, which I hadn't noticed because it was hidden within the paneling. "This is where we keep your father's manuscripts."

She looked at me as if curious to witness my reaction to her mention of my father. You knew everything all along, I thought, but I wasn't intimidated by her anymore. I figured she was Magnus's pawn, just like everyone else.

"You're good at keeping secrets," I said.

She pushed the door open, and flicked another switch. "I'm an actress. It's my job to be whoever other people want me to be. In the case of your father, it's been my pleasure to act as custodian for these books. They're really no trouble at all. In fact, it's been a great deal easier to hide them than it has been to hide myself."

I barely listened to what she was saying. I had eyes only for the manuscripts, which were arranged on shelves around three walls of a plain, windowless room. She said, "They're all yours. Do your thing. That laptop is for you to make notes on. It doesn't leave this room." They'd provided a brand-new MacBook. I flipped it open. It was already set up for me and, no surprise, it had no internet access.

Tracy gave me a fob of my own, which she said would let me into the tower and the manuscript room, then left me there, shutting the door firmly yet quietly behind her, and I took stock.

The only entrance and exit was the door we'd come through. Artificial lighting had been designed to show off the books and was dimmed to conservation levels. In the middle of the space there was a large desk, where the laptop lay alongside a book stand and a lamp for examining the manuscripts.

The books waited silently on the shelves; they had a quiet, confident presence. I made a conscious effort to empty my brain of distractions, so that when I opened the first book, my memory would be primed to preserve copies of every page I looked at. Confiscating my iPhone might stop me from photographing the manuscripts and sharing them, but it couldn't stop me from recalling every detail. And I needed to. My burner phone was too basic to have a camera. It was only good for making and receiving calls.

I ran my fingers gently along the spines of the books and thought of all the people who'd handled them before me, the scribes, illustrators, bookbinders, booksellers, and owners. My father and grandfather. My mother, too. I supposed I could count her, since she'd spent one afternoon with them. And now me. It was hard to think of any other objects in my life that had been handled by my mother, father, and me.

I decided to make an inventory first, a list of the books with a description of each. Then I could organize them by type, for serious study.

As I contemplated them—there were so many—a surge of doubt rose like nausea, doubt that I couldn't deliver the standard of scholarship Magnus wanted. My heart thumped, but I had to start somewhere. I picked out a book at random and laid it on the cushion beneath the light, and I heard Mum's voice, the same way I always did when I handled a precious manuscript.

Books connect us to the past and teach us how to map our future.

I hoped so. So long as I had what it took, these books could save her life.

I worked on the collection for hours without stopping. Compiling my list was slow going because I kept getting distracted. Every book I took from the shelf was breathtaking in its beauty and rarity. Time flew, until I suddenly realized I needed food, and fresh air. I went downstairs, collecting my phone on the way.

Once I'd left the dead quiet of the manuscript room and the tower, I wasn't sure where I was allowed to go. Instinctually I kept away from the busier areas of the castle, which wasn't hard, since the place was so big. I found a side door and slipped outside to find myself in an area of the grounds that was out of sight of the castle's main rooms. It was a perfect, private place to call Mum from.

I tried her phone and when she didn't pick up I called the ward again.

The nurse was upbeat: "Rose is doing much better today. I'll transfer you to her bed."

"Mum!" I said when she answered. "It's me!"

"Hello, darling."

"Why didn't you answer your phone?"

"Viv took it downstairs to pay for some drinks. I'm so bored with this place. Tell me what you're up to. I want to know everything."

"I already started work on the manuscripts." One of the books I'd looked at that morning had an especially gorgeous binding. I knew she'd love to hear about it. She missed her work. I weighed telling her about it, and figured it was fine because she'd only seen those books once, many years ago, and like everyone else, she thought they'd burned.

"One of them had a gold repoussé binding with encrusted gems. It was stunning."

"Oh, wow. This is the drink of water I needed. Tell me more."

I smiled and then I made a mistake. My brain had a runaway moment. Maybe because it was bliss to escape into the fantasy that life was okay, that St. Andrews was everything it had promised, and that Mum and I could chat about our shared passion. I started to describe another binding to her when she snapped, "Say that again."

"It was a clasped gold binding with filigree work, showing the Adoration of the Magi."

She said nothing.

"Mum?" I said. "Hello?"

The silence stretched further and stifled that little bit of pleasure I'd let myself feel, and with a horrible sinking feeling, I knew that I'd said too much.

"Darling, I need you to listen to me very, very carefully. Are you alone?" Mum asked.

"Sort of." I'd wandered around the back of the castle. There were vans parked, back doors open, caterers and chefs unloading yet more stuff. A team of landscapers was tidying up the garden nearby.

"Go somewhere no one can hear you. Go now. I'm going to call you back, because I don't want to talk on this line."

"Okay, but when you do, use this number." I got out my burner phone and read the number out to her, then hung up and walked across the garden, to a quiet spot at the edge of the woodland where I was hidden from people and out of hearing. I waited, nerves building, for her to call, and caught it on the first ring.

"I'm alone," I said. "What's wrong?"

"I need you to be completely honest with me. Do you promise? Don't hold anything back because you think it will hurt me or make me cross."

Oh, God, I thought. What did she know? Had she found out about Dad's involvement in the clinical trial? I braced myself to fight with her over it.

"I promise," I said.

"Okay, listen carefully. I'm going to ask you some questions. Remember, be honest. Lives depend on it."

"Mum—" I started.

"No!" she interrupted, so forcefully it made her cough. "We haven't got time for feelings, and I need to give this phone back soon. First question: Were those accurate descriptions of the bookbindings?"

"Yes."

"Both of them?"

I hesitated. I had a bad feeling.

"Anya," she coaxed.

"Yes, they were," I said.

"I know those books and I know where they're from."

"That's not possible."

"Anya, I heard St. Leo's clock chiming when we spoke the other day. You were in Cambridge, and those bindings are from books in your father's collection."

"You can't possibly know that. You only saw his collection once."

"I might not have told you the truth about that."

"The collection burned!"

"Did it?" she asked. "Now I'm wondering."

My legs felt as if they might give way. I sank down and crouched against a wall.

You can't keep secrets from me, Anya. I always know.

She broke the silence. "The clinical trial. There's a reason I'm suddenly accepted and fully funded to join it, isn't there? What have you done?"

"Nothing," I said. *Please, God, don't let her refuse this.*

"Let me give you some context. After my diagnosis, when I heard the prognosis for this disease, I contacted your father for the first time in over a quarter of a century. I sent him an email asking if he would help me access the best possible treatment, whatever that might be. I told him if he didn't want to do it for me, he should do it for you, because you only had one parent. He replied promptly. Do you want to know what he said?"

"Yes," I whispered.

"He said no."

I shut my eyes tight. The world spun around me.

"I know him better than most people. Whatever he's up to now, he showed me who he is then. And not for the first time. So, if I'm accepted onto a clinical trial, fully funded, including travel to a posh clinic in the US, I'm pretty sure someone has struck a deal, and I'm pretty sure that person can only be you. What did he promise you, Anya? His collection? Has it survived? You must tell me."

I needed to think. I wanted to give her an answer that would guarantee she had the best possible chance at living, but I had no idea what that might be. Truth or lies?

"Yes," I said eventually. "We struck a deal."

She swore under her breath. "Darling, listen to me. I'm never going to tell you anything more important than this. None of this is what you think. It's bigger than either of us, or him, and much, much more dangerous. Anya, are you hearing me?"

Clio

Clio quickly discovered two things from police databases: that Zofia Danek had been registered as a missing person in St. Andrews for just under six weeks, and that she'd been found at the end of that period.

She phoned the officer in charge of the case. "Zofia Danek disappeared after a hike on a bitterly cold day in Aberdeenshire," he told her. "She left her car behind, and we found her passport and what we assume were most of her personal belongings in her cottage. It took a while, but we traced her to London. She'd managed to apply for a new passport from the embassy there and had already made her way back to Poland. We worked with the Polish police to find her and eventually spoke to her. She'd changed her name, and she requested that we keep her exact location a secret. She didn't want her old employers to know where she was."

"Her employer being the Institute of Manuscript Studies in St. Andrews?"

"Right. She said she felt threatened by them, but she wouldn't go into detail. We didn't pursue it because there didn't seem to be any lawbreaking. She'd had a rough time of it because she'd had personal problems, too. She told us she'd been stalked by a colleague's husband, so obviously, once we'd established that she was safe, we respected her wishes to remain hidden. We told the Institute we'd located her in Poland and that the case was closed but didn't give out any more information."

"Do you think she'd speak to me? I'm hoping she can help with an investigation."

"She might. There's no harm in trying. I'll send details of our contact in Poland."

Clio hung up. This case was exerting a strong pull on her. She could feel it in her gut. It wasn't just because of the connection to Lillian, though that was stirring up feelings; it was also a sixth sense that this went deep. She knew she couldn't let it lie.

It was hard to make sense of Izzy suddenly being pulled off the Diana Cornish murder. She thought about calling Izzy to ask if she'd learned anything more, but it was probably too soon. She called her boss instead. Tim might know something, but she'd have to be careful what she said. She wasn't supposed to be working on this.

She called him, told him she'd had an emergency dentist appointment but was on her way in. "By the way, do you know Tony Axford?" she asked.

"Why?"

"Just heard something about him, that's all."

"Anything I need to know?"

"No."

"Then get off the phone and get into the office. We've got work to do."

In the office, she exchanged emails with the Polish police when she could. At lunchtime, she made another excuse about her teeth and raced home from work. She let herself into her flat in a hurry, threw down her keys and bag, opened her laptop, and clicked on a Zoom link.

Zofia Danek appeared on screen. She had long, gray-blond hair that almost covered one side of her face. She'd blurred her background.

"Hello," she said.

Clio introduced herself. "Thanks so much for talking to me. I really appreciate it."

"How can I help?" She sounded wary.

"I'm working on an investigation that may involve your former employers in St. Andrews. I know some of the details about why you left, but I'm hoping you can tell me a little more."

"What do you want to know?"

"Why did you leave the way you did?"

"The Institute recruited me to start in September 2022. They offered me many things at the time, a really good package, but when I arrived, nothing felt right. They wanted to control the work I did. There is a piece of embroidery in the British Museum, a fragment. They were obsessed with it. They wanted me to spend all my time working on it, but it had already been studied. There was nothing to learn. The first year in the job I tried to please them, I did everything I could think of to shed light on this scrap, but it got ridiculous. It was so small and in such bad condition there was nothing more to know about it. And there were other things I wanted to research. When I told them I'd done everything I could, they said okay, so now we have to find the missing part." She made an expression of absurdity. "I mean, this was a crazy treasure hunt they were trying to send me on because this missing piece of the embroidery disappeared after it was stolen, everybody knew that. It's famous. And I'm not a treasure hunter or a detective. I'm just an expert on textiles. Well, I was."

"Have you changed jobs?"

"I had to. You know, there aren't many of us working in these small corners of academia. Put it this way, if you gather us all for a symposium you don't need to book a very big room. We're rare. Our interests are esoteric, they're not mainstream. If I stayed in the textiles field, the Institute would find me very easily. So, I changed jobs."

"Can you tell me more about what happened at the Institute?" Clio was making notes as Zofia spoke, her pen racing over the page.

"The more pressure they put on me to find the embroidery, the more I started to notice that nothing there was what it seemed like.

Not everyone there was working on manuscripts. They were doing other things that they were secretive about. Then I started to have trouble from one of my colleagues' husbands, a guy called Paul. It was nice at first to connect with him because I was lonely when I arrived, but it became scary. He got obsessed with me, sent me lots of notes, always trying to talk to me if I saw him in the street, which was often, because St. Andrews is a very small place. He told me he believed we were soulmates, but I hardly knew him. He had even followed me on the day I decided to disappear. It was frightening, and he nearly ruined everything."

"Did you ever confront him?"

"No. I lived alone. I tried not to engage with him. If I'd stayed longer, I would have reported him, because it was getting scary. I had started to keep a record of everything he did."

It didn't wholly explain why Zofia had left in such a dramatic way. Clio pressed her on it.

"A new hire started this time last year. September 2023. A woman called Minxu Peng. After she'd been there a little while she confided in me what I already suspected: that some of the women in the department were not really academics. She said they were involved in stuff that seemed dodgy. They hired her to scrub the internet and set up secure networks for them, or something like that. I didn't really understand what she told me, I'm not an IT person, but it validated what I was already suspecting, and I didn't want anything to do with it. Minxu was afraid of them, too. She told me she was planning to leave as soon as the academic year was over. She wanted to go home to her family. She missed them. I hope she managed to do that. Do you know?"

"I don't," Clio said. "But I'll look into it."

She paused to look back over her notes. She circled the words "embroidery" and "expert on textiles."

"Would you mind taking a look at something if I send it to you?" she asked.

Olivia

Olivia Macdonald's phone was ringing. There weren't many people she dropped everything for, only her husband, Judge Henry Macdonald, or another senior member of the Order of St. Katherine. It was the latter calling.

She stepped out of the church where she'd been helping to arrange displays of fresh produce for the harvest festival service and took the call in her Range Rover. It was a crisp, fresh morning, the parking lot and graveyard littered with the first fallen leaves, still bright and pretty, a light mist lingering in the folds of the valley.

Olivia appreciated none of it the way she usually would. She was stressed. The Order of St. Katherine was facing an unprecedented crisis. Information from the nurse, Viv, who they'd placed with Rose Brown had revealed a hole in their intelligence gathering and created a new set of problems.

Her contact didn't bother with niceties: "Diana Cornish has been murdered."

Heavens, Olivia thought. She was profoundly shocked. She hadn't seen that coming. There had been so many bodies. Eleanor Bruton picked off by the Larks and possibly the academic from China, too. Then there were the problematic individuals the Kats had disposed of themselves. How many more?

"Who did it?" Olivia asked. Nobody in the Katherinite Order had given the command, so far as she knew, and it was the sort of decision she would expect to be involved in. The hairs on the back of her neck stood on end as the caller described how and where Diana had been found. "They mean it to look as though we've done it."

"I agree," Olivia said. She had the horrible sense that everything was slipping through their fingers.

Through the Range Rover's windshield Olivia's eyes tracked a woman walking past hand in hand with her child, who held the sweetest little basket of apples for the church display, but her mind was miles away, already thinking about what it would take to mop this mess up—it absolutely had to be kept out of the press because of the St. Katherine link—and what it meant. "It's a provocation," she said. "They're escalating. Why?"

"If Viv's information is correct, and the Larks have hired Anya to study her father's collection, it could mean that some of the manuscripts survived the fire at his library. Otherwise, why take her up to Scotland and have her work in such secrecy?"

"I agree," Olivia said, through gritted teeth. If true, it was painful to admit that they hadn't known or even guessed at this until now. They should have. It would have changed everything. Now they were vulnerable, and the Larks were ahead of the game.

She tried to focus on the issue at hand. "Is the supposition that they killed Diana in this way to divert our attention while Anya closes in on the prize?"

"Maybe. I'm confident that we can manage the fallout from Diana's death so it doesn't touch us. But what we really have to think about is whether this means that the Larks are close to finding *The Book of Wonder*. If some of those books survived the fire, they may have been able to unite the embroidery with whatever we suspect Rose Brown hid in Magnus Beaufort's collection."

"I'm not sure we suspect any longer," Olivia said. "I think we *know*." There was silence on the other end of the line. She wasn't the only person finding this painful. "We were so close to getting to *The Book of Wonder*, and now we have nothing," she said.

"Our information wasn't good enough. But we can't dwell on it."

"No," Olivia said quietly. "We can't." Her mind was racing, seeking solutions. "We can still use Rose Brown," she said. "Just differently."

"Indeed, and I want to talk about that, but before we do, there's something else you need to know. Before she died, Diana Cornish and Charlotte Craven met with Bridget Farley, at Commerz Credit in London. Now, if Bridget's involved, it likely means they're ready to put funding in place for their foundation, which indicates that things are happening much faster than we anticipated. Their time scale has shrunk. To me it's another sign that Anya Brown may be close to a breakthrough on finding the book and they think they're going to cash in."

"How do you know this? Is one of ours married to a Commerz Credit banker?" It was nice to know that their intelligence gathering was effective in some areas at least.

"Yes, but we assumed the Larks would be alert to that connection," her colleague said. "So we placed some catering and reception staff there. A coffee lady brought us this information."

"Ha," Olivia said. For all their work for women's rights, the Larks' Achilles' heel was social prejudice. Laughable, really, but she was in no mood for levity. Her thoughts were sharpening into strategy. It was time to play their trump card.

"We must tell Viv to abduct Rose Brown now," she said. "It's time to exert some leverage over Anya." A controlled excitement was building in her. Was it too much to imagine that kidnapping Rose could allow them to flip Anya?

"That's exactly what I thought. Good. I'll give the order."

"We *were* prepared, then," Olivia said. It mattered to her that they hadn't failed entirely to predict what might be needed. Granted, they'd been keeping tabs on Rose for the wrong reasons, but that didn't matter if they could use her now. This could make all the difference.

After she hung up, Olivia sat in the car for a while, regrouping and thinking about next steps. When she was certain of the detail, she sent a message calling for a meeting of the most senior members of the Order.

Then she sent a message to Henry. Love you, darling. Can't wait to see you at the weekend x.

He wouldn't know about Diana yet, and when he learned, he would be devastated. Their affair had been long and passionate. So, best to remind him that his wife was a loving constant in his life, no matter what he was going through, and best to remind him before he even knew he'd need that little bit of comfort.

Anya

Mum's voice was low-pitched and intense. "Anya, listen to me. There are two very important things hidden in your father's collection. One is a letter and the other is a glossary. The glossary is *the key to deciphering the Voynich manuscript*."

"What?" I wanted to laugh. All that tension, for this? It was a spectacular delusion. They must have her back on morphine. The Voynich manuscript was one of the most famous in the world. People had been trying to decipher it for centuries. Maybe Mum was thinking about it because of the offer I'd had from Yale, because the manuscript lived in their Beinecke Library. It was the most-visited item on their website and had spawned serious academic studies in cryptography and linguistics, as well as a world of wild and rampant speculation online. I felt almost addled with relief that this was a figment of her imagination.

"Oh, Mum," I said. "What have they given you?"

"Just ibuprofen. I promise. Check with the nurse if you like. I'm aware of how crazy this sounds, Anya, but you *need* to listen. The worst thing you can do right now is ignore me. I'm completely sentient."

"Okay," I said, to appease her. "Tell me more."

"The glossary consists of four pages of vellum, which have been cut up into eight pieces and hidden inside the binding of another book. The letter is hidden with them. I know this because I did it. You need to retrieve them and destroy them, because the Voynich is not what people think it is. It's not an end in itself; it's a means to an end. It's the key to something else, something incredibly valuable that's been hidden for a very long time. I don't know exactly what this thing is, but I do know that some people badly want it, and I mean *very* badly. People have died for this, Anya. Lives have been lost because of it, and I won't let them take your life, too." Her voice shook.

"Mum," I said slowly. I wondered if she had any idea how insane she still sounded, first the Voynich and now a mysterious hidden object that it was the key to finding. She interrupted me.

"Anya! You *must* take this seriously. I need you to trust me and to do what I say. I know you're thinking I've lost my mind, or that I'm addled on morphine, but test me. Ask me a question. Ask me anything. Let me prove that I mean every word of this."

I tried to think. The pressure of coming up with something quickly was a lot, but if there was one thing Mum couldn't do when she was on morphine, it was crosswords or word puzzles. The drug confused her too much.

I asked, "What do banyan trees and rhinoceroses have in common?"

She fell silent, and my heart beat the inside of my rib cage like a drum as I waited for an answer.

After a moment, she said, "That's easy, darling, it's us. You and me: bANYAn and rhinoceROSEs."

I felt my blood run ice cold in every artery, vein, and capillary. *She was absolutely herself.* "Okay," I said. "What do I need to do?"

"You need to find the manuscript and take it. If that's impossible, split its binding and extract the gloss and the letter. There are nine pieces of vellum altogether, inside the front and back covers. As soon as you have them, leave. Then you and Sid need to run, and you need to hide so well that nobody can find you. Can you do that for me? Are you with the manuscripts now?"

"I'm just outside the building."

"What's security like?"

"I don't know." I looked up at the castle and felt daunted. It was as solid, imposing, and unforgiving as any place I'd ever visited.

"Pay attention to it when you go back in."

"How do I do this?" I asked. "How do I do any of it?"

She paused. "You'll have to work that out. I have faith in you. But whatever you do, do it now. Hello?"

I heard another voice in the background. Mum said something muffled. When she spoke to me again her voice was artificially bright and chipper. "The nurse is here. She needs her phone back. Can you do as I say?"

"Can you tell me what the book looks like?"

"Ask me anything you want about it." It was obvious that she couldn't talk openly.

"Is the binding remarkable in any way?"

"No. It's as plain as can be. Darling, I really must go. Just one more very quick thing. I've been wondering if you and Sid had considered getting a pet? It might be a lovely thing to do now that you're settled. Viv saw a very nice black cat for adoption. It had beautiful lantern eyes. Anyway, it's up to you of course, but I just wanted to mention it, and I've really got to give this very kind nurse her phone back. Bye now."

The line went dead.

CHAPTER THIRTEEN

Clio

Clio searched the internet for mentions of Minxu Peng and found nothing. She tried the police databases and got a hit. Minxu Peng was a missing person. Just like Zofia. The difference was that Minxu's body had recently been pulled out of the Thames.

She exhaled sharply. A job at this Institute in St. Andrews was starting to look like a poisoned chalice. When they were in the British Museum, Lillian had told her that one of the groups of women was likely embedded in academia. What if some of them were based in Scotland?

Something else was needling her. When they spoke at the British Museum, Lillian had also mentioned a "dear friend" who she'd lost.

She wanted to find out who this person was. Tim might know, but she hesitated to ask him. If she was to take Lillian's advice seriously, she'd already said enough. Too much, possibly, though her gut was to trust him.

She thought back to Lillian's funeral. The attendees had been a mix of former colleagues and a couple of distant family members. Clio's grief had been overwhelming that day and she hadn't lingered after the service. In fact, she'd barely spoken to anyone and she regretted that now. But there was one person who might be able to identify this friend, someone who'd been working in their building longer than Lillian, someone Lillian had formed a bond with. Clio picked up the phone and asked the switchboard to put her through to the cafeteria.

Ethel was in. It didn't surprise Clio. Ethel was always in. She ran the canteen and was a friend to everyone. Clio asked the question.

"What's it worth?" Ethel cackled.

"A box of Ferrero Rocher?" Everyone knew they were Ethel's favorite.

"Lillian palled about for years with Pippa Wade. You couldn't separate them if you tried. But Pippa died."

"What happened?"

"She was shot during a raid. Awful. I don't know the ins and outs of it, but Lillian was never the same after."

Clio googled the name, found what she needed. Philippa Wade was buried with police honors in 2011. She had died in the line of fire during an undercover operation and was survived by her husband, Geoff, an engineer. No kids. It was easy to find Geoff. He lived in Chiswick. She grabbed her bag and headed out.

Geoff Wade's house was in the middle of a well-kept Victorian row. She rang the bell. Geoff was dapper, gracious, and amenable to talking to her. His home was immaculate, but she felt as if loneliness was lurking in its nooks and crannies. The air was so still, the surfaces so clean. From the look of the décor, she'd have put money on the fact that this room had looked exactly the same the day Pippa died. Prominent on his mantel was a framed photograph of a beautiful young woman.

"Is this Pippa?" Clio asked.

"It is. It was taken on the day we got engaged. I miss her every day, even after all these years." He fixed Clio with a stern look. "I'm not sure why you're here, but if you're truly a friend of Lillian's then you're a friend of mine. Otherwise, you can leave now."

"Lillian meant the world to me. She was my mentor. I'm here because just before she died, she mentioned Pippa in the context of something she was working on, and I wanted to know if you could shed some light on it."

"Why aren't you asking your colleagues?"

She hesitated. Geoff didn't seem like a man who suffered fools gladly. She chose her words carefully. "It's sensitive."

He looked interested. "Okay, let's stop talking in code. Pippa was murdered by one of your own. I knew it, Lillian knew it. We could never prove it. The police claimed her death was accidental, unfortunate, you name it, but there were far too many coincidences that day for it to be true. Pippa was pulled onto an operation last minute. It was undercover. She'd never been undercover. She was put in the line of fire with inadequate briefing. In the debrief, it was implied that the so-called accident happened because she had a lapse in judgment, but if there was one thing she absolutely was not lacking in, it was judgment. Pippa didn't have lapses. She was whip-smart, the most extraordinary person I've ever known. It was all a lie."

Clio felt as if there was ice water dripping down her spine. "Why would they lie?"

"Because she knew something she shouldn't. She'd been working on a case with Lillian. Two groups of powerful women, out to get each other. Pippa had told Lillian she'd made a breakthrough, but they needed to meet in person. It wasn't something she was willing to say over the phone."

"But Pippa never made it to the meeting," Clio guessed.

He shook his head. "She was pulled onto this operation instead. She and Lillian were due to meet at the British Museum. Lillian said she knew, as soon as the meeting time passed and there was no sign of Pippa, that something was wrong. Pippa was never late."

"Do you know where in the museum they were supposed to meet?" Clio asked, although she suspected she already knew.

"There's a piece of medieval embroidery on display there. Doesn't look like much to my eyes, but it meant something to the case. Pippa never told me what. They were supposed to meet in front of it."

Clio felt as though someone was walking over her grave. "Who was running the operation that Pippa was working on?"

Geoff's face clouded as he fought yet more emotions. She was rattled by how fresh his anger and grief still were, even after all this time. "An asshole called Tony Axford," he said.

It was the second time Clio had heard that name today. More coincidences. Far too many.

"Did you know Tony?"

He shook his head. "No, but he was very close to Tim Keenan at the time. It was a boys' club. I expect it still is. Lillian always suspected that Tim was moved to head up Art and Antiques to keep an eye on her after Pippa died. And FYI, Tim's job should have been hers."

Clio felt sick. She should have listened better to Lillian's warning not to talk about the case internally.

Geoff said, "I see you're shocked. I'm sorry. But if you're here now, with me, it's because Lillian wanted you to be, and it's best you know everything so that you can protect yourself."

Anya

As I walked back to the manuscript room I paid attention to security for the first time.

I noticed cameras everywhere, many of them positioned discreetly. I had no idea how to do what Mum wanted.

In the tower room, a camera was trained on the bottom of the spiral staircase. Its range included the table where I was asked to leave my devices, and I put my iPhone back there before going upstairs. The burner phone stayed in my pocket. Another lens was trained on the top of the stairs, and it seemed also to cover the door that led into the paneled room and the manuscript room beyond it.

Otherwise, there were no obvious signs of security, but the cameras might be hidden. I had to assume that they were watching what I did in those rooms.

I stood in front of the shelves of manuscripts and tried to think straight.

What had Mum said? Just that the binding was unremarkable, but she'd also asked me that strange question.

I've been wondering if you and Sid had considered getting a pet? It might be a lovely thing to do now that you're settled. Viv saw a very nice black cat for adoption. It had beautiful lantern eyes.

It wasn't a riddle, exactly. So, what did she mean? Black cats were associated with witches, everyone knew that. They appeared in all kinds of images. Should I be thinking of one I'd already seen? Was she asking me to use my memory? There were a few images I could recall that would match that description. Or was she referencing something in my dad's collection? That felt the most likely.

The problem was, I'd only examined a few of the books this morning, and there were almost two hundred altogether. I began to pick out the ones with plain bindings and look through them, but, conscious of surveillance, I was careful not to rush. I tried to work methodically.

As I worked, I thought about the symbolism of the black cat. They were associated with witchcraft. Perhaps there was a witchcraft collection here. They could also symbolize sensuality, predatory skills, good or bad luck depending on the culture, darkness and shadows, sharp eyesight, a silent traveler, an emblem of the moon, or a shape-shifter. Black cats were charioteers for the Norse goddess Freya, the bearers of nine lives.

As I eased open the cover of yet another book, I also considered the lantern eyes Mum had described. Was that another layer of symbolism? The lantern represented safety, a sanctuary, a place to flee, sometimes a clandestine signal. Did it create another meaning altogether if I juxtaposed it with the cat? It was the sort of complexity

Mum enjoyed, but I was struggling to put the images together and find anything meaningful. What was I not seeing?

I finished looking through one shelf of books and started on the next. It was getting late. I didn't know how long they would let me stay here.

The first three volumes on the new shelf were law texts, then there were two medieval gardening manuals, with illustrations of fruit trees, insects, butterflies, and birds that were delightful but not helpful to me. The next four volumes were medical texts. Again, no cats. There was a copy of an ancient gynecological manual called *The Book of the Conditions of Women*. I saw drawings of the female anatomy and descriptions of stomach-turning treatments for female ailments. There was an early Bible. No cats. No lantern eyes. I opened the second-to-last book on the shelf, feeling despondent.

It was a bestiary, a book of animals, real and mythical. On a first look, I noticed a colophon on the last page that told me it had originally been made for the library of a basilica in Galatina, in Italy, in 1452. Bestiaries were designed to illustrate the breadth of God's creation, and it was a suitably luxurious book. I leafed through it, transfixed by the illuminations. Here was a whale, an elephant, a griffin, a unicorn, and here: a black panther. Its body was drawn in profile, but its head faced outward, yellow eyes staring into mine, a large rodent hanging limply from its mouth.

A black cat with lantern eyes. This had to be what Mum meant. There was no symbolism. She'd given me a literal description of an illustration. My stomach dropped.

I closed the book and examined the binding. It wasn't original. I guessed that the bestiary had been written and illustrated in the fourteenth century, and the binding had been applied a few centuries later. Maybe in the seventeenth century. It was common practice to keep bindings like this on old books, even if they were later additions. But a lot of them needed restoration, which is where Mum must have come in. She'd done a superb job, and if I was right, there was a glossary hidden inside it.

It was a decent-size manuscript, and would be difficult to sneak out of the castle. I would have to open the binding and remove the glossary. But how?

A loud noise made me jump. A door slamming. Then I heard a soft knock on the door of the manuscript room before it opened slightly. Tracy's housekeeper peered in. "I'm sorry," she said. "We need everyone except essential staff off site because some of our guests are arriving sooner than we were led to believe. We need to take you home now."

"*Right* now?"

"Our guests are people who prefer anonymity. Just like Tracy. So, if you wouldn't mind?" It was a polite question, but her tone said that "right now" was exactly what they needed.

"I'll pack up," I said as normally as I could, but my heart was thumping. There was no way I could get the bestiary out now. I would have to come back.

She waited in the tower, leaving the doors between us open. She turned away from me as she looked toward the window. I swallowed. My mouth was dry with nerves. I was still holding the bestiary. If she turns back, I thought, I'll reshelve it, but she didn't. I draped my coat over my arm, so it covered the manuscript. I would take my chances, I thought, and try to walk out with it. It was reckless but I didn't have any better ideas.

I left the manuscript room, shut the door behind me, and heard the lock click. "Ready," I said, praying she couldn't hear the fear in my voice.

As I followed her downstairs, I felt the camera's eye on me. I knew it was possible that what I'd done had been seen already if someone was watching the security footage live, and I could feel a hand on my shoulder in the next few moments. Even if they reviewed it later, it was surely only a matter of time before they would come after me. Terrified of letting the coat slip from my arm, I picked up my phone and laptop awkwardly, but the housekeeper didn't seem to notice. She was ahead of me, preoccupied with getting me out of there as quickly as possible.

The castle felt bigger than ever, the route to the main exit neverending. There was no one in the dining room and the florist had gone. Outside, all the vehicles had been cleared from the drive. I stood on the steps. It was freezing, but sweat beaded on my hairline and under my arms.

The housekeeper said, "If you wait here, the car will come round in a minute."

It felt like I waited for an eternity. It was dusky out there, the moon visible, rising above the trees just like it had on my first visit here. Floodlights snapped on, bringing the building to life as darkness swaddled it. Eventually the car came, and the driver hustled me in quickly. I didn't know her, but she seemed harassed. I sat in the back and hugged the manuscript to my chest, trying to look calm, to quiet my breathing. The car took off down the drive, much faster than usual. I heard the crackle of a voice from the driver's earpiece, and she braked hard.

Lights and noise filled the sky as a chopper appeared suddenly from behind the trees and then banked sharply and landed on the field beside the driveway, coming down right in front of us, its blades bowing the grass, severing leaves from nearby trees. As soon as the blades stopped turning, the driver hit the gas and my head snapped back. The gates opened automatically as we approached at speed. I looked back as we slowed momentarily to turn onto the lane.

Magnus was getting out of the helicopter. I was sure it was him, even in the semidark. And as he did, Tracy emerged from the castle to meet him. When he reached her, they kissed like lovers.

I was shocked but not surprised. It confirmed what he'd hinted at and it intensified my disgust for him. When I turned back to face the front the driver was watching me in the rearview mirror. I had the feeling I wasn't supposed to have seen any of that, but they hadn't got me out of there in time.

As we drove through the countryside, I hugged the manuscript tighter. Surely I wasn't going to get away with taking it. What if Magnus wanted to look at his books while he was here?

I'd seen a similar manuscript sell at auction. Whether Mum was right about the glossary and the Voynich or not, I'd just made off with roughly three million pounds' worth of my father's property.

Sid

Alone in the cottage for the first time in a few days, Sid felt claustrophobic and afraid. The shocking news about Diana's death didn't help.

It weighed on him that he hadn't told Anya what he'd read online about Folio 9, but he told himself he'd done the right thing. A single comment on a message board wasn't proof that Folio 9 was forged, of course, but if he mentioned it, it could get under her skin and fuel her insecurities, which was the last thing she needed. He still felt it was best to see what more he could find out before saying anything. He was very much hoping to discover that it wasn't true. If it was, Anya would be deeply embarrassed at best, and, more likely, devastated.

But first, he wanted to talk to Mel, the private investigator, again. He wanted to tell her what Paul had said about Zofia, because he didn't think she knew that another young woman had gone missing. On his way to the lab he knocked on her door. She didn't answer, and when he peered through the window the cottage looked empty. He'd call or message her later, he decided, if she wasn't back when he got home.

Moving on, he found himself glancing over his shoulder as he walked and scanning faces in every group of students he passed or stood among as he waited to cross the road.

When he reached the lab he found a quiet cubicle and tried to revisit the dark web chat about Folio 9, but it had been deleted.

Every nerve in his body jangled. He tried more searches, desperate to learn anything useful about Folio 9 or about Zofia, but couldn't find anything. It was getting dark as he walked back to the cottage. He called next door again but Mel wasn't back. Anya wasn't home, either, and he hadn't heard from her.

He searched for Mel's card but he'd mislaid it. While he waited for her and for Anya, he went to his office and attempted to work on Lucis, but all he could think about was the possibility that the walls had eyes. Their little paradise was a panopticon.

The waiting got so painful that he took a walk. Students were in the shops, buying dinner, or gathering in pubs and bars. He wandered the center for a while, but the crowds were too much, and he found himself drawn to the quieter streets, then heading in the direction of Paul and Giulia's home. He thought he might try to talk to Paul again. He needed more clarity. At the very least it would be helpful to have Zofia's surname.

There were lights on in their house. As Sid approached, Giulia appeared at the window, looking out, and Sid froze. He was partially hidden by parked vehicles, and the birch in her yard had just enough leaves on it to obscure her view of him. He watched her as she stared up the street toward the ruins. It was a shock to see her in person now that he knew she wasn't who she said she was. It had been one thing to learn it, but it felt more real, more of a deception now that she was in front of him. She looked put together, as usual, though her expression was peculiarly blank and hard, and he wondered how Diana's death had affected her. She didn't seem to see him, but Sid stayed stock-still until she'd lowered the blinds, then backed away so as not to have to walk past the house and took the long route back to the cottage.

The windows in Mel's cottage were dark and Anya still wasn't home. He waited awhile, nerves building, and sent Anya a message to which she didn't reply. His anxiety escalated.

He was searching again for Mel's card, when blue light filled the cottage suddenly, bright and eerie, pulsating, startling him. It came from the back lane. His stomach lurched even though he knew it probably had nothing to do with him. He ran out of the back gate and toward the commotion.

An ambulance and police car were parked in front of the cathedral complex, lights revolving. The chain securing the gates had been severed and two police officers were on site, walking toward the ruins with flashlights. A dog walker watched from the pavement, his face pale with shock. "I saw someone on top of the ruins," he said. "Walking toward the tower. And—" He was visibly shaken up.

"*Jesus*," Sid said. He entered the site. Nobody told him not to. The police raked the ruins with the beams of their flashlights. Sid followed, his heart in his mouth. The flashlight beams converged to illuminate the stump of a column. A body lay broken over it, limbs abnormally crooked, neck bent back unnaturally over the edge of the stone, eyes open but seeing nothing.

It wasn't Anya. He almost vomited with relief, but as he got closer, he realized it was Paul, and he did retch then, painfully and as silently as he could, before backing away into the darkness so he wouldn't be seen.

It was enough. Enough people dying, disappearing. He needed to find Anya now.

At the gate, more people had gathered, rubbernecking. Sid avoided it. He climbed the wall to get out and tried to call Anya as he walked the few hundred yards home. She didn't answer. His nerves were stretched so taut he felt like he might snap, but as he got closer to home, he saw her getting out of a car at the end of Gregory Lane and the relief almost brought him to tears.

He waited in the shadows until the car had pulled away before he stepped out, then he put his arm around her as if he was hugging her and whispered in her ear that they had to leave. Now. He wasn't going to risk them staying another moment in that place.

In the filmy darkness he could see the whites of her eyes. Beneath his arm he could feel her tension. She nodded and tilted her head to whisper back.

"We grab only what we need. We're not coming back."

He stiffened. It was like she already knew they had to go. He dreaded to think why, but there was no time to ask.

Inside, he picked up their passports, his laptop, and the car keys and couldn't think of anything else that mattered. All he needed was Anya.

His car was parked down the street. He glanced back at the cottage as they were getting in. A pair of young women stood outside their front door. He recognized them. Before he could warn Anya, she slammed the car door shut, and their heads turned toward the sound in unison.

Sid jumped in, got the car started. In the rearview mirror he saw the women running toward the car. They were fast. He pulled away, foot down. The last Sid saw of them as he braced himself to take a corner as fast as he dared was a pair of dusky silhouettes in the middle of the road and a flash as one of them photographed the car's license plate.

Anya

We wanted to get as far away from St. Andrews as possible but were worried Sid's car could be traced. We drove to Edinburgh and left the car on a residential street in the suburbs and walked until we found a hotel.

The journey was grim as we exchanged news of Paul's death, and of what Mum had told me and what I had done. Once we'd checked into our room, I tried to call Mum even though she'd told me not to. I wanted to tell her I had the bestiary. She didn't answer.

"Viv should have given her phone back by now," I said.

Sid shook his head. "I don't trust her."

I phoned the ward number and it rang and rang. Sid said, "It's probably shift changeover time, maybe try again in a bit," but I held on, gripping the handset so hard my knuckles whitened, until eventually they answered. "Your mum's fine. She's asleep," the nurse told me.

"Can you tell her I called?" I asked, and she promised she would.

The hotel room was small and basic. Sid double-locked the door and closed the curtains. I laid the bestiary on the bed.

"Holy shit," he said.

The book was bound using two boards, front and back. Embossed leather was glued onto the outside of each cover, and plain parchment on the inside. I used my fingernail to separate the parchment from the front cover.

Carefully, I eased out four small sheets of vellum covered in writing. I did the same for the back cover and extracted another four sheets.

It was just as Mum had said. It was unbelievable.

My hand shook as I put the pages together. I was holding a glossary, a list of words translated from Voynichese into Latin in closely written text. I checked the binding again. As Mum had said, there was one more thing hidden there: a letter, written in Latin.

It felt like a miracle that they'd survived. At first glance there were enough words listed in the glossary that I should be able to translate the entire Voynich manuscript. It would take time, but I felt confident that it could be done.

"This is huge," I said.

"What does this say?" Sid was looking at the letter.

I took it from him. It was written in Renaissance Latin. I could read parts of it easily, but others would take some work.

"It talks about a manuscript, which must be the Voynich, although this refers to it as the *Liber mulierum*, which means the *Book of Women*."

"So where does the name 'Voynich' come from?"

"From a guy who bought the manuscript off the Jesuits in the early twentieth century and spent the rest of his life trying to hawk it for maximum profit because he was convinced there was something special about it. But he failed; there were no takers. It was still in his possession when he died, and it was eventually gifted to Yale. *Liber mulierum* is a really interesting name for it, because there are pages of pictures of naked women in the Voynich and nobody knows what they're supposed to represent. That title reminds me of another famous medieval text called *Liber de sinthomatibus mulierum*, which means *The Book of the Conditions of Women*. It's basically an OB-GYN book for medieval midwives. My father actually has a copy of it in his collection. But this is fascinating because it could suggest that the Voynich was written specifically for women."

"How old do you think the gloss and the letter are?"

I pointed to the last line of the letter. Sid read it out.

It was the author's sign-off, in brown ink dark enough that I thought it must be made from oak galls, just like the ink in the Voynich.

Vale. 5 Iunius 1461.

"June 5, 1461," I said.

"Vale?" he asked. "Is that who wrote it?"

"It's pronounced 'vah-lay,'" I said. "It's a Latin sign-off. It means 'goodbye.' I can't see the author's name, but perhaps when I translate it, I'll find it." I had butterflies in my stomach. This was historical treasure.

"How long will that take?"

"A few hours for a rough translation."

"Do it."

Sid emptied the minibar of snacks and sodas to keep us going, and I got to work. As the night ran into the small hours the character of the letter writer emerged and made itself known with unexpected strength. She was a woman, unnamed, and was in turns witty, learned, and bitter.

By the time I finished Sid was dozing beside me, and I nudged him awake.

"Have you done it?" he asked.

I was buzzing. "It's just like Mum said, I think this writer is implying that the Voynich is the key to something else, and it might be another book."

CHAPTER FOURTEEN

Anya

Sid and I abandoned the car and took the train to London very early the next morning. We'd had only a couple of hours' rest. It was still dark when we hurried on foot to the station beneath the glow of Edinburgh's streetlamps, our footsteps overly loud on the cobbles, street cleaners hosing the pavements slick, rain spitting.

We found seats and fell asleep. After a few hours I woke to find I had an email from an unknown address. The subject line caught me.

To: Anya Brown
From: RB
Subject: READ CAREFULLY, ANYA
Date: September 23, 2024

My darling girl,

They told me you called last night. You'll want to know how I am. I'm feeling much better today, so don't worry.

I don't have much time to write this, and I'm doing so on another borrowed phone. I don't have mine back yet. The lovely young man who cleans my room helped me set up this email address and use his phone.

Everything I'm about to confess is true. Believe it. There's no time for doubt. Delete this after reading it.

I should start by explaining how the glossary came to me.

A few years before I met your father, I attended a conference organized by the Society of Bookbinders. I was there because I wanted to hear a woman called Josephine Dunne speak. She was very elderly by then, and a legend in our business because she was a female pioneer in the industry. She was also well known to be very reclusive, so it felt like a once-in-a-lifetime opportunity.

At the conference Josephine ran a daylong seminar and workshop for women bookbinders. Attendance was selective, we had to apply in writing and with examples of our work. I was delighted to be accepted, alongside just three others, and even more delighted when she apparently took a shine to me, approaching me at the end of the session and asking me, and only me, to come to tea with her. The others were jealous, but I didn't care. She was my heroine.

She told me so many stories when we were alone together that afternoon and asked me so many questions. When we parted, she gave me a gift: a red leather bookmark she'd made that day as part of a demonstration during our workshop. It was made from the softest leather and tooled in gold with a beautiful design. She made a few that day, to demonstrate different techniques, each with a different Shakespeare quote on it. "Coronet weeds," this one said. Do you remember it? When you were a child, I kept it in the little drawer in my workshop, the one you loved to rummage through.

About a month after Josephine's funeral, and out of the blue, a courier arrived at my studio in Cambridge and handed over a package. Then I understood that she'd been vetting me that day.

The package contained the glossary, an old letter written in Latin, and a note from Josephine explaining that, together, the glossary and the old letter were the key to decoding the Voynich manuscript.

I could hardly believe it. Suddenly to find yourself in possession of the key to unlock one of the most enigmatic manuscripts in existence was quite astounding, but her note warned me that there was far more to it than that.

Josephine wrote that the glossary was important not just because it was the key to decoding the Voynich, *but because the Voynich is the key to finding something else*. Something far more valuable and important. She didn't say what it was, but she wrote, "Lives have been ruined or lost searching for this object and for that reason it's best that it's never found."

She told me I should hide the glossary and the letter somewhere no one would find them and keep them hidden for as long as I could. She'd chosen me to bear this responsibility, she said, because she had no daughter of her own or any other female descendants and it was important both artifacts were in the care of someone who could understood their power and who knew how to keep them safe.

I didn't know about that. Nor did I know what to make of any of it or even whether to take it seriously. It sounded unreal. But the woman I remembered wasn't a fantasist, and her reputation as a pioneer and a craftswoman was stellar. I decided that whatever I thought of her claims for the glossary, I would honor her wishes.

A solution presented itself. It so happened that the glossary and the letter appeared at my studio a few days before that short window of time when I had access to your father's collection of manuscripts. I knew that it wasn't uncommon to find the remnants of old manuscripts in the bindings of newer ones—I'd made some discoveries like that myself—so I decided to do the same with the glossary and the letter, as you've hopefully found out by now. I carefully took the glossary apart and hid the pieces, and the letter, within another book. It was the most secret place I could think of, and the safest, because your grandfather had installed extraordinary measures to safeguard the collection. Magnus never suspected a thing. Nor did anyone else. I was hopeful that I'd done my bit and that I could leave the book there for years, decades, without having to think of it again.

My sense of security didn't last long. Within weeks I found out I was pregnant with you and my relationship imploded. A few months later strange things began to happen to me. There were hang-ups on my landline and a couple of nights when I was certain someone followed me home from my studio. One morning I found the body of a mutilated owl on my doorstep, a beautiful creature. I was terrified. I knew it wasn't coincidence. It was a message. Josephine had run a tiny independent publishing house called the Owl Press. Someone else wanted the glossary, and they'd found me.

Women are tigresses, never more so than when pregnant, and never more so than when the father of their child has told them he wants nothing more to do with them. I was beside myself with worry. I thought they might hurt me and that I might lose you.

I didn't want the responsibility for the glossary or the letter any longer; I didn't think I was the right person. I wanted to give them to someone else, but I'd lost the ability to access them. Your father had rejected me so completely, I couldn't even think of a way to get myself inside the family home, let alone his library.

There was only one solution I could think of: destroy them. I didn't care if I was destroying history, as long as that meant I could keep my child safe. I waited until nobody was home, and I burned your father's library down.

It was the most terrifying and necessary thing I've ever done, but afterward I was able to sleep at night, knowing that you and I were safer.

But imagine how I've felt over the past few days, knowing that the glossary and letter survived because the book I hid them in had been moved before the library burned. Knowing that you have been recruited to work on it. Knowing that someone has pieced some or all of this together and is using you.

Terror doesn't describe it adequately.

I introduced you to my world because I hoped it would give you joy. I never dreamed it would put you in such danger. When I disabled the fire protection system your grandfather installed, and I lit that flame, when I ran from it and felt its heat on my back after it grew large, and hungry, when I knew the glossary would soon be ashes, I thought I'd saved myself and you.

Josephine told me that some objects hold tremendous power. Not because of what they are, but because of what they represent. The glossary and the letter are two such objects. I don't know why. I only know that the people who want them are very dangerous and have powerful backing.

If you've managed to find them, you should put a match to them and finish what I started.

It's the only solution to keep you out of danger.

Whatever you do, don't come to me. They will know where I am. You should go into hiding for a while. You're resourceful and brilliant. I know you can do it. It won't be forever.

If all this sounds melodramatic, or crazy, it isn't. I may be unwell, but I'm still sharp, and I'm the person who cares most about you in the world. I love you so much.

One more thing. Don't contact me, either. Not for a while. It's too dangerous. If I don't hear from you, I'll know you're safe. Nothing else will persuade me you are. But I will be sending love, as always and forever.

Mum xxxx

Viv

Viv sat quietly beside Rose's bed as the doctor examined her chart. He was a very good-looking man, very distinguished. She sat up a little straighter, but he didn't look at her. He was focused on Rose.

"How are we feeling today, Mrs. Brown?" he asked.

"It's Ms. Brown, and not too good. I had a bad night," Rose said.

Viv glanced at Rose, surprised. Viv hadn't been at the hospital long this morning, but Rose looked much better than yesterday, even if she was a little quiet. Viv had put that down to Rose being upset that Viv hadn't brought her phone to the hospital. "I'm so sorry," Viv had told her when Rose asked for it. "I was rushing to tidy the house before I left, and I forgot to grab it." She hadn't, of course. The phone was in her handbag, which was sitting at her feet, but Viv didn't want Rose to have it just now.

He stabbed a finger at her chart. "Judging from this, I should say you're ready to go home today, aren't you?" he asked. "Have you had any new symptoms overnight?"

Rose hesitated. "No," she said. Viv frowned at her reluctant tone. Rose was normally desperate to get home from the hospital. Viv didn't like the way that Rose was looking at her, either. It was like Rose was assessing her. Suspecting her? Viv didn't think she'd given Rose any reason to, but Rose was sharp.

"Just a bad night's sleep then," the doctor said, "in which case I'm happy to discharge you. I'll write up some antibiotics for you to take home with you. Do you live alone?"

"No," Rose said. She didn't meet Viv's eye. Viv took note of that, too, but if Rose was becoming suspicious, it was nothing Viv couldn't handle, nothing she hadn't planned for.

"I live with her," she said, and the doctor nodded approvingly. "Excellent. Then you're all set."

"I'll be back in a second," Viv mouthed to Rose as the doctor gave the nurse some instructions. Rose nodded. Viv went to the visitor bathroom on the ward and locked herself in. She used the encrypted app the Order had installed on her phone to send a message to her mentor:

They're discharging her today.

She got an immediate reply:

You know what to do.

Anya

King's Cross Station was crowded when Sid and I got off the train. I was still reeling from Mum's email. We wove through the crowds to the exit and crossed the road straight into St. Pancras Station next door and then out the other side of it, to the British Library.

It was the best place I could think to hide while I studied the glossary and the letter more closely.

Sid settled in the café. I had a reader's card for the library, so I went to the manuscript room, where you could hear a pin drop among the low stacks, and each desk was furnished with a cushion to rest the precious books on. A few other readers had heads bent over their work. The librarians worked quietly behind their desks. The slow mechanisms of library life were familiar and soothing; I felt my head clear.

I was tempted to dive into the glossary but decided to refine my translation of the letter first, to fill in gaps where I hadn't been able to find the right words last night.

After a couple of hours, my neck and shoulders had seized up, but my translation was done. It was still clumsy—I couldn't capture the fine, nuanced Latin of the original in such a short time—but it was a finished draft, and once again I was captivated by the voice of the letter's author. I felt as if she were whispering to me across the centuries, and it moved me.

> *To my sisters of the future,*
>
> *I have been reluctant to write, delaying the moment of change, but to remain so would constitute a sin against women.*
>
> *There is a book,* The Book of Wonder, *an ornament of our sex, that has been hidden from men who are prone to ridicule women, in word and deed. This book encapsulates such power, such knowledge, such excellence and eloquence that men would take offense if they knew of it. It exists to nourish women, to nurture them and feed their courage, their very souls.*
>
> *It came into the possession of my aunt, a virtuous, extraordinary woman of great learning. The book was her most prized possession, but my aunt came to fear for its safety. She was afraid of the jealousy and destruction of men, so she hid* The Book of Wonder *out of their reach.*
>
> *She then bade her nieces, my sisters and me, to help her encode its resting place so that it would never be lost to the women of our family.*
>
> *Our* Book of Women *carefully folds the location of the other volume into its pages.*
>
> *To make demanding the task of finding what is hidden, we sisters*

tested ourselves to elaborate on a silly, whimsical family language, first invented by us girls to communicate beyond the reach of our tutors and our brothers.

Beyond their gaze, our aunt provided money to buy us parchments and ink from her bookseller. Two sisters had the talent to draw and illuminate God's creation on its pages, and when walls confined us in the city, women as we are, our good friend the artist who painted our other sister in fur and cloth resplendent and pure among salamander, horse's rump, and dragon's-kill bones allowed her the perusal of his sketchbooks, where chalk and line were, unknown to him, muse for our book.

That done, we four sisters and our aunt tasked our fair hands with the job of scribes to write the book in our secret language, using every technique and discipline our tutor instilled in us.

But now, as age and poor health soften my courage and my memory, I share my aunt's fear that as one generation gives way to another the means to find The Book of Wonder *will be lost to our family. Our language has not been passed on to my sisters' daughters, and I have no offspring. The chain will break.*

I have asked often in my life, what can I, a woman, do? As I lie facing death, I narrow the question. What can I do to preserve this secret for our sisters of the future?

I answered thus.

I will gift this knowledge to the good women of the wider world. I will send the Book of Women *in the company of a gray lady who will travel north with it to Augsburg and lodge it in the silence and safety of her order there. I will send with it this glossary, which reveals the working of our family's private language. Thus, I offer to all sisters of the future a means to translate the* Book of Women *and thereby to find* The Book of Wonder.

And for this effort, this gift, indulge me now, for I have a sweet dream of the woman who has the skills to translate our words and read our Book of Women.

May she be worthy to lift its finer sister, The Book of Wonder, *from its cell and use it for good for the other women of the world.*

I dream that this worthy woman looks at the world through the eyes of a lynx, not a rabbit. I dream that the world she lives in rushes to offer a woman like her abundance, prosperity, and kindness, not bitterness or chains, that it doesn't entrap her with men's words that conjure only weakness and insufficiency out of her existence.

Across time, I long to touch hands with you, dear friend, with your wondrous flashing gaze. If you have the mind for it, I gladly offer you this glossary with this letter, both together the key to find The Book of Wonder.

To you, dear sister in time, I ask, indulge me one small thing, in return for this. Before you seek the greater prize, first enjoy the flavors of our family in these pages, the sketches of our days, of our laughter, our love, our whimsy, our innumerable squabbles. Allow a moment in time for our souls to shine again, however fleetingly. Let sunshine bathe the meadows, fields, and flowers of Cyanum once more.

But when the moment comes to sharpen your attention and pull back the veil to reveal the location of The Book of Wonder, *then it will be the last page of our* Book of Women *that commands you, and with it the page of nine circles.*

Read well. Read with lightning in your eyes.

Vale.

June 5, 1461

The Book of Wonder. It must be what the Institute was looking for.

I scanned the letter again. Several things leaped out. I needed to think about each of them in turn. I started with the stuff that sounded strangest, feeling as if I was trying to solve one of Mum's riddles.

Salamander. Horse's rump. Dragon's-kill bones. A woman in fur and cloth. An artist's sketches. It didn't take my memory long to place the images. These were all elements of a fresco I'd seen.

Its subject was St. George and the Dragon and it was painted by an artist called Pisanello. I remembered that half of the fresco was well preserved and that it included horses, one with its back facing outward, and a princess beside it, finely robed, in profile. The other half was badly damaged, but still visible, though barely, were a salamander and the remains of the dragon's kill.

I googled it, confirming it was located where I thought: on the wall of the Pellegrini Chapel in a church in Verona, Italy. I dug into the identity of the woman in it. She was supposed to represent the princess of Trebizond, from the St. George legend, and at first, I couldn't find anything about who might have modeled for it, but then it popped up, a small piece of research suggesting that a woman recently engaged to one of the sons of the Pellegrini family may be depicted in the fresco. Her name was Laura Nogarola.

I looked her up. She was from a large and prominent family in fifteenth-century Verona. She had many siblings and a famous aunt, as the letter suggested: Angela Nogarola, a poet. She also had a very famous sister: Isotta. I clicked on a link to her bio.

Isotta was a well-educated and brilliant feminist writer, a clear voice advocating for women all the way from fifteenth-century Italy. The more I read about her, the more I became convinced she was the letter writer and that she and her aunt and sisters had coauthored the Voynich manuscript.

The reference to a "gray lady" caught my attention, too. The description of her taking the Voynich to Augsburg and leaving it in the safekeeping of her "order" suggested she was a religious woman, probably a nun. I knew it was a journey she could have made in the fifteenth century. Centuries earlier, the Romans had built a road over the Alps directly connecting Verona to Augsburg.

I discovered an order of women who went by the name of beguines and who typically wore gray habits. They owned a network of female-only houses and convents across Europe at the time, including a property in Augsburg. This fit what was known about the

Voynich, too. I found an article claiming that long before Voynich himself got his hands on it and gave it his name, this strange book might have been owned by a doctor who lived in Augsburg. It wasn't a huge leap to think he could have somehow got it from the beguines.

I was pretty much convinced already that Isotta was the mystery author of the letter, but I found one more piece of proof.

The word "Cyanum" had leaped out at me. I knew it related to the nymph Cyane from ancient mythology but not what it might have meant to Isotta, if anything. I dug deeper and found a collection of letters and poems that she'd written. Among them was one titled "Elegy on the Countryside Around the Spring of Cyanum."

I read an analysis of the poem. It noted that the verses referenced the Nogarola family's country home, just outside Verona, comparing its location to the mythical and beautiful setting of Cyane's spring. Isotta's obvious love of nature also fit with the pages of botanical illustrations in the Voynich.

Evidence was mounting beyond doubt. I needed to tell Sid what I'd learned.

I packed up quickly and found him in the café downstairs. I showed him the fresco and my translation. As he looked at both, I told him what I'd discovered, leaning across the table, keeping my voice low, aware of all the people sitting around us.

"I've worked out who wrote this letter. I'm certain it's a woman called Isotta Nogarola, a famous poet and scholar from fifteenth-century Verona. She was from a prominent noble family. Amazingly for the time, she and her sisters were all educated to the same level as their brothers so they could easily have done this. I wonder if anyone has ever considered that the Voynich manuscript could have been made by women."

Sid listened carefully as I told him everything, taking it all in. When I'd finished, he had a question: "So if this *Book of Women* that Isotta mentions in her letter is the Voynich manuscript, what's the nine-circle page she talks about?"

"I think I know that, too."

We went onto the Beinecke Library's website and pulled up their scans of the Voynich, and I found the famous rosette page, a foldout with nine circles, one in the center and the others arranged around it at regular intervals, each linked to its neighbor with fantastical drawings.

We pored over the screen together. Now that I had Isotta in mind as the author of the letter, I saw all sorts of details in the manuscript that suddenly made sense. "There's so much here that fits with the Voynich being made in Verona," I told Sid. "See this little castle here?" There was a small line drawing of a tower and some battlements, almost hidden among the more indecipherable imagery. "The crenellations in that drawing is unusual; they're called swallowtail or fishtail merlons because of their shape. You don't find them everywhere, but they're all over Verona."

I showed him a photograph of Verona's Castelvecchio, a castle with a famous bridge beside it. Both structures had stunning swallowtail merlons.

"These were built before Isotta was born," I said. "You can find merlons like these in quite a few locations in northern Italy and southern Germany, and in some places in France and Switzerland, too, but the coincidence with the Nogarolas must relate these in the Voynich to Verona. And look at the pictures of domed buildings in the central rosette. You see architecture like that in Venice, which Nogarola definitely visited, but also in Verona." I clicked back to the image of Pisanello's St. George fresco and pointed to the fantastical buildings at the top. "See here: there are even similar domed buildings in this fresco, which, incidentally, was painted in around 1435, precisely the period when they estimate the Voynich was made, based on scientific analysis of the parchment. Everything fits!"

"So, what, we need to go to Verona now?" Sid laughed but he'd voiced what I was thinking, and I was deadly serious about it.

"Why not? What else are we going to do? I don't think going

abroad is the worst idea right now. We have our passports. What's stopping us?" I paused. The gravity of our situation weighed heavy. I knew I was going to go, with or without him. "I *need* to do this, Sid. For Mum. For us."

"How do you explain any of this to your dad? Won't he be trying to find you?"

He had a point. I had no idea if the women who'd chased us as we drove away from the cottage were working for Magnus, or for the Institute. But deceiving my father was a risk I would have to take if I was going to do this. "I'll tell him I'm traveling for research. He doesn't have to know where. He might buy it for a day or two."

Sid didn't look sure, and neither was I, but I couldn't see I had any other option. People were hunting for me, for us, but I thought that if I could find *The Book of Wonder* before they found me, it could help us bargain our way out of danger. Even if I was wrong, I didn't have any better ideas.

Sid nodded and I felt a surge of enthusiasm and of hope. We looked up cheap flights. By 4 p.m. we were on a train to Stansted Airport, and by 6 p.m. we'd held our breaths as we passed through security, with the bestiary hidden in my bag, purchased toiletries, booked ourselves an apartment in Verona that we couldn't afford, drunk a beer at the bar, and were about to board.

For those few hours, we were energized by an illusion of control, a feeling of unstoppable momentum.

I had a window seat on the plane. As we took off, London shrank and flattened below us. We were rising through a blanket of clouds when reality bit. A clock was ticking. At any moment we could be traced to Verona. At any moment, Mum might need me, and I wouldn't be there. Also staring me in the face was the fact that I didn't know exactly what we were looking for in Verona. All I had was a *feeling* that I might find something and that could amount to nothing.

The plane banked as it turned toward Europe and juddered as

the dense cloud cover enveloped us. I shut my eyes and squeezed Sid's hand. This felt incredibly reckless.

Clio

Clio sat in her flat. It was evening, dark, but she hadn't put the light on or shut the curtain. Best no one knew she was home. She'd left Geoff's house earlier with alarm bells clamoring.

She sat cross-legged on the floor, her laptop on her knees, working in its glow and that of the streetlamp right outside her second-floor window, which settled a sticky orange light over everything around her.

She hit the Zoom link that Zofia had sent her. Zofia appeared in front of the same blurred background as before.

"I can't be long," she said. "And I can't do this again."

Clio nodded.

"But I looked at the embroidery, and the poem. If you put the two pieces of the embroidery together there's still a chunk missing, I think about half a centimeter where it's frayed." Clio nodded. She'd seen that when she'd tried. "But you see a few things. There's some lettering I don't have an explanation for, and the portraits I can't identify in such a short time. Because they're of women, it's less likely we can find a name for them because history rarely records the names of women. What I can tell you is that there are two heraldry shields in that section in the middle. One got ripped through and it's impossible to get anything from it. The other is damaged but complete and I think I might know which family it relates to. Honestly, I'm not sure I would have figured it out without the clue I got from Eleanor Bruton's poem, the line that says, 'He who on the ladder has the sacred bird displayed.'" Clio nodded, and Zofia went on. "So, I think, if you look carefully, that we can just make out the outline of a ladder in this shield and there are a set of bird wings above it, both of which are mentioned in the poem. Do you see?"

Clio peered at the photograph on her phone. "I *think* so," she said but it was really hard to tell.

"The ladder and eagle are emblems for the Della Scala family, from Verona, in Italy," Zofia said. "A very famous family. They ruled Verona for centuries. And look, the blue and the yellow? Those are the colors of the city of Verona. The Della Scala family was famous for hosting the poet Dante when he visited Verona. Okay? So, I was looking at Dante. This is what he wrote: 'Your first refuge and your first inn shall be the courtesy of the great Lombard, he who on the ladder bears the sacred bird.'"

"That's a line in Eleanor Bruton's poem!" Clio said.

"And the man who hosted Dante was a powerful aristocrat called Cangrande. Which in English means Big Dog. Eleanor Bruton had worked out that this came from Verona, I think."

"Wow," Clio said. "Thank you."

"That's all I have on the embroidery, but I think it has more stories to tell. It was nice to see it. It's very rare to have a book covered in fabric at this time from Italy. It was more common in England."

"Do you think we can find out who the women in the portraits are?" Clio asked.

"I would need a library. It's too risky for me to do more. I left all this behind for a reason."

Clio heard the plea in her voice. "I understand," she said. "Thanks so much for everything."

"Can you promise me something?"

"Try me."

"Will you look after the new girl? I have a Google alert, and I know the Institute just hired someone. A young academic. I'm worried for her."

"Of course. What's her name?"

"Dr. Anya Brown."

In the quiet after the call ended, Clio looked up Dr. Brown. There was an impressive press release about her work, including a photo of a young woman with a sweet but hesitant smile. She'd only just started at the Institute. Clio wanted to talk to her, but she needed to know a bit about her first. You could find a lot of murk beneath the surface of even the nicest-looking people. The easiest way to do it would be to run Anya's name through the systems at work, but she couldn't log on from her flat.

She messaged Izzy, asking her if she'd do it, without explanation, and waited nervously for the reply, wondering if it was too soon to ask a favor.

She got a quick reply. Can you talk?

Sure, Clio wrote back.

Give me five.

She picked up on the first ring. Izzy was clearly outside. Wind whistled down the line.

"I just stepped out of the office," she said.

"You're working late."

"Yeah. Listen, I take it you're still interested in the St. Katherine case?"

"Definitely."

"The boss is going up to St. Andrews to interview the staff at the Institute. I overheard him talking about it. One of the lecturers' husbands just died in suspicious circumstances. His body was found on the site of some old ruins. Suspected suicide. It looks as if he climbed up there and threw himself off. His partner said he'd been struggling with his mental health for a while. Autopsy is happening tomorrow."

"Seriously?"

"That's not all. This Anya Brown you asked me about has gone away."

"Isn't it the beginning of term?"

"Maybe it's a work trip or something personal, but the boss thinks it's odd."

"Do we know where she went?"

"I thought you might ask. I did some checking. She boarded a flight at Stanstead an hour ago; she's due to land in Italy in forty minutes."

"Where in Italy?" Clio felt the buzz she got when the pieces of an investigation began to slot together, even if she couldn't see the big picture yet.

"Verona."

"Huh," Clio said.

"Also, the boss wanted to know what we looked at in the evidence room. He was being weird about it."

"What did you tell him?" Clio held her breath.

"I told him we signed everything out, but didn't have a chance to examine it before he called to let me know I was off the case."

"Thanks."

"He let slip that he already knew how long we'd had the evidence out for. He'd checked."

"Do me a favor, Izzy, keep your head down, don't change that story, and don't show any interest in that case. You need to be deaf, dumb, and blind around it, okay?"

Izzy was silent for a beat, then spoke softly, "Understood."

"You and I should stop speaking, for now. If anyone knows we talked tonight, tell them I was calling to get advice on joining the criminal investigations division."

"But—"

"Just tell them that, Izzy. Got it?"

"Got it."

"And watch your back."

Clio hung up. The murky light in the flat seemed electric, suddenly, charged with danger.

After a few minutes thinking, she went back online and booked herself a flight to Italy first thing in the morning.

CHAPTER FIFTEEN

Anya

I woke early in the bedroom at the back of the apartment we'd rented in the heart of the ancient city of Verona. I'd slept surprisingly well, but I felt disoriented, and my nerves were humming.

Sid was already up, opening the shutters at the front. The apartment was on the second floor of an old palazzo, overlooking a cobbled pedestrian street not much wider than the Roman carriages it was designed for. Its ceilings were twelve feet high, the floors parquet. A balcony with a chunky stone balustrade ran along the front of it.

We opened the French doors and stepped out to take in the view of the shops and cafés, saw how the pavements were made from huge slabs of creamy and pale coral marble, softened and shined by centuries of footfall. Generous windows and handsome balconies ornamented the shoulder-to-shoulder buildings, life spilling from inside out on multiple levels, exactly as it must have done for centuries. The city felt brimming with life and style and wore its history in mellow colors: ochre and peach, dusty yellow and terra-cotta, shutters in greens and soft grays.

I turned to Sid. His eyes were shut, his face turned toward the rays of early sunshine.

"We definitely can't afford this place," I said.

He shrugged.

I set up at the kitchen table. I had my laptop to type the translation into and Sid's beside it, with the Voynich up on his screen. I also laid out the fragments of the glossary and pieced them back together.

We kept the internal door to the apartment double locked and fell quiet whenever we heard the scrape of feet on the stairwell or across the landing, breathing again when no one paused outside our door or knocked on it, but I left the French doors to the balcony open, because it made me feel part of the city. My senses absorbed its sounds and smells as I worked; I was breathing in the same air as Isotta Nogarola had.

I pored over the glossary, trying to puzzle out the meaning of the last paragraph of the Voynich manuscript. The glossary wasn't a dictionary, it only gave translations of a small selection of words, so I had to puzzle out the rest.

It really tested me. I felt as if I was working at the limits of my ability, and a voice in my head began to insist that I couldn't do it. Sid told me to ignore it. Mum would have said the same. I wished she were with us.

After a few hours I was done, my concentration shot. I wasn't finished but I needed a break. "Let's go out," I said. I wanted to walk the streets and see if I could find traces of the city that Isotta had known. I felt like it might help me.

The streets were full of stylish locals and rubbernecking tourists. We blended into the crowds feeling safer than we had in London, though not relaxed, and headed to the tourist office to pick up a map.

I had my eyes open for anything in the city that would have been there when Isotta was alive. I was trying to edit out the new and see it with her eyes. It was much easier than I'd anticipated. So much of Verona was ancient.

The tourist office was beside the Roman amphitheater, so we began there. We climbed up the chunky stone benches to sit at the top. We had a view of the hills around Verona and the whole of the oval amphitheater, set up for a concert that evening. Verona's church spires surrounded us. We saw swallowtail merlons on more than one building, which bolstered my feeling that we'd come to the right place.

Seated just below us was a well-dressed older woman, in chic dark glasses, her hair cut into a classy bob. She was with a much younger man—her son? He was beautiful, too. They looked away as we passed, but I felt a moment of jealousy that they could spend the day sightseeing without fear.

I forgot them once we'd left the arena. We had so much to see and absorb; I felt like the city was drawing me in. We started by visiting the churches. There were at least four or five that were already built when Isotta was born and that she would have known.

Everywhere we went, my excitement grew. We hunted down anything that could have inspired the Nogarolas. In the basilica of San Zeno, we saw a medieval clock that looked like a drawing in the Voynich; on the ceiling of the tiny San Zenetto there was frescoed foliage almost identical to a plant in the botanical section of the manuscript; in the ancient Christian church hidden beneath the newer church of San Fermo there were more echoes of Voynich imagery in the early Christian frescoes. After a few hours running around I'd seen traces of the manuscript everywhere in medieval Verona, in its architecture and in the detail of the surviving artworks.

There was also a surprise: Verona was a city shaped by water, and in more ways than one. The River Adige was ever present, bordering three sides of the ancient heart of the city, but Verona's churches and squares contained multiple fonts and fountains that could have inspired the mysterious bathing scenes in the manuscript. I didn't need any more convincing that we were where we needed to be.

We finished up at the Basilica of Santa Anastasia to see the Pisanello fresco in the flesh, craning our necks as we stared up at it. As high up as it was, it was still stunning. Sid was so absorbed in it that he stepped backward without looking where he was going and trod on a woman's foot. She yelped and I realized she was the same woman I'd seen in the amphitheater with her son, who was here with her, too. I noticed she wore a distinctive brooch on the lapel of her coat, a spiked wheel. It reminded me of the rose windows all around the city, and of the wheel of St. Katherine we'd seen in both a fresco and sculpture in the Castelvecchio museum.

Sid apologized, and I smiled at the woman, but she didn't smile back. She still had her dark glasses on, even in the relative gloom of the church. The man took her arm, and they walked away quickly. He was older than I'd first thought. Something about the moment left me feeling unsettled.

In the piazza outside Santa Anastasia, my phone buzzed with a message from Magnus that made my heart thump:

Where are you? I know what you've done.

Viv

Viv walked down the cottage garden and let herself into Rose's potting shed. It was musty in there, full of cobwebs. It was a long time since Rose had been well enough to use it. Viv shut the door and made a call.

"You've done well. Excellent work," her mentor said. The praise made Viv swell with pride. She felt replete with it. This is what happiness is, she thought. It's being both needed *and* appreciated.

"If Rose Brown is well enough to travel, we'll take her today," her mentor continued. "It's time."

"She's well enough."

"Good. We left you something to give her. Check where you leave the empty milk bottles. Slip one pill into her tea or coffee later today. Just one. We want her alive, for now. Message me as soon as it's done, and someone will be there within an hour to help you move her to the car. Don't try to do it yourself."

Viv hung up and took a pair of shears from the shed. Back in the house she put her head around the door of the sitting room. Rose was dozing in front of the television.

"It's such a lovely day, I thought I might do some pruning out the front," Viv said.

"You're a dream, Viv," Rose said. Viv hesitated. Was Rose's tone a bit off, again? Sarcastic, even? She felt a flicker of annoyance but let it go. No point in a petty argument now.

Tucked between the wire basket where they left the empties for the milkman and the cottage's crumbling wall, Viv found an envelope containing a foil strip of tablets. She slipped it into her pocket and spent a few minutes snipping at some whippy branches and one or two plants she thought were ugly.

She was excited. This was the first stage of the plan for Rose, and Viv's information had been instrumental in bringing them to this point. She hoped they would let her stay with Rose, even after they'd taken her from her home. Viv wanted to demonstrate that when the time came she could deliver on her promise that she was willing to end Rose's life if necessary. It could work wonders for her reputation in the Order.

When she was done, she went back inside and popped her head into the sitting room.

"Do you fancy a coffee, Rose?" she asked.

Rose wasn't smiling anymore. She'd propped herself up, frail as she was.

"Do I have a choice?" she asked.

Viv stared at her. So she knew. But it wasn't a problem. Rose was clever, but you could be as clever as you liked. It didn't matter if your body was failing you and you were dependent. Viv smiled and said, "Not really, dear. No."

Clio

Clio called in sick from the departures lounge at Heathrow Airport first thing in the morning, boarded her flight, and landed in Venice sixteen hours after Anya Brown had arrived in Verona.

She got off the water ferry at St. Mark's Square after a fierce internal debate over which was the lesser of two evils: coming to Italy when she'd called in sick in order to work an investigation she wasn't allowed near, or breaking international law by not informing the carabinieri she was here. She figured the odds of Tim finding out she was here were minimal, even if she did make contact with the local force. She was the only one on their team who had a contact here, from an old case. Better to risk it than to risk landing in an Italian jail if things went pear shaped.

She wove through throngs of tourists on St. Mark's Square to reach the huge wooden doors of the Carabinieri Command for the Protection of Cultural Heritage, on the square's south side, and pushed the tarnished brass buzzer. She intended to behave confidently, as she would if she'd been sent here officially. She didn't think anyone would bother to check. Each of the heavy wooden doors had an elaborate door knocker, a ram, with curved horns and a worried look on its face that Clio thought appropriate to her profession.

It turned out to be a pleasant and helpful visit. She spent a bittersweet half hour in their offices, marveling at the size and strength of their operation, the value they put on cultural heritage. It was something to aspire to, though she knew it would never happen in London.

Even better, her contact helpfully made a call to the force in Verona to let them know she'd be there. She was given permission to interview Anya Brown without oversight but warned that if she got a sniff of any laws being broken, including those involving cultural heritage, she should let him, or the local force, know immediately, and she'd have the full force of their resources behind her.

On the train from Venice to Verona she made a call she'd been thinking about all morning, to the British Museum, requesting CCTV footage from inside the museum on the morning she and Lillian had visited. It had been niggling at her that Lillian had taken her there. If the situation had been so dangerous, why do something so brazen when she could have just shown Clio a photograph of the embroidery or sent her a link to the Museum's catalog entry for the piece, where there was a high-resolution image?

The scenery from the train was a mix of industrial, beautiful—a clock tower in Padua, mountains, vineyards, a bridge over a wide, milky-green river near Vicenza, terraced hills embracing Verona—and voyeuristic, where the tracks ran behind private gardens and apartment buildings and she got glimpses into other people's lives.

There were two parts of her job that Clio took very seriously: upholding justice and protecting people from crime. It was why she was proud to call herself a police officer. She shifted uncomfortably in her seat. She couldn't shake her unease that she was breaking rules to be here now. Nor was it lost on her that she was starting to get a strong whiff of corruption, and she had no one to turn to.

As the announcer told her, first in Italian, then in English, that they were arriving in Verona, she received a message from her Italian contact: an address for where Anya Brown was staying.

Whatever else was going on, at least she could try to ensure this young woman remained safe.

Anya

"Ignore the message from Magnus," Sid said.

"I think he knows I took the bestiary."

"I agree, but please ignore it for now."

"He's powerful, Sid."

"I don't think he can possibly know you're here, for one, but also, he *needs* you, which means you have some agency. Don't forget that. You don't need to respond immediately."

I knew he was right, Magnus didn't have all the power, but I felt the creep of paranoia. "You know that woman whose foot you stepped on in the church? I saw her earlier, in the amphitheater."

"Verona's a small city. We're bound to see the same people doing the same things. There's a tourist circuit here."

"I think we should go back to the apartment for a bit." No matter what he said, I was suddenly nervous to be out on the street, and I felt like I'd seen enough to know that we were right to come here. Now I needed to go back to the manuscript and look at it with fresh eyes, to try to identify possible locations within the city where *The Book of Wonder* might be.

"Sure," Sid said. He took my hand as we walked. "Tell me about the last paragraph of the Voynich. What have you managed to figure out so far?"

I smiled. "It's kind of charming, like Isotta's letter. It talks about *The Book of Wonder* and explains that it's been hidden, and why. Like the letter, it refers the reader to the rosette page, that big fold-out page, and I *think* it says something along the lines of 'You can find it there.'"

"Meaning the rosette page contains clues for finding *The Book of Wonder*?"

"I think it might and in relation to the location, it mentions a word that I'm not sure how to interpret: 'tegumentum.' It means cover, or skin, sometimes clothing. It could refer to the book's original binding, but that's lost. The binding that's on the Voynich today was put on more recently. I'm also wondering if 'tegumentum' could mean something else. Sometimes old manuscripts were stored in bags."

"And this binding or cover could be the key to the location of *The Book of Wonder*?"

"It might be, but 'tegumentum' could also be a metaphor."

"Right. What about the words on the rosette page? Can they give a clue?"

"They seem to be names, but I can't make anything of that yet."

"It'll come. Give it time."

I wished I had his confidence in me. "But what if it doesn't? What if I'm only as good as my memory?"

He squeezed my hand. "Don't go there, Anya. Have faith."

We'd been walking along the banks of the river, not paying attention to where we were going, and found ourselves back near the Basilica of San Zeno, where we'd started out. I took a second look at the two ancient towers, one a typical pointed medieval tower, similar in style to a drawing on the rosette page of the Voynich, the other with swallowtail merlons, another echo of the manuscript. I looked up at the basilica's façade, at the rose window, shaped like a spoked wheel.

Images from the morning and from the manuscript flipped through my mind.

"Sid!" I pointed. "Do you see that window? It looks just like one of the circles on the Voynich rosette page. And remember the oval shape of the amphitheater? There's a shape like that on the rosette page, too. What if each of the rosettes represents a specific site in Verona?"

"Like a map?"

"Yes! Maybe!"

I needed to be off the streets, to write down my thoughts, draw connections, do more research on Verona's churches and sites, to be doubly certain which ones had existed in Isotta's time. There were already theories that the rosette page was a map, of the skies, the celestial bodies, or a geographic area, but as far as I knew, no one had suggested it was a map of a specific city.

We hurried back to the apartment, propelled by a new sense of urgency, or was it hope? The most dangerous emotion.

When we turned the corner onto our street, I grabbed Sid's arm. "Stop."

Standing outside the entrance of the building was a woman, her back to us, looking up at our balcony.

Clio

Clio sensed eyes on the back of her neck and turned to see a young couple, holding hands, watching her. The street was busy with people, passing through, shopping, chatting, laughing, but this pair stood still, staring, like deer in headlamps. She recognized Anya Brown and gave what she hoped was a small, friendly wave. She made her way toward them. They stayed where they were, though they looked ready to bolt, and Clio wondered why.

"Anya Brown?" she asked.

"Who's asking?" the man shot back.

She pulled a badge from her bag. "My name is Detective Constable Clio Spicer. I'm from the Scotland Yard Art and Antiques Squad. If you can spare me some time, I'd like to have a chat about Professor Diana Cornish."

"It's a long way to come for a chat," he said.

"And you are?" Clio smiled, kept her tone friendly, trying to defang his defensiveness.

"Sid Hill."

"Good to meet you, Sid. I'm here because it's an important case." True, even if she wasn't being entirely honest with them.

"Do you have jurisdiction here?" he asked.

Anya hadn't said a word yet. She was watching Clio intently.

"I don't. But I don't need it unless a crime has been committed. The local police know I'm here; you can check with them if you want. It's entirely up to you, Anya, as to whether you're willing to chat to me or not. We're just trying to get as rounded a picture of Diana and her associates and activities as possible."

"Sid, it's fine," Anya said, eventually. "Where do you want to do this?"

"Your place?"

They exchanged a glance, some hesitation passing between them. "Sure," Anya said after a beat.

Sid let them into the building and ran up the stairs, entering the apartment first. As Clio followed Anya inside, he was coming out of a bedroom. "Just clearing up," he said, and she wondered what was so important that he'd had to rush ahead.

They sat in the kitchen. It was small, the table taking up most of the room, cabinets on either side, and, Clio noted, it was overlooked by the building opposite.

"When did you last see Diana?" she asked.

Anya spoke about Diana introducing her to her father at his house in London, then taking her to a bookshop in London where they debriefed. "I was upset with her for springing the meeting with my dad on me. After I left, I didn't see her again," Anya said.

"Can anyone confirm?"

"My father and his wife. His driver. The bookseller."

"Had you never met your father before?"

"No. He and Mum were estranged before I was born."

"And he is *the* Magnus Beaufort?" Clio wanted to confirm. He was famous. Fame complicated everything.

"He is."

"And did you agree to work with him?"

"I did." Anya Brown spoke quietly, calmly. If she had big feelings, she kept them locked behind the eyes. "My father wants me to be involved with the library he's building in Cambridge. It's a big legacy project for him, and apparently"—she raised her eyebrows a little—"it's always been a dream of his that I work with him on the collection. I don't know my father well, but he has a lot of grand ideas, and this is one of them."

"I take it you don't feel enthusiastic about the collaboration?"

"My feelings about him are complicated." Anya's gaze was as steady as her voice. Brave, Clio thought. Outwardly controlled.

"How did you spend the rest of that day?"

"I traveled to Cambridge to see some of the books in his collection. They were at his house. I also visited the site where he's building the library. When I got back to London that evening, I had a call from my mum's carer saying she'd been taken to hospital, so I took the train to Bristol to be with her."

"Is she okay?" Clio asked.

Anya nodded but twisted her lips. Not great, then, Clio thought, but she held back from asking more.

"I know you've just started work at the Institute, but I need to ask if you've noticed anything unusual about it."

The question seemed to electrify them. They exchanged a glance, another silent communication. They were close enough to read each other's thoughts easily, that was obvious.

Sid was the one to speak, cautiously at first, then warming up. Two names Clio recognized came out of his mouth: Minxu Peng and Zofia. He'd been told they'd disappeared and believed they'd been killed. The person who'd told him—the husband of Anya's colleague—had died the night they'd decided to leave St. Andrews. He'd seen the body. Clio could tell it was haunting him. She recognized the look in his eyes.

She'd seen it on her colleagues. When he stopped talking, Anya took over, filling in gaps in the story she'd just told about Diana and her father, describing a hidden letter and a glossary that was the key to the famous Voynich manuscript, important because the Voynich encoded clues to the location of an object that some dangerous people were looking for.

Anya stopped speaking, and they all fell silent. Clio's mind was racing to join the dots between what she was hearing and what she already knew.

A bell tolled nearby, four strikes, after the last of which something slammed so heavily from somewhere inside the building that all three of them flinched and glanced toward the door.

"Can you take a look at something for me?" Clio asked.

She took out her phone and showed them photographs of both pieces of the embroidery. Anya pored over the images, flicking between them. Her focus was intense.

She got up suddenly and disappeared into the bedroom, returning with a laptop and some pieces of an old manuscript and a letter that she laid out on the table.

"This is the glossary and the letter that were hidden in my father's manuscript." She turned the laptop so Clio could see the screen. It showed a high-res image of pages from the Voynich. "And I think the embroidery pieces could be from the Voynich's original binding. When you put them together they're the perfect size. Where did you find the missing piece?"

"I can't divulge that yet," Clio said. Anya didn't have to know everything.

"Have other people seen it?"

"It was discovered by a woman who we believe kept it hidden to study it. She seems to have written a poem about it."

"Can I see it?"

Clio watched Anya carefully as she read Eleanor Bruton's words. Her cheeks were flushed when she looked up. She said, "Whoever wrote this linked the embroidery to Verona, but that's all. They didn't connect it to the Voynich. Can you tell me who wrote it?"

Clio explained about Eleanor Bruton, without naming her, and about the two groups of women, one with links to St. Katherine.

"Oh my God, the couple we saw earlier. She was wearing a St. Katherine brooch," Anya said.

Clio thought of the remote island where Eleanor Bruton died. "It's possible they've followed you here. These women are dangerous and well resourced."

"Should we tell the Italian police?" Sid asked.

Clio considered it. If she stayed under the radar, the carabinieri wouldn't be in touch with her office in London, but if she involved them, chances were it would get back to the UK quickly. There were protocols. "Nobody's broken the law, so let's watch and wait for now."

"But you said they were dangerous."

"They are. But we can't be sure that the people you saw are involved with the group. St. Katherine is a popular saint, and this is a Roman Catholic country. Let's not be hasty."

They seemed to accept it and she felt a pang of guilt for the ways she was misleading them. She would have to make sure she kept them safe.

"Can you show me how the embroidery links to the Voynich?" she asked.

"It's so intricate, it probably connects in loads of ways, but this is one of the more obvious." Flipping between the photos of the two embroidery pieces on Clio's phone again, Anya pointed out the five embroidered circles, each containing a portrait of a woman in profile, including the one that had been ripped in half. "The letter I translated, from Isotta Nogarola, says that the Voynich was made by five women from her family: her, three of her sisters, and their aunt. I think these profiles are portraits of them, and I think that because each one has her initial beside her, and a plant that's relevant to her name, growing through it. Juniper for Ginevra, laurel for Laura, basil for Isabella, honeysuckle for Isotta, and angelica for their aunt Angela. She and Isotta were famous poets. What's exciting is that you can see drawings of these same plants inside the Voynich, on the botanical pages. And look here, I think the Nogarola family crest is also in the embroidery. Do you see here, where it's been ripped?"

Clio peered at it.

"I think it's another heraldic shield," Anya said. "You see there's one that's intact below the central roundel?"

"Yes," Clio said. Zofia Danek had mentioned two shields but she hadn't been able to identify the torn one.

"If the embroidery hadn't been ripped in that exact place, this destroyed shield would have been the more prominent one. And look, on each piece we can *just* see the ends of a pair of kinked lines that would have run diagonally across the shield. That's the Nogarola family crest. And those kinked lines appear as a motif in the Voynich, too, twisted to make the shape of the roots in one of the botanical drawings." She found the page on her laptop.

"It's playful," Clio said.

Anya nodded. "You get a sense of what the family were like. It's nice." She smiled. Clio warmed to this side of her. She read everything Anya showed her, looking most carefully at her translation of the final page of the Voynich. "What does this mean?" She pointed at a row of capital letters that Anya hadn't translated yet.

"I'm not sure," Anya said. "It's been a bit of a puzzle figuring out these letters from the Voynichese, and I'm not sure I've got it right. The Latin doesn't translate easily."

She copied the letters out onto the side of her tourist map of Verona:

HYPOEUMSNTMRSSUNT

Then, eyes narrowed, played with them, rewriting them a few different ways until she had:

HYPO EUM SNT MR SSUNT

"'Hypo' is Latin for 'beneath,'" she said, "but it's a prefix. 'Eum' is a demonstrative pronoun, I believe, so what I'm about to say doesn't quite make sense, but at a stretch it could be translated as 'beneath *that*,' or '*him*,' but the grammar isn't correct for either word. On first glance at the other groups of letters, I'm seeing an abbreviation. The letters could stand for Santa Maria Assunta, Saint Mary of the Assumption. Churches are commonly dedicated to her." She frowned, thinking aloud. "Which means that the gender for 'eum' is also wrong."

Clio interrupted. "Are there any churches dedicated to this saint in Verona?"

"The cathedral."

"Is that the one with the Roman remains beneath it?" Sid asked.

"It's built over two older churches and a Roman site, and it has a separate baptistery with a famous font." Her eyes lit up. "And it's right beside the river. You know, water is a huge theme in the Voynich."

"Should we go back there?" Sid asked.

"I'll go," Clio said. "You two should stay here, especially if you suspect you were being followed."

"But you'll need us," Sid said. "Well, you'll need Anya to interpret what you're looking at, and I'm not letting her go without me."

He got up and went to close the doors to the balcony, then froze, and stepped back from them.

"What is it?" Clio asked.

"The woman and man we saw earlier."

"Where?" She stood beside him, both of them in the shadows. He pointed out a younger man and a middle-aged woman, looking in a shop window opposite. Doubtless, they weren't shopping but using the reflections to see behind them and tell them who was entering and exiting Anya and Sid's building.

In that same reflection, Clio could see the St. Katherine's wheel brooch on the woman's lapel.

"Is there a back way out of here?" she asked.

CHAPTER SIXTEEN

Anya

Sid and I stuffed everything into our packs. We didn't know if it would be safe to return.

We ran downstairs and searched the dim corridor. There was no back exit. Clio hammered on the door of one of the apartments. A young woman with a baby in her arms opened it. Visible behind her were doors that opened onto a courtyard at the back.

"I'm so sorry," Clio said. She pushed past the woman; Sid and I followed. The woman held her baby's head to her shoulder and shouted at us. Clio pulled a plastic table up to the courtyard wall and we climbed over, dropping down hard on the other side into a narrow alleyway.

The sun had just gone down. Away from the main streets, some light spilled from streetlamps and apartment windows, but the shadows were dark and deep. We headed toward the cathedral.

Outside Juliet's House the crowds were still thick, everyone trying to catch a glimpse of the famous balcony. Clio dove into the throng of people, and we emerged on the other side near the Scaliger tombs, which were creepy at night, as was the silent church beside them where I knew Isotta and her family had worshipped.

We took the path by the river, the breeze on our faces, moving quietly past busy restaurants, ducking away from the glow of their garlands of lights, until the path ended, forcing us back into a labyrinthine warren of narrow streets that eventually led us to the cathedral.

A mass was underway. One of the cathedral doors was open. We could hear the organ and over it, the priest's voice, intoning the mass through a microphone, his voice sonorous and mesmeric. I stared, my eyes caught by the stands of flickering candles. I was trying to ignore a growing feeling that this location wasn't right, that I'd got it wrong. This place was so touristy. If Isotta had hidden something here, it would surely have been discovered by now.

The baptistery entrance was at the back of the cathedral. It was a small hall, ancient, remnants of frescoes on the otherwise plain walls, the star of the show the huge octagonal marble font carved with bibilical scenes that I tried to relate to the Voynich but couldn't. I felt despondent. My gut was still insisting that the answer lay elsewhere, that coming here was a mistake.

"Anything?" Sid asked, and I shook my head.

"I need to look at the manuscript and the embroidery again. This doesn't feel right."

"We can get a hotel," Clio said.

Outside, the street was empty, apart from a woman and three men, standing a little way down, conferring. My heart skipped a beat. "It's them," I whispered.

We walked fast around the side of the cathedral, and as soon as we rounded the corner into the square, we ran. Clio was ahead. She led us into a narrow passage beside the cathedral steps. It was unlit and claustrophobic, hemmed in by tall ancient walls. We emerged into a small square on the riverbank. We heard the water below. A portico sheltered the entrance to another church, even more ancient than the cathedral. I tried its massive door handle, tugged it, rattled it, but it was firmly locked. "Over here," Sid said. Opposite was a low, tunneled entrance, cutting through a building, our only option.

We ran through it and found ourselves in the corner of a shadowy cloister. I reached for my phone, to turn on the flashlight, but as I did, we heard voices approaching. Spotlights came on suddenly around the cloister and in the garden, showing off its beauty, forcing us to melt back into the shadows.

A large party of tourists entered the tunnel, following a guide who held up a sign saying "Verona by Night." She stopped them at the mouth of the tunnel and talked about the remains of Roman mosaics that had been unearthed beneath the cloister. The group huddled around her. Her voice rung out clearly in the quiet space. She spoke English with a lilting Italian accent.

Clio whispered, "Follow me."

She discreetly joined the back of the group, and Sid and I followed. When the guide moved around the cloister, we went with them. The group was large enough that nobody noticed. I glanced toward the entrance. No one was looking for us here yet.

"So, this is a very special place," the guide said. "Verona is home to the oldest working library in the world, and where we're standing right now is the site of the ancient scriptorium. We have the first written record of it in the fourth century CE. All that remains of it is this cloister, because . . ." She talked on, and I barely listened. I knew of the library. Dante had studied there. Isotta would have known it, too.

Sid nudged me. A man had appeared in the doorway to the cloister, staring in. He was tall and scarily well built, and he was scanning our group. We all three moved so that we were obscured by other members of the group.

My phone pinged once, then again, loud enough that people turned around to look. I fumbled in my bag to find it. Three more messages came in—*ping, ping, ping*—all from Magnus, before I managed to mute it. I shoved the phone in my pocket without reading them. I could hear my heart pounding in my ears.

The man in the entrance was still there. He looked adrenalized but hesitant. I willed him to leave. The guide kept talking throughout, explaining how the library had been affected by a series of disasters over the years, devastating floods from the river it was built directly above, raids during war with Napoleon. I glanced at Clio. She was facing the guide, but I could see the whites of her eyes. Her gaze was trained on the entrance.

I glanced back there to find that the man had gone. I felt a moment of relief before I realized he could easily have slipped into the cloister's shadows. He could be closing in on us.

"Then there was the time the library was almost totally destroyed," the guide said. "The Allies landed a bomb directly on it during the war, and it burned. Flames reaching up into the night, their reflections in the river. Can you imagine that? If you come back here in the daytime for a tour of the reading rooms, you'll see shrapnel scars on the spines of some of our books from that explosion. They were dug out from the rubble afterward. But it wasn't the end of the library, because at the start of the war a clever librarian had packed up fifty-three boxes with our most precious books and sent them to a monastery in the mountains for safekeeping. So, they were spared, and they're here today in the collection."

The story reminded me of Magnus's collection, saved from flames, but it also made me think of the Voynich, and all the botanic illustrations in its pages. I'd been connecting them to the frescoes around Verona, thinking they related to the churches here, but what if they were more literal than that? What if the drawings of flowers and plants, and even the water imagery, hinted that *The Book of Wonder* had been removed from the city and taken to the countryside instead, just like the books from this library? I remembered something else: Isotta's poem, the one that mentioned Cyanum, was also about her family's idyllic country home. What if *The Book of Wonder* was there?

"Okay," the guide said. "So, we move on to visit our city's beautiful Roman bridge, the Ponte Pietra. Follow me!"

We stayed with the group as it left the cloister and wound its way back through the narrow passageway and into the cathedral piazza. There was no sign of the man. Mass had just finished in the cathedral and the congregation was pouring out of the building, filling the square and the nearby streets. It was the perfect cover. We slipped into the crowd and got away.

THE HOTEL CLIO BOOKED US WAS A SMALL PLACE, IN THE ANCIENT CENTER, but on a quiet street, a little off the beaten track. The room was small and bland but clean, two double beds made up with gold, satiny quilts that felt gross to the touch. It had a view of the Castelvecchio and its bridge, the rows of swallowtail merlons lit up like rows of jagged teeth.

We logged onto the Wi-Fi. "We need to find out where the Nogarola family had their country villa," I said.

It didn't take Sid long to figure it out. "They had a house in a village called Castel d'Azzano. It's still there, but it's not a private home anymore. It looks like it's used by the town council and they call it Villa Violini." He pulled up Google Maps. "Castel d'Azzano is about a half hour south of here by car."

"We'll go there first thing in the morning." It was too late and too dark now.

"We should try to get some sleep," Clio said. She'd been very quiet since we got to the hotel, watching us and listening to our conversations, but not contributing. It reminded me that she was a stranger, and a cop, and that we really didn't know her at all.

She took one of the beds, and Sid and I shared the other. I couldn't sleep. My mind kept picking over my latest plan, finding reasons that a countryside location was dumb, that it wouldn't work just to show up at this house, which looked huge and mostly locked up. I became convinced it was just another dead end. I felt in over my depth, slapped by waves of panic and self-doubt.

I was also desperate to speak to Mum. She'd told me not to call her, but she was the only person who might be able to help. I knew it wasn't a smart move, that it might even be a dangerous move, but I got out of bed and locked myself into the small bathroom.

Viv answered.

"Could you give Mum the phone, please." I had no bandwidth left to generate politeness.

She laughed. "I'm not your personal assistant."

"Viv!" I was shocked. "I'm not joking. I need to speak to her urgently."

She snapped. "No! You listen to me, you ungrateful little bitch. You can't speak to your mother because she's not here. *They have her.* Do you know why? It's because you prioritized yourself and your career. You were so self-important, it was beneath you to care for your own mother, your own flesh and blood. Did you ever wonder whether I really wanted to spend all my days caring for her? Did you really believe that was enough for me? Big mistake, Anya. I'm an esteemed member of the Order of St. Katherine. I matter!"

I couldn't believe what I was hearing. "Where's Mum?"

"Gone. Good luck finding her."

"Where is she?" I shouted. "Tell me!"

"You heard me, and guess what, Dr. Anya Brown, everyone knows that Folio 9 was forged. They did it to lure you in. And now you know how it feels to be used, you can stop pretending how clever you are, because you're not!"

She was screaming. I felt sick to my stomach. She hung up, and when I tried to call back, it went to voicemail. It was the same when I tried her number. We had no neighbors at the cottage, no one I could ask to go and check on Mum. I threw my phone at the bathroom door.

Sid rattled the handle. "Anya! What's wrong?"

I unlocked the door. Clio was standing on the other side with Sid. I told them everything.

"I should call this in," Clio said.

"What if that puts Mum in more danger?"

"We need to find out what's happened here."

"No," I said. "Please. Let's just think about this. If the police get involved, the Katherine people might do something to Mum, but if I find this hidden book, I can offer it to them to get her back."

"If a crime's been committed, it's my duty to report it," Clio said, but then she seemed to reconsider. "Okay. We think, but when I say it's time to report it, we do."

I told them what Viv said about Folio 9. "She can't be serious, can she?" I asked Sid. "Surely she was just trying to get at me." My stomach dropped when I saw how he looked. "Oh, my God. You knew this already? Is it true?"

"I've seen it said before, in a chat room online. Someone claimed that Alice Trevelyan had the forgery made. I thought it was gossip. It probably is!"

"When did you see it? Why didn't you tell me? What the hell, Sid!"

Clio interrupted. "Can I interject?" Her voice was calm. Her training was showing.

I couldn't let it go. "This makes me a fraud," I said. "I was right all along."

Clio raised her voice. "Who is Alice Trevelyan?"

"She's a professor at Oxford. She supervised my PhD, and she was the person who showed me Folio 9 for the first time. She told me it was a new discovery. She also encouraged me to take the job at St. Andrews." I remembered something Sid had said. "Didn't you tell me Diana and Trevelyan studied together? Oh, God. They set me up years ago, didn't they?"

"It sounds as if they were grooming you," Clio said. "I think I'm only just starting to understand how far their influence reaches. They're not just dangerous, they're really sophisticated, too. And that goes for both groups."

"Why didn't you tell me before?" I asked Sid.

"Your mum had just gone into hospital. I didn't think you needed to hear it right then. I also wasn't even sure it was true, and for what it's worth, even if it is, I don't think it makes any difference to your achievement. You were still the only person to translate it."

"It makes all the difference! I'm a fraud."

I felt ashamed and appalled. I thought of the press release, the job offers. All of it seemed hollow now. It made me an embarrassment. I'd been used to get to Magnus, that was all.

Worse still, I thought of Mum's pride in me and how painful it would be to shatter it. That is, if I ever got the chance. But the thought brought me back to myself. I should stop being selfish. We needed to find Mum. Viv's words echoed, chilling me: *"They have her."*

It had never been more urgent to locate the book, and I'd never felt so incapable of finding it.

Clio

Clio got into the elevator, saw herself reflected in the mirrored wall, and looked away.

Was she a civilian or an officer? She had to decide. All she knew for now was that she shouldn't be here, but she didn't know what else she could have done.

Her sense of duty, usually rock steady, an anchor for her, had come untethered from her moral compass, and that was a nauseating feeling.

She hit the button for the ground floor. Sid and Anya needed space, and she was going to ask a colleague to make inquiries about Anya's mother, no matter what the two of them wanted. It was her duty.

There were people in the lobby. She tucked herself into a chair in a quiet corner, and checked her mail while she considered whether to call Izzy and ask for another favor regarding Rose Brown or report it directly. It was late, but she could get some messages sent off so people would see them first thing in the morning.

Anya Brown would be upset, angry even, but Clio wasn't working for her. She'd taken an oath, and she had to believe in it. A woman's life might be at stake.

While she considered how best to proceed, she noticed that the footage from the British Museum had arrived in her inbox. She clicked play. The entrance footage didn't tell her anything. Too many people. She didn't spot any familiar faces or red flags, but they'd be easy to miss, especially as she was so tired. On the footage from the Medieval Europe gallery she watched herself and Lillian come into the gallery and enter the Everly Bequest room where the embroidery was kept, but the camera didn't have a view into the room. It was hard to watch Lillian, knowing what was about to happen to her. A few others entered and left the gallery. Clio saw the guard pass by the entrance to the Everly Bequest room, pausing on a second pass to take a closer look in, then moving on and speaking into her radio.

She took note. That could be something or nothing, a coincidence. Or not. She rolled her head, trying to get the kinks out of her neck, and ran the final piece of footage she'd been sent. The camera was trained on an area just outside the gallery entrance, where there was a café. She caught Lillian arriving, visible from behind, then herself, about ten minutes later. The café filled up soon afterward. A man on his own working on a laptop, earbuds in. A woman reading a novel. A grandma and a mum with two small kids who were creating mayhem. She watched until she saw herself and Lillian leaving, this time catching a glimpse of Lillian's face.

On the footage, Clio was walking slightly ahead of Lillian, so on the day she hadn't noticed Lillian take a hard look at the two women sitting at the table with the kids. Nor had she noticed Lillian taking another look over her shoulder before they went out of shot. They walked downstairs right after that, Clio remembered, and exited the museum, which was when Lillian became agitated. On the footage, the older woman watched them leave, then got her phone out and sent a message. Her face was grim. She put the phone back in her bag and pulled one of the grandkids onto her lap. The younger woman said something to her, but she didn't notice. She was still looking toward the staircase.

Clio reran the footage, screenshotted the woman's face, and sent it to Izzy with a message: Can you run facial recognition on this for me first thing?

Izzy replied right away.

I don't need to. That's Mrs. Tony Axford, my boss's wife.

Clio zoomed in on the picture. It was blurry, but she was pretty sure Mrs. Axford was wearing a silk scarf with a Catherine wheel symbol on it. She'd been blindsided.

Anya

I barely slept that night in the hotel, worrying whether we could easily be found there. When I did doze off, it was in snatches of time. In the dark hours, fear of my mother coming to harm danced grotesquely through my dreams and my waking nightmares, hand in hand with an excoriating feeling that I'd failed her. Viv was right. I should have been less selfish, less sure of myself. Mum was what mattered, not a career move that turned out to have been a bait and switch.

The stakes had been raised to a level I could barely comprehend. Viv's suggestion that Folio 9 might have been forged was unproven and very possibly a lie designed to hurt me, but I couldn't stop thinking about it and wondering: If it *was* true, what else had I got wrong? It made me question every leap of logic I'd made, yet by 5 a.m. I'd been over everything multiple times and couldn't see things differently. Trusting my gut felt dangerous, but it was all I had.

Isotta's country home. Was *The Book of Wonder* there? It was my best guess and I had to run with it.

I picked up my phone. Magnus's messages from last night were still there, unread. More had arrived since. I glanced through them, terrified I might learn that he was closing in on me, but they just contained more threats and said horrible things about me and Mum.

I tried to put him out of my mind as I looked on Google Maps at the Nogarola family villa at Castel d'Azzano.

The villa was still intact, but the original building had been extended and altered a lot over the ages. It had swallowtail merlons on its roof, which was good to see, though the internet wasn't clear about when that part of the house had been built. I could see that a river ran behind it and that the villa bordered a nature park, and I thought Isotta might have been pleased to know something of her idyll had been preserved. But as Sid had said, the house itself was used by the town's council now, and there was almost no trace left of the building Isotta would have known.

It still felt right to me in theory that *The Book of Wonder* might be hidden there but doubts were creeping in. Why hide the book on private property, where most people would be denied access, or which could change hands? This solution also felt too easy. Isotta wanted the book to be found by a "worthy woman." Had I done enough to solve the puzzle she'd set? I wasn't sure. I felt as if I might have missed something even though I'd read her letter and my translation over and over.

I thought about Mum, how she and Isotta shared a love of language and how, in her riddles, Mum never knowingly put one meaning into words when she could put two. It occurred to me that maybe I'd been looking in the wrong place. Was there a chance that Mum had put a hint in her email, something that might not be in the glossary or in Isotta's letter but could have been handed down with them, something that would either tell me I was on the right track or point me in a different direction? I couldn't be sure Mum had been well enough to pull off anything like her usual word tricks, but—

Verona was dark when I crept out of bed. The swallowtail merlons on the Castelvecchio Bridge were still lit, its terra-cotta bricks glowing. Clio and Sid had been restless all night, too, but both were lightly asleep as I got up.

Quietly, I slipped my phone off the charger and found Mum's

email. As I reread it, I thought of Isotta, of double meanings, of the importance of our choice of words. The paragraph where Mum described the bookmark she'd been given by Josephine Dunne stood out. There was too much detail in it for such a minor recollection.

"'Coronet weeds,' this one said. Do you remember it?" Mum wrote about the bookmark. "When you were a child, I kept it in the little drawer in my workshop, the one you loved to rummage through."

I remembered the drawer. There had been a bookmark in it, but it wasn't made of leather, nor was it red. I searched online for the words "coronet weeds" and found them easily. They were from *Hamlet*, a description of Ophelia's flowers, the ones she had when she died.

It dawned on me, then. Mum was steering me toward a picture we'd seen together on our first-ever visit to the Tate Gallery: John Everett Millais's famous painting of Ophelia's corpse floating ethereally in the river, after her death, surrounded by flora. "Who's that flower girl?" I'd asked, and she'd explained the play's sad story. It was the words "flower girl" she wanted me to remember, I realized with a jolt, and everything fell into place.

The Nogarola women had been made into literal flower girls on the Voynich's binding. I pictured their portraits on the embroidery, saw their initials tangled in the delicate foliage that framed each portrait: A, I, G, L, and I.

I played with the letters, wondering if I could insert them into the baffling words from the last paragraph of the Voynich to make sense out of them. It didn't work. I was about to give up when I noticed that the letter G and one of the I's had a tiny star embroidered beside them. There were another five of them beside the letter A, but nothing beside the L and the other I. Could the stars possibly represent numbers, telling me which letters to use, and how frequently? It was my best guess. Holding my breath, I tried different combinations until I had something.

HYPO EUM SNT MR SSUNT

became

HYPOGEUM SANTA MARIA ASSUNTA

I googled it and the results stunned me. My heart was pounding. This, surely, was the answer to the puzzle.

I glanced at Sid. He was awake, watching me. I put my finger to my lips and beckoned to him to follow me. I didn't want to wake Clio. I didn't trust her not to force me to hand over *The Book of Wonder* to the local police if I found it.

I quickly packed and took my backpack with me as we snuck out of the room. The hotel corridors had the emptiness of the quiet hours. The lobby downstairs wasn't manned overnight and was empty apart from the eye of a camera trained on us. We sat close together on the small sofa. I leaned toward Sid and told him what I wanted to do. I turned my face away from the camera so no one could lip-read my words.

He didn't like it, but I was ready for that. I knew how to convince him.

He ran his hand over his forehead after hearing me out. His face was already drawn with fatigue and worry, and my plan was worsening it.

I said, "Sid, it's going to work. I don't see any other way."

I had to remind myself to breathe as I waited for him to weigh everything up, knowing better than to rush him. Finally, he said, "Okay, if you're sure."

He went to the front desk and rummaged behind it until he'd found a pad of paper and a pen. I wrote a note, keeping it out of sight of the camera and gave it to him.

"Do you have everything you need?" he asked.

I nodded.

"Be careful." He hugged me tightly.

"I will," I told him. The words seemed too small and too ordinary for the moment. Everything else we meant to convey seemed to be glittering in the air around us, not needing to be spoken; the way it does when you love someone and they love you back. I knew he felt it, too.

He went to the elevator. The note was in his hand. As soon as the doors closed, my stomach dropped; the air stopped glittering and darkened.

I took a card for a taxi firm from a rack on the reception desk, scanned the QR code on it, ordered a car, and waited for it outside. There were glimmers of light to the east, and their reflections glinted on the river's surface.

It wasn't a long drive. I sat in the back of the taxi and stared out the window. Housing petered out and gave way to agricultural land, pastures and fields that rested softly in the languid dawn, everything dewy and quiet. The land was mostly flat, cradling patches of soft mist where it dipped. To our right and ahead hills rose steeply, terraced with vines; switchback roads zigzagged up them.

I didn't want the driver to know exactly where I was going, so I asked to be dropped in the middle of the village and used my phone to navigate the last bit of my journey on foot. It was a beautiful, quiet, pastoral spot off the beaten track, ringing with birdsong, a rich tang of the season in the air.

This wasn't Isotta's country home, but this place had surely meant something to her.

I was betting everything on a hunch that it had.

The church was simple, built from stone and brick in the same sand and coral palette as Verona. It stood on the corner of a road, the Via Pantheon. In front of its doors was a small square with a few modest houses around it. A black cat with yellow eyes watched me impassively from the top of a tall wall; it felt like an omen, but I didn't know how to interpret it. Otherwise, the place was deserted.

I knew from the reading I'd done that morning that the church hadn't been built when Isotta was alive. In her time there was a smaller church here, but it was rebuilt from scratch about the same time that she died. Pretty as it was, I didn't think it was worth looking inside. Nothing from Isotta's time was likely to have survived.

I was much more interested in what was directly below it: the Hypogeum Santa Maria Assunta.

I'd learned from Google that it was an underground system of tunnels and chambers used by the Romans to worship water nymphs, nymphs like Cyane. After the Romans, St. Zeno of Verona had baptized people in the underground spring. By Isotta's time, it was an important place of Christian pilgrimage.

I was convinced that Isotta would have known of this place and visited it. She wasn't just an educated woman with an interest in mythology, and Cyane in particular, she was devout, too, and had the means to travel.

Just as compelling as the hypogeum's history were the photographs of it that I'd seen online. Deep underground was something so remarkable I couldn't believe more people didn't know about it: an ancient, incredible ceiling decoration. I'd never seen anything like it before and it looked so much like some of the most mysterious imagery in the Voynich that it had taken my breath away.

For centuries no one had been able to explain the weird imagery of water pipes, tubes, and bathing pools that appeared on so many pages of the Voynich manuscript, or the naked women who bathed in them. But if you linked them to this hypogeum and to Isotta's poetry, you surely had the answer: the women were water nymphs.

Finally, everything felt right. This was the place where everything came together. The evidence, my gut, and a sense of connection with Isotta that I couldn't deny told me *The Book of Wonder* was more likely to be here than anywhere else. The site's history didn't put me off. The hypogeum may have been in use over centuries, but it had been a holy place, preserved intact, no intensive archeology or modern development for tourists. Of all the sites I'd considered, this seemed the one where secrets had the most chance of remaining hidden for centuries. I felt sure that even if I didn't find the book down there, I would find another clue to where Isotta had hidden it.

The entrance to the hypogeum was behind a closed and padlocked metal gate. Through it, at the bottom of a flight of steps, I could see the mouth of a tunnel, dark and unwelcoming.

I wasn't sure when the hypogeum would next be open to the public and I couldn't wait. I rattled the gate, making a small space between it and the post, but it wasn't wide enough for me to get through. I thought the gap above the gate might be. It looked be tight, but not impossible.

I took my backpack off, climbed up the gate, dropped it over—no going back now—and squeezed myself through the gap, falling down heavily on the other side. I got up and dusted myself off, feeling as if the thud I'd made must have alerted someone, but the square remained deserted, the cat still watching, its tail flicking.

I walked down the steps and was soon underground. The darkness was so complete it was as if someone had thrown a hood over my head, as if I'd stepped into every story that had ever terrified me. The outside world had gone. There was no noise or light in front of me, just blank silence. My brain screamed at me to retrace my steps and get out, but I turned on my phone's flashlight, and kept going.

At the bottom of the steps the beam of my flashlight revealed a niche in the wall, with a statue set into it of a man dressed in a toga, the first trace of the ancient origins of this place. To my left was another dark passageway. The torchlight only illuminated the first few meters. I was hyperaware of what might lie in the shadows and my breathing sounded too fast and too loud, a sharp ebb and flow of hot fear disturbing the dank, still air. If there were predators down here, they would easily mark me as prey.

I heard water flowing, a strong trickle, but the sound was muted, as if the water was separated from me, perhaps running somewhere deeper, beneath my feet or behind the wall. I guessed I was hearing the underground spring.

I'd memorized the hypogeum's layout from a plan I'd seen online and knew this was the second of three tunnels I had to go through to reach the main complex of chambers where the walls and ceilings were painted. I tried to swallow my fear as I pushed on, but claustrophobia got a grip on me, and I was panting by the time I emerged into a small, square space carved out of rock.

A marble mausoleum lay along one wall, squat and heavy. I ran my hands over it, feeling how cold and smooth it was. I looked for inscriptions but there were none. The lid was far too heavy for me to move to see what might be inside. I was starting to realize that this was no place to hide any book, let alone one as valuable as *The Book of Wonder*. It was too cold and damp down here. I pinned my hopes on seeing something that would tell me what to do or where to go next.

A low stone lintel marked the entrance to the final tunnel. Its ceiling was very low—I would need to stoop to walk through it—and it was horribly narrow.

I took off my backpack again. With the bestiary inside, it was bulky and heavy, awkward to stoop in. The tunnel seemed to last forever. I felt as if the walls were closing in around me, as if the oxygen would run out. My heart raced. Light from my phone bounced off the rough stone walls and floor. It felt like I was walking to the center of the earth. When I finally emerged, the space around me opened up and I lifted my head gratefully.

I was standing in an atrium, an explosion of color and pattern above and around me, covering the walls and ceiling. It was shocking to see such incredible work hiding all the way down here. It was powerful and marvelous.

On either side, the atrium opened out into two chambers. My light gave me glimpses of their mosaic floors and semi-domed ceilings. I was looking for the paintings that had lured me here, and I caught my breath when I got my first glimpse.

I'd never felt such a sense of wonder before, but it was shattered in an instant. From somewhere close behind me I heard footsteps.

CHAPTER SEVENTEEN

Clio

Clio was alone in the room when she woke up. There was no sign of Sid or Anya, and she was grateful, because her cheeks were wet with tears that she didn't want them to see. She wiped them away roughly.

She hadn't got to sleep until four in the morning because she'd been trying to work out what to do, wondering how deep this went in the force, and if Lillian had left her so abruptly on the steps of the British Museum because she was trying to get away quickly. Had she known that they'd been seen?

Clio's brain had worked on the problem while she slept and the answers made her feel a little dead inside, as well as desperately sad.

Lillian had to have known that her death was imminent, and she'd tried to force it into taking place in such a way as to make Clio suspicious of murder. Why else would she have chosen one of the most surveilled places in London to meet Clio? Even though the exterior cameras had been disabled somehow, whoever murdered Lillian hadn't got to the ones inside the museum. Lillian had likely gambled on it being impossible to put every camera out of action, and hoped Clio would figure it out.

She'd sacrificed herself to expose evil.

And I did figure it out, Clio thought. She threw back the covers and got out of bed. She'd slept in her clothes. In the bathroom, she splashed water on her face, scrubbed away her tears, and looked hard at herself in the mirror as she swallowed her feelings. Not now.

She heard a soft knock on the door of the room and the sound of it opening cautiously. "It's me," Sid called.

She let herself out of the bathroom. He was alone. "Where's Anya?"

She'd eventually decided she wouldn't report Anya's mother missing yet. If these organizations had enough of a grip on the police force to get both Lillian and her friend killed, then their reach was very deep. Triggering an investigation into her whereabouts would almost certainly put Rose Brown in more danger.

Sid said, "Anya's gone. She left a note." He handed it to Clio. He looked cut up.

She read it: "'Wait at the hotel. I'll be back later. Don't worry.'" She glanced at Sid and his gaze slid away. The man was a bad liar. "Where did you find it?" she asked.

He hesitated. Another tell. "Downstairs."

"At the desk?"

He nodded.

"I thought it wasn't manned until seven."

He shrugged.

Clio's phone pinged with a new message from Izzy. Clearly, she never slept.

> Just took another look at that CCTV grab. Isn't the younger woman Tim Keenan's new wife?

Clio was shocked all over again. How deep did the influence of these women reach? She messaged back: Is it?? I've never met her.

Tim kept his private life private around her, but she'd heard on the grapevine that he'd married someone much younger, and once overheard him complaining about starting another family at his age. It was his second round, and it had deepened the bags under his eyes. Serves him right, she thought now. Probably the mother of his first children thought the same.

I'm sure I've seen her in a photo Axford showed me on his phone, Izzy wrote. They all socialize together.

Can you try to confirm and let me know?

Yeah. Are you still sick?

Clio hated lying. She stared at the phone, then typed, I owe you one.

Sid was in the bathroom. Clio sat on the side of the bed, testing out an idea, a way to bring Tim and Tony down, a way to keep herself safe. It was a good idea, the kind that shoots a bolt of energy through you. Lillian would approve. Lillian had been ten steps ahead of her all the way, and she probably still was.

When Sid came out of the bathroom, Clio said, "You need to tell me where Anya's gone. I know you know."

Anya

I held my breath, waiting to hear someone entering the hypogeum behind me but there was only the sound of gurgling water. Perhaps fear was playing tricks with my imagination.

I looked up. The inside of the half-domed ceiling was decorated with rows of multiple short tubes, stacked vertically, each painted a different color, cream, yellow, blue, and red. It was weirdly modern, deeply strange, and as I'd thought when I'd found the images of the ceiling online, by far the closest thing I'd ever seen to the strange pipes illustrated in the Voynich. I was transfixed.

In the opposite chamber, the ceiling was painted blue and covered in stars, another strong Voynich echo. Painted scenes from the Old and New Testaments covered the walls, bold and frightening. Their crude style told me they were very old. I felt awed, as if I'd walked into an Egyptian tomb or a cave of prehistoric paintings. When I returned to the first chamber to stand beneath the strange tubular forms again, I felt as if I'd walked into a page of the Voynich.

But I saw nothing to tell me where *The Book of Wonder* might be, or even hint at it. I searched all three spaces carefully, sending torchlight into every corner, closely examining every painting, desperate for a clue—a sign, a symbol, anything—to tell me what next. Since I'd come this far, I felt like the solution should be staring me in the face, but the art was so simple, the spaces so empty otherwise, and I couldn't find any reference to a hidden book or to the Nogarolas or anything else relevant. I felt hopeless.

The sound of the water must have masked the footsteps. By the time I heard them again, they were close. Someone was coming and I only had moments to decide what to do. I switched off my flashlight and the space turned black.

There was no other way out apart from a tunnel that had been chained off. It wasn't open to the public. I knew from the plans I'd seen that it led deeper underground, to the spring, almost certainly to a dead end, but I thought I could hide there at least. It was my only chance.

As quietly as I could, I felt along the walls until I found the tunnel's opening and ducked beneath the chain to enter. I felt my way along it, my palms on the rough walls to guide me. It was narrow and the floor was uneven and jagged in places. As the tunnel descended, the water level rose and soaked through my shoes. Within minutes, I was wading through a couple of inches of freezing, fast flowing spring water and I was afraid of how deep it might get.

When I glanced behind me I could see light raking the tunnel walls. A man's voice called my name, and it echoed menacingly.

My heart raced harder. I pushed on even as the water rose to my knees, moving ever slower and struggling to keep my balance until I couldn't any longer. I tripped and cried out as I fell, smashing my shoulder against the rock wall.

Another shout came from behind me, sharper and more urgent than before. Light fell on me momentarily. My fingers grasped for purchase on the slippery rock wall; I pulled myself up and pushed forward harder until I reached a bend in the tunnel where the flooring seemed to drop off a shelf and had no choice but to carry on. I stepped into icy water that came up to waist level, making me gasp, and within moments I was shivering. I didn't know if I could go much farther. I cinched my backpack straps as tightly as possible to raise it up my back. The bestiary and glossary were in there. I couldn't let them get wet.

Behind me I heard splashing. Someone was getting closer.

Hands trembling, I managed to dry them enough to turn on my phone light.

The light picked out the shape of a metal bar set into the wall a few feet away. There were more above it. It was a rudimentary ladder, set into the side of the tunnel. It looked like hope. I had no way of telling how deep the water beneath it was but I waded toward it, praying I wouldn't step off another ledge.

My hands slipped off the rungs when I tried to pull myself up. I tried again. This time my foot found a rung beneath the surface of the water, giving me some leverage. I looked up and could see the dimmest crescent of light above. I climbed as fast as I could. I was in a well, I realized. It narrowed as I climbed. To reach the top I had to wriggle my backpack off and carry it with one hand. I barely fit in the narrowing space. I was afraid of getting stuck and the muscles in my arms and legs screamed with effort.

At the top, planks covered the circular opening. Bracing my back against the side of the well, I pushed at them, but they didn't move. I propped the backpack on a rung in front of me, holding it in place with my abdomen, and used every last bit of strength I had to slam the palms of my hands into the planks. Pain shot down my arms, but I did it again, and again, until one of them shifted.

As it did, light filled the shaft of the well from below, spotlighting and almost blinding me. A man was directly beneath me, shouting in Italian. I heard my name again. I tried to climb up, through the narrow gap I'd made, but now I was stuck, wedged against my pack. I wriggled desperately until I'd freed it, but holding on to it was awkward. For a second, I was tempted to drop it, to save myself, but with what felt like the last of my strength, I managed to shove it up through the gap.

But the man was climbing up toward me, fast, and he'd almost reached me. I got my head through the gap, then my shoulders. My arms shook with the effort. I thought my strength would fail me. He was right below me now, reaching up, and he grabbed at my foot. I screamed, kicking him away, and made a final effort to pull myself out just as he tried again. The plank splintered my flank and my thigh savagely but I made it.

I looked back down into the well. He was staring up at me. I saw the whites of his eyes, the glow of his flashlight, but he was stuck. The well was too narrow at the top for him. He shouted at me again. I hefted the plank back over the top of the well, leaving him in darkness, and looked around.

There was a stack of masonry, broken stone, and marble piled against a wall. They looked like fragments of tombstones. I heaved a few pieces on top of the planks. Just in case. I didn't know how many people were down there, if there was someone my size who might be able to follow me up.

I took stock of the state of my body. Blood stained my T-shirt, and my trousers, but I wasn't feeling pain yet, adrenaline doing its job. I needed to get away. Even if they couldn't climb up the well, it wouldn't take them long to get out of the hypogeum and find me above ground. I put my backpack on. It was still dry.

I was in an old building, a small, dusty, low-ceilinged room lit dimly by daylight coming through a little window. It seemed to be part storeroom, part priest's room. Old-fashioned, formal chairs with ornate wooden arms flanked a large table. Vestments hung from a set of brass hooks. A glass-fronted cabinet contained books and a crucifix. Rows of tarnished brass candlesticks stood in orderly rows on a shelf, beside boxes of pamphlets and a painting, turned to the wall.

The floor was grander than the rest of the space, made from huge slabs of marble, just like the pavements of Verona. One or two of them had inscriptions, too faded to read but I realized they were ancient gravestones. I figured I was in a building adjacent to the church and quickly realized what I was looking at was the floor of the more ancient church that originally stood on this site, in Isotta's time, before it was rebuilt.

That older church's footprint must have been a little different from the current building's. I felt a little surge of hope, that maybe something remained of the older building, that maybe there was still a chance of finding a clue Isotta could have left here, but the hope quickly drained away. I could no longer hear shouting from the well, which meant the man was almost certainly on his way up. I had to get away.

I looked through the window but saw only an enclosed courtyard strung with an empty washing line, a hose lying uncoiled on a patch of grass, a terra-cotta pot spilling with geraniums beside an open door. I thought of trying to escape through there but the window was painted shut.

I turned to the door, afraid someone could be waiting for me behind it already. The doorway was low and narrow, the door made of thick planks of oak, with a forged latch. It creaked as I opened it and I stepped right into the nave of the present-day church.

Inside the church it was hushed and still, but men's voices were audible from outside. I looked around for a place to hide, but there were slim pickings. The confession box, but they'd find me in a heartbeat. Maybe behind the altar, but it would hardly offer me cover. The pews were too open; I couldn't even crouch between them. I turned to retreat back into the little room when the doors burst open and a man entered.

"Anya Brown," he said in heavily accented English. Behind him I could see the village square, a blast of morning sunlight that made me squint, and another man, the same one who tried to follow me up the well. I was dripping wet and hurting. I was cornered. I had no option except to face him.

"Yes," I said.

"Your father wants you."

Sid

The taxi traveled down a long, straight road. Sid and Clio sat silently in the back.

Sid had a view of the imposing house at the end of the road, a large, three-story edifice, fortresslike, U-shaped in plan, two arms extending to enclose the front lawn: the Nogarolas' country home.

They drove through the remains of a pair of very old gateposts, remnants of the building's earlier lives, and pulled into a parking lot in front.

Close up, the villa looked shabby and unkempt. On the ground floor of the central section, three huge arches enclosed a terrace. You could see through to trees and parkland on the other side.

Sid knew from a YouTube video that this was the original part of the building, the part the Nogarola family had used as their summer home. The rest was added on later. There were other buildings on the grounds, too, of mixed use. Some looked like homes, others were offices or storage.

Anya should be here somewhere. He knew he'd betrayed her by bringing Clio to this place, but he was afraid for her.

Clio asked the driver to wait for them, and he cracked his door, lit a cigarette. His radio played 1990s pop tunes.

"Wait here," Clio told Sid. He watched her approach the building and enter a section of it that had a sign out front.

He ignored Clio's instruction to stay where he was and walked up to the terrace, looked out the other side. There was a shallow river behind the house, and the park, a hint that this place had been isolated and in unspoiled surroundings, once, but the steps behind the terrace were covered in bird shit and the doors off the terrace were locked. Anya couldn't be back here. He scanned the front, watched Clio come out of one of the buildings, frowning. He watched her look into a few more entrances until she'd exhausted them all. He was getting a bad feeling that Anya might have lied to them both.

He got out his phone. Reception was terrible, just one bar.

"What are you doing?" Clio had spotted him and was striding toward him.

"Nothing," he said.

"She's not here, is she?"

"I swear I thought she was."

"She could be in serious danger, Sid. That's my priority right now, and I know it's yours, too."

He hesitated fractionally. Clio was right, but he was loyal.

She held out her hand. "Sid! Her life could be in danger. Show me your fucking 'Find My.'"

Anya

One of the men seized me by the arms. There was no getting away. I was no match for his size and strength. I could feel the violence in him, smell his sweat.

My body shook as I stood in his grip in the middle of the central aisle. Shafts of watery sunlight streamed through the windows of the church, but they weren't strong enough to warm the air. Cold crept through my wet clothing and into my bones.

The other man shut the church doors firmly. He paced energetically in front of them as he made a call, big with the energy of capturing me. He spoke in Italian, and I couldn't understand it, but I got the gist: I may not have found what I was looking for, but they had. I was treasure to them, and they were getting instructions for what to do with me.

I tried to stand tall. I didn't want to give them the satisfaction of displaying any submission. I didn't want it to get back to my father that I'd shown weakness. That, at least, I could do for Mum.

Suddenly, the tone of the man's voice changed. He glanced at me, and his expression transformed from victorious to angry. The man holding me saw it, too. He tightened his grip on me and barked a question. The answer was barked back. The atmosphere shifted. I sensed fear in them and steeled myself because I didn't understand why or what it meant.

I was roughly dragged up the aisle toward the doors, where they had another angry exchange over my head, close up, spittle flecking, and I flinched at every word. I was looking for a chance to get away but not finding one. I was shaken like a doll as they shouted at each other. I cried out, and the man let go of me suddenly, shoving me away. I fell hard into the back row of pews and was struggling to sit up, when they fled, and the church door swung shut behind them.

The silence in the church felt loud. The patches of sunlight seemed to be burning. The animal smell of the man hung on me. All my senses were in overdrive, and it took me a few moments to come back to myself. I was very sore. I moved, gingerly, to sit in a pew but I couldn't get comfortable because I was still wearing my backpack. My arms and torso ached as I slowly wriggled to get it off, and as I did, my shadow moved against the wall beside me, and something there caught my eye.

In a shallow side chapel, windowless and unadorned, a wooden chest was pushed up against the wall. It was very old, the lid warped, the sides carved. It stood a few inches off the ground on solid legs and was about four feet long. It looked as if it weighed a ton. Hidden among the carvings on the front of it, I saw the faint but distinctive outline of the Nogarola coat of arms and beneath it, a line that I recognized from my translation of the Voynich. I caught my breath.

Even if nothing of the original church building had survived, apart from its floor, might this object be a survivor from that time? A chest that could relatively easily have been saved from the older building and moved into the newer church after it was built? A chest obviously commissioned by the Nogarolas and perhaps gifted to this special place?

The lid creaked as I lifted it. The chest was packed full of altar cloths and vestments. They were dusty and moth-eaten, but neatly folded. I pulled them out, dumping them in heaps beside me, and ran my hands over the inside of the chest, looking for somewhere, anywhere, that *The Book of Wonder* might be hidden. It felt like this had to be its resting place, though it wasn't long before I realized that was wishful thinking: the book wasn't there. I sat back on my heels, exhausted. Disappointment scythed through what felt like my final chance of hope.

Dust motes swirled in a shaft of sunlight above me as I reached out to touch the chest and my fingertips traced the outline of the Nogarola crest and the familiar words carved beneath it. A dog barked outside, and from somewhere in the distance, I heard the faint sound of police sirens.

I felt exhausted, ready to give up, but I realized there was one more place I could try. I leaned down and tried to see beneath the chest, but it was too dark. The sirens were getting louder. They were for me, I realized. They were the reason the men had left. Somehow, the carabinieri had caught up with me. But they weren't here yet.

I ran my hands beneath the chest and felt a protuberance where someone had built a compartment into its base that was invisible from the inside and outside. It was the right size to house a small manuscript. I lay on the ground and used my phone's light to get a better view, but I couldn't see where it opened. I felt all around it, getting frustrated. It was a sealed box, apparently, with no opening. I wished I could upend the chest, but it was far too heavy. As the volume of the sirens increased, I tried again, forcing myself to take it slower, to be more careful. This time, one side of the box slid cleanly away beneath my fingers and clattered as it fell to the floor.

I reached inside it. I had to explore it by touch, because it was impossible to get an angle to see. I felt a spine and a hard cover, and caught my breath. My fingertips dug gently around it until I felt the soft edges of vellum leaves. The sirens were screaming now, but I had to remain patient, to ease the book gently out of its hiding place. It came painfully slowly and reluctantly, as if afraid of seeing the light of day, and then, finally, I had it in my hands.

The Book of Wonder. It looked like a dusty little volume but that meant nothing. I lifted the cover to a random page, and its beauty and brilliance took my breath away. I could see at first glance that it was the equal of any of the finest manuscripts in the world, jewellike and perfect, exquisite craftmanship in the illustrations. The *Mona Lisa* of manuscripts. Pages of text—tantalizing—that I had no time to linger over because the sirens were right outside now, tires were squealing, car doors slamming, and footsteps were approaching, at speed.

I seized my backpack and shoved *The Book of Wonder* into it, then threw the piles of fabric back into the chest and shut the lid. As the church doors burst open, I turned to face the door and fear rippled through me. Two carabinieri burst through it with weapons raised and they trained them on me.

Clio

Clio jumped out of the taxi as it pulled up behind four carabinieri vehicles parked haphazardly in front of the church where Anya's phone had located her. She heard Sid's footsteps close behind hers as she ran across the square, but they were stopped outside the church by an officer who held them there even when Clio showed him her badge. He spoke no English. He wasn't interested in her attempts to persuade him to let her pass.

Once she and Sid had located Anya, she'd felt she had no choice but to call her contact and ask him to send the local carabinieri to help Anya, because they had the best chance of reaching her first. Clio had covered her own back, too. To mobilize her colleagues with maximum urgency, she told her contact about *The Book of Wonder*.

But now she was afraid she'd made a terrible mistake. During the taxi ride here, worry had begun to eat at her as it occurred to her that if these women's groups had successfully infiltrated the police force in the UK, they might have done the same here in Italy.

She hadn't said anything to Sid about her doubts, because he didn't need to know—should *never* know—but as she stood outside the church, she was terrified she'd just delivered Anya and *The Book of Wonder* right into the hands of the Kats or the Larks.

"There she is! Anya!" Sid said.

Anya stood at the top of the steps, framed by the doorway of the church, a foil blanket around her shoulders. She looked small and vulnerable. She was with a female carabinieri officer, and Clio's tension rose another notch. She thought of Anya's mother, of how Anya wanted to use *The Book of Wonder* as leverage to get her mum to safety, and her stomach twisted with apprehension.

"Anya!" Sid called again, and she looked toward them but shook her head minutely. *Not now.*

Clio and Sid watched as Anya and the officer talked. Anya removed her backpack. She put it on the ground and knelt beside it. "What's she doing?" Sid asked. He stepped forward. Clio put a hand on his arm. She didn't need him getting in the way. She was paying close attention to where all the officers were, how they were armed. She was trying to calculate her next move if she needed to make one, whether a move was even possible, or if it was too late for that. Her heart was in her mouth as Anya reached into the bag and removed a small, ancient book, which she handed to the officer.

The officer smiled as she took it. She cracked it open briefly, just long enough to glimpse a page or two, then closed it and handed it to a colleague, who took it to his car. Anya was safe, but they might have just condemned her mother to harm.

Sid whispered, "Why did Anya just give away her father's bestiary?"

Had she? Was he right? Clio felt the world go still.

She held her breath as Anya walked down the steps toward them. The officers were standing down and leaving, car engines starting.

Anya was shivering and her clothes were dripping, leaving trails of droplets down the steps in her wake, but she was smiling and hugging her backpack to her chest. Clio could see the outline of something heavy in it, something rectangular.

The Book of Wonder.

"Oh," Clio said under her breath. "Clever girl."

Anya

I chose the venue. The Piazza Isotta Nogarola was a nondescript square in a quiet, residential area of the city where tourists didn't venture. Verona had dedicated one of its least auspicious piazzas to one of their brightest daughters. But it suited me.

A steady stream of quiet traffic passed through the square. There was a roundabout in its center and parking bays around its edges. Beneath low-rise apartment buildings painted in pastel colors, the shop fronts were home to a newsagent, a hairdresser, a women's clothing store, a real estate agency, and two cafés.

Sid and Clio sat in one. I crossed the square toward the other. It was on a corner, beneath a prominent red awning, a row of black plastic tables and chairs out front. Pastries were displayed alongside silk flowers in the windows.

A bell jangled as I opened the door. I picked a table beside the window and in the corner, with a view of the whole room. The café smelled of coffee beans, fresh bread, and the bright tang of confectioners' sugar. Good-natured shouts volleyed between the staff out front and their colleagues in back by the ovens.

It was the safest place I could think of.

Tracy Lock arrived first, representing the Fellowship of the Larks. I was expecting her. I'd contacted her via Sarabeth. I want your most senior representative, I'd told her. Don't mess around with me. No one else will do. I have *The Book of Wonder*.

Those words were all it took to summon the women in power. Both arrived in Verona and signaled that they were ready to meet within twelve hours. If I'd been in any doubt that the book had been their ultimate goal, I wasn't anymore.

Tracy arrived wearing shades, a scarf, and a hat. She was low key. No one in the shop would have guessed who she was.

I still wasn't sure who would take the third seat, but I was confident Tracy had known who to reach out to from the Order of St. Katherine. Where there was power, there were always back channels. Why would these groups of women be any different?

She arrived soon after: Cece Beaufort, my father's wife. It took my breath away to be meeting with his mistress and his spouse. She and Tracy nodded at one another, unsmiling, and Cece took her seat.

The Order of St. Katherine versus the Fellowship of the Larks. Magnus should have kept his eyes open wider.

I needed to keep mine open, too. It had never been more important. I still didn't know where my mother was, but I heard her voice as loud and clear as ever.

Be strong. Trust your judgment. You can shape more of your destiny than you think.

"Shall we talk about *The Book of Wonder*?" I asked.

I laid out my conditions. If they met them, I said, I would give them the book. They listened and asked me for some time. I moved to a table on the pavement out front and watched them through the glass as they talked. Across the street, Clio and Sid were waiting and watching, too.

After a while, Tracy made a call. When she hung up, they beckoned me back inside and explained that an agreement had been reached. They wouldn't reveal details, they said, but soon I would have proof that they were telling the truth and that my conditions had been met.

"How?" I was afraid they were outmaneuvering me.

Cece said, "We wait until midday, and you'll see. Are you still getting messages from your father?"

I nodded. Magnus was still violently angry that I'd evaded him. Every time another message arrived from him it sent a chill down my spine.

"We'll check in with him a little bit later and I think you'll find he's not a threat anymore," Tracy said. Neither of them would say more.

Time ticked. The city's ancient bells chimed in the distance. There was no small talk and a lot of silence. Both women sent and received messages, moving pieces on boards. We ordered food that we barely touched, took turns stretching our legs on the square. I messaged Sid, keeping him and Clio informed. They were starting to have doubts. They questioned whether it was becoming dangerous. I told them I wanted to wait.

Almost two hours had passed when Tracy received a message and said, "It's done." She looked up, meeting Cece's gaze, and something profound seemed to pass between them, something that looked like a mix of sorrow and relief.

"Is it online yet?" Cece asked.

Tracy nodded.

"Show Anya."

She handed me her phone and I read a breaking news item posted just three minutes earlier.

"At least one dead after chopper crashes near St. Andrews, Scotland."

It took me a moment to understand what I was reading, and what a shockingly brutal and efficient thing they'd engineered. "Is it him?"

Tracy nodded. "I'm afraid Magnus has been the victim of a tragic accident. As you know, he liked to pilot his own helicopter. I believe he was on his way south to deal more directly with the matter of finding you. I'm sure you'll have some feelings about his death, but this is for the best. It makes it possible for Cece and me to come to an arrangement over *The Book of Wonder*. You'll get what you want. Your mother will return home safely, and we'll honor Magnus's commitments to her regarding the clinical trial. We'll ensure the safety of Clio Spicer. The Order of St. Katherine will become custodians of the book. In return, Cece will donate its equivalent value to the Fellowship of the Larks, enabling us to build and run our foundation and continue our good work helping women. As the sole primary beneficiary of Magnus's will since their children are still underage, she's in a position to do this."

The relief I felt was indescribable.

"We'd also like to discuss your future," Tracy said. "We would both like you to remain working on the manuscript collection. It will still be a foundational part of the library."

"I won't work in a library that carries his name."

"How does the Rose Brown Library sound to you?"

"I'll think about it. I want to speak to her."

Within moments they'd got Mum on the phone. She told me she loved me, and I said it back. When I hung up, they were both watching me impassively, and I found myself looking at them with new eyes.

They were so different from me, so calculating, so powerful, so dedicated to elevating women's lives and probably more realistic about what it took to change a man's world than I might ever be. They were terrifying. What they were willing to do, and had done, was horrendous. Part of me felt like I'd just made a deal with the devil, but I knew I'd had no choice.

"Of course all of this is contingent on us taking possession of the book," Cece said.

"You don't get the book until we get the money," Tracy said.

I messaged Sid and Clio, and they met us in the street.

I asked Sid to give the book to Tracy, and he handed her a simple cotton tote bag containing a priceless manuscript. Cece watched every move. I'd looked into the eyes of both women, and I knew they'd never stop fighting each other to get what they wanted, but this might bring some temporary peace between them, perhaps enough to last a generation, perhaps not.

A town car pulled up, sleek and shiny, and out of place in this neighborhood. Tracy and Cece left together. I couldn't imagine what they might be saying to each other in the car.

I leaned into Sid and felt safer than I had for days, but I also knew I'd never feel safe again, not the way I had before that email from Diana Cornish dropped into my mailbox.

We said goodbye to Clio. She took a cab. Sid and I decided to walk. I was thinking about Magnus, trying to work out how I felt about him now.

After we'd been walking in silence for a while, I asked, "Do you think either of those groups are really doing good? Considering their methods, are they truly helping women or are they seeking power for its own sake?"

"Both," Sid said. "What do you think?"

We'd reached the riverbank, which was gently sloped, and we walked down onto a pebbly beach. The water ran fast and clear; it was a beautiful shade of turquoise. Sid skimmed stones and I sat on the beach and watched. On the opposite bank the city of Verona rose up, centuries old, as timeless and beautiful and proud as ever, but it had been built by men.

After a while I'd worked out my answer. I said it aloud, even though Sid was too far away to hear me. I didn't need him to.

I said, "They did what it took."

AUTHOR'S NOTE

A fictional explanation of the mysterious Voynich manuscript can be found at the heart of this novel. The historical figures, places, and many of the artworks it's based on are real.

ACKNOWLEDGMENTS

Heartfelt thanks to my long-standing and outstanding editor, Emily Krump, at William Morrow for having faith in such a wild pitch and guiding this novel toward its potential. Knowing the state of the first draft of this book, I imagine editing it might have felt something like herding cats. I'm super grateful for your talent, acuity, vision, and word-wrangling skills.

Warmest thanks must also go to Liate Stehlik and Jen Hart at Morrow for your backing. And heaps more gratitude is due to Paige Meintzer, Camille Collins, Amelia Wood, Hope Breeman, Elsie Lyons, and the wonderful sales team.

To the outstanding HarperCollins team in Canada. I'm indebted to Cory Beatty. Thanks for having my back, working your sales and marketing magic, and being so fun to spend time with since the beginning. Thanks to Rebecca Silver and Brenann Francis for everything you do. You're a pleasure to work with. And to Leo Macdonald: you might have retired but I will always be grateful for your generosity and support while you were steering the ship.

Huge thanks to Jade Chandler, who saw the fun in this novel and brought it under her wing at Baskerville in the UK, and to Rebecca Folland, Helena Dorée, Louise Henderson-Clark, Zoe King, and

Sophie Jackson from the rights team, who have found wonderful homes for it in more countries than I dreamed of. Warmest thanks to Zulekhá Afzal, Alice Herbert, Ellie Bailey, Kyla Dean, and Megan Schaffer. For an outstanding cover design, thanks to Lydia Blagden, and last but by no means least I'm incredibly grateful to Jocasta Hamilton and Nick Davies for your support.

Warm thanks, too, to Katy Loftus for suggesting such a smoking-hot title.

To Helen Heller and Jemma McDonagh, I'm hugely grateful to you both for finding such wonderful homes for this novel in North America, the UK, and Germany. Thank you.

Thanks to Professor Clare Bowern of Yale Linguistics, who kindly gifted me the idea for the discovery of a glossary that would facilitate a translation of Voynichese. Thanks also to Carm Del Guercio, who advised me on internet security. Any mistakes I've made or liberties I've taken in these areas are all mine.

To my author friends. Thank you for being so inspiring and supportive. To the booksellers, readers, bloggers, and reviewers who support my books, I'm grateful for you all.

Jules, thank you for the chicken Caesar salad.

Rose, thank you for unscrambling my brain, for remaining unflappably cool and brilliant, and for providing weeks of invaluable editorial support and suggestions during the drafting and editing of this novel. I couldn't have done it without you.

Max, thank you for suggesting I take a look at a mysterious manuscript named after Wilfrid Voynich when this book was in the planning stage. You unleashed a beast.

Rose, Max, and Louis, thank you for setting such incredible and energizing examples with your tenacity in riding the ups and down of a creative life, your commitment to exploring possibilities and embracing creative risk, and the energy you put into producing your best work. The three of you inspire me every day.

Gilly Macmillan is the internationally bestselling author of eight other novels, including *The Manor House*, *The Perfect Girl*, *The Nanny*, and *The Long Weekend*. She lives in Bristol, England.